6/16 c2013 5c(2cpR1)
2015-6÷5=1.2

ALLEGIANCE

TOR BOOKS BY BETH BERNOBICH

Passion Play
Queen's Hunt
Allegiance

ALLEGIANCE

BETH BERNOBICH

A TOM DOHERTY ASSOCIATES BOOK
NEW YORK

ALLEGIANCE

Copyright © 2013 by Beth Bernobich

Maps by Jennifer Hanover

A Tor Book
Published by Tom Doherty Associates, LLC
175 Fifth Avenue
New York, NY 10010

www.tor-forge.com

Tor® is a registered trademark of Tom Doherty Associates, LLC.

The Library of Congress Cataloging-in-Publication Data is available upon request.

ISBN 978-0-7653-2219-7 (hardcover)
ISBN 978-1-4299-4549-3 (e-book)

Tor books may be purchased for educational, business, or promotional use. For information on bulk purchases, please contact Macmillan Corporate and Premium Sales Department at 1-800-221-7945, extension 5442, or write specialmarkets@macmillan.com.

First Edition: October 2013

Printed in the United States of America

0 9 8 7 6 5 4 3 2 1

TO DELIA SHERMAN,
for her wisdom and kindness

ACKNOWLEDGMENTS

Ilse's journey began many years ago, with numerous false starts and more than a few rewrites. Much the same happened when I sat down to write *Allegiance*. I knew exactly how the book should end, but the rest was little more than a grand collection of scenes.

A number of people helped me take these vague ideas and turn them into a coherent narrative. Delia Sherman explained the care and feeding of trilogies to me. Ed Greaves provided invaluable insight into the true theme of the book. My editor, Claire Eddy, offered her usual splendid advice on how to make the story stronger. Thank you all! I am grateful for your comments, critiques, and insight.

Most of all, I thank my husband for listening, for brainstorming, and for believing in me.

MANTHARAH

RASTOV

KÁROVÍ

Duszranjo Valley

Solvatni River

DUBRO

RYZ

VERAENE

Telč River

LENOV

KRANJĚ ISLANDS

MELNEK

MUNDLAU

HALLAU ISLAND

W

E

S

DONUTH

to DUENNE

Gallenz River

TIRALIEN

to MORENNIOÙ

FULDAH

KONSTANZIEN

LENIZ

KLEE

OSTERLING KEEP

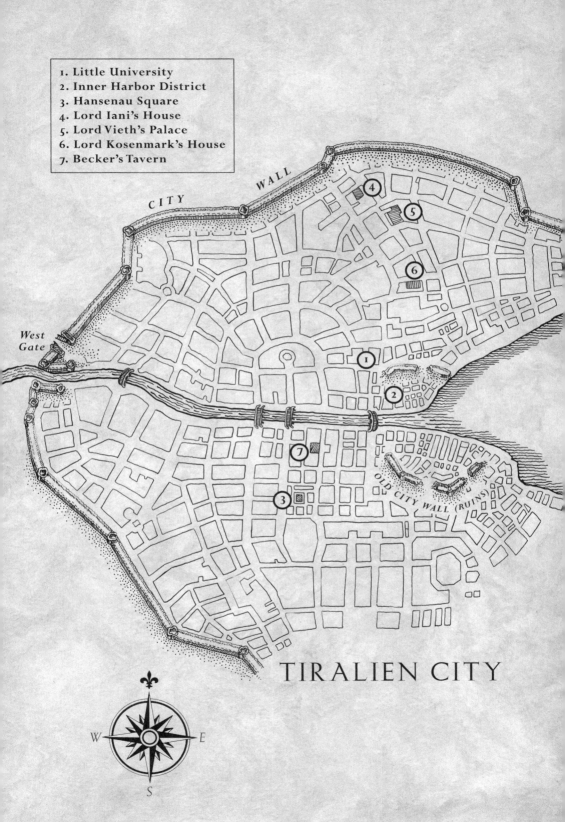

1. Little University
2. Inner Harbor District
3. Hansenau Square
4. Lord Iani's House
5. Lord Vieth's Palace
6. Lord Kosenmark's House
7. Becker's Tavern

CITY WALL

West Gate

① Little University
② Inner Harbor District

④ Lord Iani's House
⑤ Lord Vieth's Palace
⑥ Lord Kosenmark's House

⑦ Becker's Tavern
③ Hansenau Square

OLD CITY WALL (RUINS)

TIRALIEN CITY

W E
S

1 Royal Palace
2 Duke Kosenmark's House
3 Tanja Duhr's House
4 Central Square

NORTHERN HILLS

to OURNES

to TIRALIEN

Gallenz River

to YSTERIEN

to FORTEZZIEN

DUENNE

W   E

N

S

ALLEGIANCE

CHAPTER ONE

ENDINGS, THE POET Tanja Duhr once wrote, were deceptive things. No story truly came to a final stop, no poem described the last of the last—they could not, not until the world and the gods and time had ceased to exist. An ending was a literary device. In truth, the end of one story, or one life, carried the seeds for the next.

The idea of seeds and new beginnings offered Ilse Zhalina little consolation.

It was late summer, the season tipping over into autumn, and dawn wrapped the skies in murky gray. Six weeks had passed since she had abandoned Raul Kosenmark on Hallau Island. Her last glimpse had been of him fighting off an impossible number of enemy soldiers. Ten days ago, Leos of Károví, once called the immortal king, had died, and she had witnessed Lir's jewels reunited into a single alien creature, who then disappeared into the magical void. Endings upon endings, to be sure, and some of them she had not yet begun to comprehend. And yet she lived on, she and Valara Baussay.

Ilse crouched over the ashes of their campfire and rubbed her hands together, trying to warm them. The air was chill, stinking of sweat and smoke. In the first few days of their flight, Ilse had been convinced they would never survive. Inadequate clothing, inadequate supplies. She had since acquired a knitted cap and a woolen coat, once the property of a man much taller and heavier than she. He was dead now. A sword slash, ringed with bloodstains, marked where she had killed him. Underneath, she still wore her own cotton shirt from Hallau Island. If she allowed herself, if she let imagination take flight, she might catch the faded scent of days long past, of that brief interlude with Raul Kosenmark.

Raul. My love.

She pressed both hands against her eyes. She was hungry, hungry and cold and consumed by an emptiness that was greater than any physical need. She wished . . . oh, but to wish for Raul was impossible. She would only start weeping, and she could not grant herself the luxury of grief, not yet. Not until she and Valara Baussay had escaped this hostile land.

Her breath shivering inside her, she wished instead for a scalding hot fire. A perfumed bath, too. At the thought of scented baths in this wilderness, she almost laughed, but it was a breathless, painful laugh, and she had to pause and recover herself before she could continue her list of wants and desires. Clean clothes, strong coffee, a book to read in warmth and quiet. A feast of roasted lamb, fresh melon, and steamed rice mixed with green peppercorn.

Her imagination failed her at the subsequent courses. There could be no fire until daybreak, not unless she wished to signal her presence to any chance patrols from the western garrisons. The skies had lightened with the approaching dawn, but day came as slowly as the night, here in the far north of Károví. It would be another hour before she could risk a fire. She shuddered from the cold and the thought of enemies in pursuit.

Her companion in this madness, Valara Baussay, slept wrapped tightly in a blanket, and as close to the fire as possible. In the dim light, only the darkest and largest of her tattoos, at the outside corner of her left eye, was visible—an elaborate pattern of interlocking squares, drawn in reddish-brown ink, that formed a diamond. A second, simpler pattern under her lower lip was indistinguishable in the shadows. Symbols of nobility or rank, Ilse guessed, though Valara had said nothing of their meaning in the few months of their acquaintanceship. It was difficult to remember, when Valara slept, that she was a queen of Morenniwhere. Awake, it was impossible to forget.

We have never been true friends, not in any of our lives. But from time to time, we have been good allies.

Not in every life. They had been enemies as well, or if not true enemies, then in conflict with each other. Four hundred years ago, in one of those past lives, Valara had been a prince of Károví. As Andrej Dzavek, he and his brother had stolen Lir's jewels from the emperor, then fled to their homeland, in those days a princedom of the empire. In that same life, Ilse had been a princess betrothed to Leos Dzavek in a political marriage.

Andrej Dzavek had regretted his treason. He had led the imperial armies against Károví and his brother, only to die on the battlefield. Ilse Zhalina had attempted to negotiate a peace between the kingdoms. Leos Dzavek had executed her, and with the jewels' magic, lived on for centuries. At some point, Ilse and Valara Baussay would both have to confront all the complications of their past lives.

Her hands were as warm as she could make them. Ilse tugged her knitted cap low over her forehead and drew her hands inside the sleeves of her ill-fitting coat. Moving as quietly as she could manage, she crept up the slope and peered between the two slabs of rock that overshadowed their campsite. From here, she had a clear view of the surrounding plains. They had made camp, such as it was, in a narrow fold of land, its banks strewn with rocks. Pine and spruce once grew here, but now only a few dead trees remained. At the bottom of the fold ran a stream, fed by summer rains and meltwater from the western mountains. A cold uncomfortable site, but for now, she was grateful to have wood for fire, water to drink, and a shelter to hide in.

All was quiet. Rain had fallen in the night, and a cool damp breeze blew from the west, carrying with it the tang of mountain pines, like magic's sharp green fragrance, and the earthier scents of mud and grass and wild-flowers. Even as she watched, a thin ribbon of light unfurled along the eastern horizon, changing the black expanse into a pale ocean of grass, bowing in wave after wave, like those from the far-off seas. That looming mass of shadow to the west would be the Železny Mountains, which divided the Károvín plains from the kingdom's westernmost province of Duszranjo. Within a day's march was where she and Valara were to meet with Duke Miro Karasek.

A flicker of shadow caught her eye—a blurred speck of movement in the grass. Ilse unhooked the buttons of her coat and checked her few weapons—the sword at her belt, the knife in her boot, and the one in her wrist sheath. All were within easy reach. She stared at the point where she had sighted the shadow. Not a patrol, she told herself. It was too small and swift a movement. A solitary rider?

Then the light ticked upward, and she saw what it was—a fox, gliding through the tall grass. A breath of laughter escaped her. She eased back toward the banked fire. Valara stirred and muttered in her own language. Was she dreaming of past lives?

I've dreamed. I've never stopped dreaming since Leos died.

She rubbed her forehead with the back of her wrist.

. . . Leos Dzavek's hand tightened around the ruby jewel, its light spilling through his fingers like blood . . . Magic burst against magic, and the world exploded. When she could see again, she saw Leos crushed beneath the marble pedestal, his eyes blank and white, like a winter snowfall. He was dying, dying, dying but he would not release his hold upon her, and she felt her soul slipping into the void between worlds . . .

No! Dzavek was dead, his soul was in flight to its next life, and the jewels had returned as one to the magical plane. She had fulfilled her obligations to the gods. She pulled off the cap and raked her fingers through her knotted hair. The lurid images of her nightmare faded into the pale red light of sunrise.

She drew a sharp breath in surprise.

Valara Baussay was awake and studying Ilse with those brilliant brown eyes. Though Valara's expression seldom betrayed anything, and even those few clues were often deliberate indirection, Ilse had the impression of being constantly assessed by her companion. In that she was much like Raul.

"You didn't wake me for my watch," Valara said.

"No. You were tired and—"

"—and you were afraid of your nightmares. Was it the same one as before?"

Her voice was uncharacteristically gentle.

"The same one, yes."

"Ah. I have them, too."

Ilse glanced up, suddenly wary. "You never said so before."

Valara shrugged. "I don't like to think about it."

Ah, well. Ilse could understand that.

"I'll restart the fire," she said. "We can eat breakfast and make an early start."

"Breakfast." Valara's mouth softened into a pensive smile. "I've dreamed of breakfast, too, from time to time."

She stood up and stretched. She wore the dead courier's gloves and his shirt over her own. Valara had rolled up the sleeves and tied a makeshift sash, but her thin frame was almost lost in the folds. Even dressed in such a mismatched costume, she had the air of one about to issue a royal decree— yet another similarity to Raul.

"What is wrong?" Valara asked.

"Nothing," Ilse said quickly. "Nothing we can change."

Valara regarded her with narrowed eyes. "As you say," she murmured.

She headed downstream to the trench Ilse had dug for their latrine. Ilse collected tinder and a few larger branches, and coaxed their fire into life. She set a pan of water to boil and refilled their waterskins. A brief inspection of their supplies was discouraging: a handful of tea leaves, enough smoked beef for a good breakfast but nothing for midday, and a few dried apples. They had eaten the last of the courier's flatbread the night before. Karasek had provided them with as much gear and provisions as he could spare, but it had all been so haphazard, those final hours at the

Mantharah. Hiding all traces of their camp, including their magic. Working out their escape, and how Karasek might lead the search in the opposite direction. What came next, after they were certain they were safe.

Ilse blew out a breath. After. Yes.

If I were wishing, I would wish for Raul. I would wish we were together in Tiralien, without any fear of war between our kingdom and Károví. Without balancing every act against what Markus Khandarr might do against us. We could be Stefan and Anike, two ordinary people, living ordinary lives.

Impossible wishes. Ilse had promised Valara she would sail with her to her island kingdom, a hostage for peace, in return for Valara's help in recovering the last of Lir's jewels. She could argue the vows no longer applied. Dzavek was dead. The jewels had departed from the ordinary world. All the variables she and Raul had depended upon had vanished or changed in unpredictable ways.

Including Raul himself.

We are creatures of nothing, she thought. *Caught between lives and obligations. We have no certain ending, nor any sign of what comes next.*

Or perhaps she had not understood the true import of her previous lives.

It was an uncomfortable idea.

WITHIN THE HOUR, they broke their fast with hot tea and smoked beef, saving the apples for midday. Their stomachs were full, at least temporarily. With the sun glancing over the fields, and the frost melting under the summer sun, Ilse and Valara cleared away all signs of their camp, refilled their waterskins, and set off on foot over the Károvín plains.

Progress was slow. Foraging proved less productive than they liked.

Even so, by late afternoon, they were within sight of their destination. A midday hailstorm had ended, leaving intermittent rain showers in its wake. Clouds still veiled the skies and the air shimmered wet and gray.

They took cover in a thicket of scrub and sapling pines, while Ilse scanned the open ground ahead. A grassy slope dipped toward a shallow ravine and creek swollen by rain. A stand of trees on the farther ridge marked a more substantial streambed beyond. According to all her calculations, every landmark, and instructions from the man himself, those trees and that streambed marked where Duke Karasek had appointed to meet them.

An empty landscape met her eye. She saw no sign of movement, other than needles trembling under raindrops, but she had been deceived once before. She wore the memory of that encounter.

*. . . a startled man dressed in military garb. His grin as he saw two women
alone, on foot. Ilse drawing her sword, speaking words of magic to blind him.
Moments later, the sun slanting through leaves spattered with blood . . .*

The nearest garrison lay almost fifty miles away, she told herself. Patrols
were not likely. Nor should they encounter any trappers or chance travelers
in this wild region. She leaned toward Valara and whispered, "I'll scout
ahead. Wait for my signal."

She rose slowly to her feet, checked her sword and knives, then crept
forward into the ravine, down, step by cautious step, across the bare ground,
to the meltwater stream at the bottom and up the farther side.

At the top of the bank, she peered over the edge. More thornbushes
covered the ground here. The stand of pines lay directly ahead. From a distance came the rill of running water. A bird, a tiny brown wren, flitted from
one branch to another, but otherwise, all was still.

She whistled, a brief warbling cry, to signal all clear. Valara scrambled
down the bank and across the open expanse to join her. No sooner had she
done so than Ilse heard the distinct whicker of a horse.

Valara froze. "More patrols?" she whispered.

"Or our friend." Then Ilse broached the subject she had not dared to,
five days before, after their encounter with the courier. "We might need to
use magic—"

"I cannot. I— Never mind why. I cannot."

*You were ready that other time, in Osterling Keep. You killed a dozen men
with words alone. And on Hallau Island, too.*

But not once since their confrontation with Leos Dzavek.

Yet another subject for later.

"Wait here," she whispered. "I'll scout ahead. If that horse belongs to
Karasek, I'll give our other safe signal. Otherwise, make your escape, and
I'll do whatever I need to."

Valara nodded. She understood. They could not risk discovery. If Ilse
were attacked, she would kill their enemies with sword and magic.

Ilse crawled forward, wriggling through the mud until the thornbushes
gave way to the pine trees. Cautiously she rose to a crouch and continued
farther into the trees. Saplings grew thickly among the older pines and the
air was ripe with their tang. As her eyes adjusted to the shadows, she could
make out a clearing ahead, and three horses on the far side. Two of them
were plain, hairy beasts, as short as ponies. The third was a long-legged
creature, a mount fit for a royal courier—or a duke.

The hiss of a branch was her only warning. She sprang to her feet and reached for her sword. Before she could slide the blade free, an arm crashed into her face. Ilse staggered back, tucked into a ball to roll free, but a hand grabbed her shoulder and swung her around. She slammed against the stranger's chest, breathless and stunned.

But now the hours of drill with Benedikt Ault took control. Ilse kicked back, driving her heel against her attacker's shin. The moment his grip loosened, she spun around and drew her sword.

"Ei rûf ane gôtter . . .

". . . ane Lir unde Toc . . ."

Two summonses to the magic current. Two invocations to the gods, delivered in old Erythandran. The air split, as though divided by a knife, an infinitesimal void running between Ilse and her attacker. Bright magic rushed through. It filled the clearing with a sharp green scent, overpowering the pine tang. Like a wind diverted from a larger storm, it blew hard against Ilse's face. Ilse gripped her sword, trying to peer through the brilliant haze of magic. Her own signature was strong and unmistakable, starlight glancing through clouds. His came fainter, sunlight reflected from snow-crested mountains.

I know that signature.

She whispered the words to recall the magical current. The brightness faded.

Miro Karasek crouched a few yards away, his sword angled up and outward, ready to strike. The branches above swung to and fro, casting raindrops over them both. It was hard to make out much in the gray-green shadows, but Ilse could see the dark circles under his eyes, the lines drawn sharp beside his mouth. The past two weeks had cost him much.

Miro bent to massage his shin. "I warned you against using magic."

Ilse ran her tongue over her swollen lip. "And I do not like games. Why did you attack?"

"My apologies for the roughness," he said. "I didn't recognize you."

And thought her a brigand—or worse. Her hands shaking, Ilse sheathed her sword. "You have news?"

He nodded. "Where is her highness, the queen?"

He did not say whether the news was good or bad, and Ilse did not press him. She gave a short shrill whistle to signal all-safe. Within moments Valara appeared, pushing the low-hanging branches to one side, as if they were curtains in a palace. She spared a glance toward Ilse, but her attention was for Miro Karasek.

His gaze caught hers, then flicked away. "They are hunting north and east," he said. He gestured toward the clearing. "I can tell you more after you eat. You will be starving, and I want you able to pay attention."

Before long they were seated close to a campfire and shedding their filthiest, dampest outer garments. It was not exactly Ilse's dream of wishes, but nearly so. She greedily drank the soup Miro Karasek offered, followed by a mug of tea. The tea was strong and black, sweetened with honey. Before she had finished it, she found a second panniken of soup waiting, along with a flat disk of camp bread.

Valara waved away her second helping of soup. "Tell us what happened at Rastov. No, before that. Start from the day you left us."

Her voice was short and sharp. Ilse stiffened. Would Karasek recognize the panic?

Karasek stirred the coals, betraying nothing of his thoughts. "There is not much to tell. You remember how we worked to mislead any trackers from Duke Markov? I decided that was not sufficient. Markov has a number of mages in his employ, not to mention his ally, Duke Černosek. If they once decided to search beyond Mantharah, they would overtake you within days. So I prepared other clues farther to the east."

As he fed the fire with more sticks, he told them of creating the apparent signs of a large camp between Károví's capital city of Rastov and Mantharah, then a distinct trail leading northeast toward a remote inlet. It had taken him the entire day and half of the next.

"I returned to Rastov by the following morning—"

"What did they say about the king?" Valara said.

He regarded her with a long, impenetrable look. "They say he died. And that someone killed him."

Valara subsided. It was a matter of technicalities, who or what had killed Leos Dzavek. Ilse had distracted him. Valara had infuriated him. In the end, Lir's jewels had unleashed the magic to kill the immortal king, but they could not have done so without each small step and sidestep in between. *We are all complicit, including Leos himself.*

"What about those horses?" she said. "You didn't take those from a garrison."

"The horses are for you. I acquired them discreetly, along with these maps . . ."

He went to his mount and extracted several scrolls from a pouch. These were maps of the regions, wrapped in oilskin against the uncertain summer rains. Now Ilse could see clearly the reasons behind his instructions from ten days before—the way they had circled around Rastov toward the mountains, how their path would parallel his as they proceeded south into the central plains, and the point where they would turn east into Karasek's duchy of Taboresk, where he would rejoin them.

"I have new provisions and more gear," he continued.

Obtained from garrison stores, and at the risk of discovery.

Ilse hesitated to ask. Valara had no qualms. "Does anyone suspect?" she asked.

This time there was no pause before he answered.

"Duke Markov might," he said. "I arrived, almost coincidentally, at the crisis. I took it upon myself to track the assassins. In his eyes, that will appear unusual enough for suspicion. But he cannot afford to offend me, nor I him. What of you?"

"We survived," Valara said. "Anything else is superfluous."

Karasek's eyes narrowed and he studied her a long moment. "As you say," he said slowly.

HE DIVVIED UP the chores and watches with no more consideration than if they were his most junior recruits. Ilse dug a new latrine away from the stream and their camp. Valara took the early watch, which included tending to the horses and washing all the dishes.

I am a queen of Morennioù, she thought with a rueful smile. *I should not have to wash dishes.*

She remembered what her father said once, years ago, when Valara and her sister had rebelled against tending to their own horses. She was a princess, Franseza had declared. She would not care for such dirty creatures. Certainly she would not muck out their stalls.

"Then you can never be queen," Mikaël of Morennioù told his daughter. "This horse is your servant. You owe her this service in return for her service to you. If you refuse this small task, then you refuse the throne and the crown. Else how can I trust you with the greater duty of ruling the kingdom when I die?"

Shocked, Franseza never again protested such chores. Nor had Valara, even though she was the younger daughter, and therefore not called to the throne. Of course, that was before Franseza and their mother died at sea.

I want to earn that throne, Valara thought. *I want to be queen, the way my father was king.*

So she bent herself to scrubbing out pots.

She soon needed more water to rinse the dishes. Valara took up the largest waterskin and set off to find the stream. Miro had pointed out the direction before he went to sleep, but he had not mentioned how thickly the trees grew. She had to pick her way between and around the saplings and underbrush, pausing now and then to free her sleeve from a prickly vine. By the time she reached the lip of the ravine, the camp was no longer visible. There was not even a glimmer of firelight.

I will not shout for help.

As if in answer, one of the horses snorted. Valara laughed softly. She fixed the direction of that helpful snort in her memory and turned back to her task. The ravine's bank was steep. She had to scramble down from out-cropping to outcropping, sometimes on her hands and knees, and barely missed falling into the stream itself. Cursing to herself, she filled the wa-terskin and dried her hands on her shirt.

The last of the sunlight had bled from the sky during her climb down the bank. The skies had turned violet, with wisps of dark clouds obscur-ing the stars. A breeze from the east carried with it the scents of summer from the open plains. Farther and fainter came the cold scent of the com-ing winter.

Home seemed so very distant.

She blew out a breath. *Let us eradicate one obstacle after another.* She slung the waterskin's strap over her shoulder and clambered up the bank. She had almost attained the summit when a shadow loomed over her. Valara started back. Miro Karasek caught her by the arm before she tumbled down the bank.

"You were gone longer than I expected," he said.

"You were watching?"

"No. But the horses woke me."

He helped her up the last few yards of the bank. To her relief, he re-mained silent as they threaded through the bushes and back to the camp. Even so, she remained preternaturally aware of his presence at her side, and later as he settled easily onto his bed of blankets, his gaze resting on her. Valara knelt by the fire and took up the next pot, adding hot water and soap before scrubbing it clean. "It's not time for your watch," she said. "You should sleep."

"I will later. I had a question or two."

When he did not continue, she swiped the rag inside the pot. She rinsed it clean of suds and set the pot upside down on the stones next to the fire where it could dry. The next was a metal pan, suited for baking flatbread. She dipped the pan into hot water and tilted it so the suds swirled around.

Once, as Leos Dzavek's brother, she had wanted to murder the man who later became Miro Karasek. Once, as Morenniwhere's queen, she had wanted to make him her consort. Now? Now she was no longer certain. He had vowed to give her aid, to ensure she could return home. And yet she found it difficult to trust.

Debts are like wounds, her father once said.

"You intend to hold her to her promise?" Miro said.

Valara twisted the rag between her fingers to recover her self-control. No need to ask whom he meant by *her*, or what promise he referred to. In the weeks before she and Ilse Zhalina had escaped to Mantharah, Ilse had offered to accompany Valara to her homeland. In return, Valara had promised to help Ilse recover the last of Lir's jewels.

Since then, the jewels had rejoined into one and returned to the magical plane. With Raul most likely dead, there was no reason for Ilse to keep her promise. It was Valara who needed Ilse to confirm Valara's account of what transpired during her long absence. The council might have named another ruler in these intervening months. It was even possible that certain factions would accuse her of collaborating with the enemy. Ilse Zhalina could testify against that.

"I cannot release her from her promise," she said shortly. "Not only do I value her advice, I will need a second voice in my own council. Surely you can understand."

Her palm ached. She rubbed it absentmindedly.

. . . Lir folded her hands around Valara's. Toc clasped both of theirs within his. The gods' lips did not move, but their voices filled the air with rippling tones, like raindrops on a canopy of summer leaves. With a flicker of memory, she saw her two hands plunged into the Agnau's silvery depths. Three jewels rejoined into one called Ishya, who stepped from Valara's palm and with every step grew in height, until he, she reached the center of the lake and vanished from sight . . .

If Valara were still able to work magic, she could transport herself to Morenniou with a breath and a thought. But Lir or Toc had excised her ability for magic, as cleanly as a plain-surgeon's knife. She no longer possessed any, not even the ability to work the simplest of spells, such as lighting a candle—a clear warning that the gods watched her.

Her council would prefer it. The kings and queens of Morenniou were forbidden to use magic, after all. She might even work the loss into a sign of favor. But in the larger world of kingdoms and politics and negotiations, such a loss would be seen as a weakness.

"It is necessary," she repeated.

Karasek nodded, but said nothing. For a terrible moment, she wished she could read his thoughts. For an equally terrible moment, she hoped he could not read hers.

MIRO KARASEK WOKE Ilse a few hours past midnight for her turn at watch. The skies had cleared, true dark had fallen, and the stars were bright pinpoints against the black expanse. Ilse dragged herself from the depths of much-needed sleep and rolled over to one side. Karasek offered her a mug of hot, spiced tea. Ilse downed a swallow, coughed, and drank the rest. Her mind cleared at once. "What is that?"

"A special brew, concocted for soldiers in the garrison. Are you awake now?"

"Awake enough."

She staggered to her feet. At some point, she had reassumed the coat and cap she had stolen from the dead courier. She fastened the buttons with clumsy fingers.

Miro crouched next to the low-burning fire, his hands splayed as if to capture its warmth. "You had some trouble in the past few weeks," he said quietly.

Ilse shuddered. "Once. We . . . I had to kill him."

"Was he a soldier?"

"A courier, we think."

She went on to describe their encounter with the solitary man who thought two women alone were defenseless. Ilse had proved him wrong. She had blinded him with magic, then run him through with her sword. Together she and Valara had removed every bit of identification from his body, and examined his saddlebags for further clues. They had found one packet wrapped in oilskin, with a message that contained a report of the king's death.

"Do you have the packet, or did you burn it?" Miro asked.

Wordlessly, Ilse handed the letter over to Miro, who scanned its contents, then set it aside. For a long interval, he said nothing, but studied the star-speckled skies. He seemed lost in contemplation of some faraway puzzle.

"How do they take the news in the garrisons?" she said at last.

"Badly," he said. "They are afraid. *I* am afraid. We've grown so accustomed to this one king that his sudden disappearance has loosened our customary restraints. I expected maneuvers from Markov, but not the others. That was a mistake . . ."

He shook his head. A dismissal of one problem, before he addressed another.

"I have been thinking about how to introduce you into my household," he said. "Let us say that you are two sisters, cousins from my mother's family. You are seeking a place with a distant relative along the coast. I invited you to visit me first at Taboresk, but bandits attacked your entourage. Only you and your sister escaped."

Ilse nodded. "That . . . could work. What about your servants, however? Do they know your mother's family very well?"

"No," he said quietly. "Not anymore."

Ah, that question about his mother had scraped against some deeply buried grief. "But two strangers arriving just weeks after Dzavek's death. Will the coincidence be too strong?"

His glance dropped to the ground. He wasn't certain either, she could tell, but he only said, "It will serve for now. The current rumors speak of one young woman from foreign parts, not two. The queen's appearance is nothing like a Károvín, but I have a plan for that as well. We can discuss all that tomorrow. There is one last thing I must tell you, however." A long pause followed. Ilse thought he had lost the thread of their conversation when he said, almost unwillingly, "He lives."

Ilse's head swam. She dropped into a crouch and stared at Karasek. "What do you mean?"

"He lives," Miro Karasek repeated. "My captain reported the news to me in Rastov. Your Lord Kosenmark lives."

Though he continued to speak, Ilse could not take in the rest of his words. *He lives,* she thought. Raul lived. He had survived that impossible battle on Hallau Island.

"I can go home," she said.

"No. Not yet."

Her gaze swung up to meet his. "Why not?"

"I need . . . a very great favor."

More promises. More expectations.

"Tell me this favor," she said softly.

Miro Karasek chafed one hand inside the other, as though he were seeking the right words, and there were none to be found.

"I have no right to ask this," he said, "but I will. Ride with the queen to Taboresk. It's too dangerous for either of you to travel alone—your encounter with that courier proves it—and I must report to the rest of the northern garrisons before I see you and her safely home."

"And if I do?" she asked. "What then?"

"Then I send you home to Veraene by the safest means I have."

One risk for another.

"Why would you do such a thing?" she said. "For me, or for her?"

The hands stilled. When he spoke, it was as though he spoke to others watching from beyond an invisible veil. "Because I failed a dozen times before. Each time, I salved my conscience, saying I had proved my loyalty to my king. And yet, by doing so, I had lost my honor and allegiance to the gods. Once, as you might remember, I executed you for treason, but there were other betrayals in other lives. I must do better in this one."

There could be no possible answer to such a declaration. Miro did not seem to expect one. He lay down next to the campfire, on the opposite side from Valara.

Ilse let her breath trickle out. *So and so. We are not yet done with our obligations.*

She stood and paced the circuit of their camp. For two weeks, she had told herself she had lost Raul for this lifetime and she could only hope to find him in the next. All that was overturned by two words.

He lives. He lives and I will go to him.

Oh, she would keep her promise to Miro Karasek. Keeping that promise would forge new alliances between his kingdom and hers, between theirs and Morennioù. But even as she considered the future, she came back to the news that Raul Kosenmark lived.

She found she was weeping for joy.

CHAPTER TWO

THE NEXT DAY, Valara Baussay woke to the sun slanting through the pine trees. Above, the branches were limned in silver, and the air smelled clean and damp, as if rain had passed over them in the night. It was like a spring morning in Morennioù, except for the absence of salt tang in the air.

She let a soundless sigh trickle from her lips. It bothered her, how much she missed her homeland. It had started with sympathy, she thought. A dangerous sentiment, as her father always warned her. That led to regret, which led to any number of self-indulgent emotions. Court did not allow that. Her mother's and sister's deaths had only confirmed the lesson.

Nearby, she heard voices—Ilse's and Miro's—talking in undertones. Valara turned her head toward them, and saw Ilse crouched by the campfire, stirring the contents of a cook pot. A second pot sat on the coals. Valara sniffed and smelled roasted oats and the rich scent of coffee. Karasek must have brought a fresh sack of the beans, because she and Ilse had drunk nothing but infusions of herbs and bitter bark these past ten days.

Miro stood a few paces farther off, by the horses. One butted its head against his chest. He laughed—the change was so startling, she nearly exclaimed. When had she last heard him laugh? Not for a dozen lifetimes. Not since . . .

. . . *since their lives together in Morennioù, when she took him into her bedchamber and they made love. The next morning, a ship had arrived with orders from the emperor, demanding his return to the continent.*

Valara flung her blanket away and sat up. Ilse immediately glanced toward her. Faint lines creased her face, sharpened to ink-black strokes in the firelight, as though she had not slept well. The laughter vanished from Miro's face. He turned away and busied himself with the pile of saddlebags.

Ilse poured a mug of steaming coffee and handed it to Valara. "Drink quickly. We have a great deal to discuss."

Yes, the plans for the next stage of their journey.

Valara gulped down the scalding coffee. The drink tasted like smoke on her tongue; it sent warmth coursing through her bones. If she were to miss anything about these miserable lands, it would be this scent, this flavor, which was like a mouthful of fire. Awake now, she combed her hair and braided it anew.

They ate breakfast quickly—boiled oats mixed with dried fruit and hunks of toasted bread with melted cheese. At last the pot of coffee was empty, the oats and bread devoured. Ilse took their mugs and set them to one side.

"What comes next?" she asked.

"For you," Karasek said, "shelter in my domain. Once we are there, you shall have privacy and I shall have the means to arrange for a ship. You two are sisters, distant cousins of mine from Duszranjo, who intended to travel to the coast, to visit another, more distant cousin. But bandits attacked your party, late enough that you could not turn back . . ."

"So we continued to your household," Valara said. "Yes. A long journey. The attack. The loss of nearly all our possessions. That would account for a great deal. But"—she gestured at the ill-fitting cloak and boots she wore—"perhaps not quite everything."

He smiled briefly. "No, not quite. I can provide for that, however."

He fetched the largest of his saddlebags and set it before Valara and Ilse. After a puzzled glance toward Ilse, Valara unbuckled the bag and peered inside. Clothing. A generous quantity. She extracted the first item— it was an embroidered tunic, cut to fit a woman. She set that aside and took up a skirt, which was split into two, perfectly suited to riding. Underneath were two long woolen coats. Valara hardly dared to ask where he had acquired them. If their plans succeeded, she would not have to concern herself with any rumors left behind.

"I also brought this," Karasek said. He took a many-folded square of paper from his shirt. "Your letter of introduction to my steward, Sergej Bassar. Your name will be Matylda Zelenka," he said to Ilse. "Yours," he said to Valara, "is Ivana."

Karasek handed the letter to Ilse, who read it through before she gave it to Valara. Valara scanned its contents. A typical letter of introduction, she thought, allowing for the differences of language and custom, informing one Mestr Sergej Bassar that Duke Karasek had invited his two cousins to enjoy his hospitality, etc., etc. So many details, so many points where the plan could fracture and miscarry.

"Are you certain they won't question us?" she asked Karasek. "I look nothing like your people."

"You don't," he agreed. "For that, I brought another kind of disguise."

He took a square wooden box from the bottom of the saddlebag and unlatched the lid. Inside were several tins of ground spices, which sent up a pungent cloud of scent. Miro washed out their cook pots and fetched a skin of water from the stream. As he mixed and measured the spices, he explained that certain Immatran spies used the dye to color themselves so they were not so conspicuous outside their own kingdom.

"Where did you find the ingredients?" Ilse asked.

"Various sources."

Valara's skin rippled in apprehension. Discretion was one matter. Concealing information from your allies was another. "You found it lying by the roadside?" she asked, her tone as light as his was not. "Or did you requisition these supplies from your last garrison?"

His gaze snapped up to meet her. Angry. Good.

"I took no unnecessary chances," he said softly. "Not for the clothing. Not for the dye itself. These are all common ingredients, which is why our spies, and those of other kingdoms, like the method."

Throughout the exchange, Ilse Zhalina had observed them both with strange intensity.

What did she see? Valara wondered. The first flaw in an enemy's shield? A reason for pity or sympathy?

She rubbed her forehead. She could not think of what to say. To her relief, Karasek continued with the next installment of their instructions.

"Head south until you reach the Ostrava Hills. You will find a small lake, fed by streams from the hills. A trail leads directly east from the lake. Four days should bring you to a valley that marks the western edge of my lands. Follow its southern slopes for another day and you will come to my household."

"Any obvious dangers?" Valara asked. "Other than soldiers hunting for the king's assassins."

That provoked an almost smile. "No human dangers. It's the wrong season for trappers. But the animals they hunt pose a greater risk—mountain leopards, wolverines, lynxes. My father died hunting leopards in these same hills."

He spoke dispassionately, but the sense of lost possibilities teased at her.

Karasek stirred the dye. It looked like dark brown mud, with a strong, biting smell that Valara could not identify. "Brew another batch when you reach the hills," he said. "A second application should last a month or two."

Long enough for him to acquire the ship and for her to leave this kingdom behind.

Silently, the three of them watched the mixture as it bubbled and spit. From time to time, Karasek bent close as though to examine its consistency. Then, though Valara could see no difference, he apparently decided it had cooked enough. He wrapped his cloak around his hands and transferred the bowl to one side to cool.

He would visit the next three garrisons heading south, he told them, then ride directly to Taboresk so as to arrive before them and prepare his people. It was much like their last few hours at the Mantharah, with Karasek giving precise instructions for concealing their presence. Latrine buried. Trash burned and the ashes covered in dirt. The supplies redistributed between their three horses.

The dye had cooled long before they finished.

Valara eyed the viscous concoction. It looked like fresh horse dung, and smelled worse. "Do you expect me to strip?" she asked drily.

Color edged Karasek's cheeks—a most unexpected reaction.

"No," he said. "Cover as much of you that shows—face, neck, arms, and hands. You can dye the rest before you reach Taboresk. I want to make certain, however, that your first and most obvious appearance is correct."

Of course. That answer helped Valara to steady her own heartbeat as she pushed up her sleeves and applied a thick coating to her hands and arms. The dye stung, and its acrid smell made her eyes water. She took up a smaller scoop and applied it to her face, working the dye into the crevasses beside her nose, around her mouth and eyes.

"How long until it takes?" she asked as she continued to apply the paste to the rest of her exposed skin.

"Not long. Less than an hour."

Valara bit her lip. An hour. She could bear it. It was no worse than when the priests had inked her first and second tattoos, proclaiming her as a princess royal, then heir to the crown. Far less painful than when the gods had burned away her magic.

Ilse stood. "I'll fetch more water so you can wash."

She picked up a waterskin and headed toward the stream.

Karasek stood and paced around the camp. As she applied more paste to her throat and behind her ears, Valara glanced at him surreptiously. It did not require much insight to note his impatience to be gone. Did he expect his enemies to count the days between his departure at one garrison and his arrival at the next? Or was it simply the habit of a soldier?

She tilted her head to one side, to reach the back of her neck. Drops from the paste trickled into her eyes. She hissed, caught herself before she rubbed her eyes.

Karasek spun around and hurried toward her. "Hold still. Close your eyes."

She squeezed her eyes shut. All her other senses leapt to awareness. She heard the rustle of pine needles as Karasek knelt down, much louder than expected. The slither of leather. Taking off his gloves? Then a faint brush of air as he lifted his hand toward her face.

He wiped the liquid away with his sleeve, then said, "Your eyelids. We forgot those."

His fingers touched her eyelids. She shivered. Karasek paused, but she could hear his breath, amplified, it seemed.

"I'm sorry," she said. "Please. Go ahead."

Karasek daubed the still-warm paste over her eyelids. More paste went on her eyebrows and in the slight creases beside both eyes. With swift light strokes, he worked the paste into her skin.

Her eyes watered. His hand withdrew, then returned to wipe away the tears with a soft cloth. Beneath the stink of the paste, she could breathe in his scent, a blend of horse and leather and the sweat from riding through the wilderness.

There was a pause. She felt fingertips brush over her cheek. No, that had to be her imagination, because when Karasek next spoke, his voice seemed remote.

"Now we let it set," he said.

Her eyes still closed against the dye, she heard him pace around the camp. Once, twice. His footsteps were slow and deliberate. More than once he stopped, then his boots creaked slightly. She pictured him kneeling to pluck up a nearly invisible clue.

She recited the litany to summon magic. It did her no good, but the words and cadence were familiar enough to calm her nerves.

I did what you asked, she prayed to Lir, to Toc. *I made mistakes, but I tried to do right, in the end. Can you understand? Please?*

Silence answered her questions, and eventually, her thoughts drifted into the same almost-resignation that plagued her since Mantharah. The gods would do as they wished. She would discover their intentions only in the aftermath.

Ilse returned with the water. Valara waited until Karasek gave the signal, then splashed her face to wash away the excess dye. She scrubbed her skin, dried her face with the corner of her cloak. She repeated the process twice more and ran her fingers through her hair to catch the last bits of herbs and spices. When she looked up, she found Ilse studying her closely.

"How do I look?" she asked.

"Like a Károvín."

Hard to read anything from that bland tone. Even more unsettling was Karasek's dispassionate gaze. "And you?" she said sharply. "How do I look to you?"

He smiled briefly. "Just as our friend said."

An unsatisfactory reply. She wanted to demand an honest answer, but Karasek was already mounting his horse. His gaze met hers, just for a moment. "Until Taboresk," he said.

ILSE WATCHED HIM ride west and south with an uneasy feeling. She had known this man in a dozen lifetimes, but the memory of each was blurred. Twice he had executed her at Leos Dzavek's command. Now he meant to make restitution. To her. To Valara Baussay.

And yet he is not easy with his compromise between allegiance and honor, she thought. *Not when the two do not coincide.*

Nor did Valara Baussay appear easy with trusting a man who had so recently been their enemy. In the days after they parted from Karasek, the other woman rode silently beside Ilse over the sun-baked plains that spread like a varicolored quilt of green and gold toward the west and south. They had little cover, except for the sudden narrow ravines carved out by rainstorms and melting snows, or the occasional stand of trees. It was a relief when Ilse at last sighted the Ostrava Hills. Another day brought them to Karasek's lake, and the trail heading east toward his domain.

Domain. An interesting term. It could mean simply a region granted by the king to a faithful retainer, but the older definition implied the lands of a prince. Yet Károví itself had been called a princedom in the old empire days.

When Ilse calculated they were a day from the valley and Karasek's lands, she called for an early halt. They built a generous fire and tended to the horses while the dye brewed. This time Valara stripped and painted herself completely with the mixture. She did not speak, but her movements were dogged, her expression remote. If she noticed Ilse glancing in her direction from time to time, she made no comment. Nor did she object when Ilse checked over her work.

It was only the pulse, beating swift and light at her throat, that told Ilse how much her companion's mood resembled hers.

We are both afraid. In one more day, we come to the true test of our disguise.

After dinner, they dressed in the finest of their new clothing. By agreement, because she spoke the truest Károvín, Ilse took possession of the letter. They buried their borrowed cloaks, their clothing from Veraene, and anything else that might not fit their new roles as Duke Karasek's distant cousins from Duszranjo. The last two objects they cast into the trench were Valara's box of dyes and Ilse's sword.

The sword was the most difficult to give up. She had this blade from Raul, a gift from their days together in Tiralien. He had brought the sword to her, after she and Valara had fled from Osterling Keep.

"You might keep it," Valara said, in a rare display of understanding.

"I might," Ilse said, "except that such a sword was made for a woman of my height and strength. It would draw too much suspicion."

She laid the sword in the pit and covered it with dirt.

The following day they woke to a mass of iron-gray clouds on the horizon. By midafternoon the wind blew raw and cold. They drew rein at the bottom of a dry streambed. Ahead the land climbed through scattered pine forests to a high exposed ridge at least two miles away. Ilse wrapped her new coat tight around her throat and checked the presence of their letter once more.

"Do we stop," Valara said, "or ride forward?"

Ilse gazed upward to the bare ridge. No cover there, but the streambed would hardly shelter them once the rain started, and she could smell its approach. "We keep going. I suspect we will find better shelter on the other side of that ridge."

They started off at a fast trot, but once they entered the pine forest, the ground turned rough underfoot and their progress slowed. The storm hit before they covered a mile. The sky turned black, and rain swept down, rattling through the branches. She thought it might come to hail soon. Once they cleared the last band of trees, Ilse pulled her hood low over her forehead and urged her horse into a trot. The ridge was much closer, the ground rising steeply ahead. She glanced over her shoulder to see how Valara did, when she caught the flicker of movement off to one side. Had she imagined that?

Lightning crackled, illuminating a horse and its rider galloping toward them.

Bandits, Ilse thought. Karasek's lies had become truth. "Ride!" she shouted.

She bent over her horse's neck and dug her heels into its sides. The horse surged forward. Above the growl of thunder, Ilse heard Valara's cries to her own mount, encouraging it to run, to gallop, to race the storm. Their pursuer veered toward the ridge, on a path to cut them off, but they still had a chance. Then, to her dismay, a second shadow burst from the gloom. Ilse cursed Miro Karasek and his orders not to use magic. She called out the invocation to gods. Cold fire sprang up from the ground, cutting off the rider. It was enough to let her gain the ridge first, with Valara close behind. Over they went, down the treacherous hillside, into a twisting gorge . . .

Three more riders blocked her path. Ilse tried to veer to one side, but one of their pursuers had overtaken her and was riding in parallel. "Stop!" he shouted.

She drove her horse into his. The two of them slithered halfway down the slope; she thought she could break free, but then he grabbed the reins from her and dragged her and her horse to a halt. The horse squealed its distress. Ilse reached at once for her sword. Gone. Buried with the rest of her old belongings the day before.

She struck out at the man, then grabbed the reins away. The man only grinned, his teeth a flash of dull white in the murky light. "No fighting. You couldn't best the lot of us."

Six or more shadows were milling about. Was one of them Valara? Yes. There she was, tall and bone-thin, her manner that of a queen.

Three more riders approached. Far, far too many for her to overcome with magic. One of them signaled the others with an uplifted hand. The leader?

Whoever it was walked their horse toward Ilse. It was impossible to tell much about the person. They wore a dark cloak, streaming with water, and a hood pulled low over their forehead. A sword hung from the person's hip, and no doubt they had more weapons hidden from view.

"Who are you?"

It was a woman who spoke.

"We are travelers," Ilse said carefully.

"That was not my question. *Who* are you?"

Ilse wet her mouth. "We're travelers bound for Duke Miro Karasek's holdings. He expects us. But if you think to rob us, you're too late. Bandits attacked our party five days ago."

A brief silence followed. "Is that true?"

"That we have no possessions, or that you aren't robbers? The first is true. As for the second, I cannot tell. Not from your manner."

At that, the woman laughed. "No, we are not robbers."

She raised a hand and spoke a few words in Erythandran. For a moment the wind seemed to hold its breath. Then came the strong invigorating scent of magic, like summer wrapped into a single moment. Light bloomed in the air. It cast a nimbus of silver in the steady rain, and by its glow, Ilse could see the woman's face. Square-built, a dusky brown so dark, she might have come from Veraene's southern coast, except for the folds at her eyes, and the slant of her cheeks that said Károví.

"We are patrols for my Duke Karasek of Taboresk," the woman said, "charged with keeping his domain secure. I ask again. Who are you?"

It was all wrong. This confrontation. The anger and suspicion, even before they had a chance to give the story Karasek had manufactured for them. Drawing a breath to steady her nerves, Ilse met the woman's gaze.

"We come from Duszranjo at Duke Karasek's invitation," she said. "Ask him, if you doubt my word."

The patrol members were whispering among themselves, but the woman herself did not change expression. "His grace is not here," she said. "He last wrote to us from the capital, and he gave no news of visitors."

"The duke wrote his steward, not his sentries," Ilse replied.

Her answer provoked a tight smile. "I am Bela Sovic—captain of this patrol. The steward would notify me of expected visitors." She glanced from Ilse to Valara, who sat uneasily on her horse, her hands flexing and unflexing around the reins. "Pardon my own caution, but do you have any mark of passage from my duke?"

"A letter." Ilse gestured at the rain. "I would rather not open it here."

"I can solve that difficulty."

Sovic spoke again in Erythandran. The green scent of magic intensified as the silver nimbus expanded to enclose them both. It was like a cousin to the shield of secrecy Ilse had used more than once. Not far away, Valara watched the scene with a strange avid expression.

Sovic held out her hand.

Silently Ilse handed the letter to the woman.

The patrol captain examined the envelope with its neatly written address. Then she unfolded the paper, which Karasek had left unsealed, and read it through slowly. Her expression did not change, but when she glanced up, Ilse sensed a difference.

"My apologies, Lady Matylda. We've heard rumors of trouble in the region."

Ilse nodded slowly. "I quite understand. We have met more than rumors ourselves."

"Just so, my lady." She returned the letter to Ilse, who tucked it back into her shirt. "We are not far from the duke's household. No more than an hour. Can you manage that long, my lady?"

Ilse exchanged a glance with Valara, who nodded. "Better an hour of riding than a night in the wet."

Bela's mouth twisted in a smile. "So I've often thought. And you, my lady?"

Valara lifted her chin. "I can ride."

One brief phrase, carefully chosen. Could Bela hear the false intonation?

Bela gave no indication of that, however. She scattered her magic to the air, then delivered a series of commands to her patrol. One rider rode ahead. The rest fell into formation around Valara and Ilse. Another command, and the company set forth.

ONCE THEY HAD cleared the next ridge, the patrol veered into a thicket of pine. The trail wound through the forest, dripping with rain, the trail muddy and uncertain. Their progress slowed and they rode single file. Only a madman—a Károvín madman—would attempt an assault on Taboresk's heartland, Ilse thought. It was a telling detail, this attention to patrols in such a wilderness. If she weren't so cold and wet, she might have attempted to work through the implications. As it was, she huddled inside her soaking cloak and kept her eyes upon the horse and rider in front of her.

Soon they came to the edge of the trees. Here the land dropped away abruptly. Ilse could just make out a trail, a dark ribbon snaking down through the rain-soaked grass.

"Very soon," Bela said to Ilse.

The trail brought them down to a well-maintained road. The rain had eased, and the dark red of the setting sun broke through the clouds over the western horizon. They made faster progress then, trotting at times. At last they came to a high stone wall, interrupted by a formidable gate. As the patrol approached, two sentries emerged from a shelter, while three more were visible behind the gate. Far beyond, Ilse saw a massive building, its windows illuminated with golden light.

Karasek's home.

She had expected a mansion, such as Raul Kosenmark's, or a palace such as Lord Vieth's in Tiralien. What she saw was more like a mountain, rising abruptly from the ground in turrets and towers all of blue-gray stone, with wings thrusting around the courtyard. She had the sense of entering the household of an ancient prince from the empire times.

An army of servants swarmed from the house. Some helped her and Valara to dismount. Others took possession of their horses. More servants unloaded their few saddlebags. An older man, with several attendants carrying rain screens, approached them. "My ladies. My name is Sergej Bassar, steward to the duke. Welcome, welcome to Taboresk."

He led them through a set of wide double doors. The relief from wind and rain was painfully exquisite. Ilse had the blurred impression of a vast entry hall, laid with dark blue tiles, and a high-domed ceiling overhead. Around her the hum of servants, the glow of lamps, the corridors stretching out in all directions.

"The captain sent word ahead," Bassar was saying. "I have rooms prepared for you both."

He took Ilse and Valara up the main stairs, along a stone passageway to a wide corridor that extended as far as Ilse could see. The air felt cool and stale, as though few people frequented this wing.

Bassar stopped by a low square door, constructed of thick golden wood, and carved with leopards and other wild creatures. A young man in livery stood at attention, while from within came the murmured conversation of servants at work.

"My lady," he said to Ilse. "Your rooms. I've taken the liberty of providing you with clothing from our stores, until we can supply you with better."

Ilse paused before she entered. "And our cousin, the duke?"

"He has not yet arrived. I will send him word as soon as he does."

An incomplete answer to all the questions she had, but Ilse did not insist. The man had told her all he knew, or that he thought appropriate to relay. She called up a smile, one appropriate for the trusted servant of her distant cousin, and passed through the doors.

* * *

VALARA ENTERED HER new rooms cautiously, taking in all the details.

A fire blazed in the enormous brick-lined hearth. Several maids had already arrived with hot bathwater, which they were pouring into a tub in the dressing room. Others brought trays of refreshments: hot soup, wine, steaming bread. Beyond, a low, arched passageway led into the bedroom.

She had not known what to expect of Miro Karasek and his home. *Home.* Her lips puffed in silent laughter. What an inadequate word. Her first glimpse had reminded her of the ancient fortresses of Morennioù, all bare stone, carved from mountains. There were no true mountains here, only pine-forested hills rolling away in all directions, but she could tell this building had stood through centuries, its floors and stairs polished by the passage of many, many servants and nobles. And this room . . . Only the multicolored woolen rugs and a series of round windows relieved the impression she had stepped into a cave, however bright and warm.

She disliked this separation from Ilse. She disliked more Karasek's unexpected absence. Her thoughts ran through all the possibilities, none of them good. Karasek delayed. Karasek arrested on suspicion. Karasek betraying her to Markov and the council.

And yet, the steward had not questioned their poverty. He had not even asked to see the letter of introduction. Apparently Sovic's judgment was enough.

"My lady," the steward said.

His name was Bassar, she recalled. Valara nodded, not quite trusting herself to speak yet.

"I have sent word for a seamstress," Bassar said. "My lord duke will make good your losses. Until then"—he gestured toward a trunk by one wall—"we can provide you with suitable attire from our stores."

He paused, expectant.

I must get alone. I must think.

"Thank you," she said, taking care to speak as Ilse Zhalina taught her. "I . . . I am tired. I need to eat and rest. Alone, please."

She bowed her head, as if weary.

(Not a lie. She was weary—weary of pursuit, of dissembling every moment, even to her companions. Court had never demanded quite so much.)

"Of course." Bassar motioned for the servants to withdraw. "If you should discover anything lacking, please send a runner. I shall have one waiting outside your door."

The moment she was alone, Valara threw off her sodden clothing and sank into her bath. The maids had left an astonishing array of soaps and brushes and cloths. She used them all, reveling in a luxury she had not known since Morennioù.

Since Karasek had brought a thousand soldiers to her kingdom.

She shivered in the cooling water. Six months had passed since that day. She could not guess how many more until she regained her homeland.

From far off a bell rang, rendered faint and dim by the stone walls. Valara rose from the bath and dried herself. The maids had hung a selection of clothes by the fireplace. She dressed in a loose gown and drew a robe over that. Her chambers were warm, but she needed the familiar weight of layers upon layers. It was the closest she could come to feeling at home.

Eventually, she remembered her dinner. She ate with little attention to the food, wondering what other plans Karasek had laid, what other schemes he had not revealed to her. Her thoughts drifted from Karasek to Morennioù and then to Jhen Aubévil, once her best friend in childhood, in a court where friendship was little valued. Later, because his father held great influence at court, and because her father valued that influence, they had arranged a marriage between their houses. Her sister's death and her own ascension to heir had changed the balance but not the substance of their relationship—

Oh, but that was too painful a thought. She had last seen Jhen in the company of his father, riding toward the castle gates. Had they broken through the line of Károvín invaders? Or were they among the many dead she had passed on the way to the ships?

I cannot, cannot think of that yet.

She set her plates aside and paced the room. Her circuit took her past the doorway leading to her bedchamber. She flinched away from the memory of other stone passageways, other lives, where she felt imprisoned by walls and unhappy decisions. She paused by a tall mirror on its stand and examined her appearance.

The stain had darkened her skin from golden to the copper brown of Károví. Her flat, full cheeks, her otherwise sharp features, all of them so common in Morennioù, now looked startlingly different. She stared harder at this new picture of herself, trying to see her face as Bassar the steward might. As Bela Sovic might.

I will pass. I have to.

A knock sounded at the suite's outer door. Valara spun around, startled.

With an effort, she recalled herself. The visitor would be Ilse Zhalina, most likely, come to discuss their situation. Even so, her nerves buzzed with suppressed alarm as she crossed to the door and opened it.

Miro Karasek stood outside, a shadow against the dim light of the corridor. He had changed his clothes. Gone was the plain dark uniform of the soldier, the hair bound in its utilitarian braid. Now he wore a neat linen costume—loose trousers, a shirt with banded collar, and a voluminous jacket gathered by a cloth belt—the whole a subtle shading of blue upon darker blue.

"Lady Ivana," he said quietly. "My apologies for the delay. I understand you and your sister had a confrontation with my sentries."

"A fortunate encounter," Valara murmured. "At the last."

His smile was brief but genuine. In a softer voice, he said, "Did you think our script had turned into reality?"

"Yes. No. But it worked to our advantage."

To her eye, he was like a friend strangely altered, clothed in elegant linen and his hair, still damp from the rain, gathered loosely in a ribbon. He even wore scent, one as subtle as the shading of his cloth. Then she realized she had only ever seen him as a soldier, and not a lord, even in lives past. She wondered, for the first time, how he viewed her.

"Have you dined?" he asked. "Do you have everything you need?"

"I have everything," she said. "For today. I thank you."

His glance shifted down the corridor and back. "I told the servants your nerves were badly shaken by your ordeal with the bandits and that you wished for privacy. It seemed reasonable."

He spoke in a great hurry. She could not read his expression. It seemed a mixture of distress and indecision. Just when she expected him to say more—about their plans, about what she might expect the next day—he turned away. "I must go. We can talk tomorrow. I will send word to you."

Before she could answer, he was pacing down the corridor.

Valara leaned against the door and pressed both hands and her cheek against it. She heard a ringing of boots over stone fading in the distance.

She drew a breath. How to decipher that brief exchange? Experience said he regretted his decision to give them aid and shelter. Her instincts—but her instincts had proved so very wrong these past six months—but if she believed them . . .

Abruptly she walked to the nearest window. The storm had passed, leaving the silvery skies clear, except for a cascade of stars. The stars reminded her of Lir's jewels. Her palm ached from where the three jewels had merged into one.

Death erases us, she thought, recalling the poet René Chartain's essay. But she remembered the essay's next line: *Death reminds us*.

From that she took what comfort she could.

CHAPTER THREE

IT WAS THE quiet that woke Ilse the next morning.

The quiet had infiltrated her dreams—an unfamiliar silence more absolute than any woodland, or even the hush throughout Raul Kosenmark's pleasure house, in the hours when courtesans and clients both slept.

As quiet as death.

Her eyes blinked open. There was a long moment of taking in the bare details—the sense of being dipped in blue shadows, how every movement caused her to sink further into a soft and all-encompassing sea of blankets and down-filled quilts. She tensed, still caught between dreams and waking. Then came recollection—the confrontation with Karasek's sentries, the long ride through the soaking rain, and late arrival at Karasek's household.

She sat up and pushed aside the curtains around her bed. The hour was barely past dawn. Light spilled through the windows, a pale silvery tide, pouring down the walls and reaching high toward the ceiling of stone. The fire in her grate had died to ashes; the air felt chill and damp. Ilse fumbled into the woolen robe she had abandoned last night and padded over to the stand with its basin and pitcher.

A tapping sounded at the bedroom door. "My lady?"

One of the servants. "Enter," she said.

A young woman dressed in a dark smock and skirt opened the door, and immediately sank into a curtsy. "My lady. I am your maid Anezka. The steward assigned me to attend you. Is there anything you wish?"

I wish I could open a door from one city to another.

That was a request for Miro Karasek, however.

"Has my cousin, the duke, arrived?" she asked.

"Last night, my lady."

Good. She smiled at her maid. "Then I would like breakfast. Hot tea and bread, or whatever the cook has ready. And please send word to his grace that I would like an interview with him as soon as possible."

Anezka's eyes widened, but she merely replied she would do as her mistress required.

Once the girl left, Ilse closed her eyes and cursed Miro Karasek. He had planned for every circumstance with Leos Dzavek's court, but beyond an introductory letter, nothing for his own household. She wished she had questioned him more closely during their last rendezvous in the wilderness. She wanted more clues to their supposed situation, what quarrels or loves or history lay between his mother and their fictitious family. Were his mother's people nobles or landowners? Did they correspond regularly? So many tiny clues that could betray them all.

She brushed out her hair and wound it in a loose plait as she passed from night-cold bedroom to the parlor, where a generous fire burned. Too restless to sit, she continued to pace, working through how to address her concerns to Karasek. Now that she had delivered Valara Baussay to Taboresk, she could return to Veraene at once. Only how? And what of her own uncertain status? Alesso Valturri had arranged to disguise her disappearance as murder, but she could not be certain if Markus Khandarr had penetrated that ruse. She would have to arrive secretly and swiftly.

Her other difficulty lay within herself. She had promised Valara Baussay to accompany her back to Morennioù. Now all the reasons for that promise had vanished, but she knew Valara would insist she keep the vow.

She wants an ally, a witness to these past six months.

From what Ilse knew of Morenniou's Court, she could understand.

But I must go to Tiralien. I must tell Raul about the jewels.

A conflict of allegiances, to self, to kingdom.

Before she had made a dozen circuits, the girl returned with a tray laden with an enormous silver teapot and several covered plates, which she suspected contained more than just bread. Apparently the cook wished to provide a proper breakfast for the duke's visitors. "Breakfast, my lady."

"And the duke?" Ilse asked.

"He rides with his steward, my lady. On inspection." Anezka laid the tray on the table and poured steaming tea into a round glass cup. "But he left messages for you and the Lady Ivana."

She indicated an envelope, tucked beneath a plate.

The moment Anezka curtsied and withdrew, Ilse plucked up the letter. No magic or wax, she noted in passing. The letter itself was short, written in strong sure brushstrokes.

Lady Matylda Zelenka, My regrets for the misunderstanding with my sentries, and especially for my delayed arrival. I have begun arrangements for you and your sister to continue your journey to our cousins in the east. I hope

*to have more news by this afternoon. Until we meet again, you might find my
library of interest. My stables are at your service as well. You have merely to
send word to my steward or the stable master, so they can arrange for a horse
and a proper escort.*

—*Miro Karasek*

A public message, judging by the lack of protections, but she could read
the private interpretation easily enough. *He means to reassure us. He does not
wish to speak with me alone. Not yet.*

So. Which to choose? Ilse's first inclination was to visit the library—to
discover the enemy within his own domain. But then she remembered that
Duke Karasek was riding on inspection. Perhaps she could arrange to encounter him.

First she applied herself to breakfast. Her appetite had awakened at the
sight of the sumptuous meal the cook had provided: hot cakes spread with
bittersweet jam, and tiny balls of egg yolk and grated cheese—the kind of
breakfast Ilse's grandmother had loved because the dishes reminded her of
Duszranjo. Ilse ate to her fill, drank the tea, brewed hot and strong in the
northern fashion, then called for her maid.

"I would like to ride," Ilse said. "Please send a runner to the stables for
a horse and escort. And leave word with my sister for when she awakes."

That request, at least, did not provoke any surprise. Anezke sent off the
requested runner toward the stables, then helped Ilse into a riding costume
from the trunk the steward had supplied. These were much like the clothes
Miro Karasek had acquired for them during their journey, but of a much
finer cloth, and a much more elegant cut. Voluminous trousers of fine wool.
A shirt of the same material, soft and embroidered along the collarless
neckline. Another jacket that swept over her hips and flared outward like a
gown. Someone had stitched up the hems to match her other clothes. The
fit was loose, but it would do well enough for today.

A second runner guided Ilse down the staircases and through a broad
hallway that led toward the rear of the house. Lamps illuminated all the
passageways. Several fireplaces interrupted the smooth walls along the corridors, throwing out a bright welcome glare. Taboresk House was old, built
close to the end of the empire, she guessed. She wondered what role the
family had played in the wars.

How many of them did I know as a princess of Károví?

Ilse wiped a hand over her face. No time to speculate about past lives.
She must press forward into the new.

She arrived at the stables to find Bela Sovic waiting by two dark brown mares, both saddled and ready. Several stable boys and girls, and a young man dressed in riding gear, stood off to one side.

Ilse paused. She took in the young man's obvious irritation, the curiosity of the stable hands, and Sovic's own sardonic smile. Her pulse leapt upward in alarm. Whatever she expected, she had not anticipated the patrol captain's presence.

Sovic nodded. "My lady. I hear you wished to ride."

Ilse kept her expression as bland as Sovic's. "That is true. I had hoped my cousin could show me his estates, but I understand he is otherwise occupied. Are you my escort this morning?"

The other rider muttered something Ilse could not decipher. Bela's lips twitched into an almost smile. "Let us say that I often ride a circuit of the grounds in the morning—call it a private ritual—and I thought you might prefer a guide willing to speak and answer your questions."

So. Possibly Karasek's captain of the guard felt particularly protective of her duke. Ilse could test that hypothesis, which might answer other questions of her own.

She smiled. "You thought correctly, Captain. Let us ride."

They mounted. Sovic led the way through a tunnel and into a paved courtyard, surrounded by a low wall topped with ironwork and lit by the rising sun. The bars curved in patterns that echoed those in the stone, black against the brilliant sunlight, and topped by a deadly row of spikes. Beyond the gates, a pair of guards flanked the opening, and another pair walked the rounds. All the clues pointed to a far more dangerous situation than she had first expected. Ilse slowed her horse and glanced back to the house. Its walls rose up in a straight gray expanse five stories high, crowned by spires. Lesser wings swept out to either side—foothills to the grand central mountain. She thought she could spot the windows of her own rooms.

"Very grand," Bela said.

"Very," Ilse agreed. "My cousin is a wealthy man, but everyone knows that."

"So they do," Bela said. "Shall we ride, my lady?" She indicated a wide path that circled around the house, then another narrower path leading into the fields. "We have gentle trails and rough ones, or there is the road leading to the nearest village. Whatever you like."

"You said you made a private survey," Ilse replied. "I would like to see that."

"My ride is a long one."

Her companion smiled. A warning or a challenge?

"If I tire, I will let you know," Ilse said.

Bela's answer was a soft laugh. Definitely a challenge.

They set off with Bela in the lead. A grassy expanse spilled out from the courtyard to a wilderness beyond. The path—no more than a narrow ribbon of bare dirt—led them through a break of trees, over a stream, and up a steep incline. Up they climbed, along a winding path that gradually brought them into the foothills on the northern edge of the valley.

Bela dismounted and walked her horse along the ridge. Ilse followed. They came to a crown of boulders. A few feet farther, the trail ended in a ravine cut by a rushing stream.

They tethered their horses to a nearby tree. Bela crouched by the edge of the ravine itself. Ilse stopped a few steps behind and followed the direction of Bela's gaze as she surveyed the duke's lands.

The early mists had burned away. The sun had lifted into the skies, a disk of gold casting shafts of light through the clouds. Far to the east, Ilse could see farmland and open fields where cattle grazed. Closer by were several villages, strung along the stream they had crossed. Directly below them stood Taboresk House, a solid gray anchor amid the greening fields.

"My favorite," Bela said. "It was how I first came into this valley, as swift and direct as I could, not knowing that sometimes the longer path is quicker."

Her voice was soft and pensive.

"When did you first come here?" Ilse asked.

"Fifteen years ago. Two years before the duke returned from Duszranjo. Of course he was not the duke then. Not even the heir."

The air went still, or so it seemed to Ilse. From far off came the faint reverberation of an hour bell.

"But, of course, you knew of that," Bela went on. "You had to, living in Duszranjo."

I should. But your duke never schooled me on the necessary details.

But even this glimpse of the man's past explained his reaction to her earlier questions.

"His grace never told us when you came into the family's service," she said.

"He would not," Bela replied. "It was his father who bought me from the prison. I had tried to fight the pirates on my own after they killed my sister and brother. I— I was less able to distinguish between the enemy and someone merely ignorant, or greedy, and I killed the wrong person. Several wrong persons. The king wished to punish me. I cannot say I disagree, but the old duke believed in mercy. He paid the blood price and took me from the prison. He sent me with a horse, money, and a letter of introduction to the captain of his guards."

She spoke fervently, as if that long-dead duke stood before them and she was reaffirming her vow of allegiance. Ilse could not think how to reply.

"You loved him?" she said at last.

Bela laughed. "Oh, no. He was a hard man, the duke, at least to his soldiers and his guards. But I respected him, and for what he—and his son— have done for me, I would do anything in return."

She bent close to the waterfall and cupped her hands in the spray of water for a drink. The ordinary gesture broke the mood. When she glanced around, her expression was faintly mocking. "Shall we ride on, my lady? Or have you seen enough?"

I have seen your loyalty to the duke, Ilse thought. *Possibly to his son.*

To Bela, she only said, "Lead on. I would like to see more."

VALARA WOKE TO bright sunlight falling on her face. She bolted upright and grabbed for the bedpost, gulping for breath.

It was the dream all over again—fists pounding on her door. Her father shouting to the guards, *Attack! Attack!* And the jewel, Daya, at her breast humming its magic speech, a jumble of bright notes and dark despairing chords.

My father is dead. Daya no longer exists in this world.

Valara wiped a hand over her face. Tasted the tears and sweat. It was the stone that affected her so. Stone walls. Stone tunnels. She had sensed it the night before, but only in her dreams had she understood how much Taboresk House reminded her of Morennioù Castle.

Gradually her pulse stopped its hammering. Her vision cleared from dreams and memory to the present. *We are safe. Safe enough,* she told herself. Karasek had promised his assistance. Proof lay before her, in this luxurious room and the attitude of his steward, even that grim Captain Sovic. She had only to act the part of his cousin, and she could overtake all the obstacles between here and Morennioù.

One moment at a time. She could manage that.

She rose and took her robe from its hook. Someone had removed her filthy discarded clothes. In their place, a selection of clean costumes hung over a rack near the fire. Next to the rack stood a stand with its basin and pitcher of water. The water was steaming, as if newly poured from its kettle, and scented with oils and herbs. She could almost taste the magic used to keep it warm. More luxury, more forethought that so precisely guessed her preferences.

"My lady?" said a woman's voice outside the door.

Valara let the breath trickle from her lips. A maid or runner, of course. "Come in."

A young woman opened the door and curtsied. A maid, judging from her plain dark smock and skirt. "Mestr Bassar sent me to serve you," the young woman said. "Shall I bring you breakfast?"

Her dialect was strong, but the words were comprehensible enough. Valara waved her hand. "Please. Yes."

Alone again, she released a breath. Soon enough she would have to speak more than a few brief phrases. Until then, she would have to listen closely to Karasek's accent, and that of the higher servants, to catch the right lilt and cadence for a Károvín. Ilse had learned the language from her Duszranjen grandmother. Valara had learned it from books and tutors, whose knowledge dated from centuries ago, in the days before Morennioù concealed itself behind its magical veil.

She returned to the washbasin and scrubbed the sleep from her eyes. Brushed the tangles from her hair and braided it afresh. Once more she examined her face in the mirror. It felt so strange to see those dark features and know them to be hers. How long would the stain last? Long enough, she hoped, to see her to the ship.

She paced around the outer parlor and came to an uneasy rest by the windows.

Below, a narrow garden ran the length of the wall. She could just make out a gravel path winding between ornamental pines and laurels. Here and there were stone statues. Even from this distance, she recognized the attitude in each. Lir grieving. Lir laughing. Lir the ancient, implacable judge of humanity. And once, Lir with her consort, both of them old and powerful. In Morennioù they called the goddess by other names, but it was all the same.

I should know. I have talked to them.

Her skin rippled at the memory. She had told herself a dozen times since that she had misremembered, but her dreams refused to forget. Toc, with bright suns in place of his eyes. Lir, holding out her hands for the jewels. She had met the gods, and they had allowed her to live. After a fashion.

A tapping recalled her. Valara's maid entered with a tray and laid out dish after covered dish in an enormous breakfast. Flat cakes, sour cream, smoked fish, a dish of honeyed fruit, and strong tea. As she took her seat before this feast, Valara was not surprised to find an envelope.

"Thank you," she said to the maid. "You may go."

"Yes, my lady. I shall be outside the chambers. You have only to call if you need anything."

Valara waited until the girl closed the door before she took up the letter.

The outer flap bore her new name, Lady Ivana Zelenka, written in strong, precise brushstrokes. No magic, however, not even an ordinary spell to seal the letter. Her breath caught at the possible implications of its absence. Impossible, she told herself. He could not possibly guess her loss.

With greater apprehension, she opened the single sheet to find a brief note in Karasek's hand.

> *Lady Ivana Zelenka, Please excuse the disarray of my household. Certain obligations to the kingdom delayed me, so that I could not be here when you first arrived.*

No disarray, she thought with a return of bitter humor. Even that initial confrontation with Bela Sovic took only moments to resolve. She read on.

> *Duties of house and kingdom require my attention at this moment. Later, if you would grant me the favor, I would like to escort you and your sister around the grounds, when we can discuss your journey to the east. Should the hours grow long or weary, send word to the stable master if you wish to ride. Or may I direct your attention to the library, where you might find books to entertain or enlighten you.*
> —*Miro Karasek*

She set the letter aside. She no longer found the absence of magic sinister. Undoubtedly he did not want to provoke curiosity among his servants. A man of details, he must be thinking of the weeks and months ahead, in case of visitors from Rastov. She would be far away in Morennioù, but he would remain behind.

At the thought of Morennioù, her appetite awakened. She ate quickly as she considered what to do for the morning. A ride might allow her the freedom of exploration. And yet she had spent too many days riding a difficult horse. The library, on the other hand, would contain books on Károví's history. It might even include books that referenced Taboresk. She could hardly hope for a map to Miro Karasek himself, but his possessions might yield more clues to his character. One unguarded moment, her father had always said, could draw a finer picture than any public declaration.

She summoned her maid. "Do you have word of my sister?" she asked. "The Lady Matylda?"

"She went riding, my lady. She has not yet returned."

Interesting. *And so as she chose to ride, I shall visit the library.*

She dressed with her maid's help in the unfamiliar clothing. Tunic, skirt, sash. The layers themselves reminded her of home, but little else did. The ties instead of buttons or loops. The fine wool stitched with intricate designs along the sleeves and neck. Soon enough, however, she was striding through the corridors after a runner, who took her along a direct route from this half-deserted wing to the ground floor, then through a series of wide halls, one of them large enough for dancing. They were leaving one wing and entering another, before the runner paused outside a large set of doors and bowed. "The library, my lady."

Valara paused on the threshold, caught by amazement.

She knew and loved the royal library in Morennioù Castle, but it was nothing compared to this vast chamber, which extended the length of an entire wing and rose two stories into the air. Tall windows alternated with broad walls of rose-colored marble, lined with bookshelves.

She drifted forward a few steps, her gaze taking in the lofty shelves that stretched from floor to airy ceiling. Books and more books and even more. She was so amazed by the unexpected sight, she hardly noticed the door shutting behind her.

Her progress soon brought her to a stand, with a large, delicately painted map underneath a glass frame. The parchment looked ancient, its edges yellowed and crinkled, but the map's crisp inkwork seemed unchanged by time.

Taboresk, read the inscription.

A breathy laugh escaped her. She had wanted a map, though not so obvious a one as this. Well, it was a start. She bent over the glass frame to study her first clue.

The map showed the entire region, stretching from the mountains she and Ilse had skirted on their trip south, to the hills that divided Károví's plains. Taboresk was a rambling wilderness, dotted with villages and small towns. It was much larger than she had first anticipated, almost a miniature kingdom. The man who ruled here had wealth and influence enough to make good his promises. Valara felt her anxiety ease a fraction.

But there was more to discover.

Leaving the map, she approached the nearest shelves, which held rows of bound volumes. She extracted one, which turned out to be written reports from the Károvín Council. She skimmed the text, reading of land grants and taxes and laws enacted by some elder generation. More reports told her these must date from two centuries past.

Then she came to Leos Dzavek's name.

Valara snapped the book shut and leaned against the bookcases, trembling. It was the suddenness, coming across the name so unexpectedly. Not cowardice. Or guilt. Her brother was dead, dead by his own magic. She had paid her own price, as well.

You will never pay the full price. You cannot, unless you undo time itself.

The truth according to her father's mage councillor, when she once dared to ask him about retribution for past crimes. Her pulse beating too fast for comfort, she returned the book to its shelf and stared at the others.

I cannot change yesterday, she thought. *I can only look for tomorrow.*

Nevertheless, her hands continued to shake as she plucked out a second book, several rows past those council reports. This one carried no title except the name *Karasek*.

It was a family history. The first page described how Fedor Karasek, a trusted retainer of Leos Dzavek's father, received his grant of lands. Two decades later, Dzavek himself elevated the man to nobility during the Liberty Wars and awarded him these holdings.

Four hundred years ago.

Valara paused. She had found her treasure of clues, yet the thought intruded that she had no right to trespass thus. She shook away this odd, new delicacy on her part.

We cannot trust until we know each other better.

She replaced the book and searched through the volumes until she found the most recent one. Quickly, she leafed through its pages until she reached the end.

Miro Konstantin Anton Karasek. Seventeenth duke of Taboresk. Only child of Alexje Ivanic Teodor Karasek. He had assumed the title on his father's death in his nineteenth year. A list of military titles, honors, and medals followed, including his appointment to Leos Dzavek's Privy Council.

Nineteen. Younger than I am now.

Orphaned young and trained to rule. They were alike in that.

She skipped back to Alexje Karasek's entry. Miro's father had served in the Privy Council for thirty years, including an interval in Duszranjo as a general overseeing the garrisons. She found details about his speeches to the council and laws he proposed. A paragraph spoke of Miro's birth, but nothing about the man's wife except her name: Pavla Maria. And then, in the year Miro turned eight, a cryptic notation said that Alexje Karasek had named his nephew Ryba Karasek as his new heir.

Valara turned the page. Nothing about this Ryba. Nothing more about Miro's mother. Just a series of mundane observations concerning Taboresk itself. Then mysteriously, another paragraph reinstating his son as his heir. No year given, nor any explanation.

The father had nothing more to tell her. She returned to Miro's entry.

His name meant peace, she learned. (And yet she remembered the blood on his face, from when she first saw him in Morennioù Castle.) He had studied magic in Rastov's university, founded by the king. (Oh, yes. She had proof of his abilities.) He had joined his father in Károví's army at the age of fifteen. Less than a year later, he had taken command. When his father died, he had spent two years running Taboresk alone before Leos Dzavek appointed him to that same Privy Council.

Odd gaps and inexplicable changes in his life. Just like his father.

A door clicked open. Valara shut the book hastily and returned it to its shelf just as Miro Karasek entered the library.

He was dressed formally, in a loose jacket and trousers of dark blue wool, trimmed with black. She found herself responding as she would to any member of her own court and started to lift her hand, palm outward, when she caught herself. He was not Morenniòuen. He would not understand the subtleties of one palm touching another.

Karasek seemed oblivious to her hesitation. "My duties ended earlier than I anticipated," he said. "We shall talk, you and your sister and I. Your sister is riding a circuit of the grounds. Until she returns, would you like a tour of the gardens?"

A clear invitation to a private conversation between the two of them. Curiosity pricked at her. "I would. Thank you."

A short detour brought them to a side door and a small, enclosed court-yard. The skies were a clear hard blue, and the sun shone strong. Yesterday's storm had passed, leaving the trees bowed and wet, and the grounds muddy. Karasek dispatched runners to fetch boots for him and Lady Ivana.

"The seamstress and shoemakers will arrive this evening," he told her as they passed through the courtyard's gate. "You will need more than the few costumes to continue your journey."

"I am grateful for your generosity."

His gaze swung toward her. "I would only do what is right."

Valara could only nod. Karasek was an ambitious man. He risked his life and reputation to see her safely back to her kingdom. *Are you making atonement?* she had asked him at the Mantharah. Though he asked her the same, she knew he was—for the invasion he led in Dzavek's name, of course, but also for more. For past lives, and past failings.

Redemption, she thought, for us both.

They had walked in silence along a path paved with stones. The stones, but not the path itself, ended on the verge of rough grassland, overspread with wildflowers, much like the plains she and Ilse had traversed. A short distance ahead, the ground sloped down to a stream. The northern hills were visible, standing in a dark blue mass against the sky. Downstream and east, she saw the roofs and chimneys of a small village.

Here Karasek paused. "I wrote to my agent in Lenov," he said. "He has instructions to hire a ship and crew, and to provision it for a long journey of uncertain length."

She recalled the city from Raul Kosenmark's maps of the coast. Lenov. A port in the southeast corner of Károví. "Will that draw suspicion?"

He shrugged. "Everything will, these days. But I implied that House Karasek wished to engage in some private trading."

Which brought the next question. "Does the agent know?"

"Of the king's death?" Karasek said. "Not yet, but he will soon."

She noticed that he kept his gaze averted.

"Why are you telling me this?" she asked. "Why not wait until this afternoon?"

"Because I have yet more news."

Ah. Her breath escaped her in a soundless exclamation.

"A courier arrived from Rastov this morning," Karasek said quietly. "News of the king's death has spread throughout Rastov and the outlying towns. Markov has contained the worst confusion there, but there will be more troubles until Károví names a new king. Meanwhile, various nobles, my fellow councillors among them, are maneuvering for the throne."

"Are you saying you must return to Rastov?"

"I don't know yet. But I told my people the news. They had to know."

He spoke with peculiar emphasis. *A conflict of allegiance,* she thought. *Between his kingdom, his dependents, and us.*

"How might that change our plans?" she asked carefully. "Can Markov order you to return?"

He shook his head. "Not as such. We are equal members of the council. More important, I command the armies. But he has allies, and influence."

Now she understood why he had asked for this private conversation. He did not wish Ilse Zhalina to know that Károví was poised on the edge of civil war. *But she comes with me. She cannot carry the news to Raul Kosenmark and Veraene.*

A dozen different questions occurred to her: Did he trust her more than he trusted Zhalina? Did he consider Morennioù a nullity? Or perhaps he thought the Károvín troops there rendered it such. She disliked all those questions, disliked all the answers. It took great control, and the acknowledgment of her father's good advice, to speak calmly.

"Do you have a counterplan?" she asked.

"Several," he replied. "I shall need to consider the implications for each one. But I promise I will discuss them all with you, as soon as I can."

He spoke the truth. She could read that from his tone, from the grave expression he wore as he gazed over his lands. He had broken his trust in several past lives. He would not do so again. But what those vows portended, she could not say.

CHAPTER FOUR

THE KING IS dead. *I'm certain, my lord. The news came from our best agent in Károví.*

Gerek Hessler recited those words over and over as he jogged up the stairs to Lord Kosenmark's private rooms. His heart beat painfully fast, his sides ached, but he did not think of stopping. Kosenmark would want, would need, to hear this news at once.

His best intentions lasted until he gained the fourth floor, where he fell against the wall, one hand pressed against his ribs. He had eaten too well since his return from Hallau—eaten too well, and never ventured beyond the walls of this pleasure house. He was an ox again, large and lumbering.

You cannot bind your true nature, a philosopher had written. *Unless you wish to chafe your soul as rope and chains chafe the flesh.* Gerek closed his eyes and muttered a curse against philosophers and true natures both. Perhaps he would take up weapons drill, like Lord Kosenmark. An hour's bout every day would take away the fat. Then he laughed silently, to think of himself with a sword and not a pen in his hand.

He touched his shirt where he'd placed the packet with Danusa Benik's report. It had come by the usual route, through a series of trusted agents from Károví into Veraene, from there to a bookseller in Tiralien, who sent all such correspondence to Lord Kosenmark packed inside crates of old and rare books. No one had tampered with the seals, and layers of magic ensured only Lord Raul Kosenmark could read the full report. But four words written in old Immatran on the outermost envelope were enough to tell Gerek the bones of Benik's news.

The mountain has fallen.

The mountain had to mean Leos Dzavek, king of Károví. And *fallen* in the code Benik and Kosenmark used translated to *died*. Leos Dzavek had ruled Károví beyond the ordinary span of any other human reign—since the fall of the empire. It was almost impossible to believe him dead, except that Benik was no fool. She had lived six years in the Károvín Court, an anonymous runner of the lowest order, but someone skilled at extracting secrets from her companions. She would never report a rumor as truth.

Gerek knocked at the door to Kosenmark's office with a shaking hand. No answer. He knocked a second time—louder—then tried the latch. Locked, of course. Gerek rattled the latch in irritation. Without much expectation of success, he tried the spell that ordinarily would admit him, and only him, into the office. That also failed.

Has he left without telling me?

Since he and Lord Kosenmark returned to Tiralien, two weeks ago, Kosenmark spent his afternoons in his office. More than once, Gerek had come upon him on his rooftop garden, staring over the city toward the sea. He continued to receive guests in the pleasure house at night, and he met with Gerek over business matters every morning, but otherwise, he kept to his rooms.

Except twice, Gerek thought. When he vanished for a day, each time.

Kosenmark had given no explanation other than to say he'd been hunting. Hunting Lord Khandarr and his agents, Gerek suspected. Though Kosenmark had shut down his shadow court ten months ago, he still had a handful of trusted agents in Veraene. From their reports, Gerek knew that Lord Khandarr had remained in Tiralien several months after the affair on Hallau Island. Word from various agents said the king's mage hoped to collect further evidence of Kosenmark's treason, then arrest Kosenmark on his return. Khandarr had given up just a few days before Kosenmark had returned. By now he would have reported to the king, which made this latest news even more imperative.

Gerek set off to search the rest of the house, traversing each floor and wing from end to end—a long and ultimately pointless task. He found no sign of the man, neither in the many public halls and galleries, nor in the private parlors where Lord Kosenmark sometimes met with more secret visitors. Kosenmark's official schedule for the afternoon claimed he was "at home to visiting nobles."

He never is, though. Not since he lost Ilse Zhalina on that cursed island.

Gerek paused at one of the side doors that gave onto a small paved courtyard. A stone path led through an open gate to an expanse of green grass, then the formal gardens. Past the gardens lay a patch of wilderness, and beyond that, the edge of Kosenmark's grounds, which were patrolled by guards. Gerek did not venture past the door, however. *You must not leave the grounds,* Kosenmark had told him, in their first conference upon their return to Tiralien. *Markus Khandarr will not forgive you for escaping his company.*

Such a delicate way to describe kidnapping, a beating, and interrogation by magic. There had been no official call for Gerek's arrest, but as they both knew, the King's Mage did not always work through official channels.

"Are you hunting our lord, Maester Gerek?"

Gerek stiffened, then reluctantly turned around.

The courtesan Nadine leaned against an arched passageway. She was dressed for an appointment with a client, in a gauzy creation of amber lace, caught by golden ribbons at wrist and ankles. The curves of her body showed through, a dark brown shadow beneath the lace, and a faint breeze carried a trace of her spicy perfume. Kathe had once told him about wild cats she had seen at Duenne's Court, when a famed handler brought several panthers to perform before the king. Kathe had never quite decided if the handler had tamed the cats, or if the creatures chose to perform such tricks out of boredom. Gerek could picture Nadine as one of those panthers.

His throat quivered. He swallowed hard, a temporary cure at best. He hated his stutter. The damned thing showed itself whenever he was afraid or uncertain or simply anxious, as he was now. Only his elder brother, his cousin Dedrick, and now his beloved Kathe, had the patience to work through his sometimes tangled speech. Gerek swallowed again and considered several short replies that might satisfy this woman.

"So you are hunting," Nadine went on. "Like a dog homing to its master—"

"Nadine."

Kathe appeared in the passageway. She spoke breathlessly, as if she had hurried.

Nadine narrowed her eyes—again reminding Gerek of panthers—but she merely shook her head. "Kathe, my love. I thought you were in the kitchen with your mother, terrifying all the girls and boys."

Kathe smiled, a deceptively pleasant smile, except for the tips of her teeth that she showed. "My mother does well enough on her own. My business is with you this moment. You *do* remember what I told you the day Maester Hessler came to us."

Nadine rolled her eyes and gave a dramatic sigh. "That day? So like any other. The sun rose and set. Josef offended a client, though everyone laughed afterward. And your mother insulted yet another pastry cook because she could not bear to yield her place to you, or anyone else, and simply do what

she loves best. But Gerek . . . Gerek. Ah . . . yes. Now I remember. That
was the day you were eating prunes."

"No teasing," Kathe said. "Or you will find raisins in all your biscuits,
and prunes in every other dish. I can arrange that." To Gerek she said,
"Lord Kosenmark is with Maester Ault, my love."

Gerek mumbled a thank-you to Kathe and hurried down the corridor
to the drill yard where Lord Kosenmark practiced with his weapons master, Benedikt Ault. Kosenmark's usual time with Ault was in the early morning. But Kosenmark's usual schedule had proven a mere fantasy these past
two weeks.

He found them engaged in a match with wooden practice swords—one
that had lasted quite some time, judging by their appearance. Ault was an
older man, wiry and strong, with silvered hair cropped short. Like his
weapons master, Kosenmark wore a plain cotton shirt and loose trousers.
Both were covered with sweat and dust, and several long strands of hair
had escaped his braid.

Gerek waved to catch his attention, but neither man noticed. Ault circled around, grinning, then lunged quickly for Kosenmark, who just managed to parry the blow and sidestep the next attack. A series of quick strikes
followed, and both took hits as they went around and around the courtyard. Then Ault lunged again. There was a complicated set of maneuvers
with blade and foot, and the match ended with them both disarmed. Ault
was laughing. Kosenmark bent over, hands splayed against his thighs as he
caught his breath. He was grinning.

Then he glanced toward Gerek. His expression smoothed to a blank.
"Tomorrow," he said to the weapons master. "We'll fight a longer bout."

"With pleasure, my lord."

Kosenmark hung his practice weapon on the rack and wiped the sweat
from his face. "Walk with me," he said to Gerek. "We can talk while I bathe."

Gerek followed him into the pleasure house, down the winding stairs to
the immense and luxurious rooms given over to baths. Once he had hated
Kosenmark. He had believed him a traitor to the king and Vereane. He
had believed this man responsible for the death of Gerek's cousin, Lord
Dedrick Maszuryn. Then Kosenmark had unexpectedly offered him trust.

Let me tell you my intentions, he had said. *Believe me or not, but listen.
Stay in my household a few weeks longer and share my work. Judge for yourself if
I am a traitor to the kingdom or not.*

Gerek had listened, watched, and eventually found himself as entangled as all the other followers of this man. There were times Gerek loved

him. There were other times he cursed himself for succumbing to the man's influence, and yet he continued to serve him.

In the bathing chambers, Kosenmark stripped off his sweaty drill clothes and stepped into the waiting pool. For a moment, he floated on his back in the warm waters, seemingly oblivious to his secretary's presence.

He is not like other men, Dedrick Maszuryn had said, years before when he first told his cousin about his lover, Raul Kosenmark. *He chose mutilation. Some said he wanted to spare his brother. Some say he gambled his manhood for a chance to rule beside the old king.*

A king who demanded this sacrifice for all his chief councillors.

Then Baerne had died, and his grandson, Armand of Angersee, had dismissed Kosenmark from Duenne. Rumor said Lord Khandarr had offered to restore both Raul Kosenmark's manhood and his place at court—but in return he had demanded loyalty to Khandarr himself and not the king. Others claimed that Lord Kosenmark had formed a shadow court to work against the king and rule Veraene from a distance.

Both had elements of the truth, but neither was accurate.

Gerek lowered himself to sit by the pool's edge. Kosenmark sank into the bathwaters with a sigh of pleasure. When he rose again, he splashed water over his face, then took up a bar of soap. "Tell me the news."

All the words he rehearsed fled Gerek's memory. He said, "Leos Dzavek is dead."

The reaction was nothing more than a brief stillness—invisible unless you knew the man. "You are certain of it?" Kosenmark said.

His fluting voice had sunk to a soft even tone. Gerek's skin prickled in sudden apprehension. He licked his lips. "I-I have not read the report itself. Benik s-s-set spells on the paper keyed to you alone. But she wrote a message on the out-s-side, and its meaning is clear enough. She wrote in old Immatran," he added, as if Kosenmark needed this reassurance of his agent's discretion.

Kosenmark merely smiled. "What did that message say?"

"The mountain has fallen."

"Hmmmm." Kosenmark lathered his hands and ran them over his body, scrubbing away the sweat and grime from his sword drill. "So our friend Leos is dead."

"According to the code, yes."

Kosenmark gave no answer to that. His gaze had turned inward. Even after six months in the man's employ, Gerek could not read anything in that still, beautiful mask. Unhappiness, perhaps, but a philosopher might say that each emotion implied the presence of its opposite, and he had not known Lord Raul Kosenmark to express such an alien emotion as happiness, at least not in his presence.

Abruptly, Kosenmark submerged himself, then stood up, the water streaming over his body.

He *was* different from other men, Gerek thought, trying to look elsewhere and failing. Tall and well made, his honey-brown skin gleaming wet, his eyes like polished gold coins. The mage-surgeon had done his job well, but the differences were too obvious to miss. The hairless chest, the stubby penis, the blank expanse between his legs where magic had burned away the flesh.

Kosenmark studied him coolly in return. "Have you seen enough, my friend?"

Gerek flinched and bowed his head. Still with that impassive expression, Kosenmark toweled himself dry and drew on a clean robe. He left the room and mounted the stairs. Gerek trailed behind him, beset with thoughts of dogs and lackeys.

When they reached the fourth floor, Kosenmark unlocked his office door with a spell. Once they were inside, he relocked the door and held out his hand. Gerek yielded the packet and watched as Kosenmark broke the wax seal. A subtle change in the air was the only sign of magic working, but in the next moment, the packet unfolded into three closely written pages. More Immatran, Gerek could see. In addition to her knowledge of magic and spy craft, Benik was gifted in languages—another trait that qualified her for her dangerous post.

Kosenmark quickly read through the report. "This is very great news, indeed," he said softly. "Leos Dzavek believed dead. The council in turmoil, but not for long. Markov oversees the investigation. Karasek is organizing the troops. Risova controls the capital city of Rastov and the immediate surroundings. Ah, that is interesting . . ." He bent closer to the pages, humming to himself as he read, then looked up at Gerek with bright eyes. "Duke Karasek returned from his mission to Hallau Island, but almost immediately departed from the capital, first to track the assassins, then to notify the garrisons of the king's death."

"He *is* the s-senior commander," Gerek said tentatively.

"Yes, but why go himself? Why not send his captains and trusted couriers for the task?" Kosenmark shook his head. "There could be any reason—good or bad—for such a decision. What concerns me is that they have not found the body."

"N-n-no body? Then how do they kn-kno-know—?"

"By magic. When the councilors entered the king's study, they found the signs of a battle with magic. Dzavek had vanished, along with certain irreplaceable treasures—Benik cannot tell which ones. The three chief councillors—Karasek, Markov, and Černosek—refuse to admit anyone else into the rooms, including the servants. There are rumors of magical traces pointing to Immatra and Duszranjo, but no conclusive evidence . . . Various factions within are maneuvering for power . . . which makes Karasek's absence all the more puzzling."

His attention captured by one phrase, Gerek barely paid attention to these comments about councils and factions. "Irreplaceable treasures. Does that mean s-someone s-s-stole King Leos's ruby?"

"Possibly, but do not mention that to anyone, not even Kathe. Think how dangerous that knowledge is."

Oh, yes. Lir's three jewels had returned to the world. Leos Dzavek had recovered the ruby, only to lose it once again. If Lord Khandarr ever suspected anyone of such knowledge, they faced arrest and torture on the chance they also knew of its location. With even a single jewel, Veraene could launch a war against Károví and no one in the council would object.

Speaking of the king . . .

"What of Armand?" he said. "Our king. He has his own s-spies in Károví."

"Of course. I suspect Armand will read a very similar report this week or next."

Then how long until he gathers his soldiers?

But Gerek could tell Kosenmark's thoughts were not upon Armand of Angersee and his quest for war. Kosenmark had turned away from his secretary and stood with his face averted, as if gazing through one of the many tall windows that overlooked Tiralien's red-tiled roofs and the seas beyond. Gerek knew better. There was a tautness in Kosenmark's stance, at once an air of weariness and barely suppressed excitement.

He is thinking of Ilse Zhalina. He has never stopped thinking of her.

He knew better than to mention Zhalina's name. Kosenmark had not mentioned his beloved once since Gerek first came to this house.

Before he could decide what to say, how to say it, or if he should speak at all, Kosenmark gestured to the door and recited a string of Erythandran. The ripple of tension brushed against Gerek's cheek. A sharp green scent filled the air, and the lock clicked open.

A clear dismissal. Gerek bowed his head and retreated from the room.

* * *

RAUL KOSENMARK WAITED until the door swung shut behind his secretary. Only then did he return to his desk, where he spread out the pages of Danusa Benik's report. A very neat script, with few corrections, and the ink all of the same color and hue, which suggested she had written out the whole in one session.

Several key points of the letter troubled him, items he had not mentioned to Gerek Hessler.

Benik had dated the letter from eight weeks ago. That alone did not worry him. A courier traveling by swift messenger packet could sail from Rastov's port to Tiralien in ten days, given the right winds, but this letter had come by a much more circuitous route, passed from agent to agent, until it reached the bookseller in Tiralien. Dzavek's death had taken place two weeks before that. Benik must have waited until she confirmed the king's death and observed its aftermath before writing to Kosenmark. Again, the mark of a cautious, meticulous agent.

But that left four weeks between Hallau Island and Karasek's return to Zalinenka. According to the rumors Benik heard, Karasek had reappeared alone and on horseback, in the same hour as Dzavek's death. Time spent in the magic plane could account for his absence, but the coincidence of his reappearance was too strong. Why go to Zalinenka and not back to Hallau?

He rubbed his hand over his face, then shuffled the pages together and slid them into his letterbox. The air stirred as the paper slid through the narrow slot—the current briefly called to life by the box's layers of spells. He would read Benik's report again tonight and again the next day, gleaning additional clues from the words she chose, and those she left out. Even so, he knew the essentials. Dzavek dead. Karasek returned from the magic plane. And no mention of mysterious prisoners or recent executions.

Ilse lives. I know it. She and Baussay both.

He had last seen them on Hallau Island, when Karasek and his soldiers attacked at night. Karasek had seized Valara Baussay. The woman had fought free and leapt into Anderswar and the magical plane. Ilse had followed at once. A moment later, Karasek pursued them.

So what happened next?

He tapped his fingers together and closed his eyes. Baussay wanted to return home. She was desperate to take her throne and deal with the Károvín invaders. So, home to Morennioù. Except why hadn't she done so long before? Why bargain with Raul at all?

I don't know. I only know she must have been present in Zalinenka. She and Ilse.

He could picture a confrontation between the Morenniòuen queen and Leos Dzavek. Baussay had tried to steal Lir's ruby. He had prevented her. And Ilse . . .

I can't think about that now. I have to trust that she and Baussay escaped. Otherwise, Benik would have heard that rumor, and there would be no question of who killed King Leos.

He turned to a more palatable mystery—that of Duke Miro Karasek. Why hadn't he remained in Rastov with the other members of the council? Benik spoke of turmoil at court, rumors of assassins, and violent unrest throughout the capital city. Was it possible that Karasek still hunted for Ilse and the Morenniòuen queen? Again, Raul needed more information.

Which brought him to the main point: Veraene itself. Armand of Angersee would soon have the same news from his own spies. With Leos Dzavek dead and Károví bereft of Lir's ruby, Armand could make the case that now was the time to reclaim Károví for Veraene, for the empire. Raul knew Armand's reasoning. Once—if—Veraene conquered Károví, Armand could declare war against other former provinces—Hanídos, Andelizien, or even those that had never completely submitted, such as Ysterien. From there he could expand northward to the old territories once ruled by the Erythandran tribes, abandoned when they rode south into the plains.

Except Károví would not submit so easily. It would be a costly, bloody war with no clear victory. His own father had used that argument with Baerne. Raul had attempted the same with Armand with less success. In the past few years, there were fewer and fewer in Duenne's Council to speak against him or the King's Mage. After Dedrick's death, no one dared.

It is time and past to act.

He took out a sheet of paper and wrote swiftly.

Beloved Father, I wrote to you before, urging you to attend court. I told you it was all the old reasons—the king's senseless desire for war, the duplicity and ambition of his advisers. I could not say more, because I did not know more for certain myself. I advised you to watch, to listen, to use only the gentlest persuasion with the king because his unpredictable temper might harden his resolve instead of turning him aside.

I was wrong. We must, all of us, speak openly and urge the king to peace. If you can support me in this matter, I promise . . .

He paused, wondering what great promise his father would accept. What promise Raul knew he could keep. He crossed out the last few words and continued.

I will explain more once I see you at court. I have some matters to arrange in Tiralien first, but I shall arrive in Duenne within the next month.

He signed his name, then sealed the letter with wax and three layers of magic.

CHAPTER FIVE

FOR EMMA IANI, the summer season was her least favorite. Incipient thunderstorms hung above the city, and the air felt heavy and charged, as if wrapped in an excess of magic. This year was the worst that she could remember, stifling and hot, with a constant threat of storms that reflected her own anxious mood. If she were to write a poem about these days, the storm clouds would make a suitable metaphor for the kingdom and its politics.

But she had given over writing poems since Benno's return from Duenne's Court. Metaphors were too simple, too soft, and words mere lines of ink upon the page. Once she had believed the opposite, that words were sharp and dangerous weapons, but she had spent countless nights watching over Benno, waiting for the inevitable nightmares, ready to hold him in her arms, or remain quietly nearby, whichever he required. Words had not injured him, weapons of magic had. It had taken weeks before he could bear any mention of Duenne or the King's Mage without weeping.

And so I give myself over to a life of nothing, Emma thought. *To the elegant frivolity of musical evenings and conversations about inconsequentials.*

Such as this gathering at the regional governor's palace.

She surveyed the assembly hall where a dozen guests stood about in twos or threes, while a trio of musicians played a lilting recursive melody on water flutes. A very exclusive gathering, to be sure. Tall windows overlooked the city below and the moonlit seas beyond. Within, Lady Vieth had kept to the simplest furnishing so that nothing would distract from the guests themselves, all of them dressed in patterned silks cut in the highest fashion. Watching them, Emma had the impression of a costly jewel box and its gems.

Benno leaned close to her. "You are scowling."

Emma consciously smoothed out her expression to one pleasantly bland. "It was a momentary discomfort, my love. If I might be so vulgar as to mention it, my feet ache."

"Liar," he murmured. "What is wrong?"

She glanced toward the other guests. All came from noble families of impeccable lineage, patrons of the arts, with fine sensibilities toward music. And—a point she had not missed—they were all famously apolitical. Emma had briefly wondered if Lady Vieth wished to mend Emma's and Benno's reputation after the events of the previous autumn, but it was far more likely the royal governor and his wife simply wanted an evening of exquisite music.

"I fear my jewels are not bright enough for this company," she said quietly.

His mouth twisted in silent agreement. "We might go."

"Soon," she replied. Whatever she thought of the other guests, she liked Lady Vieth and did not wish to offend her. Her own dark moods were not Hella's fault. "Let us wait another half hour."

No sooner had she spoken when a stir among the other guests caught her attention. She followed the direction of their gazes toward the entryway. Her fingers tightened around her wine cup as she recognized the newcomer.

Raul Kosenmark.

He was dressed in elaborate attire of dark red silk robes, layers upon layers, with minuscule rubies sewn into the cuffs and hems. An enormous ruby hung from one ear. As he glided between the other guests, the lamplight caught each jewel so that they glittered like drops of fresh blood.

Next to her, Benno drew a sharp breath. Emma laid her hand on her husband's arm. He was trembling.

I shall murder that man for coming here tonight, she thought.

Kosenmark paused by Lord and Lady Vieth to make his formal greeting. He glanced around the room. His gaze took in the musicians and the collection of guests, passing lightly over Emma and Benno with nothing more than a polite smile. He seemed to note and appreciate a new trio of miniature paintings, hung in a position of prominence on one wall. All this took only moments. Then Kosenmark was gliding toward them, with that same polite smile on his otherwise expressionless face.

"Lord and Lady Iani."

Emma quelled the impulse to growl. Too many would witness any friction between them, and while these other nobles were famously apolitical, their friends might not be. So she smiled pleasantly. "Lord Kosenmark. I had heard you returned recently from a pleasure cruise. Alas, your presence was missed in the city."

"My apologies for my absence. The decision was borne of impulse. I wished to sample a warmer climate before the summer storms prevented me."

Emma heard a faint edge in his voice. A warning, perhaps, to tread softly.

"I hope your journey was a pleasant one," Benno said. "Lord Vieth had earlier expressed disappointment that you were not to be among us tonight. I see you reversed your earlier decision."

Raul nodded. "Another impulse, you might say. I've neglected my friends these past several months, and I wished to make up the loss."

Emma had to suppress her own trembling. *He intends to regather his shadow court.*

"Are you certain?" she asked.

His only reply was an enigmatic smile.

There was a pause as the musicians came to the end of their piece. Raul laid a hand over his heart and bowed his head, eyes closed and silent. Emma hated him in that moment. His love of music was unfeigned, she knew, but he used that love to disguise his other motives.

She shook her head. Anyone might accuse her of the same.

"What do you want?" she whispered.

"A conversation with you and Benno," he replied just as softly.

"Tonight?" Benno said.

"Yes. The matter is urgent."

Emma resisted the urge to cry out: *You abandoned us. You pretended indifference.* She was angry with him, yes, but underneath that first furious response, she was aware of other, contradictory emotions. *You were afraid, just as we were. And now you know, you've heard, something that affects us all.*

She pressed her lips together. What she thought about Raul Kosenmark the man did not matter. The welfare of Veraene and its people should be her chief concern. So she joined in the conversation discussing the finer points of the musical performance. She even managed an almost genuine laugh. Then Kosenmark continued on to the next gathering.

Benno touched Emma's arm. She leaned against his shoulder.

"He is not a restful soul," she said.

"It is not his nature," he agreed. "But think how much easier we have it. He cannot escape himself."

She shook her head. "You would see things his way."

They lingered another hour before they offered their farewells to Lord and Lady Vieth. Most of the guests remained, and Kosenmark had not departed yet, but Emma found her ability to dissemble fading. She offered a wan smile to Lady Vieth, saying that a headache had come over her, no doubt the fault of the close weather.

At home, they retired into the common parlor, which overlooked a walled garden and the pathway running between their house and the next. Emma ordered the servants to bring them refreshments—spiced tea, a jug of strong wine, another of chilled water—then dismissed them to their beds. She and Benno drank tea and spoke of the evening's entertainment as they waited.

It was not until midnight, however, that their patience was rewarded. Benno broke off in the middle of a sentence. His lips parted in a smile. Emma heard a soft scratching at the door to the garden. Benno was already moving across the room to admit their visitor. Raul Kosenmark no longer wore his gaudy costume of red silks. His clothing was dark and loose-fitting, and as he clasped Benno's hand in greeting, his sleeve fell back to reveal a wrist sheath with its knife.

"You expect danger?" Emma asked. "No, don't answer. Of course you do. You would be a fool not to."

"So glad to know I'm not a fool in your eyes," he said.

She ignored that comment and motioned to the chairs, while Benno inquired whether Kosenmark preferred tea, wine, or water. Kosenmark chose water.

There was no point in meaningless politesse. Emma asked the question she had wished to ask hours before, at Lord and Lady Vieth's affair. "You've decided to involve yourself in politics again. Is that true?"

"I never stopped," Raul said. "I only made the shadows darker, if you will. However, I received news last week that compels me to take a more open role."

Compels. Interesting. "For many years, you argued against that."

"I was wrong."

Her desire to vent her fury died at that flat declaration. "What has changed?"

Kosenmark shrugged. "The necessity of the times. My own beliefs. A sudden acquisition of courage or foolhardiness, most likely a combination of the two. You seem displeased. What has changed with you?"

The answer should have been obvious, she thought. Dedrick. Benno. Ilse Zhalina's abrupt departure, and Kosenmark's own retreat into secrecy and isolation. Dedrick had died at Markus Khandarr's hands in a prison cell in Duenne's palace. Khandarr had forced Benno to watch, then sent him back to Tiralien, bound by magic to report every terrifying detail to Kosenmark. Rumor said that Ilse herself died by a murderer's hand in Osterling Keep. She realized she was gripping both hands together. With a conscious effort, she untangled her fingers and met Kosenmark's gaze.

"I'm afraid," she said.

"So am I," he replied. "But I am more afraid to do nothing."

An answer she might have offered herself, a year ago.

She was about to tell him they had nothing more to discuss, when Benno surprised her by asking, "What next? You have a plan—it's obvious—and you want to tell us about it. Or at least selected portions."

"Selected portions, yes. More would be dangerous."

"A simple excuse," Emma replied.

Benno reproved her with a gentle clasp of hand-over-hand. Lover and friend, she thought bitterly. He would be loyal to us both.

Raul made no gesture to admit or deny what she said. "I go to Duenne tomorrow," he said. "Leos Dzavek is dead. Armand will know that soon, if he does not already. You can imagine what follows next. So I intend to demand a public audience before the entire council. It is my right as my father's heir. There I will say all that I should have said years before."

At first she was unable to speak. Dzavek dead. Raul Kosenmark returning to court and council. It was as though the gods had reached down and overturned all their lives. But immediately after came the thought, *He dissolved his shadow court, but his spies are still at work in Károví.*

She wondered what else he had kept from her and Benno.

"Will Armand listen?" Benno asked softly. "He never has before."

Another shrug, but Emma did not mistake that gesture for indifference. "I cannot tell. I also intend to speak with my father and his factions—with any faction that will have me—so that mine is not the only voice. There are others who might dislike me, but they dislike more the idea of a senseless war. They know that Károví will not yield, if they ever do yield, without a long and bloody fight."

More revelations. "When did your father return to court?"

Kosenmark smiled bitterly. "Another recent event. I wrote to him last month, during my absence."

Yes, the absence that remained a mystery.

"What of Lir's jewels?" Benno asked. "Dzavek had one. Surely—"

"I have no report about them."

She thought he had not meant to disclose even that much, because he fell silent and stared into his water cup. Arranging his lies, she suspected.

But when he spoke again, it was with obvious difficulty. And unexpected honesty.

"Last spring, three Károvín ships foundered off the coast from Osterling Keep. The survivors were taken prisoner. However, one among them was not from Károví. She was from Morennioù."

"Impossible," Benno said. "For that—"

Raul held up a hand. "I know. For that, the ships needed to cross the barrier."

The barrier called Lir's Veil was a burning wall of magic that had appeared three hundred years before, during the second and bloodiest of the wars between Veraene and Károví. History said Morennioùen mages had died working that spell, all so the island province could separate itself from the mainland. No one knew if that were true—all the ships sent by Veraene's kings to investigate the matter had vanished.

Emma Iani shivered, thinking of the magical power Dzavek must have expended to break through such an invincible barrier.

"How?" she whispered. "How could they—?"

"I don't know," Raul said. "But they did. The key is that this woman was the new queen of Morennioù. I met with her and Ilse Zhalina. The queen admitted that she had discovered the second of Lir's jewels. She claimed it remained hidden in Morennioù, while the Károvín had taken a decoy specially prepared to deceive them. I am not certain how much of her story I can believe, but the part of recovering Lir's jewel rang true."

Emma listened as he told a story of negotiations with this supposed queen, the impasse between them, and Ilse Zhalina's offer of herself as hostage. She had wondered at their break, had suspected a deception, but never one quite so complete as what Raul's words implied.

"Our plan was to provide the queen with a ship," Raul said. "Unlike Dzavek we could not draw on the jewels' magic, but we hoped to chart a course around Lir's Veil. There are several old texts that mention such a possibility . . ." Again he stared into the cup, but this time, Emma had the clear sense of absolute truth, one almost too difficult to speak of.

He drank off the water. "The Károvín found us on Hallau Island," he said at last. "We fought. The Morennioùen queen fled into the magical plane. Ilse followed her, as did the Károvín officer leading the attack.

"We waited several days," he said softly. "They did not return."

After that, Emma could say nothing. No accusations of lies. No demands to know why he had not confided in them earlier. She knew the reasons. They all ended in the words, *Because of Markus Khandarr.*

Benno shook his head. He reached past the water jug and filled all their cups with strong wine. Emma drank hers down in one gulp. The spirits burned her throat and cut through all her indecision. So, they might die. At least they would die with good cause.

"Tell us what to do," she said.

"Watch," Raul said. "Watch for any sign of Ilse, the jewels, or the queen. Can you promise me that?"

He spoke to them both, but it was Emma who replied.

"We can. We promise."

She took her husband's hand, felt the answering pressure of his palm against hers, his pulse warm and steady, and knew they had chosen the right path.

GEREK WAS IMMERSED in a dream of ships and seas when a sharp crack, like the sound of a mast being sprung, broke through. He jerked awake and swayed, thinking he was aboard a ship. *A storm* was his first thought. The ship foundering on the shoals near Osterling Keep. A dream from lives ago, or one that had never taken place. He stumbled from his hammock. Not a hammock, but a bed. His foot tangled in the linens and he pitched forward. A hand caught him by the shoulder. "Maester Hessler. Maester Hessler, wake up, please. Lord Kosenmark wishes to see you at once."

The images from that dream—of enormous waves rising up beside the ship, of the moonlight striking through a single patch of clear sky—scattered. The groan from the ship's planks was his own, protesting. The waves were nothing but fluttering shadows, cast by a single candle on a nearby table. He drew a deep breath, recognized the man's voice, which continued to urge him awake. Uli. Uli Baier. Kosenmark's senior runner.

"I-I-I am awake," he said.

"Take a moment," the man said. "He wants you with a clear head."

From somewhere, Uli produced a pitcher of water. Gerek splashed a few handfuls over his face. He rubbed the sleep from his eyes with the towel Uli handed him. Had the runner come prepared? Or were there maidservants gawking at him? He felt too self-conscious, standing naked and bleary-eyed.

"Would you have tea as well?" he asked. "And do you kn-know what he wants?"

Uli shook his head. Gerek would get no answers then, until he spoke with Kosenmark himself. If then, he thought. A week had passed since Benik's report had arrived. Since then Kosenmark had discussed nothing with Gerek outside the business of the pleasure house. No politics. No mention of jewels or Károví. No mention of Leos Dzavek.

He hurried himself into clothes. Uli lit a second candle for Gerek, who accepted it with thanks and jogged out the door.

The house was silent, the hallways dark. It was three hours past midnight, the middle point between night and dawn. Gerek took the stairs as quickly as he dared. His panting breath echoed from the walls. Had he ever traversed the house at this hour? Once or twice, perhaps, when his work kept him at his desk until late. Kathe would be just leaving the kitchen . . .

Lamps illuminated the upper landing. A second runner was just exiting Raul's office. As their glances met, Gerek caught the brief widening of the man's eyes, the shake of his head. A warning of Kosenmark's mood?

Gerek entered the room with some trepidation. He found Raul Kosenmark kneeling by the fireplace, which blazed far too bright and hot, despite the close summer night. Papers were spread around him. The letter box—that cursed magic-spelled letter box where Kosenmark stored his most private documents—stood open with all its secret contents exposed, and Kosenmark was feeding the pages one by one into the flames. At Gerek's entrance, he glanced up with a fey smile.

"I have a gift for you," he said.

Gerek paused, unable to think of a suitable reply. Or a safe one.

"Under ordinary circumstances, you would thank me," Raul continued. He stood up and went to his desk, where he sorted through a smaller stack of papers. "But you have had little reason to."

"My lord—"

"My Lord Haszler, do not pretend gratitude where none is deserved."

"I-I-" Gerek stopped again at the mention of his true name. He had to force himself to breathe steadily. He noted, as from a distance, that Kosenmark waited patiently.

"I do n-not pretend anything," he said. "If I am grateful, I-I am. If you dislike that, you should send me away."

That brought a surprised laugh from Kosenmark. "Very well. No pretense, not from either of us. So. The gift." He picked out a few pages, heavy parchment covered in small close script. Raul laid them out and touched each one, as if reassuring himself of their existence. His expression had gone pensive, though a stranger might not have noticed the change. "I am offering you this house," he said, "and everything inside, except for the contents of my private chambers. Those I will send for in a few weeks."

"The courtesans as well?" Gerek asked.

"You have a need for them?" Raul said drily.

"N-n-no, my lord."

"Good. I would hate to think you tired of Kathe so easily."

Never, Gerek thought. *Not for a hundred years. Not for a hundred lives.*

To Raul, he only bowed his head.

"I regret I cannot attend your wedding," Raul went on. "I leave for Duenne at first light."

Another surprise, another exclamation swallowed.

"I have business with the king," Raul added. "You do not need to know more. I hope . . ." And here his voice lost its faintly amused tone. "I hope this sudden break will protect you and yours from Lord Khandarr's attentions. If it does not, send word to Lord Vieth. Do not use the usual channels. Send word directly to Vieth or to Lord Benno Iani."

He handed over the sheets of parchment, all of them witnessed and stamped with the magical and wax seals of the various offices in Tiralien. Kosenmark had signed over the house itself to Lord Gerek Haszler, favorite cousin of his once lover, Lord Dedrik Maszuryn. He had also allocated a substantial sum to Kathe Raendl, and a second, lesser amount for the house expenses until Lord Gerek took formal possession. Gerek wondered what Kathe's mother would make of these gifts. He wondered what Kathe herself would think.

The next few hours were spent arranging for contingencies and various fallbacks. If Gerek and Kathe wished to keep the house, he might consider retaining the guards. If they chose to sell, the guards and staff could find employment with the duke at Valentain. And if they in turn chose to go elsewhere . . .

On and on, each permutation laid out in that fluting voice. It was much like their discussions for other, equally complicated plans, except this one carried with it an air of finality.

At last they were done. Runners carried a few saddlebags below. Others went to work in the long-concealed private chambers, packing clothing, books, and other belongings into crates for later. Dawn was approaching, but Gerek had no inclination to sleep. He watched as Kosenmark gathered a few papers together and wrapped them in waxed sheets. He noted the man did not order him away. Perhaps he was human after all.

At last Kosenmark stood and glanced around the room. His gaze met Gerek's and he smiled, a genuine one at last. "Your beloved has missed you, undoubtedly."

As does yours, Gerek thought.

He said nothing, however. He still retained some sense of self-preservation.

Kosenmark's lips curled into a sardonic smile, as if he guessed Gerek's thoughts. "Come. Walk with me, please."

It was a request, not a command—an acknowledgment that Kosenmark was no longer master and lord.

They descended the stairs, but at the second landing, Kosenmark turned into the corridors. Gerek followed. A dog to the last, he thought. But it was true, his earlier impression. Kosenmark was bidding this house farewell. They—he—wandered through the corridors and galleries, through rooms empty of clients, and down another level to the main floor, where they took a circuitous route among the parlors and sitting rooms, the common room, and then, by a twist and a quirk, into a small library, seldom used, that over-looked the gardens below, now little more than shadows in the early morn-ing light.

Kosenmark stared out the window a long quarter hour. Then, with dawn seeping through the trees, he turned away with an audible sigh. He and Gerek paced the last length of halls side by side, until they came to the front entryway where two servants waited.

There was another pause. Another searching glance that took in the high, arched ceiling, the black-and-white-tiled floor, the mosaics in the wall that depicted the goddess Lir and her brother-god Toc in all their in-carnations. Until this moment, Gerek had almost convinced himself that Kosenmark would not take the final step, that all these preparations were a pretense. But even as he released his breath, Kosenmark gave a sharp nod to the two servants. They opened the doors and he passed through them alone.

Gerek froze a moment, too startled to move. Then he hurried after Kosenmark.

Outside, Benedikt Ault and eight guards waited on horses. One of the stable boys held the reins for a tenth, riderless horse. This was no entourage of a duke's son, Gerek thought. This was a military company.

Kosenmark turned and gripped Gerek by the arm. "Be well, be safe, my friend."

Gerek could do nothing more than return the clasp. Friend to friend. Then Kosenmark was striding toward his horse. He mounted, gave the order to depart, and was away.

CHAPTER SIX

FOR THE PAST six years, Kathe Raendl had awakened to a cacophony of bellsong. She had hated the noise at first and called the bells metal-tongued monsters. Their clamor was nothing like the silvery chimes in Duenne's palace, which insinuated themselves into your sleep and lifted you to wakefulness. Subtle, much like the court itself.

She had come to love Tiralien even so—the whisper of the seas, the sense of being perched on the edge of the world and its water-filled horizon. She even came to love Lord Kosenmark's house, a place of shadows and bright-lit halls, filled with elegant statuary, rare books and paintings, its halls scented with sweet perfume and the musk of sexual spendings. But she never forgot the listening devices within, nor that Kosenmark himself was a creature of court and politics. And the bells . . .

Bellsong crashed through her dreams, waking her abruptly.

She lay there, her pulse beating far too fast, uncertain for a moment where she was. Bells continued to ring. The familiar noise anchored her in the ordinary world. This was Tiralien. The seventh year of Armand of Angersee's reign. And she was Kathe Raendl, assistant cook in Lord Kosenmark's pleasure house. She counted the peals. Eight and two quarter-hour chimes. Plus whatever bells she had missed. Call it half past ten, judging by the angle of sunlight.

Too early, she thought, and buried her face into her pillow. *Let my mother take charge of the girls by herself.*

Except she had promised Mistress Denk to review the kitchen's budget for the coming month. And there was the problem with Dana, who had run off with a stable boy the week before.

We need to hire extra staff, she thought wearily. *Another girl for the kitchen and at least two more to serve in the common room.*

She would talk to Mistress Denk this afternoon.

But Mistress Denk would insist they discuss the matter with Kathe's mother, who was the senior cook. Kathe groaned. Perhaps that discussion could wait.

She lay there a moment longer, unwilling to encounter the day just yet, but memories of the previous night stirred her into wakefulness, restless and unbidden. It had been a chaotic night in the pleasure house. Josef had quarreled with Tatiana. Nadine had tweaked and teased everyone, like a child who knew a terrible secret but refused to tell. Half the kitchen girls were in tears before midnight, and the other half seemed close to taking up knives in battle.

Then there was the quarrel with her mother.

He is nothing but a ruined scholar.

Not true. He's a good man. Lord Kosenmark trusts him.

And that is your best recommendation?

No, but—

But she could not tell her mother that Gerek Hessler, a wandering scholar and dependent on Lord Kosenmark, was in truth Lord Gerek Haszler, whose cousin was a companion to the queen of Veraene. Not to mention that his other cousin was Lord Dedrick, once Lord Kosenmark's lover. Those were his secrets, not hers.

Kathe rolled over onto her back to glare at the innocent ceiling.

I love him. I loved him ever since he first knocked on the door. He is clever and brave and . . .

An idiot would never see past the stutters, the self-effacing manner-isms, which all sprang from incurable shyness, but *she* knew better. If she had not mistaken things, so did Lord Kosenmark. Not that Lord Kosen-mark deserved much more than a knock over his head. She glanced up, as though her thoughts were audible, but there were no vents here. No one could spy on her tears or foul temper.

(Good. If there were, she might throw her heaviest pot at Lord Kosen-mark's thick head.)

So. They would marry in a week or less. Gerek had written to his par-ents and the rest of his numerous family. Other than Gerek's older brother, no one seemed to care. Was that good? A poor omen? She couldn't tell.

Kathe blew out a breath and hauled herself from the bed. Once she had washed and dressed in a clean smock and skirt, she felt more herself. She drank a cup of cold tea to wet her throat, then headed down to the kitchens.

Hanne, Birte, and Janna were already at their workstations. Janna kneaded dough for the afternoon baking. Hanna was grinding coffee beans, and Birte plucked the stems from a basket of fresh strawberries, so that late-rising guests might partake of a light meal before they departed. Steffi and the new girl, Gerda, had lingered over their own breakfast, but the moment Kathe appeared, they started up to clear away their dirty dishes. There was no sign of her mother.

Kathe greeted the girls and continued into the cold room to check the supplies of meat. Veal and lamb in adequate supply. The beef, however, seemed off. She would have to speak to the butcher. Perhaps she could use this excuse to escape the house and visit the market for fresh supplies.

Coward.

Why not?

You know very well why not.

Still arguing with herself, she returned to the main kitchen, in time to hear Janna chattering to Steffi. "Gone," she was saying. "As quick as a blink and in such a terrible mood. I even heard Micha say—"

She broke off at Kathe's appearance. Steffi gulped down a nervous laugh. Janna drove both fists into the bowl of dough. She stopped herself in time and proceeded at a gentler pace. Some day she would make a fine pastry cook, but first she would need to learn control. More important, Kathe would have to speak honestly with her mother. Until then . . .

"Do you mean Lord Kosenmark?" Kathe asked casually. "Has he gone away?"

Steffi and Janna exchanged glances. "I thought you had heard," Janna said. "He rode away at dawn. And . . ." Her gaze flicked toward Steffi. "And, well, it was sudden."

So there were secrets. No doubt Kathe would hear the details soon enough. She smiled, in that brisk manner she used to disguise her unease at Lord Kosenmark's doings. "Well, then," she said. "That guarantees us a quieter day, no?"

The girls all laughed, though it was a fluttering, uncertain laugh. Kathe held on fast to her own smile, but underneath came a stream of unbidden memories. This was just like the time before, when Kosenmark departed suddenly with a company of guards. Gerek had spent the next few weeks secluded in his office, hardly speaking to anyone except the senior runners and perhaps Mistress Denk. He, too, had abruptly left the city, and not by his free will, as she later learned.

It's not the same, she told herself firmly. *It could not be.*

Still thinking of that other time, she laid out a tray with coffee, bread, and pastries, the kind Gerek loved best. If nothing were wrong, if Janna had exaggerated . . . Well, Kathe was simply taking her beloved a late-morning refreshment as she almost always did.

Her first check to these comforting thoughts came at Gerek's office. Locked—not just with his key but with magic. Kathe was no mage, but she had lived six years in this household with its layers of spells on every door. She knew magic when she touched it.

She set the tray on the floor next to Gerek's office door and mounted the stairs to the fourth floor. Even before she rounded the next landing, she heard the commotion of servants hurrying back and forth. That alone was unusual, but as she climbed the last few stairs, she saw more signs of a crisis. No runner waiting in the alcove to carry messages. The door itself— always shut and locked—now stood open to reveal an army of servants swarming through Lord Kosenmark's office. Lord Kosenmark was not in view, nor was Gerek.

Then she caught sight of Mistress Denk, supervising the work.

"Mistress Denk."

The other woman glanced toward her. Kathe hesitated. All the questions she needed to ask, she had to ask in private, not here, with dozens of servants about. She shook her head. Denk gave her a sardonic smile, as if she understood Kathe's dilemma.

Kathe turned back toward the stairs. Now she truly wanted to find Gerek, and at once.

The wing of offices was empty. She thought she would have better luck with the next, which included a small library and several parlors, but Gerek was not in the library, nor the first two rooms she checked. With growing unease, Kathe entered the next, a favorite among the courtesans for its soft couches and the grand view of the lawns and the gardens. Doves gathered on the ledge below the window and their murmur was like a chorus of water flutes, only much softer.

Today, the parlor stood empty and quiet. Even the doves were silent. Brilliant sunlight poured through the arched windows. It was a day to tempt the kitchen girls to make excuses to visit the gardens, or loiter in the markets.

It was then Kathe realized where Gerek had gone.

She hurried to the window. Even as she scanned the grounds, a solitary figure emerged from the shadows of the house and crossed the lawn. The person was Gerek, clad in dun-colored robes. Ignoring the bench and roses, Gerek made directly for a gap in the bushes that led into a wilderness garden. Kathe knew from experience that a person could just see the edge of Lord Kosenmark's grounds from that point. Beyond were the stables and a maze of small lanes that led into the city.

My love, you must not . . .

Gerek sank onto the grass. The movement came so quickly, her own heart leapt in sudden apprehension. She spun around and nearly collided with a maid outside the parlor. Kathe called back an apology. Whatever the girl said in reply was lost on her. Kathe skimmed down the stone stairwell to the bottom floor. Hanne and Gerda were carrying trays with coffee and fruit into the common room. Hanne turned, as if to speak to Kathe. Kathe waved her aside. A dozen more steps brought her down a seldom-used corridor to a side door, which opened onto a narrow lane.

The same door where Ilse Zhalina knocked, three years ago.

She had no desire to revisit memories of that night, or of that visitor, however. Kathe sped along the lane, through a series of small alcoves bordered by more ornamental trees, until she came to the grassy lawn. There she paused and shaded her eyes, searching for the still dark figure she had glimpsed from the window.

This midday hour the grounds were empty, the air shimmering with dust and warmth. But there, ahead, was Gerek. He sat upon the grass, heedless of the unforgiving sun.

Quietly she approached her betrothed. He did not acknowledge her presence. She did not expect it, and simply knelt in the grass a few feet away. She could tell he had not slept at all the previous night. His clothes were rumpled, the skin beneath his eyes bruised and creased, and his hair looked as though crows had played havoc with it. He was a large man, built like an ox, as his mother often said. Brown and sturdy. Very clever. Dependable. Until she came to know him, she had not realized how much she wanted a man she could trust. Oh, to be sure, Kathe loved his intelligence, the warmth and passion and tenderness of his embrace, but the matter of trust was like a key to the entire treasure of Gerek Haszler.

For several moments she did nothing but drink in the scents and sights of the surrounding gardens, the proximity of her beloved. Summer had come upon them without her noticing. All the flowering trees had shed their blossoms after spring. The rosebushes were still in bloom, their scent thick in the air, and from farther away came the sharp fragrance of crushed grass. Bees hummed among the bushes.

"I-I can almost imagine it," Gerek said softly. "A whole c-city, complete, filled with . . . booksellers and scholars and merchants and artisans and all manner of people free to walk the streets. I remember . . . I remember a bench overlooking the harbor, where you can just hear the waves hissing against the shore."

"I remember that bench."

She and Gerek had met there by chance, on his first outing into the city. From later conversations, she knew that day marked the beginning of another kind of connection between Gerek and Lord Kosenmark.

Another connection, another clue to the day's strange beginning. It had to do with Lord Kosenmark, with the politics of Veraene, and certain other secret doings of that man, which Kathe was not supposed to know about.

"What is it?" she asked softly. "What has he done now?"

Gerek bowed his head. He was weeping, Kathe saw. It took all her strength to keep herself from reaching out to embrace him. It took all her strength not to ride after Lord Raul Kosenmark to demand an accounting for his behavior.

Later, she thought. *Later I shall confront him and all the rest.*

Gerek swiped a hand over his face. "He is gone. Gone to Duenne. He s-s-s-says . . . Toc damn him, i-ignorance is n-not a shield. No-no matter how much he wishes it were." He swiveled around to face Kathe. His eyes were wet, his glare as fierce as she had ever seen before. "He goes to argue with the king. He . . ." He drew another, rattling breath. "He gave us the house. Gave Lord Gerek Haszler the house. You are to have a great sum of money, and more to run the house until . . . until I-I-I-I don't know what."

He named the sums, which made Kathe's breath go still with astonishment. The house, a treasure by itself. The sum for its expenses an extravagant amount, enough to keep the house running with all its staff for at least six months. And then for her—with that much money she could set up her own household. It was a treasure, one last gift, from a man she thought impervious to gratitude.

Gerek had bowed down until his forehead touched the ground. He was weeping still, as if a dear friend had suddenly died.

And perhaps he had, Kathe thought. She reached out and laid a hand on Gerek's shoulder. "Is the house yours, then?"

"Yes, I-I s-said—"

"Can you do whatever you like?"

He nodded, an angry, frightened nod.

"Well, then," she said. "You could sell the cursed thing. We—or you—could go to Valentain. Or wherever you liked. There's nothing binding you to Tiralien."

You could be free of Lord Markus Khandarr and the rest of the shadow court.

Quite possibly, he had understood the question behind the questions, because he sighed. When he straightened up, she saw his lips were curled into a bitter smile. "S-so I might. And you might s-study under the duke's chief cook."

She smiled, though her lips trembled. "The great Adona Pavlakakis from Andelizien. My mother told me about her. It's true I would learn a great deal about fine cookery, but only if I could remain meek and re-spectful."

He laughed weakly, shook his head.

Kathe leaned forward and gathered his hands in hers. "Let me tell you my thoughts. You might disagree. Or not. But listen. I think . . ." She drew a long breath, and another. Why was this so difficult to say?

Because I love him. Because he might . . .

She pressed onward, in spite of those thoughts.

"I believe you should return to your father's house. Just for a few weeks," she added, before Gerek could protest. "There you could formally and openly receive Lord Kosenmark's letter. You can refuse it or not as you like. But you might as well take the gift. You can always sell the house later, af-ter we . . ."

After they married. If he still wanted that.

"Do you think that a good i-i-i-dea?" Gerek asked.

That he stuttered so, to her, was a measure of his distress. That she did not attempt to comfort him, a measure of hers.

"I want you to do what you like," she said, softly and fervently. "If you would rather stay at home with your family, then do that. If you would rather—"

"No, I—" He bit his lips. Made a visible effort to swallow. "You are my wife, as long as you wish. I love you, Kathe."

It was as though a great hand had loosed its grip around her. She breathed and managed a smile. "Well then. Let us go back to the house and make our plans."

They helped each other to stand, but when Kathe indicated the path toward the house, Gerek hesitated. "There is another s-s-secret of his that I-I kept from you."

Kathe silently cursed Raul Kosenmark. Of course. There were always more secrets with him. Even as a young man in Duenne, secrets had trailed after him.

Kosenmark, however, had departed. Her first concern was Gerek. "What is the secret?" she asked.

Another pause. Another visible swallow, as he collected his thoughts and commanded his tongue to fluency. "He loved her," he said at last. "He n-n-never stopped. N-neither did she. It was a ruse to protect you all. To protect them. I-I-I only knew it at the end."

No need to give any names. He meant Ilse Zhalina. The young woman, almost a child then, who arrived at Kosenmark's doorstep three years ago, bloody and close to death. She had worked hard to prove herself in the kitchen, then as Kosenmark's assistant and secretary. And as Kathe's good friend. All that had unraveled in the strange affair of Ilse's quarrel with her beloved.

For a long while, Kathe could do nothing. Even breathing came with difficulty. *She always loved him. She lied to me. They both did.*

Gerek stood solid and unmoving. Her ox. Her trusting, dependable ox. He expected her to rage. No, he expected worse. Kathe wanted to growl and shout. It was all Kosenmark's fault, didn't he see? The man seduced them all to secrecy, from Dedrick to Gerek to all his other friends. Including Ilse Zhalina.

She gripped his hair and pulled him close.

"You are both idiots," she said. "You and Lord Kosenmark. But *you,* you, I love."

His eyes went wide. Clearly this was not the reaction he expected.

"Even though I-I kept secrets from you?" he whispered.

"Even though," she said firmly.

Gerek rocked back on his heels, but almost immediately he engulfed her in an embrace and buried his face in her shoulder. "I'm sorry."

"Hush," she whispered. "You do not need to be sorry. Not to me, be-loved."

Only when his breathing had steadied, and she knew herself to be under control, did she gently withdraw from his arms. "Come," she said. "We have much to do."

NADINE WATCHED FROM the high vantage point of the third story as Kathe played out a mawkish scene with Gerek-the-fool. They sat upon the lawn, oblivious to the dust and glaring summer sun. Gerek faced the outer boundary of the property. Yearning, Nadine thought. She could see nothing but his wide back, but his mood since the famous return of Lord Kosenmark and his minions had veered between irritating bliss and equally irritating gloom. Kathe sat beside him, slim and straight-backed.

There were no listening pipes outside the house that would allow her to hear the conversation itself, but she could guess its substance well enough. All the courtesans were awake and chattering about Lord Kosen-mark's sudden departure. Nadine had not shared any of the secrets she had uncovered for herself over the past six years. A little judicious spy-ing. The practice of carelessly glancing over the envelopes the senior runner carried to Kosenmark or his secretary of the moment. All habits learned in previous houses, previous lives. And most effective, when she had discovered certain key listening devices scattered around the plea-sure house. Nadine knew about Kosenmark's political games. He might claim a higher cause for his actions, but in truth, they both wished to survive in a chance-riddled world.

Secrets are for learning, a lover had once told Nadine.

The lover had later attempted to murder her. A misstep, which he regretted, but his advice otherwise had proved to be good.

In the gardens, Kathe took Gerek's hands in both of hers and spoke energetically. *Talk, talk, talk, talk.* As if words could alter their situation. Kosenmark had vanished to his fate in Duenne. Most likely he would com-mit some unpardonable act of honesty against the king. Had he even con-sidered the fate of those in Tiralien?

Slippers trod the tiled floor behind Nadine. Even before the person spoke, Nadine recognized the strong scent of lily, Tatiana's favorite per-fume. She straightened up and laid her hands on either side of the window frame, making it more difficult for Tatiana to see past her.

"Do you think we shall open for business tonight?" Tatiana said.

"Of course," Nadine replied. "That is our purpose—to bring pleasure."

Tatiana laughed, a low, gurgling laugh that served her well with her clients. "Indeed. Speaking of pleasure, shall we go down to the baths to-gether? We've a new supply of soaps carved in lascivious shapes. Johanna tells me they were most effective with Lord Gerhart."

Kathe stood and held out her hands to Gerek, who lumbered to his feet. Nadine leaned closer to the window. More talk. More pauses and stares. Ah! Kathe gripped Gerek by the hair. She had lost her temper, then. Good. For all that Nadine had helped the fool to declare his love, she could not fathom why Kathe admired him. Perhaps she had underestimated his abil-ities in lovemaking.

"What are you watching?" Tatiana said.

"Idiots in lust," Nadine replied. As Tatiana attempted to peer over her shoulder, she gracefully swung around and ran her fingers down the other courtesan's arm. "Perhaps I shall come with you to the baths."

Tatiana eyed her with a speculative smile. "Alone?"

"We shall have to bribe the attendants."

"Done."

She kissed Nadine lightly on the cheek. It was a tentative kiss, as though Tatiana were not certain of its reception. Nadine laughed breathlessly. She let her hips sway forward—just a brief contact—then slid her hand around Tatiana's back and pulled her into an openmouthed kiss. "I shall have to repay you for the bribe," she murmured.

"You shall," Tatiana whispered back.

But as Nadine accompanied her companion to the baths, her mind ran upon politics rather than things sexual. *I must listen harder,* she thought. *I must make my own plans and not let the future catch me unawares.*

CHAPTER SEVEN

THE DAY BEGAN well before dawn for Armand of Angersee, king of Veraene.

He flung himself from his bed, screaming, arms flailing, trying to fend off the monsters swarming in from the fog-bound realms of dreams and magic . . .

Armand, Armand, wake up.

He twisted away from those cold hands. It was his father again, stinking of wine. His grandfather . . .

Baerne of Angersee's face hovered over his, like a dull brown cloud against an autumn sky. The old man's eyes were bright with madness, his lips black from chewing lime and bitter weeds. He muttered something about Lir and Toc, and the necessity for true allegiance, unalloyed by house or province. Only when you sever the flesh, he whispered, can you truly be certain of your allies.

Armand gasped and struck out at the ghostly face.

His fist met flesh.

A voice cried out. A woman's voice.

Armand recoiled. Yseulte. Not his father or grandfather. His wife.

Above the roar inside his skull, he heard the echo of many voices. His guards. Others. Then, Yseulte shouting them all down, saying that it was nothing but a dream. An unfortunate dream was all. They were to leave the bedchamber at once.

I hate them, Armand thought, twisting the pillow between his fists. They would not say anything of the king's nightmares for fear of execution. But they *knew.*

Yseulte returned to their bed and knelt beside him. "They are gone," she said softly. "No one else is here. No one. You are safe."

She brushed the sweat-soaked hair from his forehead. Her hands were cool and soft. Just like his father's. He shuddered, remembering those other nights. It bothered him that he could remember almost nothing of his mother, except for the scent of lavender and a single image of her sitting by the window, a silhouette of dark blue robes against the brilliant sky. He allowed Yseulte to stroke his cheek and hair, to soothe him into the semblance of calm. She understood. Above all the reasons of state, above all other political considerations, he had married her because she understood and still loved him.

"Sleep, my love," she whispered.

He closed his eyes and breathed in rhythm with his wife. He told himself his father and grandfather were dead. He was alone with Yseulte. Their three children were several rooms distant from this dreadful huge bedchamber. They would never, he swore, never dream of monsters as he had.

Yseulte cradled him in her arms, rocking him as though he were one of the children. Armand gratefully leaned against her, breathing in the strange conflicting scents that were hers alone. Rose and linden flower. The milky scent from nursing their youngest child, which she had insisted upon, even though a queen might summon any number of wet nurses. Her skin was warm and soft—silk touched with magic—and her pulse beat steady against his temple.

"I love you," she said.

Yseulte was not his mother. He was not his father.

He told himself that was enough.

BY LATE MORNING the nightmares had receded to trembling shadows. Those he was used to. Memories of the dreams and their aftermath lingered at the edge of awareness, however, like the dark oily waves he had witnessed in the south, the remnants of a storm.

Like the smothering darkness in your bedchamber, the one your mother decreed safe against your father's sickness, your grandfather's madness. You screamed until they lit an oil lamp. You screamed even louder at the wriggling shadows. Nothing worked until Lord Khandarr lit a steady flame, powered by magic, that swept away the darkness.

He decided he was fit to conduct the day's business, starting with his usual public audience. It was an unexceptional day. Minor nobles from outlying provinces, hoping to insinuate themselves into Duenne's Court. An envoy from Versterlant, here on behalf of her nation's council. Representatives from certain banking guilds in Ysterien, which required higher fees before they lent money to the crown, and another from Fortezzien, with their perpetual demands for lower taxes. Toward the end of the hour, a trade delegation from Melnek City, in the northeast province of Morauvín.

He spoke with great politeness with his Ysterien visitors. He needed funds unattached to any obligations. The Fortezzien delegates he dismissed with a vague promise to consider their petition. When the trade delegation presented itself, he greeted them politely, but was glad when the other members withdrew bowing, leaving their leader to address the king.

"Your name?" Armand inquired, though his steward had already provided a synopsis of the man's title, holdings, and his history within the guild.

"Maester Theodr Galt, your Majesty."

"And your demands?"

Galt hesitated, clearly taken aback at Armand's blunt phrasing.

"Your Majesty, I make no demands—"

"You do, Maester Galt, however softly you phrase them."

He deliberately narrowed his eyes and stared at Galt. The man was wealthy, he could determine that even without his steward's report. Dressed in sober black linen, trimmed in silk, the style the latest fashion in Duenne, which meant he had ordered a new wardrobe after his arrival. That same report named Galt as the chief of the shipping guild for Melnek and the surrounding territories. Galt could not be even forty years old—young for the post. Ruthless and ambitious, then.

All the courtiers were listening, a detail Armand had not forgotten, though apparently Galt had. The man tilted his face up. His coloring was dark brown, his features strong and stinking of stubbornness—too stubborn for diplomacy, and yet a fine veneer of mildness overlaid everything.

"I wish the best for Veraene," Galt said. "Let me prove myself, your Majesty. If you find me and my promises adequate, then let us further discuss my guild."

Stubbornness and desperation, a most interesting—and useful—combination. Melnek was a major trade city, inhabited by many wealthy merchants. That much money could fund a war, Armand thought.

And so he smiled upon Theodr Galt, and offered him the hospitality of the royal palace.

HE SPENT THE next hour with his ministers, discussing matters of the treasury, then retreated into a private assembly chamber with his senior advisers. This was a quiet wing in the palace, once the library for Erythandra's emperors and mages, now derelict except for this one room.

Today, however, it was an uncomfortable meeting. Large blue-black thunderclouds massed above the northern hills, turning the air stale and close. Armand's head ached. It felt as though a dozen fingers pressed against his eyes and temples. The presence of magic—the dozens of spells needed to seal this chamber from any spy—offered no relief.

His senior council appeared equally affected by the close hot room, but no one suggested they open the windows. They knew his preference for discretion. Unlike the usual council sessions, Armand would have no guards present. Even the few servants were a concession, and only because Khandarr had excised their ability to speak or hear.

"Next item," Armand said harshly. "Austerlant."

Duke Feltzen shuffled a stack of papers, undoubtedly searching for his notes about the subject. Normally Lord Khandarr acted as chief councillor and spokesman during these meetings, but Khandarr's absence these past four months had altered the usual order of things. "Austerlant," Feltzen said. "Yes. We've received official complaints about excess fees for goods crossing the border."

Armand signaled to the steward for water. He drank deeply and pressed the heels of his hands against his eyes.

Austerlant. Yes. The fees were in retaliation for previous taxes imposed on Veraenen caravans. Just as important, according to Markus Khandarr, the fees encouraged stricter laws governing the more casual border crossings between friendly kingdoms. Everyone was taxed, even if they only carried a loaf of bread for the noonday meal.

"The taxes and fees stand," he said. "If they dislike it, let them send all their trade by ship instead."

A route open only during the brief summer season.

"But your Majesty—"

"Do it."

He spoke softly. Even so, the duke flinched. Baron Quint merely smiled, but it was a weak, fluttering smile. The other three men glanced at each other, clearly uneasy.

Cowards, Armand thought. None of them dared to confront him. He had previously liked Feltzen, a man who used to challenge his grandfather. If the rumors were true, Feltzen had flirted with an alliance with Lord Kosenmark. But like his other councillors, Feltzen had turned overly cautious, overly placating. Quint was no different. They were like dogs, begging for treats.

"What comes next?" he asked. "Ournes, wasn't it?"

His senior secretary had brought him reports from Ournes, whose regional governor had abdicated his post. Feltzen named several candidates. Quint offered objections to three. Armand ended the debate by ordering the two men to provide detailed reports on all candidates by the following week. Fortezzien wanted concessions. Lord Nicol Joannis had vowed his allegiance once again to the crown, but the man could not compel every citizen to obedience. It was a never-ending task, like magical strings that untied themselves as soon as you loosed your hold on them.

We need the taxes and fees from Austerlant. We need funds to pay the soldiers, to quell the unrest before we can do anything about Károví. Even if—

He felt a twitch deep in his gut. He lifted a hand to signal for more water, when a tangible ripple passed through the room. The scent of magic sharpened to a strong green aroma, at once sickening and invigorating, as though the magical guards had suddenly gone alert. Quint's face turned gray. Feltzen gripped his useless papers in both fists.

Markus Khandarr limped into the room, leaning upon a wooden staff.

One of his councillors hissed in surprise. Armand nearly did himself.

Khandarr had never been young, in Armand's eyes. He had gained entry into Duenne's Court when he was forty-two, and Armand a child. He had served in minor positions, always grateful, always happy for whatever duties were handed over to him. Later, after Armand's father died of drink and suicide, Khandarr had offered his unquestioning attention to the young prince. He had secured Armand's rooms against all intrusions, even those of the king. To Armand of Angersee, Markus Khandarr was invincible.

But this broken old man was almost a stranger. His face had turned lopsided, one half unnaturally stiff and drawn into an ugly knot of deeply etched lines, the other sagging into pouches. Khandarr stomped onward, each step accompanied by a wince, a barely suppressed groan. His staff clicked loudly over the tiled floor.

Armand watched his slow progress with growing apprehension. And anger.

You told me you had discovered a mage from Morenniou. You never mentioned that mage bested you.

He should have guessed, however, that there was something more. Khandarr had sent only one report from Osterling Keep. It was laden with details about the Károvín ships that foundered offshore, hints of an expedition to faraway islands, about soldiers who died even as Khandarr attempted to question them, and then, almost as an afterthought, the mention of a great discovery.

Weeks of silence had followed, broken only by one brief note from Tiralien. Since then, nothing. Nothing for almost three months.

Khandarr stopped a few steps away from Armand's chair. He adjusted his grip on his wooden staff and, with obvious effort, lowered himself to one knee. His gray hair was tousled from wind and stiffened with sweat. Dust coated his clothes. He had obviously come here directly from the stables.

"Your Majesty," he said. "I request . . . an audience. A private one."

His voice was faint, his words slurring together.

Of course you want a private audience, Armand thought. *You bring news of a failure. One so shameful, you didn't dare send a report by written word.*

His councillors were already on their feet. Feltzen had crumpled his papers together. Quint barely held himself back from scrambling to escape. Armand waited, his stomach drawing into an ever-tighter knot, until he heard the door bolted closed behind them.

"Tell me what happened," he said.

Khandarr jerked his head up. Did he hear an echo of Baerne of Anger-see in that command? Another day, Armand might have treasured such a victory. Today was different. He pointed to Feltzen's chair. "Sit. Speak. If you can," he added.

It was an unnecessary bit of cruelty. Armand wished he could recall the words. Khandarr grimaced—strange how that twisted face could express such clear emotions—and raised himself to his feet. He stumped over to the chair. Once seated, he poured himself a cup of sweet wine and drank it down.

"Kosenmark," he said. "News from Tiralien. And more. That I could not entrust to messengers."

Interesting. So he hoped to convey that this long-overdue report would be the true and complete one. Armand found himself curious how Khandarr's account would compare with those of his other spies.

"Go on," he said.

Khandarr nodded briskly, a gesture more like his old self. He poured a second cup of wine, and proceeded to give his report, though still in that strange and garbled voice.

Armand listened with growing surprise and dread as his mage councillor recited the events of the past three months. Károví and its mysterious fleet. Lir's Veil breached and the jewels recovered—one of them at least, he gathered. Khandarr's speech had turned almost incomprehensible as he swiftly recounted this interview between himself and a supposed mage from Morennioù.

One part, however, was clear.

"That bitch. Morenniou's spy. She escaped," Khandarr said. "I do not know how."

The unaccustomed vulgarity startled Armand. He wanted to demand particulars about their interview, but knew Khandarr would avoid a direct answer. So he asked the second-most urgent question on that very long list he'd formed over the past few months.

"Where did she go, then? Back to Morennioù? You said she was a member of their court. A noble or emissary."

Khandarr shook his head. "To Károví. At least. So I believe."

An interesting equivocation. "And Kosenmark's lover?"

"Dead. Perhaps."

"You have doubts about the official reports?"

Armand's gaze met Khandarr's. Khandarr smiled grimly. So there *was* a question whether Ilse Zhalina lived or not. Knowing Raul Kosenmark, and the woman he called beloved, that did not surprise him.

"What brought you to Tiralien?" he asked next.

"Not important. What I learned there . . . is."

Khandarr went on to tell the story of a ship, acquired by Lord Kosenmark's new secretary, for purposes unknown. Khandarr had his spies investigate the secretary, but without much success. The man had appeared six months before with the usual letter of recommendation. An unimportant creature, but someone Kosenmark trusted.

The key point was the ship. It sailed without warning from Tiralien in late spring. A few weeks later, Khandarr's agents reported an unidentified ship sighted near Hallau Island. When the coastal patrol signaled it, the ship fled north. The patrol had to break off pursuit when the ship entered Károvín waters.

"Proof," Khandarr said. "Proof of treason."

"Are you certain? Or do you simply wish to be certain?"

Khandarr flinched. "Certain. Of course."

"Then you might wish to know the reports *I* received, just two days ago."

It was a moment his grandfather had warned him about—when a councillor, once a mentor, discovered they were not the absolute guide behind the throne. Armand braced himself for anger. He ought to have called the guards inside. Better, he ought to have a second mage in council, someone unconnected with Markus Khandarr. Belatedly, he wondered if such a mage existed in Veraene.

Khandarr's eyes narrowed to thin dark lines. "What report?"

So he did not know. That, too, was an important clue.

"It concerns King Leos," Armand said. "My agents tell me he died two months ago."

There was a moment of silence in the audience chamber.

"Then we have . . . war?" Khandarr said at last.

"So it would seem," Armand replied, "except that your Lord Kosenmark's father arrived in court last month to argue against it. He has gathered a sizable faction to his cause, that being the cause for peace with Károví. Furthermore," he added, "Lord Kosenmark has returned to Tiralien. If he is a traitor, he is a terribly discreet one. Or clumsy."

Another silence, even more gratifying than the first.

Was this the true test of Armand's trust in the man, and Khandarr's loyalty in return?

You cannot trust without need, his grandfather once said. *Nor can your men vow allegiance with no promise in return. Both are paid with the same coin.*

"I think," Armand said, "we must plan our next maneuver."

CHAPTER EIGHT

ILSE WAITED THREE days before she decided to confront Miro Karasek alone.

It had taken all her strength of will to refrain from demanding an audience that first night and day. Karasek had evaded her, Bela Sovic had distracted her—an obvious ploy, but with the unexpected glimpse into Sovic's own history and that of Karasek's father. Later, when Ilse and Valara walked with Karasek through a series of formal gardens, the air heavy with the scent of ripening fruit and dying leaves, she noted a curious and unsettling reticence on his part. He spoke of their future plans, but only in the vaguest terms, and always with a reference to possible delays. He did not mention that Ilse would not accompany Valara Baussay to Morennioù. Nor had he arranged to speak in private about Ilse's own concerns.

He was being cautious, she told herself, but when a second day passed without any word, she became anxious. She reluctantly accepted an invitation from Bela Sovic for a tour of the river valley, then submitted to the attentions of seamstresses and shoemakers, who arrived from nearby Duchova to measure Duke Karasek's cousins for new clothes, boots, and shoes. Valara was similarly occupied. Miro Karasek himself was given over to the business of running his holdings: conferences with secretary and steward, making the rounds of his lands, holding audiences with farmers and village speakers to hear their concerns. It was all quite reasonable, all what anyone might expect of relations between a powerful duke and his cousins from a remote province.

On the third day, she rose at sunrise and sent a message to Karasek, requesting an interview at his convenience. She worded the note politely, obliquely, but the abrupt brushstrokes expressed her true emotions. Even in such a short time, she knew his habits. He rose at first light and drilled with his guards. He broke his fast with bread and cheese and strong tea, then rode a circuit with this patrol or that, or sometimes he visited the surrounding farms and villages. The interval between was her best chance to speak privately with him. If he ignored this request, she would have to assume his promise of aid meant nothing.

She dressed in the first of her new costumes, loose trousers and billowing overrobe gathered at her waist by a brocaded sash. Her maid, Anezka, brushed out her hair, then, at Ilse's request, tied it in a loose braid. Her breakfast arrived soon after. Ilse nibbled at her toasted bread, unable to stomach the hot porridge with its dried fruit and spices. Her nerves were brittle and bright. It was because she acted in secret, because she intended to break her promise to Morennioù and its queen.

"My lady."

"Yes?"

Anezka curtsied. "His grace sends word he will see you."

The hour bells were ringing as she approached the entrance to Miro Karasek's private offices. She had come here once before, her first full day at Taboresk. Karasek had not been available, but the runner had directed her outside to the gardens where the duke walked with her supposed sister.

Today, the runner escorted her down the short corridor. There were no guards, but another runner waited in an alcove by the office.

"My Lady Matylda Zelenka, expected by Duke Karasek."

Bows were exchanged, and Ilse passed into the sanctuary.

At once she was reminded of her first entrance into Raul Kosenmark's private rooms above the pleasure house. A cursory glance showed all the appointments one might expect of a wealthy noble—the arching ceiling with a single elaborate chandelier, the enormous window with expensive glass overlooking a formal garden, the floor an expanse of dark blue tiles, inlaid with pale gray stones fashioned into scenes that she guessed came from Károví's history.

But another glance showed a different aspect. (And another reminder of Raul Kosenmark.) Shelves covered many of the walls, all of them stuffed with books about law, history, finance, and more. The rest was given over to maps of the kingdom. Karasek himself was ensconced behind a massive desk of rare blackwood, whose surface was entirely covered with stacks of papers, inkstones and brushes and parchment, ready for use. Here, said those clues, was a man who worked.

Karasek rose from behind his desk. "My lady cousin."

"My lord and grace."

The door closed behind her. Ilse released a breath she had not realized she held.

"I've come to redeem your promise," she said.

"So I anticipated."

Her pulse leapt up at his flat tone.

"Is there trouble?" she asked. "More than you anticipated, that is?"

His mouth quirked into a smile. "There always is. But to answer your true question. I have not forgotten my promise to you. However, the means to accomplish it is not as simple as I hoped."

"How so?"

"Originally I intended to send you with an escort to Veraene's northwest border. It's the most direct and the least defended. But recent reports from the Duszranjen garrisons say Veraene has ordered more troops along the northern mountain passes."

He was not meeting her gaze directly, she noted.

"What are your counterplans?" she asked, her voice carefully neutral. Even if she did not trust him, she did not wish to antagonize this man. She did not wish to appear desperate.

Karasek must have read some of her emotions from her face, however, because his mouth softened into a rueful smile. "You will not like my answer. The truth is, I cannot tell what to do. Not yet. Given that Veraene guards its land borders, my next choice would be a water route. If you accompany us to Lenov, I can bribe a smuggler—or better, one of the fishing fleet—to carry you into Veraenen waters. Whatever the best choice proves to be, I promise an escort and money."

She did not like the answer, but she understood his reasoning.

"Will it be long before we depart?"

"Two or three weeks. You and the queen shall be away from Károví long before winter."

"What of setbacks?" she said. "You cannot pretend there will be none."

Karasek raked his fingers through his hair, the first break in his carefully controlled manner. "I don't. And I don't know. I have plans, but the gods have greater plans still." He tipped his head back and stared upward, as though trying to see through the ceiling to where the gods dwelt. His lips were parted as though to laugh, but there was no laughter in his expression. "No," he said softly. "I don't know. I can only ask you to trust me and my honor."

ILSE SAT ALONE in her bedchamber.

Six hours had passed since her interview with Duke Miro Karasek.

I cannot trust him. I cannot.

And yet, he had told her that Raul lived. Had told her he would ensure her passage home.

So many contradictions, honestly and truly given. She could tell it. She massaged her temples with both hands.

I must go home. I must find Raul and tell him about the jewels.

The noon bells were ringing. She knew from her maid that Valara Baussay had gone out riding with Miro Karasek. Ilse had dismissed Anezka and the other servants, saying she felt unwell and wished to rest in quiet. Now she sat cross-legged on her sumptuous bed, her back against the mound of pillows. It was the same pose she had used months ago in Osterling Keep, when she had last attempted to make the leap in the flesh into Anderswar.

Her pulse beat light and quick at the memory. Her brief encounter with Anderswar had left her bruised and bitten and terrified—and that was the simplest obstacle she faced. She had never crossed from point to point alone. If she lost her way, she might fall into another world, or another time. Or she might be trapped forever in the void.

She drew a breath and concentrated on the sensation of air filling her lungs. Slow and slow, she told herself. She had made the leap once before on her own, though she had returned to the same point as before. She had made the leap a second time in Valara Baussay's company. She could do it.

Another breath, another moment contemplating the balance point of magic.

"Ei rûf ane gôtter. Ei rûf ane strôm . . ."

The air went taut. It glittered with an unnatural light.

"Komen mir de vleisch unde sêle. Komen mir de Anderswar."

The world blinked out of existence. It was a leap of flesh and not spirit alone. She could tell by the weight of her body, the intensity of scent and the vivid green taste of magic on her tongue. Ilse crouched on the edge of nothing, her fingers curled around a rim of darkness. Spheres of worlds and universes whirled below. Her stomach lurched against her ribs. She closed her eyes and swallowed hard. No, that was not right. She could not pretend blindness. If she wanted to achieve Tiralien, she had to focus on its bell towers, the governor's palace rising tall above a sea of crimson rooftops, the intricate paths through Raul Kosenmark's rooftop garden from which she could see the ocean—anything she could recall from memory.

Without warning, her perception shifted. She huddled in a stark cave, her hand over her mouth to hold back the vomit. A creature paced before her. Its hunched back was covered with feathers, its beaked mouth snapped at the air. She could hear the click and clatter of its nails against the stone floor. The air was thick with magic and the musty scent of feathers and molding leaves.

You wanted the jewels. You found them.

She staggered to her feet. Glared at the beast through slitted eyes. She hated it, hated Miro Karasek, and all the chains that bound her to this life. She had no knife, but her nails grew longer, and she felt her skin ripple beneath its coat of fur and feathers. It's not enough, she said. The jewels found their way home. Now I must. You know that well enough.

The beast paused in its circuit.

You must?

It laughed then, a harsh braying laugh that was part human and part monster. Ilse thrust past the beast, through an invisible opening in the wall, and leapt toward the void. She was not swift enough. Claws dug into her flesh and dragged her, struggling and howling, back into the nothing of Anderswar. Let me go, she cried.

Her surroundings abruptly shifted. She hung suspended in nothingness. No worlds below. No river of souls above. All was white and empty and silent. Ilse lifted a hand, but the whiteness enveloped her so completely, she saw nothing more than a dark blue shadow. She touched her face. The fur and feathers had vanished. Blood trickled from a cut over one eye, its warmth the only sign of life that remained.

I failed. I am lost.

Deep within, a voice answered. *You expected it.*

She had. And Anderswar had taken those expectations to fashion its nightmares.

Ilse closed her eyes. *If only I had a thread to my own world. Like the thread used by heroes in the old tales, when they were trapped within a maze.*

She still felt a faint tug from the ordinary world—weak and tenuous. Not enough to pull her to safety.

More blood trickled from the cut over her eye. The beast had marked her with its claws again. Ilse wiped the blood away with one hand. Drops fell from her fingertips to whirl around, like dark pearls against the white nothingness. She felt a stronger tug in her gut, and her pulse leapt. Was it possible?

She wiped more blood from her face, flung her hand outward. The droplets spiraled down and away. With a murmured prayer to Lir and Toc, she followed.

* * *

MIDNIGHT. THERE WAS no moon to infiltrate her bedchamber, no fire to cast its dim glow, but she knew by a thousand infinitesimal clues that she had returned to Taboresk and her own bedchamber. Ilse huddled on her bed. Her throat felt thick, her tongue cleaved to the roof of her mouth, and her neck itched, as though feathers fluttered beneath her skin. There was no sign of Anezka or anyone else having entered the room during her absence, but she could not be certain. She had trusted too easily before.

I cannot stay here. I must find another way back to Veraene.

SIX MORE DAYS passed since that interview. If Miro Karasek had detected her failed attempt to cross the void, he said nothing, nor did he meet with her again, except in the company of Valara Baussay, and even then only for such unexceptional activities as dining, or to walk through the gardens of Taboresk. Ilse knew a courier had set off to Lenov with Karasek's instructions to his agent, but word had not yet come back.

She dismounted and tethered the mare to a tree before unloading her saddlebags. One pack contained cooking gear and a bag of oats. Knowing what came next, the horse whuffed and stretched its neck toward the bags. Ilse poured out a heap of oats, then she unpacked the cooking gear and a tin of ground coffee.

Patterns were the key. She knew that from her time with Raul Kosenmark. It was the same in swordplay, politics, and war. So she had established a pattern of regular outings. Mornings she rode alone, always with the same mount, a sturdy and placid mare named Duska. Once or twice, she added a shorter outing before sunset. Once or twice, the stable master inquired if she wished an escort. Ilse had gently refused. After that, no one had questioned her, which meant her plans were as yet undiscovered.

Ilse let Duska drink her fill from the noisy creek, then fetched water for herself. Once the fire was alight and the coffee brewing, she unpacked the second saddlebag. This one contained two blankets, a third empty saddlebag, and a few miscellaneous items, such as a second tinderbox (purloined when the cook was distracted), salt, a paring knife, a packet of yeast, a tin of black tea and another of coffee. She still lacked a suitable knife and sword. If she could not steal these from the practice yard where the sentries drilled, she might try to recover the ones she had buried near the entrance to the valley.

The blankets and miscellaneous items went into the smaller bag, along with an extra pair of gloves and several pairs of socks, which she had hidden in her pockets. The seamstresses and shoemakers from Duchova had come and gone, leaving behind an astonishing quantity of clothing, shoes, and boots. Ilse wore a new quilted jacket and riding trousers cut loose and tucked into low boots. These would prove useful during her journey.

She buried the saddlebag between the roots of a tree, taking care to smooth out the dirt and scatter pine needles over the spot. A pale stone wedged into the dirt marked the location. She had left three other caches, marked the same way. Each of them contained extra clothing and whatever gear she could purloin from storerooms or the stable. Was it enough? She could not tell. She only knew she had to get away, and soon.

Ilse pressed her cold hands over her face.

Twice more she had asked to speak with Miro Karasek in private. Each time, he had sent back a written note saying he would see her safely across the border. And yet he refused to name the day for their departure. More distressing, he refused to entertain a different plan, one that would allow her to leave earlier.

I must go. I cannot wait any longer. Raul must hear news of the jewels.

She thought she knew the reason for Karasek's new demands. Ilse's maid had repeated the latest gossip—how a courier from Rastov brought the terrible news that King Leos was dead, assassinated by his enemies. Everyone was frightened, Anezka said. Everyone wondered who could be the next king or queen. No doubt the duke would return to Rastov to meet with the other chief councillors.

No doubt he will use what little time remains to send Valara Baussay homeward. It's a choice I would make as well.

At last the coffee smelled done. Ilse filled a tin mug and drank it down. By now the sun was well above the hilltops, and the mists in the bottom of the valley had dissipated. The sharp tang of pine tickled her nose, underneath it the rich rank scent of dead leaves and the decaying remnants of a fallen oak tree.

Ilse unbuttoned her jacket and stuffed it into the now-empty saddlebag. She drank a second mug of coffee, then stamped back and forth along the ridge, to warm her chilled feet.

Over the past week, she had visited the library several times to study its maps. The best route was to cross to the southern edge of the Ostrava Hills, then head west under cover of the forest. If she could believe Karasek, the northwest passes into Veraene were too much of a risk. She had not yet decided whether she ought to attempt a path in the southwest corner of

Duszranjo, or seek out one of the passes near Melnek. Both had different advantages, different dangers.

I don't have to choose until I reach the mountains, but I can't wait any longer to leave. I'll finish copying those maps tonight. Tomorrow, I leave at sunset.

She blew out a breath of relief. Odd how a simple decision could ease the tightness that gripped her body.

ON HER RETURN, the stable master came himself to take the mare's reins. "Lady Matylda. Do not trouble yourself with those saddlebags. I will tend to them."

His manner was agitated, and Ilse's pulse jumped. Was it possible that someone had noted her activities? Impossible, she told herself. But she could not help turning over the past few days in her mind, searching for any sign of suspicion from her maid, the stablehands, or others in the household.

Once inside the house, she encountered more turmoil—chambermaids and runners, darting in all directions on various errands. Anezka herself paused long enough to glance in Ilse's direction, but then another called to her, and she was away.

Ilse felt a flutter of unease. She turned into a side corridor and proceeded to the seldom-used set of stairs that led to her rooms.

She stopped, sucked in a breath.

Her door stood ajar. Within, someone paced back and forth, their slippers hissing over the stone. Her memory flashed back to Osterling Keep, the day Markus Khandarr had searched her rooms. Truly anxious now, she passed inside.

Valara Baussay paced the floor in long hurried strides. At Ilse's entrance, she spun around. Her face was drawn into tight lines, making her sharp features seem more foxlike than ever. In the bright sunlight, Ilse could see the tracery of her tattoos beneath the stain, as insubstantial as the stories to explain their presence at Taboresk.

"What is it?" she whispered, even though they were alone.

"Visitors," Valara replied. "Vistors from Rastov."

MUCH LATER THAT evening, Valara Baussay sat alone in her rooms, next to a dying fire. Pale moonlight spilled through the high round windows.

Her father had warned her. Her grandfather, too, through his memoirs and the histories he wrote about his own ascension to the crown. Theirs were battles of politics and not war, but the advice still held true. No plan survives its first contact with the enemy.

So, thought Valara Baussay, *I have met the enemy within Károví. And with a single blow, they have destroyed my army.*

She had spent the afternoon with Ilse Zhalina. Most of that time they spoke of their mutual cause, as if they were friends aligned against a common enemy. After some fashion, that was true, but Valara understood that Ilse's goals were those of Veraene, and very different from those of Morennioù or Károví. So the conversation had been a delicate dance of questions and answers, each designed to elicit information from the other.

Shivering, she rubbed her hands over her arms. She could not accustom herself to this strange country. At midday she sweated. By nightfall, she wanted to smother herself in wool blankets. In Morennioù, at least, she could predict the weather by the season. Winter rainstorm, summer thunder and sweltering days. Autumn, her favorite months, when the seas rolled dark and smooth from shore to horizon, and she could perch on the windowsill of her private rooms and watch the stars.

I miss my home.

Tears caught in her throat. She choked them down. Grief was another luxury that had no place in her life until she regained her kingdom.

She turned away from the useless fire and took a robe from its hook. One of dozens now, sewed with impossible haste by the troupe of seamstresses Karasek had hired. She wrapped the robe tight around her waist and tied it with its sash.

Barefoot, she stole from her rooms and glided through the maze of corridors to a balcony overlooking Taboresk House's grandest hall. Her movements were slow and silent, as subtle as twilight in the north. She doubted anyone heard her. Even so, her breath came short as she sank to her knees to observe the scene below.

Three men sat in the hall by the enormous fireplace, in great carved chairs that offered more splendor than comfort. The winecups in their hands glittered in the fire and lamplight, like a cascade of stars amid the ordinary world. Two were strangers to her—an older man swathed in robes, his thin white hair cropped short, so that his dark skull showed through. The second, younger man, held forth in animated tones and gestures. The third sat motionless, his back toward her, but Valara recognized Miro Karasek easily. Faint strains of music echoed from a nearby chamber.

No one looked up. No one seemed the least aware that anyone watched them. Valara thought back to her own days in Morennioù Castle, even before she had become heir, to nights such as these, with music from invisible players and the illusion of privacy.

She shivered again, and the letter tucked inside her gown rustled. Valara did not need to examine it a second time. She already knew its contents: *Grave news from Rastov. I will come to you as soon as possible.*

Karasek had sent the message privately, shortly after the flood of rumors about these new visitors. At his request, she had not mentioned it to Ilse Zhalina, but the implications of that request sent another shiver through her body. The susurration of paper against paper reminded her of another night, another letter, from almost two years ago, when Jhen Aubévil wrote to proclaim his love. Poor Jhen. A captive of his father and the politics of Morennioù's Court.

I loved him once. But that was long ago.

And yet he was her best friend.

From there her thoughts winged back to other evenings in Morenniou, when Giselle, her own senior maid, might have waited on the steps for Valara, listening to what took place below. Had Giselle survived the attack? Oh, but that was too painful to think about.

She stood slowly, her knees aching as if she were an old woman, and retreated to her rooms. There she rebuilt the fire in her parlor and lit a branch of candles. Silvered light overlaid the marble floor by the window. The rest of the room lay in shadows; the furniture merely darker shapes that she recognized more from memory than from sight. From far away came the tolling of an hour bell, plain and strong. Another hour at least until Karasek's visit. She took a seat by the window and prepared to wait.

To distract herself, she forced herself to read a book of Károví's early history, comparing this historical record with her own, admittedly fragmented memories of her past lives. The text held her attention better than she expected, so that when a soft tapping sounded at the door, she started up in surprise.

Karasek. She had almost forgotten him. However, it would not do to make any assumptions. Valara extinguished the candle and crossed to the door. "Who is it?"

"Miro. Let me in."

She unlatched the door. He glided into the room, noiseless, like a wolf on the trail, and closed the door. "Come with me," he whispered.

He touched her wrist—once, no more—indicating the couch opposite them. She followed him there, thinking that even in Taboresk he did not risk a whispered conversation so close to where someone might overhear.

"What is the news?" she asked. "Who are those men?"

"My cousin Ryba and Baron Gregor Skoch."

The second name meant nothing to her. The first . . .

"He was your father's heir once."

A mistake. Karasek's face went blank. A stranger might think him angry, but over the past week, she had learned to read his array of masks. Her words had called up some painful, private memory, and that unnerved her even more. "Yes, he was," he said quietly. "For a time. Until I came back from Duszranjo."

Another uncomfortable pause before he continued, "All that took place years ago. It's not important, at least not for you. The news he and Skoch bring is, however. They have a formal letter from the council, signed by all its members, requiring my immediate presence in Rastov."

He went on to explain Károvín politics. Skoch was a minor noble who had aligned himself with Duke Markov, an influential member of King Leos's privy council. The most likely reason for a summons was that Markov, possibly others, suspected Karasek of treason. It was inevitable. Karasek had had so little time to prepare the grounds, to fabricate a convincing story about his movements the night Dzavek died. Markov remained in Rastov to secure his own position, but he had ordered Baron Skoch to escort Karasek back for a trial. Karasek did not call it that, but the implications were clear.

"Then you must go to Rastov and prove your innocence," Valara said. "Ilse and I will ride to Lenov—"

"Not possible. Markov will have spies and guards on all the ports. He would not send a message before he did so. I know him."

She drew a sharp breath at his bitter tone. "Then what? We cannot remain here."

"Nor can you remain anywhere in Károví. You must risk the magical plane."

"I told you before, I cannot—"

She broke off and shut her eyes, frightened at how close she had come to confessing. *I cannot. Not unless I wish to place myself in his power entirely.*

At last, Miro sighed and rose to his feet. "I must go in case someone sends for me." But once at the door, he stopped with his hand on the latch and glanced back. "I will talk with my secretary tomorrow. Meanwhile, I will make a pretense of arranging to return with Skoch to Rastov. He is a clever man. He will have messengers ready to report if I refuse. I do not have a counterplan yet, but I will see what I can do. If anything . . . if anything goes wrong, I will come to you again. May I?"

Valara tried to read his expression, but the moonlight had changed his face into a mosaic of blue shadows. "Of course."

Miro drew an audible breath and swung away. "There is no of course. Not in anything we do. Not today, not in all our lives before."

The ragged note in his voice brought Valara to her feet. "Miro, wait." She crossed to him quickly, stopped a pace away, breathless. The air itself had changed with speaking his name.

"I lied," she said. "At the Mantharah, the gods . . ." She discovered she was rubbing the scar on her palm, where she had gripped the three jewels. Her skin prickled at the memory of magic flooding her veins when she plunged her hands into the Mantharah's strange lake. "I cannot cross the magical plane, because I have no magic left to me," she whispered. "The gods took it."

Her eyes burned with tears. She refused to weep, however. Lir and Toc had exacted their price. So be it. Oh, but she hated this void inside her, and the sense she would have to live the rest of her life unbalanced, incomplete.

She swiped a hand across her eyes and made to turn away. Miro captured her hand in his. Then the other. Valara inhaled sharply. She did not dare to move.

His hold was featherlight, his palms rough with calluses from sword work.

"Trust me," he said. "Please. I promise to deliver you safely to your kingdom."

He lifted her hands to his lips. Stopped. Held them for a single moment that to Valara felt like infinity. All the careful blankness had vanished. She could tell by the strange smile on his face that he had stepped to the precipice of a decision. And leapt.

He loosed her hands. On impulse, she reached up to touch his face. Miro's eyes were like dark moons. Very slowly, he bent down and touched his lips to hers. Warm. His breath like a cloud of magic against her chilled face. He kissed her again, a solemn, most thorough kiss that spoke of an intimacy she had not guessed at.

Miro stepped back. No need to read his expression. She could taste the passion from that lingering kiss. Without another word, he left her chamber, as secretly as he'd come.

CHAPTER NINE

FOR ILSE ZHALINA, it was a day and night spent in anxious preparation.

She sat at a table in her bedchamber, surrounded by stacks of books and scrolls on the floor, on the table, and some on her bed, all of them smuggled from Karasek's enormous library over the past week. In front of her lay a nearly complete copy of a map showing the southwestern quadrant of Károví's plains, along with its towns, highways, and garrisons. One parsimonious candle lit her workspace. She had wanted to use magic, but she did not wish to draw attention to her activities. Magic, she expected, was particularly suspect by these new visitors to Taboresk House.

Her candle guttered. Ilse lit another before it died.

Two more left. Several days ago, when she had first formed her plans, she had advertised her love of reading at night, thus ensuring a plentiful supply from her maid. Once the search began, it would be obvious how she spent this night, but by tomorrow afternoon, it would not matter. She only had to escape the house and its immediate grounds. From there she could—she hoped—vanish into the wilderness, while Karasek's visitors kept him occupied until she was truly beyond his and their reach.

Ilse finished off one last notation about troop movements, then set the map aside to dry. She rubbed her eyes with her knuckles. Her head ached; her shoulders were stiff from hours bent over this makeshift desk.

If only I could walk the magic planes.

But she could not. She had attempted once, and nearly lost herself.

All throughout the remainder of that morning, she and Valara had talked. Talked to little purpose. They were both lying to each other, but they continued to pretend an alliance. When Valara at last departed for her own rooms, Ilse felt only relief. She had not set to work at once. Instead, mindful of spies, she lingered an hour or so in a small parlor, reading a novel, then took a walk through Taboresk's formal gardens. As soon as she dared, she dismissed her maid for the night and set to copying maps.

From far away came the muted tolling of an hour bell. Three, four, five . . .

One more hour until dawn. She would have to hurry before the household woke.

She dressed in her warmest riding costume—the silk shirt, the wool trousers, socks and boots and gloves and quilted jacket. A knitted cap went into her pockets, along with several inkstones, a few brushes, and the rest of the blank pages. She had a moment's regret for soap and a dozen other amenities, but that passed quickly enough. Her expectations had altered a great deal since she ran away from Melnek.

Her last task was to collect the coins and gems from her jewelry box. Karasek had wanted her to appear the proper wealthy young woman; to that end, he had provided her and Valara with pins and pendants, earrings, and jewels for their hair. She felt a prick of guilt; *thief* was not a name she liked. But she would need money for supplies, possibly bribes as well. She would repay him once she rejoined Raul.

She stashed the jewels and coins in a pouch, which went inside her shirt. By now the moon had dipped below the horizon. The stars were little more than pale specks. The hills, just visible, showed as a black smudge against the dark gray sky. Morning was rising whether she liked it or not. Ilse was glad she had anticipated this moment, and did not need to seek out provisions or gear.

Hurry, hurry, hurry.

She lit a new candle. The copies of her map she folded into a square packet and tucked them into her belt for now. The originals she scooped up in her arms. She surveyed her rooms one last time. There was nothing left to incriminate her or point to the route she chose, unless someone knew her intentions.

Outside her rooms, she scanned the corridor in both directions. No movement in the shadows outside her circle of candlelight. Not a sound except the thrumming of blood at her temples. She took a deep breath and glided toward the nearest stairwell, then down and around to the next landing, along now-familiar passageways, the candlelight leaping over the stone walls. She deposited the maps in the library, then sped down another set of stairs to a doorway she seldom used and which led to the courtyard where the sentries drilled.

Here she paused to recover her breath. This, this was a dangerous moment. She had no good explanation for her presence here, especially at this hour.

She extinguished the candle and set it on the floor, then eased the door open.

In the short interval since she left her room, the skies had brightened to pale gray. The stars had vanished. Scraps of clouds raced high overhead. A breeze grazed her face. It was like that moment when she diverted a portion of the magic current from the invisible to the visible world.

Though Ilse had never visited the yard before, she knew what to expect from conversations with the sentries. Several weapons racks stood near the entrance, along with a chest for other supplies. She selected a sword, belt, and scabbard. Next the smallest wrist sheath she could find. She fastened the belt over her jacket and slid the sword into its scabbard. The wrist sheath fit well enough. She turned back to the weapons rack to examine the knives when she heard the faint echo of footsteps outside the wall.

A patrol? Someone arriving early to practice alone?

Ilse snatched up two knives and ran soft-footed and silent to the door. Once through, she caught up the candle and hurried into the nearest side corridor. She slumped against the wall, shaking in panic. It took her two tries before she could slide one knife into its sheath. The other went into her boot. The next moment, she pushed away from the wall and was running through the silent passageways. This turn, then this, across this hall and into the wing that led to the stables.

Her steps slowed. Here was the next danger point.

By well-established habit, she rode every morning, but the hour was markedly earlier than other days. Would the stable master question her? Or would he still be at his breakfast, leaving the boys and girls to do her bidding? They might be curious, but they would not stop her from riding out.

An hour, that is all I ask.

To her relief, a single boy kept watch. While he set to work saddling her regular mount, Duska, Ilse noted the several new horses for Karasek's visitors. One was an especially tall stallion, long-legged and wide-chested—a horse built to gallop. A second seemed of equally fine pedigree, but it was shorter and broader, suited for a heavier rider. From what Anezka had told her, the visitors had come with a sizable retinue, but the other horses were stabled in the village.

"My lady."

The boy offered her the reins. Ilse accepted his assistance in mounting. Then she was out the doors and riding through the gates.

SHE RETRIEVED THE gear from two caches by sunrise. If nothing else, she now had weapons and blankets and tinderbox, plus miscellaneous items for trapping game in the wild. She paused long enough to drink from a mountain stream and fill her waterskin with more. She badly wanted a cup of hot coffee or tea, but she did not dare to stop for so long. She had to be away from the valley within the next hour. By then, her maid would discover Ilse's absence and alert the household.

It was like running away from Melnek—the sickening terror, the endless calculations of when and where and how long. Karasek had sympathized with her situation, but she understood about the demands of one's own kingdom. She had to reach Raul Kosenmark and tell him of the jewels. Karasek . . . He had his own loyalties and his own ambitions.

By the time the sun had lifted above the hills, she had arrived at the third and last cache. As with the other two, she examined the site. No new prints from horse or human. No sign anything had been disturbed.

Ilse dismounted and tethered Duska to a sturdy sapling, then carefully searched for any trace of magic. Karasek was an expert mage—he could erase his signature, and all signs of his magical presence—but Ilse was certain he had not had the opportunity. From all she heard of Skoch from the servants, the man knew nothing of magic, nor did he employ any mages. Even so, she ran her hands over the dirt, listening with all her senses. Nothing. No traps, magical or otherwise.

She had just dragged the last saddlebag free, when she heard the unmistakable creaking of a branch drawn taut. She started to her feet, her hand going by instinct to draw her sword.

Nothing. Only the hiss of leaves against leaves. But Duska's ears pricked up and her nostrils flared. She swung her head to the left. A wolf? One of Karasek's patrols taking an unaccustomed route home? No, not the latter. Duska would know those horses and those guards. Which meant . . .

A single man on foot appeared on the western trail. Behind him five riders followed. Ilse took in all the essentials in one glance. They were all men in their middle years. Hard-faced. Dressed in dark uniforms of leather and steel, equipped with brightly polished armor and weapons. No brigands, these. These were soldiers. She grabbed a handful of dirt and rocks and shouted to the gods.

"Ei rûf ane gôtter! Ane Lir unde Toc!"

Magic burst into the clearing, bright and blinding. Ilse shielded her eyes and flung the dirt at the closest man. He stumbled backward, little more than a blurred shadow in the haze of magic. Ilse darted forward and slashed at his throat. He went down with a garbled cry. Now a shadow loomed to Ilse's left. She retreated, swinging her sword to block any attack.

Her cheek stung. Her arm throbbed unexpectedly. Now she felt the wet warm rush of blood.

She called out again.

"Komen mir de strôm. Komen mir de viur."

Fire rained upon the soldiers. Horses and riders fell to the ground, writhing and bubbling. Duska squealed and lunged away from the battle. Another lunge and she broke free, running down the hillside. Ilse fell to her knees, retching. Dimly she heard the thudding of more hoofbeats. Then a single set of footsteps marching toward her.

Ilse fumbled for her sword. Then stared at the unexpected sight of Bela Sovic standing over one of the bodies, frowning in concentration. Bela's own horse stood still and impassive, as if such a scene were nothing extraordinary.

Bela glanced up and met Ilse's gaze. "They would have killed you."

"I know." Ilse wiped tears from her eyes. When had she started weeping? "Why . . . why are you here?"

"You grieve. That is good. That means you are not yet beyond redemption."

Ilse rubbed her hand over her face. Saw the soldiers tumbled about, bloody and broken. The horses, thrashing feebly. A deep abiding cold gripped her, in spite of the late summer day. She huddled over herself, hardly aware as the other woman searched the bodies. After a few moments, she recovered enough to ask, "What are you looking for?"

"Incriminating documents. Orders concerning Duke Karasek."

"And me?"

Bela's lips drew into a thin smile. "They know you are not the duke's cousin, nothing more. I can assure you that much."

Ilse swallowed against the tight knot in her throat. "How fortunate, then, that you came here just as they attacked."

"Hardly," Bela replied. "My duke ordered me to watch over you."

Ah. And she had thought herself so clever.

Bela finished her examination. None of the guards carried any secret orders, she told Ilse, nor any messages in any language. Even so, she frowned. "They belonged to Skoch," she said. "Skoch or Markov, which is much the same thing. Duke Markov dislikes my lord."

Her tone was cold and flat. Ilse's skin rippled in apprehension. "What will you do?"

"What I must. Close your eyes. This will not be pleasant."

Bela spoke a word. The air drew taut, and a great blaze rolled through the forest, sweeping past the trees and tinder to wrap itself around the dead riders and their mounts. Ilse pressed both hands against her eyes.

"Are you able to stand?" Bela said. "We must catch your horse and leave at once."

Ilse spat the bile from her mouth and dragged herself to her feet. She bound the cut on her arm with cloth ripped from her shirt. Then she whistled and called to Duska, called again as gently as she could. The mare returned slowly, head shaking as if uncertain whether to obey. Ilse calmed the horse with a whispered spell, stroking Duska's neck and babbling nonsense until the horse ceased to tremble. "You said the duke ordered you to guard me," she said. "Did he give you a reason?"

Bela had collected the items from Ilse's cache and was packing them into her own saddlebags. "Only that he had promised your safety. He does not make promises lightly," she added. "I know that very well. Come. We must ride before Skoch discovers his men are missing. He is a stupid man, but a stubborn one."

"What about . . . my sister?"

Bela shrugged. "My lord duke will address her concerns. As for you? You must make the border, no? You have maps. So have I. And better provisions and gear than you could find. Also, a letter that you will find useful, according to my duke."

A letter. Her skin prickled, remembering a letter she had tried to deliver, centuries ago. A matter of peace between the empire and the newly declared kingdom of Kárvoí. She recalled arguments with Leos Dzavek, other more secret discussions with the emperor's envoy. Was it possible that this was the gods' purpose in keeping her alive? Still, she found it difficult to trust, gods or humans. Especially the gods.

"You are not my friend," Ilse said softly. "Nor is the duke. Tell my *why?*"

Bela heaved the saddlebag onto her mount. "No, I am not. But Duke Karasek is everything to me. Now stop arguing and get on your horse. We have a long journey, and Skoch will send a second squad when these men do not return."

RYBA KARASEK WOKE to a touch on his shoulder. By instinct, he reached for the knife under his pillow. Before he'd touched the hilt, he recognized his man Jiří. With the shutters closed, and the fire banked to coals, Jiří was little more than a mass of shadows, but Ryba knew the weight of his hand from a hundred other mornings past. The half-open door showed lamplight in the next room. Other servants spoke in undertones as they went about their chores. Ryba blinked, rubbed his hand over his eyes to clear them. Oh, yes. He'd given orders for an early rising.

"Tea," he croaked. "Strong tea. My favorite black boots. You choose the rest."

Jiří nodded and withdrew, blessedly silent. Ryba let his eyes close, not quite willing to commit to wakefulness. They'd kept a late evening, he and Skoch and Miro. His head thrummed, and Ryba queasily recalled the many bottles of strong wine consumed between them. He'd chattered too much, he remembered, a fault that Miro said was cleverness in disguise since Ryba never divulged any real secrets, only nonsense. Skoch . . . Skoch had said very little himself, other than platitudes about the king's passing, and the kingdom's need for security in these chancy times. Other than polite rejoinders, Miro had said nothing at all.

I am a fool. And my cousin is afraid.

No cleverness in that observation. He knew it from that say-nothing letter three months before, from the mask that had stiffened his cousin's normally mobile features, and most of all, from the river of tension that ran through the household. He'd heard too many rumors these past six months, and he wanted a private conversation with Miro before Skoch slithered into their company.

With a groan, he levered himself out of bed.

AN HOUR LATER, scrubbed to wakefulness and dressed to his servants' satisfaction, Ryba paced through Taboresk's passageways in search of his cousin. The family's private wing lay silent, except for two maids sweeping the hall. Ryba grinned at them. One shook her head, clearly disapproving. The older one smiled at him sweetly. She knew him from many visits past.

"No chance of my lord cousin, the duke, lying abed?" he asked.

The elder maid laughed and shook her head. The younger woman sniffed at his tone. Then she seemed to comprehend she ought not to criticize a baron, even one so feckless and foolish as this young man. She gave a brief curtsy. "No, my lord. He rode out earlier with the morning patrol, but I cannot say if he has returned yet."

"Lir and Toc never know what my cousin will do," Ryba said.

He had the reward of seeing her smile at last. She was a pretty girl, in spite of her stiffness, with bright black eyes canted in an angular face. Dusz-ranjen, he thought, or maybe from the northern provinces. If he were a roving sort of baron, like others he knew . . .

But he was not. His father had taught him better. So, too, the old duke.

He pressed two silver koruný into the young woman's palm. Another two went to her companion. "Thank you for the news and your kindness. You have saved me at least one unnecessary diversion."

Onward he went, his favorite black boots whispering over the old stones. It was a grand household, built from marble and slate mined from Taboresk's mountains. He loved it for certain memories, hated it for others. He remembered his first visits as a child, when he and Miro had explored the grounds together. Then came a summons from his uncle. He'd been not quite six years of age, and could not understand why his mother wept at the news, nor why his father had hugged him so close before the duke's emissaries carried him away. Five strange years had followed, with infrequent visits from his true parents, and a phalanx of servants who treated him as the heir of Taboresk. He told the servants they were wrong. He was no heir. It was his cousin Miro who would be duke. They all smiled at his outbursts.

He'd hated them at first. Later, he'd made friends, loved them as well as his position allowed. He understood they were constrained as much as he and his true parents were. It was all a question of politics, and of the necessity for the old duke to appear untouched by any scandal involving his former wife and the son she had abducted.

Years later, his cousin had returned, mud-soaked and bruised and refusing to speak of his time in Duszranjo, or anything else that concerned his mother.

Old and new memories alike flitted through his consciousness as he prowled through the household. The tea had taken hold. He was awake and, thanks to Jiří's ministrations, feeling steadier than he had expected. He exchanged greetings with the senior housekeeper on the stairs, the undercook Matìj in the kitchens, where he snagged a sweet bun, and finally with the senior hostler, Luba, in the stables. From these old friends he learned his cousin had risen before dawn, met with various members of the household guards, then retreated with his secretary to his private office.

Stranger and stranger, he thought as he now sped directly to the wing that housed those offices. It was almost midmorning, the village bells ringing nine long bells, but the air was still and quiet, more quiet than one might expect for a busy duke newly returned after a long absence.

At the sight of an armed sentry outside the wing, he stopped, uncertain. Another pair waited farther along the hallway. Ryba knew them—both were Miro's first recruits after his father died. "Is my cousin within?" he asked. "I would like a moment's conversation with him, if possible."

The two guards exchanged glances. Something was up. But evidently

Miro had left word to admit his cousin, because the guard closest to the door bowed. "Of course, my lord."

A complicated knock, answered by a voice within. With another bow, the guard opened the door and stood to one side. It was so unlike all the casual visits with his cousin in previous years that he almost thought he should withdraw.

Feeling anxious and contrary, he crossed the threshold.

Miro—the man, the duke, the cousin—sat behind the desk, one hand resting on a thick packet wrapped in oilskin. He had evidently just finished off one last paper, because he still held a brush in one hand. He glanced toward Ryba and acknowledged him with the briefest nod. Miro's secretary, Vasche Capek, occupied a wooden chair by the fireplace. He carried no pens, nor any of his usual equipment. Instead, he sat with his hands gripped together, his back a rigid line. His cheeks were flushed with obvious emotion, a thing Ryba had never believed possible.

"Cousin," Ryba said.

Capek scowled—a general scowl, not directed at Ryba particularly, but unusual for the man. Miro gestured toward a second chair, without meeting Ryba's eyes.

Feh. You both invited me to this quarrel, Ryba thought.

It was unlike them both. But then, these past few weeks had been nothing like the usual. He shrugged, and sank with an exaggerated sigh into the chair Miro had indicated.

"I need tea," he declared. "Strong tea. Brewed with herbs to counteract our strenuous evening. And," he added, "a dish to make up for such an uncomfortable morning."

He had the reward of seeing Miro's mouth twitch into a smile. Capek merely frowned. "Your Grace," he said to Miro. "You have heard my objections. That is all I ask."

"Hardly all," Miro murmured. "However, I do understand your concerns, Vasche. In return, I ask only that you indulge me this one time."

Ryba felt a trickle of apprehension at his cousin's tone. He trained his glance upon the tiled floor, to the square depicting Miro's ancestor leading troops against the Veraenen invaders. It was for that brave act that King Leos granted Fedor Karasek these lands and the title of duke. Four hundred years had passed since those wars, two hundred since the artisan had created these tiles. Scuff marks obscured the ancestor's face, but otherwise the scene was vividly laid out, soldiers charging with weapons raised, soldiers hacking at each other with swords and axes, soldiers dying and weeping for little more cause than a noble's pride.

Meanwhile, Miro had affixed a wax seal to the wrapping. He pressed his thumb onto the soft wax and spoke an invocation to the gods. The air stirred, and Ryba could almost hear the magic current whispering the names Lir and Toc in response. Then Miro inserted the paper into the packet and handed the whole over to Capek. "Remember," he said. "Hold that in safe-keeping until you are required to hand it over."

"Yes, your Grace." Capek accepted the papers, but he was clearly un-happy about the orders. He exited the room with his head bowed.

Once the door closed, Miro rested his head upon his hands.

Ryba let a few moments pass before he spoke.

He had meant to tax his cousin with keeping late hours, but that would strike too close to the truth. Miro's eyes were red-rimmed and dull, as though he had not slept at all since he and Ryba had parted in the family wing. And there was an air of restlessness about him. Ryba had observed his cousin in all manner of moods—from those first skittish days after his return from Duszranjo, to those of intimacy as they worked their way past the expecta-tions imposed by others, to these past few years of easy camaraderie. To honesty itself.

This. This was a new Miro, and one that frightened Ryba with its strange-ness.

"Miro," he said softly. "What is wrong?"

Miro's head snapped up. His eyes were wide, as if Ryba had suddenly turned into one of Taboresk's ghosts.

(And there were ghosts at Taboresk. Another secret that he and his cousin shared.)

"Nothing is wrong," Miro said. "Other than our king has died, and we face a war with Veraene."

So. A blunt reply. But he had asked for one, he knew.

"I'm sorry he is dead," Ryba answered. "I cannot love him as you did—"

"I never loved him."

Again, the harsh truth. Ryba wanted to reply with a joke, but he under-stood his cousin needed more from him. *I need more. We all do, all of us in Károví, no matter what we thought of Leos Dzavek.*

So. Honesty leavened with kindness.

"I never loved him," Ryba said. "But I admired him. I admired him for his courage in the face of Erythandra's might. For his willingness to take back from the empire what belonged to us alone. For how he sacrificed himself to rebuild the kingdom. No, to build it greater than before."

"He lied to us," Miro said.

Ryba suppressed a shudder. "So perhaps he did. So did all our kings and queens. What does that make them? Fallible. Just as you and I are fallible."

He was speaking on impulse, trying to plumb what mood had taken hold of his cousin. Some of it he believed. Some he had just discovered in these past few moments. And some had pursued him through life dreams, like ghosts and nightmares, and whispers of the future.

"Will you ride with us back to Rastov?" he asked.

"No," Miro said. He shook his head. "That is, not immediately. I need a week or two to settle my affairs here at Taboresk."

A lie, Ryba thought. *An all too obvious one.*

Usually Miro was more accomplished with deceit. It came from dealing with court, especially that pair of schemers, Markov and Černosek. He decided to see how far he could probe.

"What about your cousins? Those girls from Duszranjo?"

"Women," Miro said. "They are hardly children to be called girls."

Ryba had made the goad by habit. He had not expected Miro to respond. That he did, and so plainly, was another sign of his cousin's distraction.

"My apologies," Ryba said without much conviction.

No answer.

"Only they seemed rather young to travel alone."

Miro's mouth thinned, but he said nothing.

"So you do not wish to talk about these lovely young women? I assure you that Skoch does. He was quite surprised to find them here, under your protection, when no one at court had any idea—"

"Ryba. Shut up."

Ryba grinned, but only to himself.

So you are not impervious, my dear cousin.

He wanted to provoke his cousin more—it was a rare chance that Miro allowed anyone to tweak him—but then Miro covered his face with both hands and sighed. "Ryba. I must provide for them. I promised. I—"

He stopped. Rubbed his knuckles against his eyes.

"Never mind," Ryba said. "I understand."

He stood. Glanced around at the offices once more. All neat and contained, and filled with intricate secrets, some of which he knew he would never guess. He was not certain he wished to. "Then I leave you in peace, cousin, at least for the morning. Perhaps I shall imitate your good example and ride into the hills today."

"No," Miro said at once. Then, in a milder voice, "Not . . . not today, Ryba."

Ryba's gaze met his cousin's. The fleeting vulnerability of moments before had disappeared, and once again he faced the blank courtier's mask.

I said I did not wish to know, Ryba reminded himself.

Still, he had to ask.

"Is there anything you would tell me?"

Miro smiled. "No. Nothing."

Ryba hesitated only a moment longer. "I love you," he said, and hurried out the door.

VALARA HAD INTENDED to rise with the sun. Miro would, she knew. She wanted to speak with him in the daylight, to discuss in blunt practical terms how they might counter this latest, unwelcome news from Rastov. They would need privacy, an hour at least, to work through all the tangled choices he and she faced. They could not risk the cousin or that man Skoch interrupting.

But once Miro had closed the door, Valara had wandered between the two small rooms of her apartment, unable to fasten her attention on the task of undressing for bed. When the hour bells rang two past midnight, she had finally collected herself enough to remember Ilse. She owed Ilse too much for comfort. If not for Ilse and her connections, Khandarr's soldiers would have recaptured Valara within a mile of Osterling Keep. If not for her, Valara might have attempted to gain all three of Lir's jewels for herself—at what cost to her kingdom and her future lives, she did not wish to imagine.

Debt she understood, though she disliked it. Gratitude was more difficult to process.

She paced the corridor once, twice, before she at last fetched up at Ilse's door. A lamp burned within, its light leaking around the edges of the door. Valara raised her hand to knock. And stopped.

What could she say? That Miro Karasek's plans were overturned? That his vows of protection no longer counted for anything? Ilse knew it already. Perhaps she, too, was restless and wanted these quiet hours to consider her future.

So Valara had returned to her bedchamber, there to stare into the dark until sleep overtook her.

Now. Now the bells rang midmorning.

Valara washed and dressed. She refused her maid's offer to bring a suitable breakfast tray. "I would see my lord cousin, Duke Karasek," she said.

The girl's expression never changed, but Valara thought she detected a certain hesitation.

"Is my lord duke in residence?" she asked.

"Yes, my lady. I shall send him your request at once."

A palpable lie, but clearly the girl was under orders. With an effort, Valara attempted a smile. "Thank you," she said. "I believe I would like tea."

The tea arrived quickly, hot and fragrant and blessedly strong. She drank the entire carafe. Suppressed her impatience and allowed the girl to brush her hair, which badly needed attention after the previous restless night. At last, her hair was properly braided, herself dressed in a loose gown and jacket, tied with an embroidered sash.

No word had come back from Miro.

I could insist.

The thought died with its birth. She had to trust he had spent the night to better advantage than she. If only, if only . . .

She mentioned her wish to take a turn about the garden. Her maid returned with walking boots to replace her slippers, a hood to cover her hair, and a cloak. Valara escaped the household at last and hurried through the gates to the garden beyond. There an attendant waited, but he did not follow her into the leafy pathways beyond.

Once she rounded the first corner, she closed her eyes and blew out a breath. Took in the faded scent of dying wildflowers; the stronger scent of pine needles, crushed beneath impatient feet; the far, far fainter scent of damp earth and wood chips. No one observed her here, but this was only a temporary reprieve. If she did not proceed, Skoch's minions would observe the delay. Skoch alone was nothing in Rastov's Court, but Miro said the man reported to Duke Markov, a man with influence and power.

The network of paths extended in six directions. The ends of most were obscured by greening foliage, but others opened to the clear blue sky of late summer, early autumn. Valara took the path lined by pine trees left to their natural state. It wound through a sweet-scented glade, along an artificial brook, and to an open field that overlooked Taboresk's household and its neighboring village.

If only she could escape Károví so easily.

"My lady."

Miro.

She spun around. It was not Miro. It was the cousin, Ryba Karasek, the one who had briefly served as heir to Taboresk. Their voices were too much alike. Their faces, their manner, had nothing in common. She immediately distrusted him.

"What do you wish?" she asked.

He tilted his head and observed her closely.

"You have an interesting accent," he said at last.

Damn, damn, damn. Ilse Zhalina had spent weeks drilling Valara in the proper lilt and cadence for Duszranjo. Now, in one unguarded moment, Valara had undone all their secrecy.

"You surprised me," she said.

"Obviously. As you surprised me."

No possible answer to that.

"Perhaps you know where his grace, our cousin, is?" she asked.

That provoked an even longer delay, which she had not expected.

"I left him in his office," Ryba Karasek said at last.

His tone was odd, and when he turned away, Valara saw an unnatural brightness in the man's eyes. She was saved from having to find a suitable reply by the arrival of a runner in the Karasek livery. "My lady. My duke wishes to speak with you."

"Then you must not keep him waiting," Ryba said.

His eyes were still bright, but his mouth had twisted into an angry smile. Valara signaled to the runner that she would return at once. She hurried past Ryba. Instinct stopped her. She laid a hand on his arm. He was trembling. An odd portent. The once heir to Taboresk, displaced with his cousin's return. Were they friends or enemies? She glanced up to see him studying her with those great dark eyes.

"I am sorry," she said softly.

"Why do you say that?"

"I do not know."

She truly didn't. She only knew that in this moment, this man needed comfort.

He shrugged and waved her toward the household—an easy graceful gesture that was in strange contrast to his obvious distress. Later, she might question his acceptance of her vague answer. Now she had to speak with Miro Karasek and know what he meant by his words the night before.

A RUNNER WAITED for her inside—a young girl with a blunt nose and capable air. She led Valara into the wing where the duke kept his private offices, a region Valara had not explored during her stay. Miro had not invited her, nor had she asked. She wondered now if they had unconsciously attempted to avoid any conflict between her duties and his.

The wing appeared newer than the main building, but still ancient enough, built in stark spare lines. The floors were tiled with blue marble, the walls of pale gold stone. No tapestries, no other ornamentation relieved the smooth walls. Clearly this was a place for business alone, no matter how finely constructed.

Guards stood at attention at all the doorways. The runner nodded to each one. Valara could not guess if they ordinarily kept a heavy watch. She suspected not. Had it begun with the news of the king's death, or later, with Skoch's arrival?

They halted at a higher, broader door. "Lady Ivana Zelenta," the runner told the guards. "The duke expects her."

One guard knocked. The other opened the door and bowed.

Valara proceeded within, her heart beating as fast as it had when she last walked the spirit plane with magic.

Miro sat behind his desk. She had expected him to be immersed in papers and other tokens of his duties. Instead, the vast expanse of desk was empty, except for one sheet of paper, half filled with writing. A brush and its inkstone were at hand, but Miro's attention was on the window. The heavy scent of magic lingered in the air.

Slowly, Valara approached. He made no sign that he noticed. His gaze was fixed on some distant point. From this window, she could see he had a fair view of his domain—the indigo mountain range with its thick pine forest, the silver-bright river, the green fields rolling down to the wilderness and plowed fields beyond.

"I have finished my work for the morning," he said, still with his gaze on the outer world. "I hoped you might join me for a ride."

So bland, so controlled.

What did I expect?

No, better if she did not pursue that question.

"I would be pleased to," she said.

"Thank you. Let us meet in the stables."

He glanced at her, offered the barest of smiles. That unnerved her more than his absent tone, or the way his attention veered back to the window. With a curtsy and a polite reply to his order—because it was an order, however gently phrased—she exited the office and returned to her rooms. Her

maids had already laid out the new riding costume, delivered by the seamstresses the day before.

He expected me to submit. How dare he?

He dared because he held the advantage. So her father and grandfather
would have instructed her. With a shudder, Valara gave herself over to her
maids' attentions. They must have read her mood from her face, because
they gave silence for silence and worked even more quickly than usual.

Dressed anew, she exited her rooms to find a runner waiting—an older
man, with the marks of knives hidden beneath his livery. She followed
him in double-time to the stables, where Miro already waited. He, too, had
changed his clothing, from the elegant blue silks of his morning costume to
plain black trousers and shirt, armed with swords and knives and leather
guards reinforced with steel. The duke had vanished, replaced by the soldier.

A stable boy assisted her to mount. They had given her a sweet-tempered
mare with slim black legs and a coat of burnished bronze. Karasek mounted
a gray stallion, evidently fresh and in a troublesome mood. Karasek even
smiled as he brought the horse under control. He exchanged a laughing
comment with the stable boy. Valara took the hint and smiled down at her
own attendant.

It was just like Morennioù, she thought. *We play our parts for the audience. We reserve the truth for our private moments, and that only seldom.*

She wondered if today would be such a moment.

"Cousin," Miro said.

His voice was cool and contained. She matched her reply.

"My lord duke."

They crossed the stable courtyard and passed through the gates to
the outer grounds. From there, Miro chose a path into the rising hills to the
north. By now the sun shone almost directly overhead, and the air was
bright and heavy with its warmth. Once they entered the forest, however,
Valara felt a chill. She drew a deep breath of cool air, laden with damp and
the sharp scent of pines.

At last they gained the ridge overlooking the valley. Miro reined his
horse to a walk. Here the path widened, and Valara brought her mount
next to his.

"You have news," she said quietly.

He nodded. "Skoch received two messengers last night after we spoke.
My own patrols reported the presence of strangers camped in the hills.

Don't worry," he said, when she exclaimed. "They were spotted in the southern range, not here. They attempted to stop your companion from leaving, but they were not successful."

It took her a moment to parse what he said.

"Then Ilse—"

"Has gone, yes. I sent Bela to guard her."

She pressed a hand against her forehead. Too much, too fast. She was not used to so much information given so freely. "Tell me again what happened. Please."

It was a short account. Lord Raul Kosenmark had survived the attack on Hallau Island. With Lir's jewels returned to the magical plane, Ilse wished to return home. He had intended to send Ilse home by ship from Lenov, but Skoch's arrival had overturned those plans. Ilse herself had not depended on Miro and had set off alone.

"I suspected she might. I sent Bela Sovic with money and gear. We have no guarantee they will make the border, but I wanted to give her every chance."

For a moment, she heard nothing beyond the echo of her blood within her ears. He had betrayed her. He had let this woman go, in spite of knowing Valara's need to have a witness, a companion, when she returned to Morennioù.

"You lied to me," she said softly. "You betrayed your kingdom. She will tell her king of the jewels, that Károví has no defense. You cannot pretend—"

"I pretend nothing." His voice was sharp and short. "Veraene—" He released an audible breath, and when he continued, it was in a softer voice. "I cannot tell if there will be war between us. I do know that long ago, I captured a princess of Károví and executed her at Leos Dzavek's command. She was bound for Veraene with an emissary from the emperor. He and she hoped to negotiate a peace. This time, for my honor and for Károví's, I must not stand in her way."

His face was averted, as though he spoke to a larger audience than just her. Or perhaps to the gods. She shivered. She wanted nothing more to do with the gods.

"What of me?" she said. "What of Morennioù?"

"That is a simpler question," he said. "Morennioù needs its queen. You need a witness to your court and council. We cannot take any ship—Markov and the army watch the ports—and you admit you cannot traverse the magic planes. That leaves only one choice. I will be your witness. I will carry you home."

He dismounted and held up a hand to Valara. "Come with me."

Valara accepted his hand, which was warm and dry. Comforting. They had misspent so many of their lives together. She wanted to think that in this life, the gods offered another chance, but she remembered his words about bearing witness to her council. They would not forgive him for leading the invasion.

"I know," he said quietly. "I know what I do."

He helped her to dismount. She needed his arm to steady herself.

Miro spoke in an unknown language—not Károvín, but a dialect of the north. Magic sparkled in the air. Both horses snorted. He repeated the command, more insistently. The stallion bolted first, followed by the mare, the two galloping away from the strange scent and texture of the current. Miro watched them a moment before he turned back to Valara.

"Are you afraid?" he asked.

They had no gear, nothing beyond the weapons Miro carried. If they did reach Morennioù, they would need none of that. Except she knew the magical plane. It never cooperated fully. It liked surprises.

She swallowed. "Very much."

He folded her into an embrace, but loosely. She could free herself at any time. Her mother's admonition echoed in her mind. Never show weakness. But was it weakness to accept another's gift?

"What of your home?" she asked. "What of Taboresk?"

He pressed his face into her hair. He was taller than she, lean and strong. He wore a scent that reminded her of ocean winds. His heart beat quick and light against her cheek. He, too, was afraid.

"I give Taboresk to my cousin," Miro said. "He loves it as much as I do. He will do what is right with Veraene and Morennioù. Are you ready?"

"No. Yes. Please, let us go."

He kissed her once—a brief ghost of a kiss, as though he would not trespass further—then spoke the words to summon Lir's magical current. Her palm itched. Magic prickled against her skin. She clenched her fists, felt the pang of the scar on her palm where she'd held Lir's jewels tight as the Mantharah worked its impossible magic. Miro bent down and whispered, "I love you. I'm sorry I failed you before."

An apology from now, from centuries ago.

"I'm sorry I did not understand," she said.

The current roared past with the strength of a hurricane. She had one last glimpse of Károví and Taboresk before the world vanished into darkness.

Blackness. Pinpoints of light. Worlds upon worlds wheeling beneath their feet.

We are lost, she whispered. *We cannot make it.*

We can, he said. *Think of home. Think of what you most desire.*

She stared at the maelstrom around them. She searched. She saw . . . the waves breaking upon Enzeloc's shore. The sun rising behind her father's castle. For a moment, her heart faltered. Her father had died. Her mother and sister a year before that. She would come home to a land devastated by Leos Dzavek's invasion, one still occupied by his soldiers.

I want it. I want it still. I always shall.

With that thought still echoing in her mind, she and Miro Karasek plunged downward to Morennioù's islands.

CHAPTER TEN

TEN DAYS BROUGHT Raul Kosenmark and his guards to the western edge of the Gallenz Valley. Unlike the eastern quadrant of the hills, these parts had no regular roads, and for the past day, they had ridden single file along a narrow trail that wormed upward through the trees, stopping from time to time to cut through brush so the horses could pass.

As the forest trail rounded the shoulder of a hill, the trees opened up to bare sky, the land dropped away into folds to the great central plains of Veraene stretching outward and forever to the west.

Raul drew rein and gave the signal to halt. The company took up new positions around him with a minimum of fuss and discussion. They were all veterans in his service, handpicked by Benedikt Ault and himself for this mission. They hardly needed any direction from him, for which he was grateful.

It had proved a difficult journey. The ever-steeper hills. The wild oak and pine forests, interrupted by expanses of bare rock, which they had to circle around. Over six hundred years ago, in the early days of the empire, the soldiers from the Gallenz kingdom had staged their attacks against the encroaching imperial army from these heights. Eventually they surrendered. A century later, the empire had absorbed the larger princedom of Károví.

Károví had reclaimed its independence. Gallenz had never tried.

Nor had Valentain, an even older and stronger kingdom.

Raul rubbed a hand over his face. Strange how the past continued to haunt this region, or perhaps it was his mood. He returned his attention to the present and the remaining segment of their journey. The trail, now just a worn track, looped down the foothills to Veraene's central plains, which burned a brilliant gold in the late-afternoon hour. Even as he watched, the sun dipped below the horizon. Light flared upward, a surge of crimson, as if a sword had pierced the sun and a gout of blood splashed the darkening sky. An unsettling omen, he thought.

He shaded his eyes against the glare. He could just make out what had to be the dark mass of Duenne along the horizon, its towers rising up from the plains in a low irregular silhouette. A pinprick of silver winked in the dying sunlight—the Gallenz River as it flowed out from the city to the highway.

Six years since he had traveled that road. Six years since the king dismissed him from court. Instead of returning to his father's domain in Valentain, he had fled to Tiralien and established himself there.

I was a coward, he thought. *I sent others to speak my words, to perform my deeds.*

Because of that cowardice, Dedrick had died. Also Lothar Faulk, Faulk's brother Simon, Rusza Selig, and others in Raul's network of spies.

Raul's guards remained silent. Only the jangle of reins from a restless horse betrayed their anxiety with this latest, abrupt halt. Raul rubbed his face again and scowled. Self-pity was such an ugly thing.

"Benedikt, how many days before we reach the city gates, do you think?"

His weapons master, now second in command for this company, squinted and made a silent calculation. "Five more days, my lord. Four if we push the horses. Shall we make camp?"

"We will," Raul said. "But that means an early start tomorrow."

No one complained. No one had the entire journey from Tiralian, though Raul and Ault had driven them hard. Raul had insisted on long days, with watches set throughout the night, and each halt had proved an exercise in military precision.

Within an hour, they had unloaded their gear, tended to the horses, and set up a camp. One pair gathered firewood. Another dug the latrine, while the rest laid out the bedrolls. Once Ault gave the watch orders for the night, he followed Raul to the ridge overlooking the plains.

"Thinking, my lord?" he asked.

An oblique way of asking if Raul regretted this sudden upset of the past six years.

"I would like to believe I always think," Raul said. "In spite of frequent evidence to the contrary. But yes, I am thinking. About the implications and the consequences of this journey. And you?"

Ault shrugged. "I dislike the journey, but I told you so before. My lord, you are a fool to trust Armand of Angersee and his pet cur."

Raul's lips puffed in silent laughter. "I *don't* trust them. I am an inconvenient obstacle to Armand's war. If he could wish me dead, he would, and

Lord Khandarr would oblige him except he cannot without good cause. I am not Dedrick Maszuryn, a younger son of an inconsequential baron."

"Even so, my lord. There are others, in Tiralien and elsewhere, who have risked a great deal for you. What of them?"

"I did not leave them unprepared, Benedikt, but I take your point. For all my distant friends, I have a plan in case my interview with the king goes wrong . . ."

It was a simple one. Two guards would ride ahead of the company to Duke Kosenmark's household to announce his son's arrival. They would take fast horses, and if questioned, they would pass themselves off as free swords, looking for guard work in the city. The rest of the company, including Ault, would accompany Raul. While it was possible that Lord Khandarr's spies had observed their departure from Tiralien, and would therefore know how many had started with Raul, Raul doubted the information would reach Duenne faster than he did.

"If I meet with disaster, my father will be forewarned. I can trust him to carry word to Tiralien and Melnek."

Ault shook his head. "It's not enough, my lord. Nor quick enough."

Raul drew a sharp breath. "You think Lord Khandarr would attack my father?"

"No. But what if your guards are intercepted before they reach your father? What if Lord Khandarr has set a watch for your arrival at the city gates? He might send out orders to arrest your people even before the king agrees to an audience."

He could imagine that. Markus taking Gerek hostage. Markus executing the remaining members of Raul's shadow court, one by one, until Raul publicly vowed his allegiance to the king's war. He closed his eyes a moment, trying to erase that image from his imagination. He could not.

"Tell me, then. What would you advise?"

"Just one thing, my lord. Send your two guards ahead, yes, but leave one here. If the duke your father sends word of disaster, or sends no word at all, then have them ride as fast as they might back to Tiralien."

Raul nodded slowly. "Yes. That would work. Or better—keep one here. Send a fourth east a day's ride." He was working through the permutations of that—whether to tell the first two guards about the fourth one, or if breaking the chain of secrets would add another layer of security, in case the guard left here met with difficulty. However that had its own disadvantages. "A company of five is too few," he said. "Markus would surely suspect something."

"Not a problem, my lord."

Raul glanced up. "How so? Did you—? You did, you miserable dog. Am I right?"

Ault grinned. "You are, my lord. Ada Geiss waits a day's ride east of here."

They discussed a few more possible complications, then which guards were best suited to which roles. Ault set off for a walk around the perimeter, while Raul Kosenmark summoned the three he and Ault had agreed on. The first two, Markou and Soubz, had served the duke in Valentain for a dozen years before accompanying his heir to the capital and later Tiralien. Both women knew Duenne and the family. The third was a younger man named Bayt, recommended by Ault, who had entered Kosenmark's service four years ago.

"I have two difficult assignments for you," he told them. "Difficult and dangerous ones. Are you willing?"

None of them hesitated. "Tell us only what you need, my lord," Markou said.

I need a kingdom we can both serve honestly.

That, however, was a different matter, for a different day.

"You and Soubz must ride to Duenne," he said to her. "Go directly to my father's household in the northwest quarter. You remember the street? Good. There is no letter, just a message. Tell my father . . ." He paused to consider how to word this message. "Tell him, I come as promised. Make certain you give that message to no one but him. Remain in his household until you receive word I have spoken with the king, and the outcome of that interview. Then return at once to here. Start at sunrise tomorrow. Take our fastest horses."

He clasped their hands and exchanged salutes. Once they were out of hearing, he gave Bayt his orders.

"You will make camp and wait," he told the young man. "Whatever news they bring, good or bad, you will ride east, taking the same route as before. If they do not appear within the week, you do the same. You will meet Ada Geiss. Tell her what has happened. Can you do that?"

The young man saluted. "I can and I will, my lord."

"Good. Go to our stores for provisions, gear, whatever you need for the week."

Later, he would consider the great gift of trust and loyalty these three gave him. He could not now. If he did, he might never have the courage to proceed.

* * *

MARKOU AND SOUBZ were away as the sun was lifting over the horizon. Within another hour, the others had erased all signs of their camp, while Bayt removed himself, his horse, and his gear to a higher, more secluded site.

With Ault in the lead, and Raul riding at the center point, the remaining company descended along a well-worn path that joined up with a highway running from the southeast provinces. By the middle of the second day they had entered the central plains. It was a vastly different landscape from the Gallenz Valley. Like a golden sea, it extended without any visible end toward the west.

Two, three more days until Duenne's city gates. If he circled around and continued west and south, he would come to Valentain in six more weeks. Another week beyond that lay Hanídos and the mountains dividing Veraene from Ysterien and the other coastal nations. It was tempting, he thought. He might ride and ride forever, leave behind this kingdom with its tangled politics and a king too weak to resolve the very problems he had created.

I must not. I cannot.

It was as though he had considered abandoning himself. He did not even need to think of Soubz and Markou delivering his message, and his father waiting in vain.

And so the company continued forward across the next bridge to the broad highway whose course echoed that of the Gallenz River. They spent a night in a riverside inn, crowded with merchants and freight caravans and other travelers. No one questioned their presence. The next morning, they rose before dawn and set off at a quick pace.

By the time they passed the first settlements outside Duenne, the sun hung midway between the zenith and horizon. Much had changed since Raul last came this way. The farmland had given way to sheep pens, butcher shops, and several enclaves with ceramic and iron works. Carts and makeshift tents lined the highway itself. Vendors shouted at Raul, waving bits of cloth, or lifting up strings of gems that glittered in the sun. Raul had to maneuver his horse carefully through the crowds to keep from trampling the unwary.

He signaled for Ault. The other man pressed forward until they rode side by side.

"We take the lead," Raul said. "No, no arguments. Let the others keep close behind, but I must be first through the gates."

"A symbol?"

"A warning," Raul replied. "The king will know how to decipher that."

"As will Markus Khandarr. A dangerous move, my lord."

"So be it. I intend to make others. They can be friends, all my danger-ous moves."

Ault smiled wryly, but said nothing more.

Their progress was slow, but eventually they reached the gates. A dozen guards in the king's livery stood watch on the ground. More patrolled the walls above. It was well before sunset, and people passed through the gates freely as they moved between the city and the outer markets, but the guards watched closely. One of them sighted Raul. He spoke to his companions. Now all dozen stared warily at them.

"I go first," Raul said softly.

Ault's only protest was a twitch of his mouth, before he fell back with the others. Raul eased his horse forward a few paces and dismounted. It was another calculated risk, yielding the advantages of height the horse gave him, but he judged these guards wanted a confrontation as little as he did.

He held the reins loosely with one hand. With the other, he indicated that he held no weapon. The guards did not relax their attention, but their hands drifted away from their sword hilts. Good enough.

"My name is Lord Raul Kosenmark," Raul said. "These are my personal guards. May I enter the city?"

By now, all the foot traffic around them had stopped. Raul heard the swell of whispers that died away almost at once, but he kept his gaze on the guards themselves. One or two had started at his voice, light and high as a woman's. The rest were blank-faced. He knew that kind of studied blank-ness. He was recognized, then.

"Where are you bound in the city, my lord?" one asked.

"To the palace. To speak with the king."

"And you pledge your word for your guards?"

"For the men and women who serve me, yes."

The guard hesitated—his eyes narrowed, as though suspicious of how Raul reworded that guarantee—but only for a moment. He stood aside and indicated the open gates with a sweeping bow. "My lord. Welcome back to Duenne."

Raul remounted. Ault appeared at once by his side—he must have started forward the moment the guard spoke. The other five crowded be-hind.

Raul glanced around. Those who had paused to watch the spectacle had not moved away. Well, he ought not to disappoint them. "Stay back," he said to Ault. "Follow me, one by one. We'll regroup at the first square." He offered his audience a flashing smile, a wave of his hand, then rode through the gates into Duenne.

HIS SPINE ITCHED. The guards *had* recognized his name. They must have sent word at once to Armand. What if he had waited another week? Met his father outside Duenne? But his instincts had yammered at him the entire journey from Tiralien. Armand would learn of Dzavek's death from his own spies. Raul could picture what came next. Armand speaking passionately to the council. Armand insisting they launch a war, at once. A few might argue back. Very few, given the fate of those who had argued before. And so the council would reluctantly agree. Soldiers would gather at the border. And thousands would die, all because a young king wanted glory.

He might not listen to me. But if I speak to him openly, others will hear. I cannot keep silent in the shadows any longer.

A string of young girls and boys ran alongside his train. All of them were barefooted, dressed in patched clothes and too skinny for comfort. One of them stopped long enough to gesture toward his sword. She was no more than twelve, all bones and swift angles, and a ruddy complexion that spoke of her plains heritage. Her hair tumbled over her eyes. She thrust it back with a fist. Fierce. No doubt she would bite if provoked. Raul liked that. He grinned. The girl grinned back and ran ahead, thumping a companion on his back.

At the promised square, Raul and his guards closed into a circle.

"Where to first, my lord?" Ault asked.

Raul had turned over that same question in his mind as they approached Duenne. He was tempted to delay the confrontation. He could ride to his father's house, ask his advice. They had not spoken for almost ten years.

He shook his head. No more delays. "We go to the palace."

They watered the horses and set off at a slow walk.

Humorists said the politics in Duenne were so convoluted the council had outlawed any direct route within the city. That was not entirely true. There were many direct routes. They were, however, not the shortest. Raul and his company had entered Duenne at its easternmost point, north of the river. An hour passed as they followed the main avenue west to the grand central plaza of Duenne. From here, an even grander avenue, lined with statutes of kings and queens, arrowed southeast across the river and to the palace. Very little had changed in this oldest quarter. He recognized, almost as one might recall the imprint of scent and color and texture from long-ago days, the golden walls, the roofs the color of rubies, the towers, a panoply of silver and gold breaking free . . .

"Benedikt."

"My lord?"

Raul shook his head. "Nothing." Then, "Thank you."

Ault bowed in his saddle. "You have my heart and my service, my lord. I would give more if I could."

They set off for the bridge across the Gallenz. As they crossed the river and gained the smaller square on the opposite side, Raul heard a shout from the crowd. Was that his name? He listened. The shout came again, closer now. Yes. He could pick out more words. *Kosenmark. Valentain.* Impossible, he thought. No one except the guards at the gate knew of his arrival. Such a display of enthusiasm felt . . . wrong.

He leaned toward Ault. "What do you think?"

"Hired troublemakers," Ault said. "Khandarr would accuse you of inciting discontent."

A clumsy excuse. Would that make a difference?

He urged his company forward. They threaded their way from the riverside square, down the royal avenue traversed by kings on their coronation day, into the maze bordering the palace. Statues of the rulers of Erythandra, of Lir and Toc, of their older manifestations from aeons past, lined the way.

Traffic clogged all the streets. Raul heard more shouts of *Kosenmark* and *Valentain,* less frequently, *Damn the king's weasel.* He could imagine someone wishing for peace, for the end of Markus Khandarr's rule of court and king, but he could not imagine Markus himself constructing such an obvious set of theatrics as this. *Unless logic doesn't matter, and he only wants an excuse.*

"Benedikt," he said. "Get away, as fast as you can."

"But my lord—"

"Do as I say. Go to my father at once and tell him what happened here. Tell him to speak to his factions. Send word to Tiralien—"

He had no time to say more. A battalion of soldiers burst through the crowds. Ault swore and gave the signal to scatter. Raul rode forward to meet the nearest rider.

"My lord!" shouted one. "My Lord Kosenmark!"

Raul gripped his sword tight. "That would be me. What do you require?"

"Nothing but your cooperation."

"You have that already. Take me to see our king."

They had him surrounded. He tried to see if Ault and the rest had escaped, but the crowds made it impossible to see. He dismounted, handed over his sword and all his other weapons. It was laughable—two dozen guards to take one man. However, he made no protest when they insisted on searching his boots and trousers; even the mage-soldiers examined him for spells and other magical traps.

The guards blindfolded and gagged him. Raul stiffened, forced himself to breathe easily as they covered his face with a hood. Two soldiers grabbed him by the arms; another prodded him in the back and ordered him to march. It was difficult to keep his footing, more difficult to submit to their rough handling as they hustled him away from the square and through a doorway. Others caught hold of his arms and half dragged him down two flights of stairs, and into a dank dark cell, where they locked him away without candle or fire.

ONCE, YEARS AGO, Baerne of Angersee had insisted that all his councillors spend a day in prison. To make the test true, they would remain anonymous. He claimed the experience would teach them empathy toward those they ruled, innocent and guilty alike. As far as Raul knew, however, Armand of Angersee had never undergone such an experience.

It would do him good, Raul thought savagely.

They had bound him with iron shackles and chains at his wrists and ankles, then removed the gag and hood. He swayed to his feet and shuffled forward from one end of the cell to the other. Slowly he measured his new cell. Ten by ten feet. At the upper reach of his fingertips, he discovered a small round opening with faint sunlight pouring down from above. When he tilted up his face, a wisp of air tickled his forehead. An air shaft, then. Useless for escape, but at least he no longer felt as though he would suffocate underground.

Gradually the pale light in the airshaft faded to dark. Another two bells rang before they delivered to him a meal of bread and cheese. When it came, Raul tore into the bread and cheese, gulped down the water, and when the guard offered him wine for a price, he took it.

Now, three hours later by the count of bells, Raul huddled in the corner of his cell, his head resting on his arms. He wished he knew if Ault and the other had won free. He wished he could send word to his father. Ah, his father. His heartbeat caught in an imaginary stitch. He remembered the days leading up to his castration, how his mother and father had argued, how his cousin, his love, had suddenly vanished from his life. His brother had attempted once or twice to dissuade Raul, without any success except a black eye. His sisters . . .

He sighed at the memory of Heloïse's last visit. She was eleven, three years younger than he, and in many ways older. *You are an idiot,* she hissed. *I will never forgive you.*

Moonlight trickled down the airshaft. The scent of prison, of sweat and urine, permeated the air. He wondered if Markou and Soubz had reached his father's household. Most likely. If Khandarr had expected him beforehand, the soldiers at the city gates would have taken him prisoner at once.

The echo of footsteps broke the silence. Raul went still and listened. Three marched in regular formation. A fourth stumbled along at a halting pace.

The doors opened and lamplight streamed in.

Lord Markus Khandarr limped across the threshold. Raul surged to his feet. At once the air crackled. A wall of cold fire roared up between them. Raul checked himself a hairsbreadth from the flames. When he drew back a step, the fire subsided, but he sensed its presence lurking just beyond the ordinary world. Breathing heavily, he stared at Khandarr.

A stranger's face stared back, aged and ruined, the iron gray hair bleached entirely white, the features distorted and misshapen, one half drooping, the other drawn back unnaturally tight. In the cold dead light of the mage fire, he seemed more like a monster from beyond the void than a man.

Khandarr's mouth twitched open. The muscles along his throat and jaw rippled with effort. "Treason," he said. "I know. Your letters to Károví. I know. You met with Karasek."

His speech was slurred, interrupted with false stops, a faint and flawed echo of Raul's memories of the man, two short years before, when they had last faced each other in Lord Vieth's palace. Raul covered his reaction with a mask. He remembered now. Valara Baussay had spoken of a confrontation. It was like her to understate the matter.

"I am no traitor," he said.

"What you did. Says you are."

Raul shook his head. He could say nothing to defend himself, or anyone in his trust. If they used magic to wrest a confession from his mouth, he might accidentally betray his friends, but until then, he would keep silent.

"You say nothing. You admit it."

Raul shrugged.

"Your men. Dead. Ah. That . . . bothers you."

Raul lifted his glance to meet Khandarr's. Tried to read the truth from that bizarre and twisted face. The man could be lying. Or he told the truth and had killed Ault and the rest, purely to punish Raul. Both possibilities were true to the man's nature.

"Lies. Truth. Doesn't matter," Khandarr said. "Tomorrow you die. King's orders."

CHAPTER ELEVEN

MARKUS KHANDARR LIMPED down the corridor of the prison quadrant. His feet thumped painfully against the stones, sending echoes ahead and behind. Sixty paces to the stairwell. Twenty steps up to the next landing, and another twenty until he gained the palace itself, never mind how many more steps and stairs lay between there and his quarters. He would sleep badly tonight, even with a heavy dose of wine and herbs. Magic might soothe his aches, but it never lasted as long as he liked.

He almost wished he had put Kosenmark in one of the upper cells. Almost.

Six years. He has not changed. Still a fucking arrogant bastard—

Khandarr's left foot, dragging, caught the edge between two uneven stones. He stumbled, flailed, and lost hold of his cane. One of the guards caught his arm, then almost immediately let go when Khandarr struck him with a fist. "I am . . . not . . . I . . ."

His tongue tangled itself around the words. Worse than that stuttering fool of Kosenmark's. No, not a fool. Clever and sly. Damn him, damn them all, and damn that bitch from Morennioù for ruining his body. He wanted to thrust all these guards and minions away and shut himself in the dark and quiet of his rooms. But he could not, so perforce he must allow this half-wit to drag him to his feet. His curses subsided to a low hiss as he regained his balance.

"You did well," he said slowly as the man handed him his cane.

"Shall I fetch a chair?" the guard asked.

"No. I will walk."

He motioned for the man to take the lead. The other two guards arranged themselves on either side. Khandarr stared ahead, down the long corridor with its rows of empty cells, the torches sending a ruddy glare over the stone walls and worn tiles, to the dim outline of the stairwell's entry. Once more he calculated the number of steps to the end of his day. Drew a breath and thumped his cane against the floor.

"We go," he said.

The brief pause had invigorated him. He stumped at a faster pace, each footfall steady and firm, only using the cane at long intervals. True, the steps cost as much as before. He had to bite his tongue against the agony in his limbs. He would pay the cost for this display later, with drugs and magic.

Thump, crack, thump, thump.

He entered the stairwell. Paused once more, eyes closed, before he started his ascent.

Thump. Thump and crack and thump again. The footfalls came slower now. The cane used more frequently. Arrogant. That was the word for Raul Kosenmark. A useful quality in Duenne's Court. But Kosenmark's arrogance would not save the bastard from execution. Thump. Baerne's beloved pet. Thump, pause, thump.

He had hated Raul Kosenmark from the first. The boy had been scarcely fourteen and newly gelded when he came to court. Beautiful and wild and gifted with sharp-edged wit. Oh, but troubled as well. He might have ruined himself with drink, the way Baerne's son had, but then Fara of Hanau had collected the boy, as she had collected so many other bright young men and women, and tutored Raul Kosenmark in court and politics. With her guidance, Kosenmark had soared to the grand summit of influence and power.

All that had changed with Baerne's death. Khandarr remembered the month after the funeral rites. Remembered Armand suddenly freed from his grandfather's shadow and nearly incapacitated with authority. He had not hesitated about one matter, though. Very soon after he took the crown, Armand dismissed all his grandfather's senior councillors. He would name his own, he declared. The first mark of the new king and a new reign.

Khandarr gained the next landing. There he leaned on his cane, and breathed heavily. All three guards hovered around him. He could sense their urge to help, and their terror at misreading his wishes. He grinned. The muscles of his face twitched. The flesh hung useless, dead. Two years, the physician had said, until he regained full use of his arms and legs. The face might never recover.

Enough self-pity. He dragged himself up the next set of stairs, step by stone step, still plagued by memories of Raul Kosenmark. That last morning, Khandarr had summoned the young fool to his private suite and offered him a compromise. *Vow your allegiance to the king and me, and you will keep your position. You might even regain your manhood.*

Kosenmark had refused, simply and without any excuses.

Later, Armand made it exquisitely clear how much he disliked that Khandarr had made such an offer. A humiliation all around.

The main floor gained at last. Khandarr allowed himself another brief respite. His legs shook. He badly wanted his wine and herbs. And he would send for the physician to knead his muscles. If that failed, he might summon one of the girls kept in service for pleasure. He found that sexual release often served better than medicine or magic.

He swung his body around to face his next goal—the stairs leading to the private residence wing. It took all his self-control to lift one leg, plant it firmly, then drag the other forward. Momentum was the key. He stumped and staggered toward the stairs, little caring what the guards thought by now.

Eight steps from his next goal, he glimpsed a shadow approaching rapidly from a side corridor. Khandarr swung around, reeling, his lips already forming the words to summon magic, when he recognized Armand's senior runner.

The runner knelt before Khandarr. "My lord. The king wishes your presence at once."

He presented an oversized ring set with emeralds and pearls around an enormous central diamond. An ugly thing, Armand called it. As ugly as his grandfather, who had commissioned the object early in his reign. For all Armand's bitter mockery, he had kept the ring, saying tradition had its uses. Even so, he had not made use of it until today.

Khandarr gripped his cane with both hands and muttered a curse under his breath. He recognized an imperial summons when he heard it. "Of course. Let his majesty know I come at once."

"Do you wish a chair?"

What Markus Khandarr wished was to snarl and refuse, but there were too many witnesses, all of them, he suspected, ready to report any sign of disrespect to the king. A year ago, Khandarr would have dismissed their accusations easily. A year ago, Armand would have believed him. Too much had changed since then. Khandarr nodded and offered his thanks to the runner.

The runner signaled. The chair and its six carriers appeared at once. They brought him swiftly and smoothly to a nondescript corridor on the ground floor, tucked between audience chambers and the imperial library. They stopped before an equally nondescript door, guarded by six large men in plain uniforms. Only a single torch illuminated the area.

Khandarr felt the first spurt of true panic then. Baerne had favored this room, saying it allowed him to concentrate on the work itself, and not the grandeur of the office. After he took the throne, Armand had avoided the wing, and especially these rooms, saying he wanted a complete break with all that his grandfather represented.

That makes two things, Khandarr thought. *The ring and Baerne's office.*

The carriers lowered the chair, and the guards assisted Lord Khandarr to stand. Khandarr wrapped his fingers around the head of his cane. It felt sturdy in his grip. He rapped the stick onto the tiles, dragged a foot forward. Not one of the guards stirred as he passed the threshold.

Two more guards waited just inside. Khandarr barely acknowledged them. His whole attention was on achieving the king's presence as swiftly as his body allowed. He stumped and limped and lurched through the next room, into the king's private office.

It was then he understood the reason for the king's summons at this hour.

Armand sat behind the desk once used by his grandfather. A few sheets of parchment lay before him, several of them close-written in the style of reports. A leather-bound volume was propped open as though for reference, and others were stacked to either side. Off in one corner stood an enormous sand-clock constructed of priceless metals, the frame ornamented with rubies, the glass gleaming silver as it turned over to mark the next hour.

Facing him was Duke Alvaro Kosenmark. His manner was tense, his back straight and his chin lifted, as though he stood at attention. A military man, Khandarr remembered. The duke had served on the frontier with some honor, and there were rumors he continued to command a small army in Valentain. Ostensibly, the army served to hunt and contain brigands and pirates along the province's long border, but other reports said this man and his family kept themselves ready for warfare within the kingdom.

He has come about his son.

"Your Majesty," he said. Then to the duke, "Your Grace."

"You have arrested my elder son and heir," Duke Kosenmark said. "For treason—"

"The guards tell me you plan to execute him tomorrow."

Khandarr glanced toward Armand. The king did not acknowledge his presence. He sat with hooded eyes, his hands resting lightly on the desk before him. His air was utterly contained, not like his usual impassioned self. An unseen breeze caused the lamplight to flicker over Armand's face, lending it an age he had not yet attained.

He is like his grandfather. I never expected this. I ought to have.

"We have . . . evidence," he said to the duke. "Crimes—"

"Then you will not object to presenting that evidence before the council."

"We . . . We . . . do not need—"

Armand lifted a hand. Khandarr broke off at once. He wished he had been present for the start of this conversation. The duke must have waited until Khandarr was otherwise occupied before he requested this interview with the king. His spies would be good ones, cultivated through long decades at court. A steady throbbing, the result of standing and walking far beyond his endurance, broke through his calculations. He glanced around the room, but there were no other chairs. So. Armand played his own cruel games tonight.

Meanwhile, Armand laid one hand against the other. The gesture resembled those found in the ancient portraits of priest-kings. "It is not the council but the king who decides your son's fate," he said mildly.

The duke nodded. "True. But there is the matter of trust. We trust you to guard the kingdom's welfare, from the least of your subjects to those with riches and authority of their own. If your subjects perceive that your rule has become arbitrary, if you punish without just cause, you break that trust."

"You threaten me?" Armand asked, still in that soft uninflected voice.

"I merely remind you of the responsibility of your kingship."

"Very pretty words," Armand said. "But if we would speak the truth, you came to demand the release of your son."

"Nothing of the kind," the duke replied.

Now Armand glanced up, his gaze sharp. The resemblance to his grandfather struck Khandarr even stronger than before. With Baerne, especially in his younger years, before the madness took hold, such a glance presaged a cold, deliberate rage.

But all Armand said was, "What then?"

"A trial," Duke Kosenmark said. "Display your evidence. Let the accused speak for himself."

"And if his words prove him guilty?"

"Then execute him. Do it openly, with everyone to witness his fate."

He spoke bluntly—the famed Kosenmark candor. It masked deceit, Khandarr thought. Can't you see it? He chewed his lips, his weak and fumbling lips, knowing he could not say anything to Armand in front of the duke.

Armand glanced toward Khandarr and smiled faintly, as if to reassure him. "A fair request," he said. "At least on the surface. However, the court knows my wishes. They will interpret any concession as a weakness. After all, why should I grant a trial if I know the man is guilty?"

"Then you will have your war, but not the one you desired."

King and duke regarded each other in silence. Khandarr held his breath. For so long, none had dared to challenge the king. Nor had the king dared to insist on absolute authority. Was this the moment where Armand let go all memories of his grandfather? He would become king in truth, then.

"You cannot save your son this way," Armand said.

Kosenmark never wavered. "Perhaps not, but I would try to save the kingdom."

Another long pause followed. It took all of Khandarr's self-control to remain standing, silent and impassive. He was grateful for the cane's sturdiness, hated that he must depend upon it to keep upright.

"Very well," Armand said at last. "You shall have your trial, Duke Kosenmark. May you have joy in its outcome."

"And you as well, your Majesty."

Kosenmark rose stiffly. White and gray streaked his hair, which was drawn back in a severe queue, the fashion from many decades past, and when he tilted his face upward, the lamplight emphasized the lines etched in his face. An old man, past seventy, Khandarr remembered. He had married late, fathering seven children quickly. Two had died in childhood. His heir had gambled with Baerne's decree, had accepted a gelding, only to lose all influence on the old king's death. The second son had proved dependable and dull. The daughters were yet untried.

"Your Majesty," Kosenmark said, bowing to Armand. "My lord." He nodded at Markus Khandarr.

Khandarr waited until the man had exited the room, and a longer interval after that, before he spoke.

"Your Majesty—"

"Be quiet, Markus."

Khandarr choked back his arguments. Armand watched him with a veiled amusement. "You dislike my decision. No matter. Duke Kosenmark is right in one thing, though not for the reason he believes. We cannot have any secret executions. No unexpected illness. No accidents. Not for Lord Kosenmark, nor his people. Do you understand?"

Khandarr considered the two dead guards, their faces bloody and broken. He had lost his temper, a thing that happened too easily these days. Benedikt Ault and the others might survive with proper care. He would have to see to that before the night ended.

"Yes, your Majesty. I understand."

NO CHAIR WAITED for him outside the king's offices, and no guards within view. (He did not make the mistake of thinking they were not present, however.) Only a single runner, a very junior one, stood at attention. So. One runner for one message. The king had left him his own choice what that message ought to be.

"Lord Raul Kosenmark's guards," he said. "Fetch a doctor. The king's physician. Tell him, do not let them die."

Anger lent him fluency. He spoke with all the harshness he had contained the past few hours and had the satisfaction of seeing the runner flinch. But terrifying children for no cause was a petty thing after all. With a flick of his hand, he sent the boy off at a gallop.

Khandarr let his breath trickle out and considered the two flights of stairs between himself and the end of the day. He was alone, but not unwatched. No doubt Armand had left orders for the guards to keep away. He drew a rattling breath and launched himself into motion. Stump, stump, crack, thump. Up one flight. Along the next corridor. Up another flight, around the next turning, then the hundred and two more steps to his own door.

A man, dressed in dark blue robes and trousers cut in the latest court fashion, paced the corridor outside Khandarr's rooms. Jewels glinted from the hem. Metallic threads woven through the cloth glittered with every step. At the thump of Khandarr's cane, he swung around, causing the lamplight to fall over his dark strong features.

"Maester Galt," Khandarr said drily. "You keep late hours for a visit."

Galt hesitated only briefly, then swept into a bow. "My lord. I came as soon as I heard."

Easy enough to guess what Galt meant. So the man had spies in the palace. That was useful information. He also expected Khandarr to welcome an ally. Galt had a great deal to learn in that case. A test, then, to see how the man responded.

He smiled bitterly. "What have you heard?"

Galt's expression turned wary. "About Lord Kosenmark. And the king's wish for a public trial."

Very nicely spoken. He implied nothing, accused no one.

"I wished to consult with you tonight," Galt went on. "No, that is too presumptuous. I wished to ask your advice about a related matter, but I see you are ill and weary. May I send my own physician?"

Khandarr narrowed his eyes to slits, felt the ache of mere bodily discomfort ebb in the face of this new puzzle. So many assumptions in those seemingly innocuous statements, and delivered with such obvious desire to please. He did not want to owe this man a debt, but . . . It might serve a purpose to let him believe this was the case.

"No physician. Stay here. Tell me what you know."

He allowed Galt to follow him into his rooms, to his bedchamber. There, his servants waited to undress him, to remove the tight stockings he wore to steady his legs. They bathed him with hot cloths, soaked in strong herbs, which eased the trembling. Then they dressed him in layers of soft woolen robes, built up the fire, and helped him into his bed.

Galt waited until they departed before he spoke. To Khandarr's disappointment—and his relief—the man knew nothing truly dangerous. He had learned of Kosenmark's arrest through various easily bribed guards. (Khandarr asked for, and received, their names.) He knew about Duke Kosenmark's interview, and deduced its outcome based on shrewd guesses and bits of conversation he had overheard from other courtiers. The only new piece of information was the presence of the duke's daughters in Duenne. The family had its own house in the city, but one daughter had been invited by the queen to stay in the palace. A tidbit, no more, but an interesting one.

He learned more about Galt himself than the man suspected. Galt cared too much and too passionately about Lord Kosenmark's fate. It confirmed much of what Khandarr's own informants had reported on the man when he first arrived. Young for his position as master of the shipping guild, with enough enemies and allies for a man double his years. He had attempted marriage twice, the first contract broken off with numerous ugly rumors. The second, not even a contract this time, came to nothing when the girl ran away. The identity of the second girl, and her history after fleeing from Melnek, was well known. Therez Zhalina, who renamed herself Ilse Zhalina. Raul Kosenmark's lover, now presumed dead, though Khandarr doubted those reports. He let Galt ramble on about his desire to serve the king and his councillors to the best of his abilities. He wanted, he claimed, nothing more than the king and his ministers to remember him when they next discussed matters of taxation.

A man clever at his own trade, Khandarr thought, staring upward at the ceiling. *But a fool with matters he does not understand.*

"Enough," he said abruptly. "Tell me what you want. Do not lie. Do not flatter."

"I want . . ." Galt sucked in a breath. Here was the moment of truth and passion. "I want Kosenmark dead," he said. "I want his lover shamed. I know she's alive. I've heard rumors. For that, my lord, I would do anything."

He was honest, at least. Too honest to survive in Duenne's Court. But Khandarr only wanted a few months of the man's service.

Meanwhile Galt waited in obvious anxiety for Khandarr's reply.

"I want . . . your allegiance," he whispered.

"You have it, my lord."

"Good. Now . . . my orders. Listen to your spies. Bring me reports. Everything. Everything," he repeated. "Promise."

It was a temporary assignment, meant only to bind Galt to him. He thought Galt appeared disappointed, but at least the man had the wit to bow and smile. "Whatever you command, my lord."

A soft rapping sounded at the bedchamber doors. One of Khandarr's servants spoke with the intruder. "My lord. The girl you ordered."

He had not ordered a girl. A glance at Galt told him the answer.

"I will send her away if you prefer," Galt said.

"No. I want . . . to see."

He signaled to the servant. The girl slithered inside. She was young, scarcely old enough to sign the contract for her duties, though that might be a trick of her mannerisms. She was dressed in a translucent web of honey gold lace, edged with silk ribbons, the airy confection gathered around her waist with a thin sash of the same material. Her costume was hitched back with more ribbons, and her sex was shaved clean.

Khandarr took in her dark slim form, her full breasts, the way her eyes canted over her high cheekbones. It was too, too predictable. Galt was an idiot to let his urges be known so completely.

"I do not need her," he said. Then as Galt made to dismiss the girl, he lifted a hand. "Keep her. And you. Stay."

Galt paused, clearly uncertain. "My lord?"

"Use her. Here. I will watch. Then we talk . . . about how you can please me."

CHAPTER TWELVE

NIGHT IN THE royal palace reminded Nadine of Lord Kosenmark's pleasure house. Oh, there were differences. A royal palace had more guards, more servants, and kept more regular hours, at least on the surface. But as she prowled along the dim-lit corridors, lined in marble with mosaics covering walls and floors, she considered it a matter of scale, not the details themselves. Intrigue permeated the air. It informed every word and gesture, and the silences and stillness in between. It led to intricate maneuvers, to secrets given and traded. That she had succeeded in gaining a position here as a courtesan, serving the courtiers and minor nobility, only strengthened the impression.

And both had a king, of sorts. Raul had ruled the pleasure house absolutely, extending his will through loyal minions. Armand . . . With Armand, one had only to observe the men and women who occupied the lesser tiers of influence to know that two men ruled in Duenne, though one pretended to serve the other.

It was because of Markus Khandarr that she had volunteered to serve in the midnight hours. An injury had left him with bouts of insomnia, and he often sent for young women from the courtesan wing to service him with lips and hands and sex, so that sated by pleasure, he could sleep. Nadine had never visited his room, but she talked to other women who had. He seldom spoke, other than to give specific directions. Suckle. Fondle. In the vernacular of the trade, treat him like a sausage that needed skinning and sizzling. Afterward, he required the woman to massage his legs until he dozed.

A discreet man, even gripped by passion. But from time to time, Nadine collected wisps and whispers of gossip.

Tonight, for instance. The youngest courtesan, the one named Evanna, had returned from her duties brimful of news. The Old Man had summoned her, she said, but this night he had ordered her to pleasure another while he watched.

"I had not suspected such imagination," Evanna said, laughing.

"Pah!" said Georg, one of the oldest courtesans. "You cannot convince me of that. He demands sex as one might demand a drink of plain water."

Evanna pouted. "I tell you, tonight was different. He ordered the other man to take me. Told us both to strip. Said he wanted proof the other man could please him."

"The Old Man said that?" Georg's attention was snagged at last, and he rose in a fluid motion to sit upright, his lips parted and eyes bright. "And did they . . ."

"No. He only watched. But once . . ." Evanna paused and glanced around, and when she continued, it was in a low whisper that Nadine could barely hear. "Once he said a name, this while Galt was heaving and puffing on top of me."

"What name was that?" Nadine said.

"Kosenmark."

Nadine only half listened to the rest of the conversation. Then she rose and gave her excuses to the senior guard, saying she needed to visit the house physician about these terrible cramps that had come over her quite suddenly.

An hour later, she had collected more wisps, more tantalizing bits of gossip.

And such astonishing gossip it was. Lord Kosenmark taken prisoner. The old duke himself demanding an interview with Armand of Angersee, which the king, amazingly, had granted. Now this business with Markus Khandarr and someone named Theodr Galt, head of a shipping guild from the border city of Melnek.

Melnek, where Ilse Zhalina once lived.

Nadine did not return at once. She wandered the halls and galleries, taking care to visit the physician as well. If anyone investigated later, they would find she had spent a pleasurable interlude here, another there, with less exalted members of the palace staff. A sergeant twice passed over for promotion. A bored runner outside the residential wing designated for visitors. One of the kitchen girls just coming off duty. The kitchen girl gave the sweetest kisses, and Nadine was tempted to offer the girl more, but she knew she had to return eventually to her work.

She came at last to the servants' corridor between the kitchens and the king's private quarters. A risk, a very great risk, but her instincts said that tonight marked a turning point for Armand and Khandarr both.

All because of that great arrogant creature named Raul Kosenmark.

Footsteps sounded behind her. Nadine spun around.

A woman rounded the corner—a young woman, dressed in dark loose clothing, her hair tied back with a ribbon and falling free to her waist. She stopped. Her hair swung around as she drew back a step at the sight of Nadine.

"A pleasant evening," Nadine said.

There was enough light to make out the woman's features—skin the color of honey, eyes like polished copper, full flat cheeks and a voluptuous mouth. She wore loose dark trousers, a jacket of black silk gathered at the waist with a sash. Nadine's first impression was that no noble would dress so sensibly, nor deign to enter a servants' corridor. Her second was that the woman observed her as closely and dispassionately as she herself observed the other.

"Pleasant enough," said the woman. Her voice was low, melodic, tinged with laughter.

So, you are clever enough not to make excuses, Nadine thought.

She tilted her head, smiled invitingly.

The other woman regarded her steadily. She had a familiar air. Nadine cast her memory back over the past two weeks—the clients she had pleasured, the hundreds of courtiers, runners, chambermaids, scribes, and others she had encountered. None of them like this woman. Where, oh where . . .

And then, the puzzle pieces clicked together.

The golden skin. The arrogant lift of her chin. The sound of a woman's contralto voice, but in a man's body.

"You came to rescue your brother."

The reaction came far more quickly than she had anticipated. Without warning, the woman drew a knife from her belt and attacked. Nadine sidestepped the first blow—all the while admiring the speed—gripped the woman's wrist, and slid under the blade to draw her close. Its point had nicked her cheek in passing, and she felt blood trickling down her neck. She ignored it. "You must excuse my impertinence. I dislike knives."

Their dance had taken them underneath one of the lamps. Both of them breathed heavily, the rise and fall of one chest in counterpoint to the other. The other woman attempted to draw back, but Nadine kept her arm locked around her waist. Now she could discern other details, which had been invisible before. The fine texture of the woman's jacket, with a subtle pattern woven into the cloth. The scent of perfumed soap. The calluses on her palm, which spoke of constant practice with a sword.

She knows weapons, but she had never attacked another before, not in earnest.

The woman glanced down. She must have noticed the scar at Nadine's neck, because her eyes widened. "I see why you might not like knives," she said. "Why did you threaten me?"

"I did no such thing. I merely observed what was obvious. Which sister are you?"

Those brilliant brown eyes narrowed. "Which courtesan are you?"

Nadine gave a low, gurgling laugh. So quick, so clever, this one. "Guess."

Kosenmark's sister shook her head. "I have no time for games. My brother—"

"Is locked in a cell, two floors below. Your father spoke with the king. The outcome displeased Markus Khandarr. More I cannot tell you."

The tension in the woman's arm eased. Nadine, however, did not loosen her grip, nor did she move to withdraw from the embrace. There was still a chance that Kosenmark's sister might choose to kill rather than trust Nadine to keep silent.

"You must be Nadine," the woman said at last.

"So my mother told me, years ago."

A brief smile lightened the other's expression. "I am Heloïse."

The oldest of Kosenmark's three sisters. He called them all dangerous, she remembered.

"How did you learn about my brother?" Heloïse asked.

"Why did your father not tell you?" Nadine replied.

Heloïse dropped her gaze and shifted her weight, a move calculated to throw the unwary off balance. Nadine merely smiled and drew her companion closer. Heloïse had rose-colored lips, as full and mobile as her brother's. How to tell if the differences outweighed the similarities?

"I will not stab you," Heloïse said, glancing up toward Nadine through her eyelashes.

Nadine recognized a technique as deliberate as Evanna's. Or Georg's.

"No, you will not," she agreed. "Tell me the truth. You had no idea your father spoke with the king, did you? Does your entire family keep secrets from one another?"

Heloïse laughed softly, bitterly. "Oh, *secrets*. Damned, cursed secrets. We are poisoned with them, all of us. If I had only known that my fool brother intended to visit this court, I would have beaten him senseless with a club, then locked him in a prison myself."

"Your brother inspires such longings in most of his acquaintances. Where are your two sisters?"

"At home in Valentain. Standing behind you with a knife. Locked in conference with our father, discussing their future. Pick one, it might be true."

"I dislike guesses as much as you," Nadine replied. "Do you have rooms in the palace?"

Heloïse regarded her with increased wariness. "I do. The king . . . Let us say the king wishes one member of the family to reside here, and I prefer the distance from my family. Why?"

"Because *I* prefer the comfort of a soft bed to this bare corridor."

She squeezed the bones in Heloïse's wrist. Heloïse gave an annoyed cry and dropped the knife. Nadine kicked it away and stepped back. "Send for me tonight," she said. "Give whatever reason you like to your maids, whatever will convince them you prefer a woman this once—"

"Not only this once," Heloïse breathed.

Interesting. Nadine sensed that more secrets lay beneath that simple confession. But she would not let herself get distracted. "Then your excuses will be genuine," she said. "You've heard rumors. You are sick with worry. You want a distraction. You want a woman versed in massage and pleasure both." Swiftly she bent down and retrieved the knife in one swift motion. "You want," she said, "a woman who loves women best of all. That would be me."

Her gaze caught Heloïse's and to her great surprise, her pulse leapt in desire.

You are lovely, she thought. *Lovely and brave and true. Even to someone as worthless as your brother.*

It took her a moment to recollect herself, and her position. The other woman studied her with an expression that reminded Nadine uncomfortably of Lord Kosenmark.

Heloïse nodded slowly. "I believe you are right. We have a great deal to discuss. Until next hour, then."

"Until next hour," Nadine replied.

But as she wound through the palace, back toward the courtesans' quarters, her thoughts strayed from the machinations of kings and dukes and lords, back to the warmth of skin against skin, of a voice that called up an echo inside her heart, and the impulse of a desire she thought she had lost years before.

CHAPTER THIRTEEN

IT WAS MARYSHKA Rudny's favorite hour of the day—the moments just before sunrise. The night watch had returned to their homes not long ago. The rest of the village lay quiescent, with only a rill of water from the nearby river to break the dawn's calm.

She knelt beside her garden, fingers plucking the leaves from summer savory and comfrey, blossoms from red clover, the last hidden strawberries and raspberries. She didn't need much daylight to work. She knew every furrow, every root and leaf in this patch. When she finished with one crop, she laid a cloth over it and moved on to the next. Next spring, she thought, she might send a basket of comfrey roots and leaves along with Karel Hasek, when he went up the valley to trade at Dubro's garrison and the nearby town. Get a handful of jewelweed seeds, or better, a few young plants.

The raspberries were scarce this year. She washed a handful in the dewy grass and ate them, still thinking about next year's garden. The village of Ryz was hardly more than a collection of shadows at this hour, but higher up the slopes, light was trickling down the mountainside. Down and down, over the meadows on either side of the river, and across the plowed fields— none too big this year, with the rains late and Lev Kosko's old mare going lame.

A breeze gusted over the slopes, and Maryshka shivered inside her quilted jacket. That wind carried a hint of frost. Next month might see the first snows.

A poor harvest, an early winter. And rumors of troubles along the border. Duszranjo was not so far away from Veraene, for all that the mountains stood so high.

She glanced toward the eastern ranges that divided Duszranjo equally well from Károví's central plains. They stood like tall sentinels, shrouded in dark blue cloaks. Even as she watched, a scarlet ribbon unfurled behind them and a speck of golden sunlight spilled through a notch between the two highest peaks. The few remaining stars stood out like pale freckles against the blueing sky. A moment later, they, too, had disappeared.

Day. Time for cooking breakfast and chores. Even now, she could hear her mother stirring about inside the house.

Maryshka stood and hoisted the basket to her hip. Just as she turned toward the door, a movement across the river caught her attention. She paused and shaded her eyes with one hand. A shadow, large and misshapen, lumbered over the hillside opposite the Solvatni River. Her heart gave an uncomfortable thump. Was it Matej or Lev who said the king was raising extra troops for his army? Surely they wouldn't take anyone from Ryz.

We have so few already.

As she watched, the shadow lurched and swerved to one side, immediately dispelling the thought of soldiers. *They* rode in patrols of five or six, or marching in formation, not stumbling from ridge to ridge. And none of them crossed into Duszranjo from the eastern notch. They came from the north, from Dubro, along the river path.

As the shadow approached, it divided into two. Now she could make out a horse and . . . a pile of bags? A rider? Yes, a rider, slumped over the horse's withers. A smaller figure led the horse by its reins. They had gained the lower slopes. Very soon they would reach the ford.

The chancy mountain breeze swirled around and buffeted her face with a strange new scent. Green and sharp. It reminded her of winter nights, the pine kindling burning in the fireplace. Or how the grass smelled under her bare feet in the hot summer sun. A familiar scent and yet like nothing else she had known.

She set down the basket and ran to the house.

Her mother met her at the door. "What is it? What's wrong?"

"Strangers," she gasped. "Not soldiers. Something . . . different."

For one moment, her mother went still, and the folds around her mouth and eyes deepened—not in laughter, but in fear. As if she guessed all that Maryshka had sensed and seen. "Go fetch Jannik," she whispered. "I'll tell Papa and the others."

Maryshka nodded and sped up the winding dirt path toward Jannik's home. The speaker lived alone, on the highest ridge, overlooking the rest of the village. Ditka Jasny appeared in her doorway and called out a question, but Maryshka shook her head. Talk could come later. She scrambled up the slope and fell against Jannik's door, pounding the rough planks with her fist.

"Jannik!"

The speaker flung the door open. He wore only his trousers, hastily tied with a sash, and his hair hung loose, as though he'd just woken up, but he held a staff in one hand. He dropped the staff and caught her as she stumbled over his doorstep. "Strangers," she said breathlessly. "Not soldiers. Not . . . I can't explain it."

For a moment, she hung in his arms, trembling. She could not tell why. She hated that. But as he asked a few more questions, her trembling died away. How to describe that alien scent, the way her skin prickled, as if Toc himself had breathed upon her? It was all nonsense.

"I woke you for nothing," she said. "Just two strangers."

He smiled absently, his gaze searching beyond her to the village. "Not for nothing. It's always best to be prepared."

True enough. Life this close to the border meant raiders, smugglers, and the like. But she had panicked, and she knew it. She pulled away. Hugged herself close and rubbed her arms, not daring to glance over her shoulder at the approaching visitors.

"What frightened you so?" he said. "You aren't a skittish girl."

She flushed in embarrassment. "I . . . I can't explain."

"Try," he said softly. "And be quick, before Louka starts a war."

She snorted back a laugh at the thought of Louka, charging off with his wooden spear. The panic leached away, and she could talk properly now, though Lir and Toc only knew if the story would make sense, even so. "I saw a horse and a rider," she said. "The rider looked like a bag at first. All floppy and weak. And there's another one on foot. Neither of them were soldiers, but . . . I smelled something very strange, Jannik. Like fresh-cut hay, or sun on the grass, or . . ."

"Or like Lir's breath upon the world, when all was new," he said softly.

She recognized the words as poetry. Jannik Maier liked such things. He was the only one in all of Ryz who cared about books. Nonsense, her father called it. But hearing the words spoken now, with the taste and scent of strangeness upon her tongue, she thought otherwise.

"Just so," she said. "Like stars in the moonlight."

Stars that shone brighter and sharper than any she'd seen. Her vision flickered, remembering the brush with that unearthly breeze. She shook her head, but she could not rid herself of that strong impression.

Jannik nodded. "You were doubly right to warn me. Thank you. Now to deal with Louka and his warriors." He took up his staff, then fetched a shirt.

"They might be right," she said. "Remember those bandits. And there's talk of war . . ."

Though he was turning away, he stopped. "I remember. For that, I ask you to take the children and old ones into the wood above."

He headed down the footpath into the village, drawing on his shirt as he walked, to where half the men and several women had gathered. Maryshka followed to the nearest cabin. Nela Janaček had already emerged with her daughter, Agáta. "Trouble?" Nela said.

"We don't know yet," Maryshka said. "But Jannik wants the little ones taken away."

It was one of the many drills that Jannik had insisted the villagers learn, ever since Vila Maier had died eight years ago and his son took over as speaker. Arm themselves for defense. Gather the youngest and oldest and take them into the forest above Ryz, leaving the grown men and women to fight. If those strangers were more than two wanderers, if something went wrong, they could retreat into the mountains and send word north to the garrison at Dubro.

Nela disappeared into her cabin and reappeared with two knives. She gave one to Maryshka. "I'll wake Eva and help her with the babies. And you," she said to her daughter. "Go to Ela."

"I'll help Vera with her monsters," Maryshka said.

She tucked the knife in her sash and swept down through the village, past Jannik arguing with Louka Hasek. Louka and a few others carried clubs, staffs sharpened to points, and other weapons. Maryshka wanted to shake them all, even the speaker. *If those were bandits, they'd have us killed already, with everyone chattering.*

No use scolding them. It was the same panic that had infected her. She hurried to Vera Janaček's house and gave the news. Vera drew a sharp breath, but the next moment, she had scooped up her youngest and handed him to Maryshka. "Take him, please. I'll get the others."

"And a knife," Maryshka reminded her.

Vera's only answer was a wave of her hand. Maryshka left her to the rest of her brood. With a wriggling Priba Janaček on her hip, she jogged on to the next house and the next. She gathered up children and led them up the main path into the thick green forests above Ryz. Others—younger friends and cousins—followed. Maryshka hushed their murmuring, glad they listened. It was her mother's influence. They both tended Ryz's sick and wounded, which lent them a certain authority. Renata Lendl and Alexej Zenkl were another matter. Old and stubborn, they both complained without a stop as Maryshka herded them toward the path leading around the barn and up the ridge.

That left only the older boys.

"Damek!" she called to her brother.

He ignored her. Jan Hasek glanced around.

"Damek. You and your friends. Follow me." She pointed to the heights above. "I need all of you to help with the little ones."

To her relief, Jan and his brother Marek obeyed. The rest clustered around Jannik Maier with their weapons raised high. Stupid idiot boys. She marched over to her brother and grabbed his arm. "Do what I say," she hissed. "Now."

He glared at her from under his disheveled hair. Only fifteen, she thought. Too young and too old at the same time, for all the things he wanted. "I need your help," she said softly. "If you go, the others will, too."

Damek grinned. It was an obvious bit of flattery, to be sure. "Honey-talk isn't like you. But I'll do it."

He and Maryshka detached the remaining boys from the crowd. Meanwhile, Jannik Maier gave out orders to the men and women. "You." Jannik pointed to Vilém Berger and Ilja Lendl. "Come with me. The rest of you pair off and take your positions behind the houses and barns . . ."

The boys raced each other up the ridge. By the time Maryshka overtook them, she discovered that Priba Janaček had escaped his mother and was sitting in the grass on the hillside. Maryshka shooed him back under the trees. She slid the knife from her sash and crouched behind a boulder. Her father was stationed by the barn with Martin and Ditka Jasny. Matej and his son Pavel squatted next to the speaker's house. Others made a loose guard around the village.

She watched as Jannik leaned close to Louka Hasek, who had remained behind. The older man made a rude gesture, but finally he, too, retreated to his post. Jannik glanced over his shoulder—Maryshka had the strongest impression that he could see into the dark green shadows of her hiding place. Only two remained with Jannik—she recognized Vilém's striped shirt and Ilja's unruly hair—but even they lingered behind as Jannik crossed that last and lonely stretch to the Solvatni.

ILSE ZHALINA SLOWED her pace and looped the reins around one hand. "Zp'mali," she said softly to her mare. "Slow, slow, soft and slow." Obediently, Duska came to stop and began to crop the grass. On this side of the river, the fields grew wild, overrun by thornbushes, patches of clover, and thick stands of coarse grass. A few hundred yards ahead, the land sloped down to a narrow river, where a stony ford broke the water's dark surface. Beyond, on the opposite shore, planted fields and plowed fields, and higher up, a dozen or so wooden huts with a dirt path looping between them.

She knew from the maps where she was. Ryz. A tiny village at the south-west corner of Duszranjo's winding length. This narrow river was the upper end of the Solvatni River. From here, the land rose upward toward the mountains dividing Károví from Veraene.

But it was the people in Ryz that concerned her the most.

"They are awake," she said to her companion.

Bela Sovic laughed softly, though she clung tightly to her mount's neck. "What else did you expect? They are farmers."

Farmers who expected trouble and knew they could not depend on Dubro's garrison to defend them. Ilse had not missed the sudden tumult, as a dozen or more of Ryz's occupants appeared from their huts, all of them wielding some kind of weapon. Their voices carried across the river, and though she could not hear what they said, the tone was not a happy, welcoming one.

More arguments, more debate, took place. Now the farmers scattered to take up posts around the village. *They don't trust strangers.* A sensible attitude, but one that might cause trouble for Ilse and Bela.

Three men circled around the planted fields to approach the river. Ilse laid a hand on Bela's shoulder. The woman's jacket was soaked with fever sweat, and her skin was hot to the touch, even through the cloth. A strong residue of magic clung to them both. Magic might erase that same scent, but she suspected it was too late.

"Should we go back?" she said.

Bela's answer was hardly more than a sigh. "I think we must stop here, if they let us."

That alone told Ilse how ill her companion had become. She tugged the horse's reins, and with soft words, urged Duska forward at a walk, until they reached the banks of the river.

On the opposite side, the men paused as well. Two of them were young, only a few years older than she was, she guessed. The third was older, his dark hair threaded with gray. Deep grooves marked his face, some from laughter, but more from grief and hardship. He had the same ruddy brown complexion as her father and grandparents, the same high cheekbones and a face running in swift angles. A touch of anger, which did not surprise her, here in Duszranjo. He wore nothing but a pair of patched brown trousers and a shirt tucked into them, laced halfway up.

The older man, the leader, gestured to his companions. They both halted and fell into a waiting stance, their staffs held ready. Their leader swung his staff around and came forward, until his bare feet broke the current.

"Who are you?" he said.

His voice was mild, but she could tell from the lift of his chin, the way he gripped his staff, that she had not mistaken that anger. Strangely enough, she welcomed it.

"*Dobrud'n,*" she said. "Hello. We are travelers."

He tilted his head and regarded her warily. "Most travelers come from the north," he said, "when they come here at all."

He senses our magic, she thought. *And he doesn't like it.*

She met his gaze steadily. "My companion is injured and sick. I've used what magic I know to keep her alive, but it's not enough. She will die if you turn us away. She might . . ." Her throat closed against the rest of her words, but she could not stop herself from thinking them. Bela might die, all because these men—these *Duszranjen* men—were afraid of magic.

Bela stirred. Her hand brushed Ilse's hair. "I might die anyway," she whispered.

"I'd rather give up after you do, not before," Ilse said.

Bela only laughed, a rocking wheezing laugh that held not a drop of humor. Ilse laid a hand on the woman's shoulder, and murmured an invocation to the magic current, in spite of the staring men across the river. The current swirled around them, flowing from invisible to invisible, as Tanja Duhr once wrote. Its sharp green scent revived Ilse; its warmth seeped into her bones. Bela, too, breathed more easily.

Still angry, Ilse rounded on the men. She saw with some satisfaction that all three had drawn back several steps. "So," she called across to them, "do we die here, my friend and I? Or shall you let us pass so we might die in the mountains instead?"

Their leader hesitated. Perhaps he heard the desperation in her voice, because he glanced over his shoulder at his companions. "Ilja, go tell Ana Rudny she might have a patient. Watch for my signal, though, before they come down from above. Vilém, stay where you are."

"What are you doing?" Vilém demanded. "Jannik, you said before—"

"I know what I said before. Maybe I was wrong. I might be wrong now. Whatever the case, we'll need Ana and her daughter."

Ilja and Vilém exchanged scowls. Then Vilém shrugged and Ilja jogged back to the village. He didn't stop there, Ilse noticed, but continued up the slopes to a boulder-strewn ridge. Jannik watched, too, as if he wanted to make certain his orders were obeyed. An interesting clue. His authority wasn't absolute, then.

Jannik turned back to Ilse. "I am trusting you."

"Only a little," she replied.

He smiled faintly. "True. I'd like to examine your friend. Will you allow that?"

"You are a healer?"

"No. But I have good eyes."

And he wants to make certain I'm telling the truth before he gives Ilja and the others that signal.

She nodded. "Do as you must, then."

Jannik picked his way through the rushing water. Ilse wondered why the ford existed, if most visitors came from the north. Traffic from the eastern plains must have been more frequent once. No longer, because she could see how the stone bed of the ford had shifted and sunk, leaving deep holes in spots. He seemed to know the best path, because he never once paused or lost his footing.

He stopped at the near bank, the water swirling around his ankles. This close, she could see that he was not as old as she first guessed. He was built lean and muscled, and his gait as he crossed the river spoke of strength and grace. It was the silver-threaded hair and the lines etched into his face that had misled her. A life in Ryz would do that, she thought.

Jannik stretched out a hand to the mare, which sniffed at him suspiciously, then blew a rattling breath. He smiled, a much warmer smile than he had offered to Ilse. Then his gaze flicked up to Ilse. "It will be easier," he said, "if you do not stand next to me."

Wordlessly, she handed him the reins and stepped back. He drove his staff into the ground and gathered the reins in one hand as he ran his other over the horse's nose, crest, and neck. The air stirred, and she caught a whiff of green. Ilse's skin prickled and she remembered Jannik's comment about having good eyes. She glanced across to Vilém, who waited almost patiently. Whatever she sensed, it was not strong enough to carry across the water.

I'm tired. I'm dreaming up new dangers. Nothing more.

Now Jannik touched Bela's shoulder, just as he might the shoulder of another horse. Bela's eyes slid open. They were red-rimmed and glazed with fever. Her face was mottled with a hectic coloring.

Ilse reached for her friend, but Jannik blocked her path. The scent of magic intensified. From the air, from her own heightened sensibilities, Ilse could read her signature and that of Bela's, that of starlight glancing through a mist of clouds, the shape of a hawk, hovering overhead. A magical signature was more than an image or a scent, but humans were wont to translate the extraordinary into the everyday.

Her vision darkened. For a moment, it was as though the dawn had re-turned, and she saw its edge of light creeping over the dew-laden grass. A fragment of poetry hovered just out of memory's reach—of magic and its nearly invisible imprint upon the ordinary world. Not Tanja Duhr's words. A different poet, from a different life.

She blinked, and saw Jannik studying her with narrowed eyes.

"What is wrong?"

Her voice came out too quick and breathless.

"I wanted to ask you that same question," he said.

Again, she had the impression of strong emotion beneath that outward self-possession—more emotion than the situation could explain. She shook her head, uncertain how to translate those brief sensations into words. "Nothing that matters."

"I don't quite believe you," he said. "But we can talk about that later."

He turned and flung up a hand. Vilém came alert. "Get Ilja and Nikola," Jannik called out. "And several blankets. Big ones. Hana or Zofie should have what you need."

Vilém nodded and jogged back to Ryz. A shout echoed down from above. Ilse glanced toward the ridge where Ilja had disappeared. Someone—several someones—had emerged from the fringe of trees. Ilse counted three people. One of them slowed long enough to hike up her skirts before she raced down the hillside.

"Is that Ana Rudny?" she asked Jannik.

"Her daughter," he replied.

VILÉM RETURNED WITH Ilja and another man, who carried several blankets. While Jannik and Ilse fashioned a sling, the others lifted Bela from her horse. Bela hissed. Sweat was pouring over her face. Ilse quickly untied the scarf from around her head, knotted it several times, and set the cloth between the other woman's teeth. Bela bit down hard.

"What happened?" one of the men asked.

"Rockfall," Ilse said shortly. "It killed our other horse."

It had nearly killed Bela, who tried to roll free of her mount. She had not succeeded. Ilse recited the list of her companion's injuries: Three ribs cracked. One foot crushed. Her leg scraped raw by the gravel, when she and the horse had slid helplessly down the mountainside. Ilse had managed to stop the bleeding with magic, but the wounds healed only partway. Within a day, they had begun to fester.

She rubbed a hand over her face, suddenly aware of how exhausted she

was. Two weeks since they had fled Taboresk. Five days since the rockfall.
It seemed a dozen lifetimes.

A hand rested lightly on her shoulder. "We will do what we can," Jannik said. "Come. Let us get your friend to Ana and Maryshka."

The men carried Bela across the river. Ilse followed, leading the horse.
A half dozen men and women had gathered just below Ryz. All of them
carried weapons. All of them watched silently. Ilse resisted the urge to
summon the magic current, or to reach for her sword.

Two men came forward, both gray-haired, their faces weathered and
lined. Strong men. Angry ones. Jannik hurried to meet them halfway. An
argument broke out. Ilse could not hear what they said, but the gestures
were eloquent.

A young woman ran past the men. She was thin, like the edge of a
shadow. Her hair was tied back with a rag and fell in tumbles over her
shoulders and down her back. At her orders, Vilém and the others lowered
their burden carefully to the ground. Bela herself must have fallen into a
stupor. She lay silent and sweating, her chest rising and falling in shallow
breaths.

The young woman knelt. She thrust back her hair and laid a hand
on Bela's forehead. Her mouth thinned. She touched two fingers to Bela's
throat and her lips moved rapidly. Not an invocation to the gods and magic,
not here in Duszranjo. As she continued to examine Bela with swift light
touches, her movements recalled the figure running down the hillside.

Ana's daughter, Ilse thought. *Maryshka.*

Maryshka glanced over her shoulder at the still-arguing men. "Jannik,
she's dying. Louka, if you insist, I can make the pledge myself to Lir, Toc,
and your blessed honor, that she won't hurt anyone or anything."

"What about the other one?" Louka said.

The young woman's gaze swung around to meet Ilse's. "What do you
say? Shall I pledge myself for you as well? Speak quickly."

"I pledge whatever I must," Ilse said. "Only help her."

Louka gave an angry snort and spun away. Jannik continue to speak
with a handful of others, but most of the villagers had dispersed to their
own huts.

"They won't bother us," Maryshka said. "Tell me what happened."

Ilse described the accident and what she knew about Bela's injuries.
Throughout her recitation, Maryshka continued to examine her patient,
her brows drawn together in a frown of concentration. "I cannot promise
anything," she said quietly. "We are not surgeons here."

"If you can stop the fever . . ."

The frown eased somewhat. "That much is possible, I think. For the rest . . ."

She stood and gestured for the men to lift the sling once more, then directed them toward the nearest of Ryz's huts, where a woman waited in the doorway. Easy enough to tell that this was Maryshka's mother, Ana. By that time, a stream of children poured down from the upper slopes, followed by several women and older boys and girls. One, a boy with rough-cut dark hair that fell over his face, slipped between Jannik and the rest, so that he came up on the other side of Ilse's horse.

"I can take her," he said. "The horse, I mean. I'm good with horses."

His smile was a bright flash against his sun-brown skin, but Ilse saw how his gaze was on her sword, not the horse.

To her relief, Jannik intervened. "We'll tend to the horse, Damek. Your father needs you in the fields." To Ilse, he said, "Follow me. We'll get you and your things settled. You can trust Ana and her daughter long enough for that."

Ilse disliked leaving Bela alone, but it was a matter of trust, hers for theirs. *Besides, I have to sleep at some point.*

But as she turned away to follow Jannik, she caught a glimpse of the boy Damek staring after them. She had seen such a look before, with Galena Alighero, back in Osterling Keep, with others throughout her lives, and her skin prickled with apprehension.

We've met before, you and I.

CHAPTER FOURTEEN

JANNIK LED THE way up a broad, well-worn path that wound between Ryz's households. Ilse followed with the horse, glancing around as she went. The village was much larger than others she had sighted while crossing the mountains. A dozen log huts, most with thatched roofs, but a few with wooden shingles. Sheds cobbled together from bits of planking. A number of the larger homes had stone chimneys, but many more had just a hole in the roof from which the smoke escaped. On the upper slopes, at the forest's edge, stood a large rambling structure, with expertly cut planks instead of the split logs, and a door hung on metal hinges. Like the ford, the building seemed a remnant of more prosperous days.

"We've empty stalls for both the horse and you in the barn," Jannik said, nodding toward the building. "Unless you want to sleep with Alexej Zenkl's goats in their shed. We aren't so rich here that anyone has an excess of room in their homes. Except for me, but you'd find the barn more comfortable than my floor."

"I've slept in worse places," Ilse said mildly.

His cough sounded suspiciously like a laugh. "You mean the goats, or me?"

She had not expected humor from this man. She smiled, if wearily. "I like goats."

"Hmmm." Jannik rubbed his mouth. "I should not have provoked you. Here, let us tend to your horse so you might hurry back and pester Ana and Maryshka at their work."

Inside the barn, she found more clues of once-prosperous days. A dozen sizeable stalls lined one side, with a hayloft running above them. Opposite stood a wooden rack that she first took for a weapons rack, but then realized it was meant to hold farm tools. Once this barn must have housed at least a dozen cows or horses. Now, all but one stall stood empty.

With a snort, the barn's solitary occupant, a dark brown horse, lurched forward to meet Jannik's hand. Its muzzle was white, and it limped. Surely the village possessed more than one old horse and a few goats.

Uncertain, she asked, "Does it matter which stall?"

Jannik scratched the horse behind its ears, then fended off its attempts to lip at his shirt. "No. This old girl is friendly, and we've only two cows at the far end. I'll throw down some hay for yours. You can stow your gear in the next stall."

Working together, they soon had Ilse's horse fed, watered, and rubbed down with some old sacking. The gear made a tidy stack in the far corner of the barn. The stall next to Duska's had only a bare dirt floor, but Ilse didn't much care. She had blankets for warmth, and after two weeks in the wilderness, she would be comfortable enough.

"Done," Jannik said. "Now back to your friend, for you, and to the fields for me."

They parted outside the barn. Jannik took a side path that circled around the village, while Ilse headed down the main route to the Rudny household. Many eyes watched her progress—she glimpsed a face in one window, caught a swirl of movement as several children vanished behind another, larger house, and heard the bleating of goats disturbed at their feeding.

She knocked. Someone—Maryshka, she thought—called out, but hurriedly, as if they were preoccupied. Ilse went in.

Bela lay on a rough pallet in front of a blazing fire. Her feet were bare, her boots now a shredded heap of leather. Ana Rudny bent over her, knife in hand as she cut away the rest of Bela's trousers. Her daughter knelt on the hearth, just now lifting a pot of boiling water from the fire. Several baskets and stone jars stood on a nearby table, and next to them, a mortar and pestle. The air smelled of wood smoke and pungent herbs and the sickly stink of a wound gone putrid.

Maryshka glanced over her shoulder. "I'm glad you are here," she said to Ilse. "We want you to talk to your friend while we work."

Ilse knelt and wrapped her hands around Bela's unscathed foot. "Oh, my friend."

"It is not as awful as you would think," Bela whispered.

Then Ana slid the bloody rags from beneath Bela's legs, and Bela arched her back, flailing wildly. Ilse scrambled around and gripped Bela's hands in hers. "Hold on to me," she whispered. "Just as I did to you, that night I took sick and could not stop throwing up. You blamed that handful of water I drank from the stream. I said it was impossible, not from a stream running fresh and cold. We argued and argued until I threw up again, all over your shirt." She continued to babble, dimly aware of Maryshka by the table, the scrape of a knife against stone, Ana's murmured commentary to her daughter. "Do you remember?" she said. "How I cursed and wept from the cramps. How you told me to show a little fortitude. That's when I cursed you instead of my guts."

Bela wheezed with laughter. "I remember. I remember thinking you knew more curses than I did, and me the soldier."

Then her eyes squeezed shut. She gave a gasp and went limp.

Quickly Ilse touched her fingers to Bela's throat. A faint but steady pulse beat there.

"She sleeps," Ana said. "Just as well."

She gestured to Maryshka, who came at once to her side with rags, a bowl of weeds, and the boiling water. Ilse watched, open-eyed, as mother and daughter uncovered the flesh scraped raw by the gravel. A conversation followed, technical and brief. Maryshka fetched a mug from the table, filled with a bitter-smelling brew, which they forced down Bela's throat. Bela struggled until Maryshka pinched the woman's nose shut. Bela gave a spasm, swallowed, and swallowed again. Maryshka set the mug aside and studied her patient with narrowed eyes. A long interval later, Bela relaxed into an obviously deeper sleep.

"Good enough," Ana commented.

"As good as we can hope," Maryshka replied. "Do we cover the leg with a poultice until the skin grows back? *Will* it?"

Ana's gaze flicked toward Ilse. "It might. Worth a try."

Ilse gripped her hands tightly together. "Whatever you must do, whatever you can, please do it."

Another whispered conference, spoken in a stronger dialect than before. Ilse took the hint and wandered outside into the morning sunlight. A few older women had gathered outside another of the larger houses, knitting and sewing as they talked. Idly she wondered how they had obtained the metal needles or the thread. Not far away came the murmuring of the river, the rhythmic *thunk* of hoes biting into the ground, the bleating of goats.

Her strength gave way without warning, and she flopped onto the ground.

"Ei rûf ane gôtter. Ei rûf ane strôm . . ."

She drew a long breath and pressed both hands against her eyes. No, no magic here. None. She had come to Duszranjo, land of her father and grandmother. Whatever she had claimed to Raul Kosenmark when she first came to work for him in Tiralien, magic was not a simple thing in this valley. Even Miro Karasek, once a hostage of his mother's and father's private war, could not neatly separate himself from his heritage.

For a long while, she crouched in the dirt, breathing in the scents of flowering herbs, the dankness of the nearby river, her own sour sweat from days upon days of struggling through the mountains. She heard a groaning within the Rudny house. A thin, high screech, as though someone had inhaled in sudden anguish. Panting and then a sobbing breath giving way to silence. She heard footsteps passing by. The men and women coming back from the fields.

A shadow dropped over her.

"You look ill."

Jannik stood before her, sweat-stained and covered with dust, a hoe resting over one shoulder.

"I'm . . ." She struggled to find the right word.

"You are hungry and exhausted," he said. "Come with me."

He held out a hand. Ilse hesitated a moment, then allowed him to pull her to her feet. She leaned against him, grateful for the support. He stood patiently until her bout of trembling passed, then indicated the path ahead. "Come with me," he repeated. "We can eat and talk. Leave your friend to Ana and Maryshka. They've already forgotten about you, I know. They always forget the ones who watch."

She heard the weight of memory in that offhand comment. Knew at once she could not ask what it meant. Jannik had already turned away, as though he regretted those last words. Ilse hurried after.

Jannik's house stood at the northwest corner of Ryz, directly opposite the barn. It was much larger than she had expected, with a stone hearth and chimney. One generous room served as kitchen and sitting room and bedroom. And workroom, she thought, noting the bench and neat arrangement of carpentry tools in one corner. There was even a small set of shelves with half a dozen books. The house smelled of newly cut pine, and crushed herbs, and the lingering scent of wood smoke. From the barn came a whiff of manure and hay. Fresh, clean scents that helped restore her sense of self and balance.

Then it came to her, why a solitary man might possess such a large house. Jannik Maier had once had a wife, perhaps a child, both of them dead from illness or injury. Ana and her daughter had tried to save them and could not. It explained the man's bitterness, and the impression of things amiss.

Jannik laid out bread and cheese on the table, and set a pot of water to boil for tea. Ilse took a seat on the bench and bit into the bread. It was soft and baked fresh that same day. When Jannik set a mug of water in front of her, she drank it down. Duszranjo. Her skin prickled at the thought that she had come to her father's homeland.

The water boiled. Jannik filled a stone pitcher with dried leaves and poured the water over it. He set the pitcher on the table and took a seat opposite Ilse.

"So tell me," he said. "Is Bela your lover?"

Ilse blinked. "What? No, she's my . . . my friend."

Except friend was not the right word, not as people usually meant it. Bela was her guardian, her companion, but though they had endured a great deal these past few weeks, Ilse was not certain she dared to claim friendship. Bela's allegiance was to Duke Miro Karasek, Ilse's to her kingdom. Ilse had the sense they had been allies many times in past lives, if only temporary ones.

She caught a searching glance from Jannik before he turned his attention to slicing more bread and cheese. "Eat as much as you can. I'm no healer, but even I can see you are half starved and close to falling sick. Ana doesn't have time for two patients. As for your friend, we'll work out the barter later, the three of us."

He obviously had more questions, but was willing to wait for answers. Ilse was grateful for the reprieve. Her appetite awoke, and she gladly devoured half a dozen slices of bread and cheese, then drank down mug after mug of hot tea. It was such a relief, to let others far more competent than she cook and tend after Bela. The tea was sweet, brewed from a mixture of herbs. Willow was one. It eased her headache. Others she could not identify. Only later, as her eyelids drooped, did she suspect what he had done.

"Sleep now," Jannik said as he lifted her into his arms. "We can talk later."

SHE WOKE TO a room filled with a blood-red sunlight.

She started up, already struggling against the hands that caught her. Ilse cried out, but her throat was clogged with sleep. Only when Jannik's familiar voice cut through her panic did she subside.

"You drugged me," she mumbled.

"My apologies. You were exhausted."

His voice carried no trace of regret. She had not expected it.

"You drugged me," she repeated. "I dislike that. Never mind why. I hate it. Tell me what is wrong."

"Nothing," he said. "Your friend sleeps. Ana and her daughter have drained and cleansed her wounds with some success, but she needs a proper physician. My guess is that you would dislike the attention. We'll eat, then talk about the *why* and *whens* and *ifs* of your situation."

Cold washed over her. Her situation, yes. They would care for a chance-met stranger, but she would have to tread carefully to convince them to help her cross the border.

Dinner consisted of hot soup, cooked from rabbit meat and herbs and wild onions, together with more fresh bread and plain water. Ilse doubted the man cooked for himself, not if he spent mornings and afternoons in the field. Most likely he bartered his carpentry skills, which explained his earlier comments. She ate and drank to satisfaction, then laid down her mug and stared at him.

He nodded. "We talk, honestly. Both of us." He glanced around the cabin, winced as if in painful memory. "Not here. Outside is better."

He led her up a path that circled around the barn, then veered south, up to a ridge that overlooked the valley. It was quiet here. Sunset illuminated the peaks opposite them, but Ryz's households lay in darkness. Only a very few had windows lit by firelight or lamps. Down below, the river glittered silver and black.

Jannik took a seat on a rocky ledge. Ilse stood a few paces away.

"Let us start with names," he said. "Mine is Jannik Maier. I am speaker for the village."

So much she knew already. "Mine is Ilse."

"And your companion is Bela. Not a friend, but a companion. You and she are warriors. You wear swords, and I counted several other weapons in your gear. You were also cautious enough to keep your money and other belongings secured by magic. What else? Where did you come from? Where are you bound? What more do you expect from us?"

So hard to know which words might help, which might lead to disaster. "My companion worked as a guard," she said slowly. "We carry weapons because we travel alone. Surely you can understand that."

Jannik nodded. "But you came here for a reason. What is it?"

"To cross the border into Veraene."

"For what purpose?"

She was tired of answering questions. Valara Baussay, Miro Karasek, and Bela herself had insisted on testing her loyalty to Veraene, not to mention what she could promise to Károví. With a touch of aspersion, she said, "I must find smugglers so that I can cross the border. For what purpose? For peace, if you must know. Mine, in particular, in this life and those to come."

She reached inside her jacket. Jannik tensed. With a bitter smile, Ilse withdrew a leather purse. One by one, she laid down ten golden koruný on the ground between them.

A long silence followed. Around them, birdsong faded away, to be replaced by the shrill chorus of frogs and the rill of water over the ford. Ilse had long enough to consider six ways she might kill this man. She did not want to. He might not be as innocent as he pretended, but he was surely innocent when it came to the affairs of kings and queens.

Just when she thought she might have to act, Jannik stirred.

"I can do that for you," he said.

LATER, MUCH LATER, hours close to midnight, she sat alone in the barn. Moonlight and starlight poured through the half-open door.

All around her, the night settled to quiet. Ryz's cows and horses and human occupants slept. Even Jannik Maier, who struck Ilse Zhalina as someone who spent many extra hours in the service of his village, had banked his fire hours ago.

Ilse extracted a letter from her shirt. From a distance came the bleating of a goat, but she ignored it. In spite of having read the letter's contents a dozen times or more, she had to reassure herself that nothing had changed, that she had not mistaken the writer's intent.

"Ei rûf ane gôtter. Ei rûf ane Lir unde Toc."

Magic rippled over her skin, it burned within her veins. She lowered her hands and unfolded the letter Duke Miro Karasek had entrusted to his faithful captain, Bela Sovic, who had given it to Ilse that first night away from Taboresk.

To Lord Raul Kosenmark:

Ten months ago, you wrote to me concerning matters between our kingdoms. You wished, you said, to end the centuries of mistrust and to forge an alliance of peace. I said then that my duties required me elsewhere. An unsatisfactory reply, for which I apologize, but I was not then free to speak the truth. You will have learned a part of it by now through your spies and other allies. My king ordered me to Morennioù to recapture one of Lir's three jewels, and to take the royal heir prisoner. Lir's jewels are no more. The royal heir has returned to her kingdom to take the throne. And I, I have signed over my titles and lands to my cousin, in order to fulfill other obligations, long neglected but no less important.

But though I no longer have any influence in Károví's Court, I am not

the only man or woman who wished an end to conflict between our king-
doms. Tell your king that the days of the empire are past. We are no longer a
subject people, if ever we were. But if he comes to us with an offer of true
friendship, he will find he has allies within Károví. For peace, for prosperity,
and that cause alone, I give you the names of those you can trust . . .

It was not precisely the same letter she had carried from Rastov to Duenne's representative, four hundred years before, but the semblance was
close enough to leave her shaken, no matter how many times she read this.

She recalled when she last spoke with him in Taboresk. He wore a plain
uniform of rich black cloth, decorated with embroidery, his hair drawn back
into a tight queue. A soldier, a general, a noble with influence. She could remember his face, laughing and confident and yet reticent in matters of the
heart, in a lifetime long ago. She had gone off to marry Andreas Koszen-
marc. He had led the expedition to Morennioù. In a later life still, he had
executed Ilse at his king's command.

We were both servants of our ill-thought plans.

But now, now all was different. With this letter, Miro Karasek had abandoned his title and property. He had betrayed, if one might use so strong a
word, the names of his like-minded compatriots. He had undone the deed of
centuries before.

She could do no less.

CHAPTER FIFTEEN

ILSE WOKE TO whispering voices nearby. The habit of weeks took hold even before she was truly awake, and she reached for her knife. Her fingers had closed around its hilt before she identified the voices as those of children, and the language they spoke as Duszranjen. She blinked to clear the sleep from her eyes. It was early morning, judging by the pale sunlight that filtered through the half-open doors.

Of course. The children had to be curious about their two strangers.

Smothered laughter gave way to a barely suppressed argument. Then came the unmistakable rustle of straw. Ilse eased herself onto her side. Through the slats of the stall's gate, she could make out five or six shadows creeping along the corridor. Duska nickered, but the intruders were too intent on their mission to notice.

The shadows bunched together for another argument. Ilse could not make out the difficulty. A matter of precedence? Or second thoughts? Then one voice rose above the rest. "I told you they're runaway soldiers. I'll prove it. Watch."

Damek Rudny, Maryshka's brother. Jannik had mentioned the detail in passing, but Damek's thin dark face, the tumble of dark hair, were so like Maryshka's that Ilse had already guessed. She was not surprised to find him leading this pack. She had recognized insatiable curiosity in that face. When had their lives crossed before? Not from Károví and Rastov—of that she was certain. An older memory, almost lost in the shadows of centuries past.

Damek crept forward toward the gear Ilse and Jannik had piled in one corner. His eyes gleamed bright in the early sunlight, and his lips had curled back in a grin. He was no thief, this one. He wanted to handle Bela's sword in front of his friends. Examine the genuine gear used by a genuine soldier. For that he would need to untie the strings . . .

Magic rippled through the air. Damek yelped and leaped backward, only to slip and land with a loud thump.

No use pretending she could not hear. Ilse levered herself to sitting and coughed. Loudly. With another yelp, Damek staggered to his feet. His friends scrambled toward the barn doors.

"Stop," she called out.

One terrifed squeak, and the invaders froze in silence.

Ilse stood up awkwardly. Her back and leg muscles groaned from the long days of hiking, and a night spent in unfamiliar quarters. *I am not quite nineteen*, she thought. *I should not feel so old.*

She dragged a hand over her face. Wished in vain for a hot bath, then pushed the stall gate open to survey the scene.

Damek leaned against a wall next to the gear. His mouth was pinched into a knot. His skin gleamed with sweat. Bela's magic had proved a good guardian. The others, three boys and two girls, had stopped in mid-escape in and around the outer doors. These were not Ryz's youngest children. They were all twelve or fourteen at least, older than what she would have expected, but she reminded herself that Ryz lay far beyond the usual circuit of garrisons and patrols. *We are strangers, and therefore exciting . . .*

"Damek," she said softly. "Thank you for coming so early. Duska will need water and hay. Her stall raked out, of course. And if you like, a short ride before you set her to graze. But only," she added, "if your mother and father gave permission. Would your friends like to help?"

Damek's friends rushed out the door. Damek, abandoned, stared at her with wide-eyed panic. Ilse had to choke back her laughter. Still overcome by this unfamiliar sense of antiquity, she pointed to the neighboring stall, where her horse leaned over the wooden slats to observe this strange young human. Ryz's own old mare had turned away in disgust. Clearly she had no such hopes as Ilse entertained.

"Will you care for them both?" Ilse asked. "Do you promise?"

"Yes. Yes, my lady." Then he glanced up, grinning, his eyes half hidden by a fall of black hair. "Does she like a gallop?"

He is more than curious. He is irrepressible.

She wanted to laugh and scold at the same time. She suppressed both impulses. Damek was no different from several courtesans in Raul Kosenmark's pleasure house, though his immediate wishes might be simpler or, at least, more innocent. After some conversation, she left both horses in Damek's care, then collected a set of fresh clothes and escaped the barn.

She paused on the threshold and scanned the village of Ryz.

Far away, near the river, a dozen or so men and women had already gathered in the greening fields. If she guessed right, one would be Jannik Maier.

"You must feel like a clod of dirt."

Maryshka Rudny was picking her way down the hillside, a basket filled with greens slung over one shoulder. She wore the same dark blue skirt and quilted jacket as the day before. In spite of the crisp morning air, she was barefoot.

Maryshka smiled at her. "That was rude of me. I'm sorry."

Her smile was the shadow of Damek's grin, and provoked a smile in return. "It's the truth," Ilse said. "My friend and I have been riding for too long without a proper scrub. How . . . How is she?"

Maryshka's smile wavered. "Your friend does well enough, considering. Jannik sent Karel Hasek north to Dubro to get fresh supplies. We've no animals to spare, but the farmers might be willing to trade for a calf's liver, not to mention a few herbs I cannot grow in the valley. With those, we can build up her strength. Oh, and Jannik told me to tell you that Ilja Lendl started this morning on the task you required. Into the southern mountains," she added. "If you need a translation for that, I am happy to give one."

Jannik's message was clear enough—he had sent Ilja to the band of smugglers who operated a route between Veraene and Duszranjo. It was common knowledge, Bela told Ilse more than once, that smugglers would guide spies and enemies across the border for a price. The trick was to offer enough to whet their interest, not so much that they wanted to kill and rob you.

She was not home, not yet, but she had won another step forward, and she felt the band of tension within her chest ease a fraction. "Thank you for telling me."

Maryshka was observing her far too closely for comfort. However, all she said was, "No need to thank me. You brought a spot of the unusual here. Not that Karel Hasek would thank you himself. That . . . *man*." She snorted. "I'm not being fair. He works hard, Karel does. He would battle Toc himself to feed his family. That is more than I could say for some. But he is too *grim*. I cannot abide a man who does not laugh. That is my own shortcoming."

"Mine as well," Ilse said. She had a sudden, vivid image of Raul, dressed in muddy drill clothes, laughing because she had disarmed him. Her throat squeezed shut with sudden grief. *Too many, many miles until I see you again, my love. I pray that I make it.*

She blinked away her tears. To her relief, Maryshka pretended not to notice. The young woman bent and plucked what seemed an anonymous dusty weed from the ground, then added that to her basket. "My mother gave me strict orders to bring you to our house for breakfast," she said in a casual tone. "Your friend woke more than once last night. She believes you would starve without her attention. I told her you seemed a competent woman, but she only laughed."

Ilse laughed as well. It was a shaky laugh, however, and entirely unconvincing, even to herself. "My dear friend Bela. She shows such confidence in my abilities. Thank you for the kind invitation. I should love a hot breakfast."

That won her a grin from Maryshka, one just like her brother's. "Then let us hurry," she said. "There will be grilled fish, bread, stewed greens, and hot, hot tea brewed from the freshest herbs I could collect in the fields above."

She danced down along the path into Ryz, one hand keeping the basket level as she leapt from stone to stone, and down into the village itself. Ilse followed as quickly as she might. Within her pulse beat a joyful rhythm. One man north to collect the necessary medicaments for Bela. A second south to negotiate with the smugglers. Within a week or month, they could win through and she could forget about Duszranjo forever.

SIX, EIGHT DAYS passed.

At first, Ilse Zhalina spent all her daylight hours with Bela Sovic, gladly leaving Duska to Damek Rudny's care. He mucked out Duska's stall, gathered extra hay from the fields, and badgered his sister for where he might harvest wild oats from the meadows above Ryz. He did the same for Lev Kosko's old mare. When all that proved too dull and steady, he took Duska for short gallops along the Solvatni River.

Evenings, Ilse spent alone, or with Jannik Maier, arguing poetry. They had few candles, so the arguments were conducted in the warm darkness of Károví's late brief summer, but Ilse found she liked that. Without light, she could focus on words and reason, not the countenance of her opponent.

Bela herself lay fevered and restless. Occasionally she roused herself to accept a cup of soup, or complain about the draughts Ana Rudny prepared, but mostly she lay dozing.

After two days, Ana ordered Ilse away from the house. She gave her regular chores, fetching water from the village well, carrying the family's slop buckets across the ford and into the fields beyond. Ilse did more. She washed pots and dishes, chopped roots, and carried Bela's sweat-stained blankets to the river, where she scrubbed them with rocks. Whenever she had a spare hour, she took on the young boys and girls of Ryz in mock battles.

After four days, Ilja Lendl returned with word that the fees offered were sufficient.

The transaction might require additional sums, he reported, depending on when and where the persons in question needed to make their passage across the mountains.

"Can I trust them?" Ilse asked Jannik Maier. "Should I?"

He shrugged. "I believe them to be as honest as possible. However, if I were to entrust myself to their keeping, I would sleep with my sword and knife within reach. Have you decided upon your destination?"

She had. "The city of Melnek. It lies on the border, not far from the mountains."

"You have friends there?"

A family, once. Friends. Allies of my beloved.

"Yes," she said, after a moment.

If he noticed the difficulty she had providing such a short answer, he never said anything. Nor did he question her about those friends. She began to wonder how much traffic Ryz saw from these smugglers.

What troubled her the most, however, were Bela's injuries and Karel Hasek's continued absence. Bela's mangled foot was beyond their abilities, and the rockslide had lacerated her flesh from hip to foot. Ana and Maryshka could do nothing more than bind the foot, apply herbs to the terrible wounds, and hope for the best. As for Karel Hasek, everyone could give her a hundred and two reasons why he had not yet returned. A slight injury that slowed his walk. More likely, that Vlaky could not provide the requisite supplies, and so he had to walk farther north to Dubro and the garrison itself.

"You must learn patience," Jannik told her.

"I should," Ilse replied. "I cannot."

Once Armand of Angersee learned of Leos Dzavek's death, he would seek immediate conquest of Károví. But she could not explain to him the urgency of her mission. She had trusted him as much as she dared. Eventually Jannik left off questioning her, and she was alone with her doubts.

THE EVENING OF the eighth day, well past sunset, Maryshka came to the barn, where Ilse was sharpening her sword and knives.

"Bela's fever has returned," she said. "She needs you now."

Ilse hurried after Maryshka to the Rudny household. Across the threshold, a fire blazed, sending wave upon wave of pine-scented clouds rolling through the small house. Bela lay on her pallet, twisting from side to side.

"Karel brought the liver and medicine this afternoon," Ana said. "And she seemed stronger today, but toward afternoon, she took worse. We tried all we could but—"

Ilse sank to her knees and gathered Bela's hands into hers. *Oh my friend, my friend. My companion and friend.* Bela's hands felt heavy and cold, as if the life had already begun to leach from them. No longer the hands of a soldier who wielded a sword as featly as Ilse had witnessed.

"You say the relapse came suddenly?" she asked.

Ana nodded. "Her color had improved, and at noon her appetite was much better. Then between one hour and the next, her fever came back. We thought she might take to the willow doses—she did last night—but the past hour—"

"The last hour she went cold and colder," Maryshka said. "So we sent for you."

Because you think she is dying.

"Bela," she whispered. "Live. Live, damn you."

From behind, came the sound of bickering—Damek insisting he must stay. Maryshka urging him outside. The parents in conference with their daughter. All the while, Bela's breathing grew fainter and harsher, each delay between inspiration and expiration longer than before.

Markyshka laid a hand, warm and steady, on her shoulder.

"I have sent them all away," she said softly. "But your friend—if you know magic to save her, use it now."

"I can't," Ilse whispered. "I tried before."

All her studies had been bent upon rediscovering the jewels, learning how to launch herself in spirit and flesh into Anderswar. The jewels no longer existed in this world, and all her knowledge meant nothing, nothing, nothing. She wanted to weep, to shout her fury to the gods. Except she knew the gods did not care. They could not, at least they could not care as much as she did.

Maryshka took hold of Ilse's shoulder and shook her. This was no kind and gentle grip, but someone who would not take a careless answer.

"Try," Maryshka insisted. "You have nothing to lose but her life."

All the old explanations rose up, how her father despised magic, how even her grandmother spoke of it with fleeting reserve. For all her life, she had believed this was her heritage, no matter what she once told Raul Kosenmark.

Ilse swallowed a laugh. It no longer mattered what she or anyone else believed. She drew a shaky breath, held it long past the burning in her chest, then loosed an exhalation slowly. Nothing changed except the pressure within her skull. She repeated the exercise a half dozen times before she called upon the current itself.

"*Ei rûf ane gôtter. Ei rûf ane Lir unde Toc . . .*"

The current gathered around her, the air thick with a green, pungent scent. So many ways to describe the scent, the texture, the fury and rush of magic, all of them right, all of them inadequate. She felt the familiar grip against her chest, the sense of tipping forward from the ordinary into the extraordinary.

"*Ei rûf ane Lir unde Toc. Komen mir de strôm . . .*"

Ilse laid her hands over Bela Sovic's forehead and thigh. Here the flesh burned with fever. Dimly, she felt a hand laid upon hers, another cupped around her neck, fingers lightly pressing against Ilse's throat. It was Maryshka. She must know about magic. Or perhaps she had only guessed, and hoped to aid one stranger to heal another.

Bela, can you hear me?

Nothing. Then a faint echo. *I can.*

Then live, Ilse commanded.

Bela answered with laughter. *Are you a queen? A king? To order me so? Does that matter?*

More laughter. A shudder. *No. I must live. If you could just . . . Let me show you . . .*

Rest, said another voice. Maryshka's. *I can show her what to do.*

Now Ilse felt a great pressure, as if a vise gripped her neck, forcing her to look downward, ever downward to a point between vein and muscle and bone. She stretched out a hand, felt the mass of broken vessels and flesh. Maryshka had disappeared from view. The small room enclosing them had transformed itself into mist and fog, with bright points marking the worlds upon worlds, which occupied the wheel of life. She reached out and . . .

. . . felt the touch of gods. Of a longing she could not identify . . .

Heal me, said the god.

She recognized the voice as Toc's, as he lay helpless and blind under the newborn stars. As Lir's, as she bathed her dead lover's face with her tears.

Live, she commanded Bela.

She drew a deep breath. Held it. Felt the ache of flesh bound by blood and muscle, then released the breath again as Lir once had, as she gazed upon her brother, hoping that he lived again.

"She lives," Maryshka said.

"She lives," said Jannik Maier. "And now we must talk."

* * *

NIGHT HAD FALLEN during the interlude she spent gripped in magic. Far to the north, along the valley, a faint blue and gray lined the horizon, but the skies above had turned to dark, with only a handful of stars visible through the thick clouds. Ryz itself lay asleep, except for one or two houses, their windows lit by the dull red of a dying fire.

Jannik Maier led Ilse away from the Rudny household, up the now-familiar path to his own, perched above the village. A house built for a wife and several children, now occupied by a solitary man. Ilse passed over the threshold and shivered at the thought of so many dead, and those who would never be.

A fire burned in the spacious hearth. There was no other illumination, except for faint starlight spilling through the half-open shutters, but she had not expected it. Candles and lamps were a luxury in Ryz.

Jannik motioned for her to sit. Ilse sank onto the bench by the fire, and watched with growing apprehension as he paced from one end of his house to the other. Just when she thought she would have to ask him why he had insisted on this interview, he swung around to face her.

"Karel Hasek returned today. He said there were no proper supplies to be had in Vlaky, so he went north to Dubro. There he learned any number of things he could not bear to keep secret from Ryz. Our king is dead. Assassinated by foreign spies, the rumors say. Rastov lies under strict rule by the army, while the council searches for the murderers. Since then, Duke Miro Karasek fled the kingdom to avoid arrest by the imperial representatives."

He stared at her, angry. Ryz was a border village with mixed allegiance. For months or years, that mixture did not matter, but with the news of Leos Dzavek's death, it did.

"I did not kill the king," she said.

"But you knew of his death. I can tell by your face. Are you spies? That is what Karel believes. And if I know him, he's said as much to the guards at Dubro."

"I am not a spy."

"Then what are you?"

She could lie. She could deny any connection with Leos Dzavek and his death. It was an unfortunate coincidence, the news of his murder and her arrival at the border, seeking passage into Veraene. Jannik might believe her. That he asked implied he did not wholly trust Karel Hasek's accusations.

She folded her hands one within the other. Considered the past two months. These hands had killed. They had wiped the air clean of their acts, but she could not erase her own memories. If she had learned one lesson from her past lives, it was to confront the truth.

"I was there when Leos died," she said softly. "I did not kill him. I would say he died because the gods wished it. Or he had lost his humanity. Or any number of grandiose reasons. But the truth is he died because he fought his brother, and this time, his brother won."

His face went still in shock. He rubbed a hand over his face, then stared hard at her. "Do you claim to be innocent, then?"

"No, not innocent, but—"

"But you did nothing to stop it."

Ilse shook her head. "There was no time. The jewels . . ." But she could not explain how the jewels worked their magic through Valara, so that they might gain their own freedom. "I did not," she said at last. "I could not. In the end, I believe he accepted his death."

"So you say." Jannik spoke in a hoarse whisper. "What brought you to Rastov? Why must you cross the border?"

"Peace brought me to Rastov," she said. "Peace takes me home again."

She felt the weight of Karasek's letter beneath her shirt. It was heavy from all the dead—Galena, Raul's guards, Dedrick, and the many others who worked for peace between the kingdoms. Even her own death, four hundred years ago.

"He thought me a traitor," she said softly. "He thought I betrayed him. That is why he had me executed, when he was a new king and we were at war with the empire."

Jannik Maier flinched. "A fine revenge then, to watch him die."

"It was not. It was . . ." Her voice broke and she felt the sting of tears in her eyes. "I never wished him dead. I wanted the end to war, then and now. I cannot tell you more, but this much I can swear: I bring a letter to Armand of Angersee, offering a chance for true peace between our kingdoms."

A very long silence followed.

Jannik stirred at last. "I cannot tell if I should believe you. I wish . . . It doesn't matter what I wish. My duty is to Ryz first, then the kingdom. You and Bela Sovic are a danger to us. You must both leave Ryz. Tomorrow."

IT WAS A compromise of allegiance, Ilse thought later, alone in the barn, wrapped in several layers of blankets against the bitter cold. In the stall next to her, Duska blew a rattling breath, as if she shared Ilse's conclusion.

My duty is to Ryz, then the kingdom, Jannik had said.

A clue lay buried in the words and the order of them. So. The king's soldiers might tolerate a connection with smugglers, but this was a far more serious matter. Someone had murdered the king. If the soldiers believed Ryz had collaborated with the enemy, they would punish Jannik, Ana, Maryshka . . . even foolish Damek. Only yesterday, Ana Rudny had commented on the dry summer, the hard winter, and how they had not had enough hands to harvest the crops that did grow.

So and so. Jannik had no choice but to turn Ilse and Bela over to the soldiers.

But he could have kept his suspicions a secret. The garrison lay directly north along the river trail. A troop of soldiers riding fast could cover the distance within a few days. Instead, Jannik had *warned* Ilse.

He believes me. He wants us to escape. But he also wants to protect Ryz.

So she told herself as she lay, fretful and uneasy, on her bed of straw.

CHAPTER SIXTEEN

THE NEXT MORNING, Maryshka had stronger opinions about the speaker's decision.

It was early, the sun just rising above the mountains. Ilse had waited until Ivo and Damek were gone—Ivo for a day of hunting in the upper hills, Damek to work in the barn, then to join his father.

"Idiot," Maryshka grumbled. "Arrogant, irritating, stupid idiot."

Ilse waited until Maryshka exhausted her outrage and her vocabulary before she spoke again. "We have a message to deliver," she said mildly. "We cannot wait any longer."

"Ah." Maryshka swung her glance up to meet Ilse's, and her expression changed to one oddly shuttered. "I see," she said. "Well, you cannot leave before tomorrow. You need provisions. Bela needs herbs. If our blessed speaker Jannik argues, send him to *me*."

She stomped over to the hearth, still muttering.

Ana had listened to the conversation without comment, but now she shook her head. "You ought not go, not yet. Your friend—"

"I can ride," Bela said, her voice thick with effort. "If you bind my foot and bandage my leg, I can manage."

"It will *not* be good enough," Maryshka snapped. "Let me tell Jannik—"

"You cannot tell him anything he does not know," Bela said. "We go. It's best for us. It's best for Ryz. Am I right?" she asked Ilse.

Ilse nodded.

Maryshka glared at them both. "I see. It's a plague of idiocy. Very well. You leave today. We best help you prepare."

BY EARLY AFTERNOON Ilse had washed all their clothes, cleaned and oiled their tack, and repacked their gear. When she returned to the Rudny household, she found Maryshka and Ana at work over the cook fire. Ana had baked a supply of flatbread for their journey, while Ivo had skinned a brace of rabbits, which Maryshka had cut into strips to roast over the fire.

There was also a package of herbs that Bela would need for her journey, she told Ilse. Herbs to dull the pain. Herbs that boiled would ensure the infection did not return.

They were generous, too generous, Ilse thought. *Jannik Maier was right to evict us.*

She could not truly repay them, but she could offer a practical gift. Along with the money she had offered Jannik Maier, it might ensure Ryz's survival through the next winter, even restore the village to its former prosperity. Silently she laid out six golden koruný on the worktable.

Maryshka paused at once. "What is that?"

"Call it reparations," Ilse said. "You saved my friend's life. You—"

"It's a fortune," Ana Rudny whispered. She touched the coins with her fingertips, as though she did not trust what she saw. Then she glanced up and stared at Ilse, her eyes widened in sudden apprehension.

She has heard rumors. Nothing specific, or she and her daughter would turn me out at once.

"It is not enough to repay you," Ilse said. "Bela would have died without your care."

"She might yet," Maryshka said. "I told you before, she needs another month before she can think of travel."

"I do not have another month," Bela said. "Have you packed all our gear?" she asked Ilse.

"Of course—"

"And my weapons? What about them?"

"Cleaned, oiled, and wrapped in cloth. What else?"

"Nothing," Bela said. "We eat and we go."

Ana said her good-byes. She had a few good hours before sunset, and she wanted to forage for greens in the fields above Ryz. Maryshka, however, loitered about while Ilse and Bela ate an early supper. After she and Ilse washed dishes, Ilse fetched Duska from the barn, and together the two of them loaded saddlebags onto the mare, then packed the fresh provisions into Ilse's backpack. Ilse accepted additional packets of herb and salt, a lump of sourdough wrapped in cloth, and other miscellaneous supplies with thanks.

Maryshka watched with bright curious eyes. "I won't ask questions, though I want to. I wish you well on your journey."

"I wish you good fortune, in whatever life brings you," Ilse replied.

"A fair wish to make," said Jannik Maier.

He came toward them from the direction of his house. He must have left the fields early, Ilse thought. Was he making certain they didn't linger in Ryz? Then she noticed he, too, carried a pack slung over one shoulder, and gripped a thick walking staff.

"You'll need a guide," he said.

"So I will. I thought you forgot."

His mouth twisted at her tone, but all he said was, "We should go. We need to make those hills before dark."

He dropped his pack and his stick to one side, and between the three of them, he, Ilse, and Maryshka helped Bela to mount Duska. Once in the saddle, Bela sat with her eyes closed, her hands gripping the saddle horn. She was sweating.

"We should wait another day," Ilse said.

"No," Bela whispered. "I can manage."

She offered a faint smile, but her color was paler and grayer than Ilse liked. "We stop at sunset."

"Later," Jannik said. "We must get well away from Duszranjo before nightfall."

He swung his pack over one shoulder and took up his staff. Eyeing him and Bela, Ilse did the same. Maryshka had not spoken the whole time, but she was gazing at the speaker with an intensity that spoke of a future interrogation.

A brief hug with Maryshka. A last farewell. Then Ilse and her companions set off from Ryz.

JANNIK LED THEM up to the familiar ridge overlooking the village. Ilse glanced down the hillside. Men and women were at work in the fields, harvesting the last crops before winter. Several older children were tending goats in the fields by the river. One slim figure stood apart from the others. Maryshka, watching them.

One last silent farewell, then she hurried after Jannik, along the ridge, to a branching path that climbed upward into the hills. As they entered the mountain forests, Ryz, its fields, and the river vanished from sight. Scraps of blue sky showed between the branches overhead, and sunlight illuminated the upper tree trunks, but the path itself remained cast in shadows. The scent of pine overwhelmed everything.

An hour or more passed as they climbed ever upward, the path winding around through the hills and into the mountains. Jannik said nothing, only stopping when he guessed Ilse was tired, or to signal a rough patch ahead.

Bela was silent, too. She seemed to have shrunk inside herself. Only when Ilse glanced back did she rouse enough to shake her head.

The sun was slanting down, and the light darkened to gold when Ilse finally asked, "How much longer?"

"Two hours," Jannik said.

He spoke with finality. And more than a bit of anxiety. Ilse lapsed back into silence.

They marched another hour, the path winding higher and higher, until it rounded a shoulder into the mountains themselves. Here the trees thinned into a clearing. A stream bounced over the rocks nearby, and judging by the firepit, Ilse suspected Jannik had come this way before to meet with the smugglers.

He and Ilse set up camp, with one shelter for her and Bela, another for him. Ilse built up a fire, while Jannik fetched fresh water from the stream. After a hasty meal of smoked venison, Ilse helped Bela to lie down closest to the fire and covered her with blankets. Bela insisted her leg was almost healed, but Ilse did not believe her. Once she saw her friend asleep, she returned to the dying fire where Jannik sat.

"Tomorrow we meet your smugglers?" Ilse said.

"Tomorrow afternoon at the latest," Jannik said. "They have a way station the next mountain over."

They reviewed the route, which Jannik drew in the dirt by the campfire, then arranged watches. Jannik would take the first, Ilse the second. It would not be necessary to stand guard after midnight. Brigands liked their sleep as well as anyone, he said, and Ilse did not argue. She rolled herself into her blankets and fell at once into sleep.

Jannik woke her several hours later. The moon hovered directly overheard, a bright full moon that flooded the scene with its eerie light. Ilse scrubbed the sleep from her eyes. She was thinking they had made a mistake, camping in the open like this. Or was that Raul's influence? Raul had always approached every situation as though it were a military affair.

"No trouble," Jannik said.

"So glad to hear it," Ilse said.

He laughed softly. "Watch for an hour or two, then sleep. We make an early start tomorrow."

She staggered to her feet, fully awake now from the chill. She blinked and took in the bowl of bare dirt and grass, now beautiful in the moonlight, the blue-black trees edged in silver. Lovely, that is, if you disregarded the bitter cold and the possibility of soldiers in pursuit. Duska stood motionless off to one side, dozing on her feet. Bela was a dark oblong in her blankets, Jannik another.

Ilse checked her weapons, buttoned her quilted jacket to her chin, and set off to walk the camp's perimeter. Though the season was late summer, her breath hung in white clouds, and her boots crunched over the frosted grass. She found herself glad of Duke Karasek's insistence on supplying them with adequate gear. Without that gear, without Bela, she would not have survived the long trek across Károví's plains.

Her thoughts winged back to Taboresk. Three weeks had passed since she and Bela had fled into the wilderness. Three weeks since Miro Karasek abandoned his title and his home to bring Valara Baussay to her kingdom.

Are you happy now? she thought. *You and Valara Baussay?*

Another impossible question to ask.

She swung around for a new circuit and paused at the unmistakable sound of footsteps over frozen grass. She quietly drew her sword from its sheath and murmured an invocation to the gods and magic.

What came next depended on who approached their campsite. Hunters and trappers often traversed the mountains in the autumn, searching for game. A reasonable explanation, except ordinary folk made their camps by nightfall. They did not wander about in the dark. Enemies, then. Most likely the king's patrol from Dubro. Or they might be mages in truth, sent by the Dukes Markov and Černosek.

Before she could think what to do, a familiar voice called out, "Ilse. Ilse, it's me. Damek."

Damek. Ilse let her breath trickle out. Of course. *Stupid, stupid boy. What in Lir's name were you thinking?*

She slid her sword back into its sheath. Resisted the urge to knock her head against the nearest tree trunk. "What do you want?"

A short pause, as if she had asked something blindingly obvious.

I suppose I have.

"Let me talk to you," Damek said. Then, with some hesitation, "Is Jannik there? Is he awake?"

"He is here. No, he is not awake. Not yet." Ilse stood up. She glanced toward the speaker, saw the gleam of moonlight reflected from his open eyes. She nodded at him. He nodded back. Good. On this they agreed. Get Damek into the camp where they could muzzle him until Jannik could drag the boy back to Ryz.

She stirred up the fire and waited, impatiently, until Damek emerged from the darkness. He wore a thick quilted jacket over layers of clothing and carried a pack.

Ilse pointed at the spot near the fire. Damek obediently sat. His eyes were wide, and there was a stubborn lift to his chin. He flinched when Jannik sat up, flinched again when Bela threw off her blankets and rolled over.

"Talk," Ilse said. "Why are you here?"

"Karel said you ran away."

Ilse suppressed a growl. "I am going home. Not running away."

"But Karel said—"

"Karel Hasek is an idiot."

"He knows about you and the smugglers," Damek said, his voice low and stubborn. "I wanted to come with you. I know all the trails. I know everything Ilja knows."

Ilse slapped her hand against her thigh. "You know nothing, Damek. Go home. We do not want you with us."

It was as harsh as she could make it. Damek shrank back. His gaze flicked toward Bela, who grinned at him sardonically, then Jannik, whose face had turned into a mask. "I only wanted to help."

Ilse suppressed the urge to say, *You can help by going home.* She remember herself at fifteen. Remembered her father's house where they had bartered her to Theodr Galt for better contracts with the shipping guild. Damek's family was nothing like hers, but she could understand the wish to escape a life she found intolerable.

So it was with sympathy that she said, "Damek. I understand. I truly do. But I must go to Veraene's king. I cannot take you with me."

Those were the right words. Damek swiped a hand over his face. "I know. I only wanted— Never mind what I wanted. I'll go back home tomorrow."

"Good boy," Jannik murmured.

Ilse suspected this agreement was only temporary. Tomorrow, Damek might sneak after them to visit the smugglers' wayhouse. However, that obstacle could wait for the morning. She held out a hand to the boy. "Come with me. We'll get you settled for the night."

Damek pushed her hand aside. "I can stand up by myself."

He had scrambled to his feet when Bela's head swung up. "Hush."

Ilse froze. So did Jannik and the boy.

She heard the hiss of pine needles sliding over the ground. Strangers approaching in stealth.

Bela bolted to her feet, staggered, and caught hold of a tree trunk. Ilse had her sword in hand even as the first armed man stepped into the clearing. He shouted at her—a warning, a demand for her surrender? She did not stop to ask. She swung her blade around. Their swords crashed together in a ringing blow. Then she danced backward to catch up a branch from the fire. She threw the brand at her attackers and retreated up the hillside. Bela lunged forward with both knives ready. Jannik had hesitated a long dangerous moment, but when Bela stumbled and one of the attackers seemed about to run her through, he seized his staff and swung it around to drive them back. Bela used the chance to haul herself upright and fling a stone into the banked fire.

A shower of sparks exploded, and the firelight flared, ruddy and hot against the moonlight. Ilse's mouth went dry at the scene. A half-dozen men and women swarmed into the clearing from all directions. Ilse recognized those uniforms. Not brigands. Soldiers. Guardians of Károví.

No time to think more. She drove her opponent back, caught up the knapsack with her money. She dropped back into the shadows, heart beating fast. Bela had fought off two or three attackers. One lay motionless at her feet. Jannik had not done as well. He had fallen to his knees, blood streaming from a slash over his forehead. Damek was nowhere to be seen.

Ilse's instincts yammered at her to flee while the confusion lasted, but she could not abandon her companions. Then Bela staggered backward and dropped to the ground a few feet away from Ilse. "Go," she hissed. "They won't miss you right away."

"No," Ilse said hoarsely. "I can't—"

"You must. They will take you prisoner otherwise. Besides, my duke commanded me to bring you safely to your homeland. If you go now, that is possible."

Bela lurched to her feet and charged at the soldiers. Ilse hesitated one moment before she fled into the darkness.

CHAPTER SEVENTEEN

IN THE WEEKS since his arrest, Raul Kosenmark had established a daily routine. He woke at dawn, or thereabouts, to a prison guard shouting his name and banging on the door until Raul staggered upright. The guard brought a water jug and empty slop bucket. He did not remove the old bucket. Raul had learned to breathe through his mouth while he drank down the entire jugful of water to ease the hunger cramps that overtook him on waking.

For two more hours he dozed. The guard returned and rattled his baton against Raul's cell door. He collected the stinking slop bucket, and left what passed for breakfast—a loaf of stale bread, another jug of water. Nothing more. After the first few days, they no longer offered to sell him better rations. Raul used handfuls from this second jug to wash his face and hands. The water was always tepid, the bread stale. He wondered idly if Markus had instructed the prison cooks to add extra foul-tasting ingredients, because the bread tasted faintly off, and even the water left a sour flavor in his mouth.

After the meal came the long and lonely stretch of an empty morning. Raul paced the circuit of his cell to warm his body and loosen his muscles. Pretending he was back in Tiralien with Benedikt Ault, he drilled with an imaginary sword, fighting against the weight of his chains, and the greater weight of despair. If at times he recalled the episode when he had imprisoned Ilse, suspecting her of treason against him, he did so only fleetingly. Thinking about Ilse, about whether she still lived, was too painful. To remember how he had wronged her was worse.

Three weeks had passed since they had locked him in this cell. The guards came twice a day with bread, several more times with water. They never spoke—orders from the king, or Markus Khandarr—but their sidelong glances were eloquent.

I am a dead man. The only question is when I stop breathing.

He had expected Armand to execute him at once. Then a week had passed with no visitors except the silent guards. Five days ago, Markus Khandarr had appeared to question him.

Raul left off his drill and rubbed the bruises on his arms.

Khandarr used magic to bind Raul—thick strands of magic that held him immobile, while Khandarr paced around the cell, thumping his staff against the floor, asking Raul the same questions over and over in that slurred and halting voice.

"When did you betray. The king. You did. No lies."

"Where is that bitch. That slut. The one from Morennioù."

"The girl. What happened to her. Not dead. I know."

And, "Tell me. Tell me. Speak. Do not shut your eyes."

Each time, Raul gave the same answers. "I never betrayed Armand. I never betrayed Veraene. I do not know where Valara Baussay is. I have done nothing wrong."

What he said made no difference. It was as though Markus were deaf to his words. Or that he used these relentless questions to batter at Raul, because true weapons had been denied him. The interrogation was nothing, Raul told himself. He suffered nothing except a few bruises, and after an hour Khandarr stalked away, but each session left Raul sweating and limp.

Enough. He launched himself into a new set of drill patterns, skewering his imaginary opponent. With each thrust, he cursed himself. For hiding in Tiralien three years while Markus Khandarr terrorized court and kingdom. For sending Dedrick to Duenne instead of confronting Armand himself and arguing openly for peace. He was an arrogant coward, and if the gods did not grant him the opportunity to make things right in this life—

He broke off at a familiar *thump, thump, thump* from down the corridor. Markus. Raul sucked in a breath. The hour was later than he had guessed.

The thumping grew louder, more irregular. Raul wiped the sweat from his face with his shirt hem. As the door opened, he straightened up to face his enemy.

Khandarr stumped inside. He was alone, without even the usual guard. Not that he needed one. The chains and magic were enough.

He gestured. Magic flung Raul against the wall, arms and legs pinned against the stone. He hated this, hated how the man exposed him. He had to swallow several times to keep from spewing onto the ground. He managed it, just, but his belly shivered with the effort.

"Confess," Khandarr said. "Confess to treason."

"Markus, I cannot—"

"Confess. Tell the truth. All of it."

Ah, there Markus had him.

The truth. The truth is that I wanted influence. I wanted to guide the king and his kingdom. I believed myself right. I still believe so. If that is treason, then I am a traitor.

He closed his eyes and hung from the magic bonds. He had no more courage to offer up. If Armand wished to execute him, he would.

He heard the shuffle of feet over stone as Markus approached. A hand brushed over his forehead, pushing the damp hair back. Was he gloating?

"The king believes you guilty."

"Then why hasn't he executed me? Why haven't you?"

The hand paused in mid-caress. "I will. Now if you wish."

The magic tightened around Raul's throat. A weight pressed against his chest, and the air turned dark. Above the roaring in his ears, he heard a voice rap out a sharp command.

"Stop."

Abruptly, the magic vanished. Raul dropped to his hands and knees. Blood pulsed at his temples. He had the vague impression of voices arguing over him. One pair of boots—Khandarr's—retreated while another pair took its place. The newcomer bent down and wiped his face with a cloth. Other boots gathered around. He was lifted up to sitting.

His vision was blurred, but he distinctly recognized his sister Heloïse, next to his father. Impossible. He had last seen her eight years ago, a skinny girl who declared she would have nothing to do with him or politics. She was more right than she knew. He let his eyelids sink shut and shuddered as the magic leaked away.

A hand jostled his shoulder. "Raul. Wake up."

His father crouched next to him. Two attendants dressed in the Kosenmark livery hovered in the background, but there was no sign of Heloïse. Perhaps he had imagined his sister. Perhaps he was still lost in a fantasy conjured up by Markus Khandarr.

His father shook his shoulder again. "Listen," he said intently. "The king has granted me permission to speak with you. But only for one hour."

He pressed a flask to Raul's mouth. Wine, unwatered.

"You want me drunk?" Raul said. His voice came out as a hoarse high whisper.

"Hardly. That was autumn wine. Take another swallow and we can talk."

Raul obediently gulped down another mouthful of the sweet wine. It softened the constant ache he had not realized enveloped him. His head cleared and he could pay proper attention now.

"Tell me who died," he said. "I need to know that first."

His father glanced upward, then to either side.

Of course. The cells would have listening devices. They could talk but only with great care.

"Two of your company died," his father said. "Kappel and Theiss. We nearly lost Ault as well, but the king sent his own physician. He will mend, though slowly."

"What of . . ." He dared not mention the names of those other guards, the ones he had relied upon to carry word back to Tiralien, in case his plans failed.

"The rest of your company is safe," his father said.

"And my friends?"

His shadow court. Emma and Benno. Eckard. Ilse.

His father shook his head. "We can talk about them later. Are you hungry?"

An obvious deflection, but he found he was not ready to hear more bad news. "Starving."

"So I suspected."

His father signaled. The attendants came forward with a tray of meat pastries, a flask of broth, and a vast dish of noodles seasoned with bits of spiced lamb. At the duke's command, they set a tray on the cell floor next to Raul and withdrew. Raul ate slowly, savoring each mouthful, as he listened to his father's report of the past three weeks.

News of Dzavek's death had arrived, as expected. Károví was in turmoil, with various factions maneuvering for control. The most disturbing detail was a rumor that Dzavek's senior general and commander of the armies, Duke Miro Karasek, had vanished days after he received a summons from the council. There were further reports of two women who had attached themselves to Karasek's household. They, too, had disappeared.

Ilse. Ilse and Valara Baussay. I was right.

"As for you," his father said. "The king agreed to a public trial."

Raul paused in devouring the noodles. "He does? He believes me innocent?"

"Oh, no. I had to threaten him before he would agree." Duke Kosenmark's lips drew back from his teeth in a feral grin. "Lord Khandarr wants you dead. He's presented evidence, or so he claims, of your treason. Armand might believe him, but he cannot afford to divide his court or his kingdom. So. The trial starts in ten days. I have insisted on a proper examination of the evidence. Witnesses to your character, and your activities these past six years." The grin faded. "We have some difficulties, however. We . . . We cannot act as freely as I would wish. Letters, for example, must be reviewed by Lord Khandarr. All interviews are subject to his approval. And he has rejected several witnesses as unsuitable or unreliable."

Raul finished off the wine and set the flagon aside. "That is not good. What else?"

"There is not much more to tell. Lord Khandarr, on the king's authority, has sent out warrants for the arrest of various . . . how did he phrase it . . . persons suspected of consorting with the enemy. He intends to hold them until the outcome of your trial. Then there are those such as Lord Joannis in Fortezzien, who deny having had any dealings with you."

Raul drew a sharp breath. He ought to have expected betrayal. But Joannis. Someone who had written so frequently and so passionately about peace.

Ah, Nicol. I should have guessed you were afraid. You told me as much a year ago. I only hope you have not betrayed anyone else.

"Have any others died because of me?" he asked.

"Many of your friends have seemingly vanished."

"How many?" Raul repeated. "Three? Five? A hundred?"

His father closed his eyes. His mouth settled in thin unhappy lines, sending a cascade of folds and wrinkles over his face. It gave Raul a sudden shock to see, clearly see, how his father had aged in the past six years.

"No word from Tiralien," his father said softly. "Khandarr has set a watch on both cities, but I believe all your friends there are safe. I cannot say the same for Melnek or Fortezzien. The king insists there will be no secret murders, but you and I know better. My guess, since you ask, is more than a dozen, less than a hundred."

Raul bent over his knees, weeping softly for the dead.

His father laid a gentle hand on his shoulder. "I am sorry."

"So am I. I am sorry I led my people into death."

"The legacy of the commander," his father said softly. "I know it well."

They were silent a moment.

Then, Raul asked, "What of our family? I thought I saw—"

"Heloïse? You did. She and your other sisters are in Duenne. They would visit you, but the king will not allow it. He only permitted Heloïse to accompany me, to see for herself that you lived, and only after a very long negotiation. Your brother remains at home, your mother, too. In case they need to defend our lands."

He paused, and glanced toward the airshaft, as though he could read the passing hours there. "There is one more thing. Not a public matter, though I care not who knows it. But I must . . . I wish . . . Raul, I am sorry."

Raul jerked his head up. "Why?"

His father kept his gaze fixed on the stone walls of the cell, and when at last he spoke, his voice strained with unexpected emotion. "Because I planted ambition in your heart, even before you were aware of it. Because I did not forbid you to fulfill Baerne's demands, though I knew how it could . . . how it would damage your future."

"It was not your fault," Raul said. "You had no choice—"

He stopped, suddenly aware of what his father had not explicitly said.

"I could have stopped you," his father replied. "I could have denied the mage surgeon. I might have sent word to the king, refusing to submit to his demands. Even better, I could have demanded a public audience to announce my disgust and dismay at his tactics. I did not, because I was ambitious, too."

He bent down and kissed his son on his forehead.

"I love you," he said. "I'm sorry."

He did not ask for forgiveness, nor did Raul offer it.

CHAPTER EIGHTEEN

THE RAIN HAD started early that morning, a heavy, soaking downpour that continued throughout the day and well into the evening. Ehren Zhalina had noted its arrival in passing when he breakfasted. A typical autumn storm, which would pass soon enough. He woke long before sunrise most days, but today the skies had remained as gray as a winter's evening and water streamed without pause over the walls and windows of Zhalina house. Here in his office, once his father's domain, he had closed the shutters against the damp, but he could not shut out the rill of water over stone. Its silver-dotted song reminded him of water flutes, and of another autumn night three years before, when his father still lived, and his sister . . .

My father and sister are dead.

He struck a line through his last calculation, then set the pen aside and chafed his hands together. It was the turning point between seasons, here on the border between Veraene and Károví. A chill penetrated brick and stone, despite the generous fires in every hearth, and the air carried a dank, damp scent. His head ached from too many hours bent over these books. If he had returned to Duenne, to university, he would have expected hours just as long, in a bare uncomfortable cubicle. The knowledge did little to comfort him.

Darkness ticked down suddenly. Night already. Ehren lit another branch of candles, then settled back into his chair. Contracts, always contracts. The issue of new fees demanded by the shipping guild, in response to the king's demands for new fees regarding ports and highway maintenance. The rumors of war, ever present, had intensified in the past few months, and the autumn negotiations reflected the merchants' fretfulness. Ehren had just recaptured his focus on the subject, when he heard a soft tapping at his door.

"Yes?"

His senior runner, Váná Gersi, opened the door. "Maester Zhalina? A message has come for you."

Metz or Pribyl, Ehren thought. He wasn't surprised. Both were newer merchant houses with much to gain, and far more to lose, in the coming contract negotiations. "Do they want an answer tonight, do you know?"

"As soon as you can, Maester Zhalina."

Ehren held out his hand for the message. Gersi hesitated only a moment before he handed over a small square of paper.

A shock of magic stung Ehren's palm. He dropped the paper onto his desk and stared at his runner. "Who gave this to you?"

"The stable master," Gersi said. "He received it from a person he knows."

A man the stable master recognized? Impossible, Ehren thought. None of his colleagues or acquaintances practiced magic. Except Gersi himself seemed unsettled, and by more than the presence of magic.

"Wait outside," he said. "I shall send for you when I have an answer."

Gersi silently withdrew. Ehren rubbed his mouth. He could smell the traces of magic—so strong, so green, as if someone had crushed a handful of new grass under his nose.

Petr Zhalina had never allowed magic within the household—he declared the money better spent on ordinary measures, but Ehren Zhalina had encountered magic aplenty the year he studied at Duenne's university. He knew there were a dozen or so spells used in everyday commerce—spells to light candles or spark a fire, spells to warm hands or ease a child to sleep. The one most commonly used by scholars and diplomats was a spell to seal a letter against anyone except the intended recipient. It did not require great skill, but it was impossible for strangers to use.

Someone who knows me sent me this letter. Gersi knows them, as well. And the stable master . . .

With a shudder, he took up the letter once more. The paper was cheap, discolored by grease and smoke, the flap ragged, as though the sender had torn the page from a larger sheet. A rusty red blotch at one corner could have been blood or wine, or the imprint left by a mug to anchor the paper.

Ehren pressed his fingertips against its edges. Strong magic flooded through his veins—he could almost sense it taking stock of his identity. He caught a glimpse of stars against a twilit sky. The next moment, the current vanished from perception, and the paper unfolded onto his desk.

Another shock, stronger than the magic.

I know that script.

The letter was brief—only three short lines—and written in obvious haste.

Ehren, I need your help. If you agree, send word back by Váná Gersi. He knows me. So does the stable master, Eda Hanzl. If you doubt them, let me only say that my favorite book was by Tanja Duhr.

No signature, but he didn't need one.
My sister wrote this.
He called out, "Gersi, I need you."
Gersi appeared at once. In his face, Ehren read tension and a great deal of curiosity.
"Bring the sender to our best parlor," Ehren said. "No, wait a moment."
His sister had disappeared twice under strange circumstances. He could trust Gersi and Hanzl, at least he hoped he could, but it was safer if he did not involve others. "Bring my visitor here," he said. "If my wife inquires, tell her I am engaged in a matter of business."
Alone again, Ehren read the message through a second time. He needed more clues, but this blunt request for assistance offered none. Or was that a clue itself? He remembered his sister as a soft-spoken young woman, as one might expect of Petr Zhalina's daughter. She had loved their grandmother. Loved him, he believed. But this . . . She had addressed him simply by name and asked for help.
He cast the paper aside and stood, too anxious to wait patiently. Three years. He'd thought her dead once, when she ran away from Melnek. Then came a letter from the man Alarik Brandt with news that Therez lived. Thief, he called her, and worse. But he also gave the address where Petr Zhalina could find his daughter. It was a house in Tiralien, run by the notorious Lord Raul Kosenmark. Petr had set off at once to fetch his daughter away. He returned without her, and when Ehren asked, he would only say, *My daughter is gone. I met a woman named Ilse.*
The following year their father died. Ehren exchanged a few letters with Ilse, but he could tell from her excuses that she would never willingly return to Melnek. Then came another message through her agent, saying she had left Kosenmark to live in Osterling Keep. Five short months later, a courier from the regional governor of Fortezzien brought Ehren the news that an unknown man had murdered Ilse Zhalina. She had made a will leaving everything to him.
And now he discovered she was alive.
I cannot bear this. She will vanish again, I know it.
A knock at the door brought him spinning around. "Yes?"

"Your visitor, Maester Zhalina."

"Come in," he said. "Please."

The door opened. A woman entered the room. She spoke quietly to Gersi, who closed the door behind her. Ehren came around his desk, but stopped almost at once when his sister turned back to face him.

He hardly recognized her. Oh, the angles of her face had not changed, not much. She had grown no taller, and that swift tilt of her head as she took in the room and his presence was just as he remembered. But her manner—the set of her lips, the way she met his gaze directly and without a trace of hesitation or shyness—it was as though a different mind inhabited the woman who stood before him.

"Therez . . ."

"Ilse. My name is Ilse."

Her voice was low and rough. Angry.

Ehren checked his own quick reply.

She has good reason to be angry with all of us.

And yet, she had come to him, told him she needed his help.

They studied each other a few moments. Ehren took in more of her appearance, more details that spoke of the years they had spent apart, and of a history he could not begin to guess at. Her hair was plaited into a single braid, leaving only a few wisps around her face. She wore loose trousers of some sturdy brown material tucked into low boots, a quilted jacket in the northern style, and gloves. The boots were scuffed, the heels worn. Her clothing had obviously seen much wear. And yet his merchant's eye could see it was all of good quality. As she drew off her hood, he caught a glimpse of a wide leather band around her wrist.

A knife sheath.

When had she learned to wield a knife? From that Lord Kosenmark? And there was the matter of her magic, another alien skill.

With an effort he recalled himself. "What do you need?"

It was the right thing to say, and the wrong one. Therez—Ilse, he reminded himself—drew an audible breath. "I need your help, Ehren."

She was clearly uncomfortable here, in what had been their father's office. "Would you rather we went to my rooms?" he said.

"No." The tension in her mouth flickered back to life. "Your people will see too much. I do not wish to bring trouble to your house. At least, no more than I already have."

"Then I will send Gersi for refreshment. We can eat and talk here."

She made no objection. Ehren went to the door, where his runner stood guard. "Go to the kitchens," he told Gersi. "Have them send mulled wine, tea, cold meat, and soup."

When he turned back, he found his sister had removed her jacket and gloves and placed them on the hearth where they might dry. She stood close to the fire, rubbing her hands together. Just as he suspected, she wore a belt hung with more weapons—another knife, even a sword.

Her face averted from his, Ilse spoke. "I hated you. You. Our mother. Even our grandmother. Especially you and Grandmother. Oh, I knew it was because *he* trapped us all, but I hated that you and she did nothing. And that night, when I came to you—"

She rounded on him so quickly he flinched.

"You are afraid of me?" she asked.

Ehren swallowed, tasted the magic lingering in the air. "I am afraid of your anger. And mine."

Ilse stared at him, her eyes far too bright. Then the hard lines of her mouth softened to more familiar ones. "So am I. So am I. It reminds me too much of our father."

So she is not the only one.

A soft knock announced Gersi's return. Ehren admitted the man, who carried a heavy tray with various carafes and covered baskets. In addition to the dishes Ehren had requested, there was a carafe of cold water, and baskets of dried fruit and meat pies. "Thank you," Ehren said. "We shall serve ourselves."

Gersi withdrew. Ehren poured two cups of mulled wine and gave his sister one. Ilse. Not Therez. With every repetition, the name came more naturally. She drank the wine, but when he offered her a plate of meat pies, she refused. "I am not starved, only wet and cold."

An answer that provoked only more questions to Ehren. He took a meat pie for himself—it would serve well enough for dinner—and gestured toward a low table set around with padded chairs.

It was a fortunate suggestion. Away from the desk, once their father's, her manner eased.

"So you wrote," he said. "Tell me the rest. If you can."

Ilse gave a smothered laugh. "Oh, so much happened. So much, Ehren."

From the sound of her voice, he thought she might break into tears. He fetched the wine carafe and refilled their cups. Ilse accepted the cup, but did not drink. She turned it around and around in her hands, staring into the dark red liquid. The rain had fallen off in the past few moments, but the rippling of water over stone and glass continued.

"I ran away," she said softly. "I could not marry Galt. By now you should know why."

He nodded. Galt had visited them the week after Ilse fled. He had demanded recompense for the broken contract, even though no contract had been signed. Petr Zhalina attempted to negotiate better terms. Galt refused. Only later, when rumors of Galt's previous engagement, and the reasons for its dissolution, became public knowledge, did he withdraw his demands. It had not stopped Galt from working against House Zhalina in business, but the private threats had ceased.

"And so I went south," she said. "It was not an easy journey."

Brandt and the caravan and all that implied. Ehren knew them from Brandt's letter, his father's own investigations, and rumors that came north. "You took service with Lord Raul Kosenmark," he said.

If he thought she would then talk about Kosenmark and her time with him, he had mistaken her. She passed a hand over her eyes, trembling. Just a moment, then she met his gaze with that new assurance that so unnerved him.

"We met with difficulties with Lord Khandarr," she said. "He threatened me, and so I left. Not long after that various . . . events overtook me. It's best if you don't know—"

"So say you," he murmured.

She acknowledged the strike home with a nod. "So I say. And that is all I *can* say for now. Ehren, I must find Lord Kosenmark. I *must*."

"Why come to me then?" he asked. "You know I have no connection to the man. How can I help?"

"Baron Eckard," she said. "He keeps a house in Melnek. Is he in the city still?"

Ehren nodded slowly. "He is."

"And do you visit with him ever?"

Ehren thought she knew the answer to that question already. "I do."

"Khandarr will have spies watching him," Ilse said. "I hoped you might—"

"Find the means to smuggle you inside his household?"

"Yes."

Ehren took several moments to absorb the implication of her request. Of course the baron knew Lord Kosenmark. They had attended court together, one as a trusted adviser to the old king, one as a senior member of the general council. Both had departed from Duenne after Armand of Angersee inherited the throne. Clearly they continued to meddle in the kingdom's politics. Just as clearly, the king and his closest adviser knew. This was a most dangerous, deadly game.

And she wants to involve me.

Had she learned this habit, too, from Kosenmark? To ask the impossible?

"You require a great deal," he said. "And not just of me. I have a wife and our mother to care for. Soon, a child. Or perhaps your spies did not relay that particular information. It is not so important to kings and councillors after all."

Ilse gazed at him steadily. There was no accusation in her eyes, but neither any gentleness. "You are afraid."

"Of course I am."

"And angry."

He opened his mouth, shut it, and swallowed whatever he thought he might say. "A part of our inheritance," he said at last.

Her gaze never wavered, but Ehren thought he saw a flicker of acknowledgment in those dark eyes. He wished they had a season apart from duty, or these mysterious doings of high politics, to do nothing more than talk. He suspected they had had much the same ruminations over the past few years, many of the same nights spent in grief and anger at their father. At each other.

His anger leaked away, leaving him with an emptiness centered beneath his heart. It was like a wound, kept raw and tender over three long years. She had come to him. He could not turn her away a second time.

"Tell me what I must do," he said.

She studied him a moment longer, as if gauging his sincerity. "Very well," she said slowly. "I need to talk with Baron Eckard. If you could visit him—tonight. Take me in your carriage as a servant, and leave me in the stable yard. You need not do anything more."

"Tonight?"

She nodded. "I cannot wait any longer. I must find Raul as quickly as the gods allow."

THEY SPOKE IN whispers as they planned how to achieve Ilse's next goal. Memories of their father crowded close around them. More than once, Ehren glanced over his shoulder, only to laugh softly. Ilse, too, felt as though she could hear the ghostly echoes of past lectures in this room. She wondered how Ehren could bear it.

"Then the baron might not be at home," Ehren said. "What then?"

"I have the necessary passwords. His people will admit me."

"You trust them as well?"

She rubbed the back of her hand against her forehead. An incipient headache haunted her, borne of the long trek from Duszranjo through the mountains, from the even longer trek she had taken from Mantharah across Károví, always having to give her trust to others. Miro Karasek. Valara Baussay. Bela Sovic. Jannik Maier and the smugglers who brought her across the passes. She wanted nothing more than to hide in a warm dark refuge.

Not yet.

"I have no choice, Ehren. Or rather, none better."

"You might stay with us. A day or two—"

"No," she said softly. "I'm sorry, but no. Never here."

He tilted a hand to one side, a silent acknowledgment of their shared history. "Then I shall have Gersi and Hanzl prepare the carriage."

They reviewed possible excuses for Ehren to pay Baron Eckard a visit. "How often do you meet?" Ilse asked him.

"Once, twice a month. But always at public affairs, hardly ever in private."

She pressed her lips together, considering. "Do you and he discuss business? Is there something of note you might want to confer with him about?"

He shook his head. "Nothing. Wait. I might send a letter, an invitation to a small dinner party. A few others in the merchant guild are worried about trade embargoes with Károví and Immatra. He might have advice on how to apply to the king's councillors."

"Armand won't agree."

"I know. We sent a delegation last month. The king refused to grant them an audience. Theodr Galt himself went to Duenne on behalf of the shipping guild, but I doubt if he'll have more success. We need to acquire the right connections in court. That gives me an excuse to bring the invitation myself and speak with Baron Eckard."

A few more details debated. Within half an hour, Ilse had resumed her jacket, gloves, and hood and followed Gersi back through the servant corridors to the side lane where she climbed into a carriage. Gersi himself, dressed in livery, took the reins. They drove around front, where Ehren climbed in.

A short journey followed, during which brother and sister did not speak. It was as though they had touched upon all the important topics, and it only remained for them to sit in a new and strangely companionable silence. *What more need they say?* Ilse thought. She had come to her brother and asked a great favor. He had agreed at once. He was making recompense for his earlier neglect, she understood. To say more, to ask about their mother, his new wife, the child they expected, seemed false and forced.

Later, she thought, *I will send him a letter and ask. If I survive, that is . . .*

The carriage slowed, then turned into a paved circle before a typically elegant mansion, its face a blank wall of stone, interrupted by square windows illuminated by lamplight. Ehren disembarked and went to the front door. A few moments, and a servant admitted him.

The next step achieved. Ilse leaned back into the cushions, as Gersi drove the carriage around to a walled courtyard in back of the house. Here, a team of stable boys released the horses from their harness and brought them under the roof. Gersi himself handed Ilse down from the carriage. She scanned the yard. The rain had died off, but rivulets ran between the paving stones, gleaming silver in the lamplight from the stables.

"I must speak with a man named Amsel," she said. "Relay that message exactly, please."

Gersi nodded and went to pass on the name to the stable master. Very soon, an older runner appeared, dressed in formal livery, and carrying a shaded lamp. "You asked for me?" he said to Ilse.

He spoke plainly. No "Mistress" or "My lady." No excessive eagerness to please her. Good. So far, the code words had produced the expected response.

"I came to inquire about a position in the baron's household," she said. "I understand he prefers someone with a knowledge of swordplay."

A twitch at the man's mouth betrayed his interest. He let his gaze travel over her, a clearly impersonal assessment of her clothing, her weapons, and the manner in which she carried herself. "What manner of swordplay?"

"The most dangerous kind."

Another twitch. Another examination of her person. "That might be possible. Perhaps you should speak with the baron after all. Come with me, please."

Ilse followed Amsel through the stables, along a narrow corridor lit by infrequent torches, which brought them after several turns to a small windowless parlor. The air was chill and damp, but a thick carpet covered the tiled floor, and several richly embroidered hangings decorated the walls. One carved chair occupied a corner nearest the empty fireplace.

Amsel fetched a torch to light a branch of candles. "Do you wish a fire?"

"It's not necessary," Ilse said.

She took a seat, but as soon as the door closed, she jumped to her feet to pace the room. So, so, so. She was home again. Home meaning Veraene, not Melnek. Only, she had felt an odd pang, seeing Ehren once more, and riding with him through the familiar streets. It was like reading a long-abandoned, almost forgotten book, and finding that certain passages were not terrible, and some even comforting to return to. She allowed herself to dwell on those passages as she waited. Outside, the hour bells rang, followed by the quarter hour.

Two quarter bells sounded before the door opened, and Baron Eckard hurried into the room. He breathed heavily, as though he had been running.

At the sight of her, he stopped and wiped a hand over his eyes, as though he could not trust what he saw. "Mistress Ilse," he whispered. "It *is* you. Amsel said a stranger came in Maester Zhalina's carriage. He gave no names, only that she offered the old passwords. I am sorry I could not come at once. Your brother stayed with me only a few moments, but I had another guest . . . Never mind about that. I am more glad than I can express to see you. What do you need?"

"Money," she said at once. "And a fast horse. I must get to Tiralien. I have news from Károví that Raul must hear."

"Good news, or . . ."

She shook her head. "Complicated news."

Eckard's mouth quirked in wry understanding. "It always is." Then his expression turned grave. "I've heard nothing from Raul these past few months—nothing official that is. He last wrote from Tiralien, a very public letter inquiring after my health, and describing a pleasure cruise he had taken along the southern coast."

Very odd, she thought. Only not entirely unexpected. Raul must have hoped to revive the story that his shadow court no longer existed. "Then I go to Tiralien, as planned. Can you help me?"

"Of course. I shall have to make arrangements with my people. You will have whatever you require tomorrow morning. Is that soon enough?"

"This very moment is not soon enough," she said. "But unless the gods transport me themselves, I will have to make do with tomorrow."

His answer was a rueful smile. "I've often made the same wish myself. At least I can provide you with a room for tonight, and the rest by morning. Come with me. I shall have the servants prepare a bed and fire. A meal, too, if you wish . . ."

Eckard continue to speak as they left the parlor and entered yet another corridor, with stairs at the end. Doors lined its length, most of them closed, but one or two opened into darkened sitting rooms.

"My people are quiet," Eckard was saying. "Quiet and discreet . . ."

"As discreet as I am, my friend."

Baron Mann emerged from behind one of the open doors.

Ilse's hand went to the knife at her wrist. Eckard eyed his friend with disfavor. "I am quite certain I saw you to the door, Josef. How is it that you are here? And without any notice from the servants?" he added under his breath.

Mann waved his hand in a dismissive gesture. "Do not blame your servants. I returned the moment I discovered I had left my gloves behind. There was no need to bother you, I told them. They were quite helpful, and went in search of my mythical gloves, leaving me unattended for a short interval. My dear and dishonest friend, did you truly think I never noticed the connection between you and Lord Kosenmark? You are very discreet, your servants as well, but the strange coincidence of Maester Ehren Zhalina's visit, and on such an unpleasant evening, together with that almost unobtrusive message delivered to you shortly after his arrival did make me suspicious. And I was right to be."

"What do you want?" Ilse asked him.

His mouth twisted into a smile. "Oh, what I would propose is very improper. So much that you would surely take offense and stab me with those knives you carry at your belt and beneath your sleeves."

She suppressed a flinch at his observations.

Mann noticed that as well, and smirked. "Mistress Therez, who is now Mistress Ilse, let me confess what I do know, from which you can decide whether to trust me. You have come to the baron's house by secret ways. You would return to your beloved, Lord Kosenmark. I do not need to know the reasons for that particular conversation. I would like, however, to know what you intend for Veraene."

Ilse expelled a breath. This, this was not the demand she had expected from a man like Baron Mann.

"You appear surprised," Mann said.

"Surprised by the unexpected," she replied. "What do you care about Veraene?"

"She is my home," he said. "I want her kept whole and sound."

"That is my wish as well."

"Then you will not dispute my motives."

"No. But I might dispute your definition of what is best for the kingdom."

He laughed. "Very well argued. I should expect as much from the girl I met three years ago. Do you wish me to pretend ignorance, or will you accept my help?"

"This is no game, Josef," Eckard said sharply. "You do not understand the danger."

"I understand very well."

Ilse pressed her lips together, watching Mann's face. He had known about Eckard's connection to Lord Kosenmark's shadow court, and said nothing. He had suspected her break with Raul to be false. Again, he had not betrayed her.

"What do you want?" she asked.

He regarded her with a long amused look. "You would not believe me if I said the truth. Therefore, let us pretend my wishes and motivations are unimportant, and that only yours count. What do you want, Mistress Ilse?"

She did not mistake his easy manner for disinterest. He cared, and did not dare to admit it.

"I want peace," she said. "I want my home secure."

He nodded, as though he had expected such an answer.

"Then let me help you. I've heard the rumors about Lord Kosenmark and his colleagues, one of whom is my dear friend Rudolfus. Others have heard those rumors and watch this house. You were most likely not observed, because you showed sense and caution, but you will have taken even greater care to enter Tiralien. Let me offer my services."

"Such as?" Eckard said.

"Such as a swift and anonymous passage. But let us continue this discussion in quieter regions."

Eckard and Ilse exchanged glances.

Do you trust him?

Not completely. But what choice do we have?

Mann's smile lengthened. "You are both so obvious with your suspicions. Very well. Let me be more precise. Mistress Ilse wishes to reach Tiralien and Lord Kosenmark as soon as possible. No, do not pretend to misunderstand. Let us assume I am correct, and that you are too modest to disagree. So, Lord Kosenmark, Tiralien, and the necessity for both speed and discretion. That is straightforward enough. The season is late, here in Melnek. I shall hire a boat for a pleasure cruise along the coastline to the southern provinces. I will break my journey in Tiralien on a whim, or the need to restock my supply of good wine. I am famous for that, as you well know."

"That I do," Eckard said softly. "I wonder how much else I should know."

"Little else," Mann said. "Not that you would believe me. You know my reputation. I am shallow and frivolous. Lord Khandarr himself would agree."

"If Lord Khandarr disbelieves you, you die," Ilse said.

"I knew that before," Mann replied.

Ilse glanced from one man to another. Both nodded.

She drew a long breath. "Very well, as you say. Let us proceed."

MANN'S VEHICLE WAITED outside the stables with the driver and horses ready. Ilse climbed in, and the driver brought it around to the front courtyard, where Mann embarked. At his signal, the driver urged the horses through the gates and into the streets of Melnek.

Ilse expected Mann to speak, but his volubility had died away in that short interval since her farewell to Eckard. He sat, his face turned to the window. There was a half moon rising over the northern hills, but clouds obscured its light, with only intermittent flashes from the streetlamps to show the ironic smile on Mann's lips, and the way his gaze seemed to look far beyond the dark streets rolling past.

"Why are you doing this?" she asked.

"I told you why."

"One reason. Not all of them."

Mann shrugged. "Very well. Then let us say I did so because I wish to."

"That is not enough."

At her sharp tone, he shifted his gaze toward hers, and by the chance gleam of another streetlamp, she could see that he smiled. "You were always insistent. I noticed that from the moment we met in your father's house, three years ago. Very well. I know our court and king. Also, your Lord Kosenmark. His methods are not mine, but I have come to see that even an imperfect alliance is better than none."

"But you aren't—"

"A political creature? No, I am not. I *am* a citizen of Veraene, no matter how frivolous you believe me. And I should not care for the dreams I should have in future lives if I were offered the choice of acting in good cause and did not."

He turned his face back toward the window of his carriage, staring out at the blankness of the night. As if, she thought, he had spent all his conversation in that one confession.

She let her gaze drop to her hands, clasped one within the other, and let her thoughts drift in silence as they rode.

CHAPTER NINETEEN

ILSE SPENT THE night in a servant's room, tucked under the eaves of Mann's elegant city house. Preparations for the journey would require at least two days, he told her. She had to admire how he combined attention to her needs with what had to be an innate sense of discretion, worthy of the best spies she had known. On their arrival, Mann summoned the servant who would see to all her needs. Within the hour, she had a stack of freshly laundered bedding, a bucket of hot coals to warm the room, and a tray with hot tea, bread, and thick soup, cooked just as she remembered from years before, when she and her brother secretly visited the servant's quarters.

Through the next morning, she read the well-thumbed books Mann supplied to her via the old servant, but even though she immersed herself in antique romances from the empire days, she found her thoughts flitting back over the past two weeks. To Ryz and Maryshka Rudny. To Jannik Maier and Bela Sovic, and whether they had survived that violent encounter with Károvín soldiers.

To Damek Rudny.

I remember him now. I remember . . .

A dark night with only a new moon. A ship plunging through high seas. A wounded boy that she tended for weary hours in the hold. Though the details from that life were fragmented and blurred, she recalled one thing with certainty. That other boy had survived. She hoped Damek Rudny had as well.

Evening had fallen when Mann appeared at her door. "We sail with the morning tide. However, I'd like you on board tonight."

"Why?" she said. "What has happened?"

"Such suspicion," he replied. "Nothing has 'happened,' as you phrase it. My secretary procured a ship by chance this morning, from a captain who had arrived lately in port. I would think you would be overjoyed."

He vanished before she could reply. The next moment, the old servant came with a complete set of new clothing. Plain dark trousers, sturdy leather boots, a tunic and sleeveless jacket embroidered with Mann's coat of arms. So she was to play the part of a guard. That would do, yes, that would serve very well.

She dressed in her new clothes, bound her hair in a tight military braid, and transferred her weapons into new sheaths. The servant brought her down the same narrow staircase to a door opening onto a narrow lane, where one of the genuine guards waited, along with two horses. The skies were dark blue, and streamers of mist rippled over the cobblestones, which gleamed wet from a recent rainfall.

Down by the docks, a crew and ship waited. Ilse embarked and was shown to the cabin reserved for Mann's guards. The ship itself was a swift-sailing craft, equipped with a luxurious private room for Mann, and generous space for his many servants and guards. Ilse spent a restless night and was up before dawn, in time to see Mann's own elegant carriage arrive, followed by two more guards, and a wagon with Mann's trunks and a crew of servants. It did not take Ilse long to note how the servants carried themselves as soldiers would.

"Did you send me ahead to guard the ship?" she asked, when he came on board.

"That is your task, is it not?" he said. In a softer voice, he added, "One of my servants reported an attempt at bribery. The questioner wished to know the extent of my friendship with Baron Eckard."

"And?" she said.

"That is all I know."

He would not answer more questions and set her to overseeing the disposition of his trunks in the hold. By the time she came above decks once more, the ship had left port and Melnek's towers were nothing more than an irregular silhouette on the horizon.

What followed were nine days of sailing through wine-dark seas, etched with silver foam. No storms. No difficulties with tides or countertides. It was like running upon a river of ice, with steel blades that neither stuck nor faltered. Nine days spent in silent conversation with herself to contemplate how to report on what transpired in Károví.

THEY ARRIVED IN Tiralien's outer sea lanes at midnight. A patrol ship met them as they approached the harbor. Ilse woke at once, but stayed in her cabin, listening.

One gruff voice called a challenge in the king's name. The captain of Mann's ship answered. Ilse could not follow the words themselves, but she recognized the pattern of official challenge and response. She lay with one hand on her sword hilt as footsteps rattled over the deck. Sooner than she expected, they retreated. Several long moments later, the captain opened the hatch to below.

"All clear. Inspection tomorrow when we dock."

Much later that following morning, the ship glided through the harbor to the docks reserved for temporary visitors. Ilse was awake this time, properly dosed with strong coffee, and waiting dressed in Baron Mann's livery as they approached the shore.

She had come this way once before, in Raul Kosenmark's private ship. This . . . this was much different. She noted all the details that had escaped her that other time—the barges and packets crowding the waters, small craft like their own that served as courier vessels, the royal battle ships that claimed a quadrant of their own, the steps upon steps of warehouses rising upward to the city itself. And there, upon the northern shore, Lord Vieth's palace, which stood not a mile above Raul Kosenmark's pleasure house.

Home, my love. Home and with news.

She swallowed her impatience. It was easier, once they approached the docks. Royal soldiers swarmed the shore, all of them armed with swords and magic. She wanted to meet Raul freely, not plunge him into fresh difficulties.

And so she stood at attention with the other guards, as the captain for Mann's ship presented his papers to the port officials. Mann himself stood off to one side, while his servants busied themselves packing a trunk with clothing and essentials for the baron's stay in the city. The officers questioned Mann—obliquely. He answered airily that he needed more wine for the voyage. He expected he would make several more stops before he reached his destination. Which was . . . ?

Mann shrugged. Fortezzien was too restless, he opined. Pommersien too wet and subject to disease. Perhaps a brief stay in Klee would suffice. He disliked strict plans. Whatever else, wherever else he visited, he would need two, possibly three days in Tiralien to replenish his supplies. Surely they understood.

The port officials rolled their eyes. The royal soldiers turned away, clearly uninterested.

Ilse let her breath trickle out. The next obstacle overcome.

Hired horses and a carriage brought them to a nearby inn, where Mann obtained several rooms for himself, his guards, and his servants. In passing, he ordered Ilse and another guard to accompany him to his suite, where he wished to discuss their plans for this interval.

Once the outer door closed, the true guard took her position before it, hand on weapon. Mann and Ilse retired into his bedchamber. "My apologies for the appearance," Mann said. "What comes next?"

She had thought through everything during the voyage from Melnek. "We write a letter and send it through the usual channels. If he can, he will arrange a meeting."

"And what are those usual channels?"

Another point she had spent hours considering. Ilse remembered every name from Raul's list of trusted agents. Over a year had passed since Markus Khandarr forced Raul to abandon his shadow court, however, and during their last, brief interlude together, Raul had mentioned how many had changed their loyalty, convinced by bribes or simply fear of the King's Mage Councillor. There was one Raul still trusted.

Isaac Haas. A bookseller, who specialized in rare books. Letters came to his shop, delivered through other messengers. Haas then delivered the letters under the cover of offering selected volumes for Lord Kosenmark's perusal, just as he did for his ordinary customers.

It was a risk. She had to take it.

"Let me write a letter," she told Mann. "Then I can give you directions where and how to deliver it."

She wrote a brief note, couched in vague terms, about Baron Mann's interest in acquiring books from the empire period, especially those concerning the poet Tanja Duhr. The baron would like to view Haas's merchandise, and could Haas arrange an appointment to discuss the matter without interruption. She used the code phrases to indicate news of political importance, the necessity for speed and secrecy, and a request for a private meeting.

Ilse pressed a blotting paper over the ink. Her hands were steady, but her pulse was beating far too rapidly for comfort. *Soon, soon, soon.* For so long she had contained all her emotions, driven by the necessities of the moment. Now that she was on the verge of being reunited with Raul, she could hardly bear it. Oh, there was much more to be done, but once she and Raul were together, everything else seemed effortless.

She folded the sheet in thirds and sealed it with wax alone.

"No magic?" Mann asked.

"Why do you believe I know magic?"

His smile was wistful, almost. "Why would I believe anything impossible for you?"

She shook her head. She wanted no compliments, not from this man. She wanted Raul. To speak with him of matters political and mundane, to sit in silence when silence gave them comfort, to feel that sense of completion in his company.

Mann observed her, still with that same pensive air. "My apologies," he said softly. "I spoke without thought."

"So you did."

He laughed, albeit painfully. "The kitten bites. I see the shadow of a lioness beyond. My apologies again, Mistress Ilse." He touched a hand to his forehead, thence to his breast. "I serve you with heart and spirit, with the last breath of this life, and the first of my next."

Ilse had no answer for such extravagance, especially when she sensed the extravagance served to disguise his own greater emotions. She handed him the letter, and gave him instructions on where and how to have it delivered.

Mann departed to summon a runner. When he returned, he asked, "Are you hungry?"

She shook her head.

"Then you must be tired. Not even that? A lesser man might believe you disliked his company, or preferred another's to his own, but as you know, I am both arrogant and self-centered. And so I conclude you must be weary of life itself. Therefore, we shall play cards."

She stifled a laugh at his nonsense, but her laughter verged on tears. Mann had the grace to ignore her distress. He produced a deck of cards from within one sleeve and laid them out in a complicated pattern.

"Do you know the game of Victory?" he asked.

She did not.

He explained the rules of play, and a few key points of strategy. It was a game with complicated rules, played with a specially painted set of cards, but one that absorbed her attention more than she thought possible. They played until midnight. Ilse won a dozen hands. Mann won several others, and the rest were draws.

"You are gifted with strategy," he observed as he shuffled the cards for another round.

She shook her head. "Hardly. If anything, I have had good tutors."

"A good tutor can only supply the finish to what already exists. One more hand, then we are done for the night."

Ilse won that round, and this time, she was certain she had done it herself.

"Until tomorrow," Mann said. He bowed and kissed her fingertips.

Ilse permitted the gallantry, amused at last by his foolery, which she finally understood masked an entirely different kind of man. "You should court my friend Klara," she said.

He smiled. "Perhaps I shall."

SHE WOKE AT dawn when Agneth Friesz, the senior guard, came to rouse Ilse and the other guard for early-morning watch. Ilse rose and dressed in her new uniform, but she suspected that Mann, playing the role of an indolent noble, would not make his appearance for several hours. A short word with Friesz confirmed there was a courtyard, next to the stables, where she might drill in private.

Four walls marked off a bare dirt yard. A lamp flickered over one doorway, and smoke rose from a chimney on the opposite side—the kitchen workers baking bread for the new day. Ilse took up the first stance, gathered her concentration, and struck into the shadows.

Over and over went the drill, until her arms ached, and her clothes were soaked in sweat. Mann came upon her an hour after sunrise. He had to repeat himself a second time before she realized it. Then, she leaned down, one hand pressed against her thigh, her sword held loosely to one side.

"Any word?" she said.

He shook his head. "Not yet. Shall we ride through the city, you and I?"

"As you wish, my lord baron."

He rubbed his hand over his mouth. "Yes, I do wish. We shall have breakfast and go."

It was midmorning before they departed, Mann, Ilse, and the younger guard. Still no word had arrived from Raul. The bookseller would first have to arrange another delivery to the pleasure house, which might require at least another day. Reluctantly she submitted to a tour of Tiralien, starting at the docks, going past Lord Vieth's palace, and through a pleasant avenue lined by shops. Once she had starved here. Once she had almost died. She tried not to think of those early, desperate days.

She succeeded, letting Mann choose their route, until they turned into the neighborhood where Raul's pleasure house lay.

"My lord . . ."

"Softly now," Mann murmured. "We shall ride past only."

Ilse nodded, but her hands were trembling as they approached.

The pleasure house was just as she remembered—a square of golden brick, rising four stories, and surrounded by narrow lanes from its neighbors.

This early in the morning, she expected no activity, but it was impossible to miss the *emptiness* she saw. No guards at the gates or patrolling the lanes. No candles in any windows. No servants passing in and out on their errands. It was as though the house had died, and taken all its inhabitants with it.

"My lady?" This was Mann.

"You forget yourself," she murmured.

"Never. However, if you prefer, I shall call you guardswoman. So, I see what bothers you, guardswoman. A house left empty, or nearly so. I thought I saw a face in one window . . ."

"Whatever you saw, we should not stay here," Ilse said.

"Agreed. Let us continue our tour of the district. We can return to the inn for our midday meal. Undoubtedly a message will await us."

They proceeded to the next square where Mann purchased more wine, to be delivered to his ship. Ilse pretended to converse with the other guard but with only partial success. The man did not know what to make of her, she realized. She might be the baron's secret lover. She might be a connection from his court days. Better that, she thought, than what she was. If Khandarr questioned them, they could only answer with what they knew.

On their return, a servant brought Mann a letter.

"A timely response from our bookseller," he observed, reading through it. "Such diligence heartens me." To the servant, he said, "Send word back that I will visit him after I dine. I cannot bargain with an empty stomach." He gave the innkeeper orders to feed his fainting guards, and to have fresh mounts ready for their excursion.

Two hours later, Ilse and Mann arrived at Maester Haas's antiquarian shop. The bookseller waited for them, a parcel at his side. "You will find other goods in the back rooms," he said. "Do you wish to examine them yourself, my lord baron?"

"No. My guard shall do so. She is a competent woman and knows my requirements. Let us, you and I, discuss these other rare and lovely objects over a glass of wine."

Ilse barely paid attention to his last words. Her pulse was thrumming as she passed through the indicated door, to the back room where Raul waited. Ten months, three weeks, five days, since she left Tiralien. Five months since Hallau Island. She had kept an unacknowledged ledger of their time apart, as if she could present such debts to the gods.

A shaded lamp stood on a high shelf, casting light and shadows over the small room, which was piled high with wooden crates. Several of the crates were open, their contents unpacked and stacked upon a broad table next to a journal book, where someone, Maester Haas or a clerk, recorded the inventory. The air smelled of paper dust, ink, and old leather. There was no sign of Raul himself.

Ilse paused. Her hand slid to her sword hilt, her thoughts fell inward to the balance required for magic, the same balance that swordplay demanded. It could be Raul was delayed, she told herself. It could be that he, too, suspected treachery and waited until he recognized his visitor.

Then a voice behind her spoke.

"You expected Lord Kosenmark."

Ilse spun around, the sword drawn, then checked herself with a smothered cry.

Kathe Raendl came forward into the light. She was dressed in a dark blue skirt and smock. Her hair was swept back into a thick braid, wound around her head. She looked just as Ilse remembered, when they had last walked together to the market.

It took her several moments before she could speak.

"I did expect Raul. What is wrong?"

"Everything," Kathe said in a low voice. "Lord Kosenmark left us, left Tiralien the month before last. Word came back four weeks ago the king arrested him."

Arrested. Ilse closed her eyes. She barely managed to slide her sword into its sheath without dropping it. Gone to Duenne to confront the king. About what? Oh, yes. Surely he had heard from his remaining agents about Dzavek's death.

I was too slow. I ought to have dared Anderswar a second time, back in Taboresk.

She heard Kathe circle around her in slow deliberate steps. Ilse opened her eyes and regarded her old friend. Kathe stared back. Her gaze was cold and unforgiving. Her voice, when she spoke, was laced with bitterness.

"You lied to me," she said. "You and Lord Kosenmark both."

"We did. We had good reason—"

"You lied. And your beloved abandoned us with little more than a warning, and that came almost too late. Gerek . . ." Kathe pressed her hand to her throat. "Do you know," she said, her voice edging higher. "Do you know how Markus Khandarr beat my husband? Tortured him? All because he believed your Lord Kosenmark a traitor and wanted Gerek to betray the man. Even after he returned, Gerek did not dare to go beyond the grounds because he knew Lord Khandarr's agents watched the house. When the rider came with news the king had arrested Lord Kosenmark, I had to bury my husband in a barrel of garbage so he could escape the house and return to his family. So he could pretend he never met such a man as Lord Kosenmark. I wish—"

She broke off and pressed both hands over her eyes.

Ilse could not speak for a moment. "Kathe, I am sorry."

"Sorry?" Kathe gave a smothered laugh. "Oh, yes. You are sorry. But would you do the same again?"

No more secrets, Ilse thought. *Only the truth, no matter how painful.*

"I would," she said. "I would have a choice, but I would choose the same again."

Kathe uncovered her face. Her cheeks were flushed, her eyes bright with unshed tears. "For an honor higher than the king's," she said softly. "For Veraene. Yes, I understand. I should. I lived in Duenne's Court and Lord Kosenmark's house."

There was a strange finality to her words.

Ilse had to make one last effort. "Are you safe?"

Kathe's eyes widened. "What do you mean?"

"Are you safe?" Ilse repeated. "You and your mother, Mistress Denk, Nadine and Josef, and everyone else. Are you *safe*?"

Kathe hesitated a long moment, as though she had not expected such a question. "We are," she said at last. "Gerek is with his family. I had word he arrived safely, though I cannot tell what might happen if Lord Khandarr decides to investigate. Lord and Lady Iani have vanished. I do not know where. Many of the guards went to Valentain. The rest of us took refuge with Lord Vieth. Except for Nadine. She left the same day and did not tell anyone."

Ilse nodded slowly. "Thank you. Thank you for telling me the truth."

She turned back toward the bookseller's front room, but paused at the light tread of footsteps hurrying after her. A hand brushed against hers—a gentle gesture, its eloquence unspoken.

MANN CONCLUDED NEGOTIATIONS and a purchase from the bookseller. As he and Ilse mounted their horses, he asked, "What is wrong? You do not have the air of someone reunited with their beloved."

"He is gone," she said softly. "He went to Duenne."

Mann said nothing for several moments. "He encountered difficulties, then."

She nodded. No need to mention the king or Markus Khandarr.

"What comes next?" her companion asked.

"I don't know. All his friends have . . . disappeared."

Mann blinked. "Disappeared? Or merely inaccessible?"

"I don't know."

"That is a different matter. Then, if I might suggest, let us return to the inn, where we can plan your next venture."

They took an easy pace through Tiralien's main avenues, which were crowded with carts and carriages this afternoon. Mann suggested a detour into the Little University, including a visit to the house where Tanja Duhr's most famous archivist once lived. He was attempting to divert her, and to provide a distraction for anyone who might be observing the baron's activities in Tiralien, so she did not protest.

As they came into the narrow street where Asa Dilawer had lived while he organized and annotated the first and most complete collection of Tanja Duhr's poetry, Ilse felt a hand skim her leg. She glanced down to see a nondescript man of uncertain years hurry past. There was nothing about him to attract attention . . .

She rode on a few moments, then casually leaned down to adjust her stirrup. Just as she suspected, there was a note tucked into her boot. She slid that into her palm, and from there into her sleeve, before she straightened up.

"A problem?" Mann asked.

"An answer," she replied. "Or so I hope."

At the next fountain, Mann called for a halt while they watered their horses. Ilse unfolded the scrap of paper into her palm and read the few short lines the message contained. *Go back to Little University to Aldemar Square. Third passage south to old stables. I have news of Raul.*

She crumpled the paper into her fist. An obvious ploy, except no one knew of her presence here, except Mann, his servants, and Kathe.

"You don't like the answer," Mann observed.

"I'm not certain. I might need to ride alone. Can I trust you to return to the inn?"

"No," he said cheerfully. "I would rather come with you. And do not think to use your sword against me, oh guardian of my heart. Someone would surely notice."

"In my next life, I shall hunt you down and make you miserable," she growled.

"That is my hope."

In the end, she allowed him to accompany her as they rode a great circle round to reenter the Little University, then into the third passage south from Aldemar Square. Their destination proved to be an abandoned stable, built from stone. Once it might have belonged to a thriving merchant. Now it was an empty dusty shell.

Just as Ilse was wondering what came next, a lean man dressed in a stained brown shirt and trousers emerged from the stables. "This way." He took hold of her horse's bridle. Mann dismounted and followed, gazing around him as they proceeded through a long corridor lined with empty stalls, then into a larger hall that echoed with the trill and coo of doves. The man gathered the reins of Mann's horse and nodded toward a ladder. "Go there. Your friends are waiting. Don't worry about the horses. I'll see to them."

Ilse climbed up first, a knife in one hand. She passed one darkened floor, then came to a second lit with shaded lamps leading off to one side. This one, yes. She waited for Mann, and they proceeded down the trail of lamplight, until they came to a small bare room illuminated with more lamps, where Benno Iani waited.

As she approached, Benno stared. "You live," he said in a wondering tone. "I was afraid—"

"My own story doesn't matter," Ilse said. "Tell me what happened with Raul. Quickly, please."

Her voice broke on the last word. Benno held out a hand and guided her inside to a bench where Emma Iani sat.

It was Emma who gave her the essential information.

"He rode to Duenne with Ault and eight guards. That was almost two months ago. Lord Khandarr arrested him the moment he entered Duenne. According to our last report, the king has agreed to a trial."

"What else?"

They took turns in delivering the news.

How Khandarr had infiltrated Raul's network in Tiralien. How Khandarr believed that Lord Kosenmark intended to sail to Károví to betray his own kingdom. Raul's absence seemed to confirm the rumors, until he reappeared two months later. His stay was brief, however. Less than a month after his return, he signed over all his possessions in Tiralien to Kathe Raendl and Dedrick's cousin, Lord Gerek Haszler.

Their last report, delivered by a friend from another friend, said Duke Kosenmark insisted on a public trial for his son. The king had agreed, but the process had stalled in bickering between political factions.

"Who are his allies in Duenne?" Ilse asked after she digested this news.

Benno hesitated. "From what I know, he has a few. Many others agree with him, but none wish to oppose the king or Markus Khandarr. However, the duke has influence. It is because of him that his son lives."

Ilse studied her hands, the fingers interlocked. "Then I must go to the duke." She glanced up to Baron Mann. "Would your purse extend to a fast horse and the means for fresh mounts between here and Duenne? It's a risk. It's all a risk. But if I ride tomorrow, I could reach the city within the week."

"That will be too late," Benno Iani said. "Lord Khandarr—"

"I have no choice, Benno." Her voice caught, and she had to swallow hard before she could continue. "I cannot transport myself with magic. I tried once. I nearly lost myself between worlds. But I cannot give up now. I have a message to deliver to Armand of Angersee, concerning Raul but much more besides. Too many people have died so I might deliver it."

Afraid she might start weeping if she thought about those who died, Ilse stood abruptly. She heard Mann thanking them for the news about Raul, then Benno's servant making his appearance to guide them back to their horses.

To be honest, she had not expected them to offer a sudden resolution to her problem. The information they provided was enough. She would ride tomorrow to Duenne. There she would seek out Duke Kosenmark. Raul would be dead, but at least she could accomplish their goal of peace. That was not yet impossible.

At the inn, Mann parted from her, saying he would arrange for horses, money, and whatever else she required for her journey. Ilse retired to the drill yard and attacked the invisible air with her sword.

Thunk. Thunk. Thunk.

Her sword buried its point in the soft wooden door. Ilse noted the flaws in her approach and attack, and resumed her practice. She was vaguely aware of the sun slanting westward, of her own shadow leaping higher and longer, but all she saw was the sword and its target.

One of Mann's guards arrived and vanished. Ilse hardly paid them attention. But when other familiar figures intruded, she paused in her drill.

Benno stood just inside the courtyard, his lean body draped in plain robes and framed by sunset. Behind him was Baron Mann—a very different Baron Mann dressed in plain dark clothes, his features settled in grave lines.

"I will take you to Duenne myself," Iani said without preamble.

"Through the magic plane. I've made such a journey before, alone and with others." He lifted a hand at her protests. "Yes, we risk a great deal, but we risk more if you ride, whether you ride alone or with a company of guards. Lord Khandarr might not expect you in particular, but he will have spies watching all the roads. And you cannot reach Duenne in less than ten days."

Ilse drew a sharp breath. "We might lose days or months in the magic plane."

Iani nodded. "It's possible. But you will certainly lose a week, or longer, by ordinary means. And though Lord Khandarr has set watch spells around the palace, he cannot spell all of Anderswar."

"What does Emma say?"

Benno's mouth stretched into an unhappy smile. "Emma said a great deal these past few hours. She distrusts Khandarr. She distrusts Armand and his court. But she agrees you must deliver your message to the king without delay. She says she will wait here for my return, whenever that return might take place, in this life or a future one."

Another promise made, another implied weight of trust.

"And you?" she said to Mann. "Will you continue your journey south?"

"Yes and no."

"The baron," Iani said drily, "has expressed the desire to accompany us."

Mann's only response was an edged smile.

Ilse eyed him. His expression was far different from Damek's, but she was uncomfortably reminded of the boy, and others who had decided to sacrifice themselves for her. "Josef," she said softly.

That brought a change to his countenance. She had not addressed him by name before.

"Josef, you know what we face," she said. "Armand will not like my news. Raul might die, no matter what. Anyone who helps me—"

"Stop it," Mann said sharply. "I do understand the danger, however difficult you find that to believe. I am not stupid. I am not a romantic, unlike you and the rest of your insufferable friends. In spite of that, I might prove useful. I have done so already."

Benno glanced toward her with a meaningful expression. She considered a moment, then shook her head. They could disable Baron Mann with sword or magic. And yet she wasn't certain she wanted to. He had proved an unexpected ally, reliable and perceptive. A good companion to have in difficult times.

"What preparation do you need to make?" she asked Mann.

"None. All has been accomplished while you skewered your target."

She eyed him with suspicion. "You expected me to agree?"

"Let us say I dared to hope."

She felt the weight against her heart lighten. Yes, he would make a good companion indeed.

"Very well," she said. "Let us go at once."

CHAPTER TWENTY

IT TOOK ILSE very little time to prepare.

She had kept almost nothing of her possessions throughout this long, long journey to Duenne—abandoning what little she had accumulated in Melnek, then Tiralien, and later in Osterling Keep. Her only weapons were those gifted by Baron Mann. The only item she had safeguarded from Taboresk was the letter from Duke Miro Karasek, now limp and imbued with the scent of her body. Once she had dressed in fresh plain clothing, she tucked the letter between her skin and her shirt.

Iani and Mann waited for her in Mann's private sitting room. Iani had curled into a padded armchair, much like a cat, and was reading a small thick book. Mann had barricaded himself behind his desk. Papers covered its surface, and he was busily writing. At her entrance, both men glanced up. Iani slid his book into a pocket. Mann scribbled a last hasty signature, then laid a blotting sheet over the page.

"Are we done here?" she asked.

Mann nodded. "My people understand that I need to break my journey in Tiralien."

"Do they? Are you certain?"

Mann lifted his gaze to the ceiling and muttered something under his breath. "Yes, I am certain. So that you know, my lady, I have a servant gifted in mimicry. He takes my place on the ship, in case the port officials show any curiosity about my doings. And while it is possible someone might miss your presence, my guards have made a point of riding between here and the ship to confuse matters further. In short, all is arranged, except your nerves. Once we have settled those, we are done."

Later, she would laugh at his speech. And about her own difficult manner. This moment was too soon.

"My apologies. I should not question you."

"You should question me," he said. "But I forgive you nevertheless."

He, too, seemed on the verge of laughter, but underneath she detected the same seriousness that had so surprised her back in Melnek. She cast her mind and memory back through the centuries, trying to remember another such soul who had offered such allegiance. She could not. Such a thing was possible, of course, but not easily explained.

"Very well," she said. "Benno, what comes next?"

"We go," he said. "Emma remains in hiding in Tiralien. If all goes wrong . . ." He drew a deep breath, the first mark of anxiety he had revealed this day. "If all goes wrong, she takes refuge with Lord Vieth. He has promised to send her and the rest of Lord Kosenmark's associates to Valentain by ship or whatever means is possible."

"And you?" Mann said. "Are *you* ready?"

For all her impatience, she wished she could give a reason for delay. She wanted to see the pleasure house once more, to touch its walls, to wander the rooftop gardens. Too late for that. Raul had shed this life as a snake might shed its skin. She would have to hunt him down in his new lair.

"I am," she said. "Let us go."

Mann called a runner and handed over his stack of papers. Once the door closed again, Iani collected them around a small table under the window. Outside, night was falling, and a salt breeze filtered into the room. As Iani explained, and Ilse knew, it was necessary for them to take hold of each other, to never relax their grip, or they would lose one another in the void between worlds.

"You have the skill to cross alone," he said to Ilse, "but the danger is time."

She knew. Time within the magical plane skipped and jumped and altered itself. She might lose days or months without an experienced guide such as Iani.

"And I would be lost forever," Mann said. "I know. I am not entirely ignorant."

He spoke with some asperity. Ilse wanted to smile. So he had not entirely misplaced his vanity. It was comforting, in a strange way. She took hold of her companions' hands. Iani's was lean, almost bare of flesh. Mann's palm was roughened by calluses, another unexpected detail, since she clearly recalled his smooth skin from three years before, while dancing in Melnek.

Her thoughts returned to the present as Benno Iani began the invocation to the gods and magic. He spoke in a low, urgent voice, the syllables of the ancient language rising in a lilt and cadence so familiar and yet made alien through the passage of centuries.

"Ei rûf ane gôtter, ane Lir unde Toc. Komen uns de strôm. Versigelen uns. Niht ougen. Niht hœren . . ."

This, Ilse thought, was the work of a master mage. For one moment, the scent of magic overwhelmed her senses, drowning out the salt tang, the beeswax and incense, and all the other familiar clues that told her they sat in an expensive private room, in the coastal city of Tiralien. The next moment, the air turned dark, the breeze vanished, leaving them wrapped in a cocoon of nothingness before the strong scent of magic blossomed once more.

"En name Lir unde Toc, komen uns de zoubernisse. Lâzen uns diese wërlt . . ."

Her soul leapt—as though it were a physical thing—against the cage of her flesh. She felt Mann's hand clasp hers more tightly. The air thickened, so thick she found it hard to draw a breath, and the magic strong enough that she could taste it.

And then, and then . . .

The world blinked into nothing.

She stood with her companions on a rim of brightness. Below their feet all the worlds of the universe spun, like multicolored threads of glass in an enormous invisible globe. Except she knew there was no depth or dimension to this plane. It was all her poor attempt to translate the magical to her human understanding.

Without releasing his hold on Ilse's hand, Iani crouched down, as though seeking the signpost that would lead them back to their own world and Duenne. Ilse tried to follow his gaze. It was like searching for a single minnow in a flashing swarm. There, there was the inn at Tiralien. There, a silvery ribbon that could be the Solvatni River in Duszranjo. One, twice, the images froze. She recognized Melnek. Blinked and saw a vast expanse of golden dunes, stretching toward an alien horizon. Blinked again, and had to narrow her eyes against the whirling specks of color.

Next to her, Mann stared fixedly at the maelstrom below. His hand trembled, and she tightened her grip. "What is wrong?" she asked.

"I am afraid. I see . . . faces."

"Close your eyes," Ilse said quickly. "Those are monsters, liars."

The worlds beneath them vanished. Clouds of smoke and ashes enveloped them. From a distance came the hiss of an enormous fire, and her skin drew tight. Her mouth felt parched from terror. She tried to remind herself this was another illusion, but she had read too many histories of magic. A mage could die in Anderswar, whether they came in flesh or spirit.

"Is this another lie?" Mann said. His voice was high and light. Ilse felt him tremble and she gripped his hand tighter.

"Anderswar lies," she said. "But a lie can kill you here. If you believe it, that is."

He gave a bark of laughter. "Oh. So glad I would never—"

Light bloomed at their feet. Now Ilse could see a wall of flame surrounding them, bright gold and rippling like water flowing over stone. A burst of wind scented with burning wood and magic struck her in the face. She coughed, then nearly choked when the flames parted and a massive cat-like creature made directly for them, ash and burning embers spinning in its wake.

Its color was as bright and golden as the flames. Its eyes were like twin white suns. Its tongue hung from its mouth, a rivulet of fire against a greater conflagration. Ilse gulped down a lungful of scorching air, and squeezed Mann's and Iani's hands even harder. Mann was shivering. Iani had gone unnervingly still.

The beast circled around them, once and twice. The third time it stopped before Mann. Its face shimmered and lengthened. *Josef. My love. I had not expected you would ever come to me.*

Mann flinched. "Mathis?" he whispered.

"What is it?" Ilse said. "What do you see?"

Mann didn't answer. The beast arched its neck until its face hovered inches away from Mann's. Mann tilted his head backward and stared, his eyes wide and blank, his lips stretched in an unconscious imitation of the beast's grin.

Benno was cursing under his breath. Ilse shook Mann's hand. She shouted in his ear. Nothing did any good. In fury and desperation, she drove her booted foot onto his instep. Mann recoiled from the beast with a muffled cry. Ilse yanked him to his knees and bent over him, her face between his and the monster's. "Listen to me," she said. "You see trickers. Tricksters and liars. *That* is Anderswar. It lies. It wants to snare you with your own fears. Do not listen."

"But I saw . . ."

You saw me, Josef. You saw the truth. If you go to Duenne, you will die.

Josef Mann sucked in his breath. He stared beyond Ilse as though he looked directly into the monster's eyes. Then he shook his head, assayed a smile that was a faint echo of his usual self. "Then I die," he said. "I will someday, no matter what. Begone, monster and liar."

The golden flames vanished. Once more they stood upon the edge of the universe. Mann glanced downward, as though he might still make a fatal leap. But when Ilse pressed her hand within his, he smiled once more. To Benno Iani, he said, "Do we go on? Or shall we hold a dance and conversation with more demons?"

"No need to delay," Benno Iani said. "I have found our destination."

He spoke a phrase in Erythandran. Light and shadow transposed themselves around them. Another bursting bloom of magic, another sudden shift in perception, and they were falling down and down and down, through a maelstrom of shrieks and brilliant, sickening colors. She had a moment of unrestrained panic. Heard screams, her own, Josef Mann's, and even Benno Iani's . . .

As always, the transition came abruptly. One moment they plunged through the void. The next, Ilse lay sprawled on a cold dank expanse of stone. Her stomach heaved. Her heartbeat echoed inside her skull. At first she could take in nothing except the hard stones beneath her. She might have landed atop a mountain, or in a city on the far side of the continent, or even in a world in another universe. She could not tell. But no, she recognized the scents of cardamom and ginger, of wood smoke from oak and pine, and then the thread of song from a distant window, the words unmistakably Veraenen.

With shaking limbs, she drew herself to sitting. Tipped back her head to see the stars she knew from childhood. The moon was the same quarter moon she had left behind in Tiralien, grown only a shade brighter and larger.

They had come to a small courtyard, bounded by tall brick walls, a gate at each end. Not a country village courtyard, she guessed. This place belonged to some grand inn. A wind drifted through, carrying with it the smell of horse and grass and plains from everlasting, of a city buried in land, no seas within a ride's distance.

Next to her, a man wept.

Still unsteady, she crawled to the man's side. It was Josef Mann. He huddled over himself, and his rough sobs echoed from the walls. When she touched his shoulder, his head jerked up and he stared at her wide-eyed.

"It's me," she said softly. "Ilse Zhalina."

"I . . . I know you."

His voice was hoarse, his words barely intelligible.

"Who was that, Josef? The one you called Mathis?"

A shudder ran through his body.

"My brother. He died of a fever. Ten years ago. I was never meant to be the heir."

He broke into weeping again. Ilse held him close as he rocked back and forth. She glanced around the courtyard. No sign of Iani. Had he mistaken their goal? Did he wander through the void even now? Even as all the possibilities tumbled through her mind, she held on to Josef Mann and whispered words of comfort.

And then . . .

The darkness rippled. A strong scent of magic rolled through the air. Then came a movement nearby, and a shadow rose from the ground. Iani. Benno Iani awake and eager, as she had never known the man.

She waited until he staggered upright, caught himself, and stared upward at the moon and stars. "Where are we?" she demanded.

Iani started at her voice. Then he grinned down at her with far too much cheer. "In Duenne," he replied. "And in good time. No more than a day or two lost. Come, we must hurry to the duke's household."

"Can you?" Ilse asked Mann.

He shook his head, but then drew himself together. "I can. It was just . . ."

Just a moment confronting your terrors, Ilse thought. "Tell me later if you like," she said. "We will not either of us die before then."

She helped him to his feet. Benno took them from the courtyard into the next main street. There he paused, uncertain. "I do not know this quarter."

Mann did, however—another surprise to Ilse, who had not expected him to be so familiar with parts outside the grand palace or its immediate environs. Evidently he had recovered from his distress, or postponed it to a later, more convenient hour. With a gesture, he took the lead and guided them through a maze of streets and alleys, to a wide boulevard. Ilse had no more than a moment to take in the sight of the palace, far to the southeast, its towers and walls illuminated so that it appeared a great golden crown against the deepening twilight. Then Mann took hold of her wrist and dragged her down another dark street, with houses leaning together overhead. She heard a flute whispering, the buzz of voices speaking in unfamiliar dialects, then they were running down a tunnel smothered in darkness.

One, two, a dozen intersections passed, and several dozen turns taken, so many that Ilse could not keep count. Then, unexpectedly, they fetched up beside a blank, stone wall.

Ilse stopped and tilted her head back. Far above, starlight edged a high, domed roof. The lower stories were as blank as the outer wall, but just under the gutters and waterspouts ran a row of brightly lit windows. She loosed a long-held breath, drew another and caught the rich mélange of incense and magic that enveloped the grounds. The duke, or his mages, had laid numerous spells to protect this house.

"Here," Mann said. "Or rather. Once we come to the gate."

They circled around the walled compound, feeling their way through the deepening shadows. Ilse stumbled once or twice. Mann caught her elbow before she fell. *Each of us supporting the other,* she thought. Mann whispered a question, but she could barely attend. She had achieved Duenne, in spite of so many impossible obstacles.

An unexpected barrier led them back into a maze of streets. Mann swore with an energy that belied his earlier terror. Then Ilse sighted the glare of torchlight up one narrow passageway. She darted ahead of her companions. Yes, there ahead were the walls to the duke's compound.

The next moment, a squad of guards materialized in front of her. Metal hissed against leather as they all drew their weapons.

Ilse froze. She heard footsteps behind her. An argument broke out. She recognized Mann's voice rising above a woman's demand that he stand back and not interfere.

"Josef," she called out. "Do what she says."

To the guards, she said, "My name is Ilse Zhalina. I must speak with the duke about his son."

SHE HAD EXPECTED an argument, or some demand for proof of her identity, but the guards sheathed their swords at once and offered their apologies. "Come with us, you and your companions," the senior officer said. "The duke will see you at once."

You should not trust so easily, Ilse thought, but perhaps the guards believed no one would dare such a ruse, or that there were other, better defenses set within the household. She had no time to speculate. She was already hurrying after the guard. A runner sped ahead, and disappeared into a side corridor. Ilse, Mann, and Iani were guided into a wider passage decorated with mosaics.

The passage soon joined a large one. Tapestries alternated with painted scenes from Veraene's history, and instead of torches, sweet-scented candles burned in their sockets.

As they neared a huge set of double doors, their guide slowed. Now Ilse could take in the height of the passage—twice that of a man's—and the airy semicircle before the door itself, which was carved from rich darkwood, and set with polished iron hinges into the walls.

She drew a breath in wonderment. A king's reception. No, the Kosenmark family had never claimed kingship. But they had once ruled a princedom.

It was as though she finally understood Raul Kosenmark's arrogance, and why Armand of Angersee feared him. Here was old royalty, dating from before the empire, from before Erythandra's tribes invaded the central plains.

The guard signaled to two attendants Ilse had not observed before. The attendants bowed and opened the doors. Ilse proceeded through them into a wide, open hall. She had no idea if Iani or Mann followed.

A bleak bare room stretched out before her. Unlike the halls outside, the tiled floor were bare of rugs and the walls bereft of any decoration. Off to one side stood a strange contraption, built of polished brass, that held a series of smaller sand glasses, each one seemingly gauged to measure a different quantity of time. In spite of the warm night, a great fire blazed in the hearth.

All that took only a moment to absorb. Her attention veered to the opposite end of the hall, where an old man sat in a well-cushioned chair, surrounded by three women. Even without being told, Ilse knew who they were: Duke Kosenmark and his three dangerous daughters. She wished she could request a more private interview, knew she could not. She advanced toward the chair where Raul Kosenmark's father sat.

A few feet away, she paused. The old man studied her closely, a strange searching expression on his face. The sisters stared even more keenly. They were of various heights, but she could see the similarity between them and Raul. The fair golden coloring, made fairer by their black hair, so thick and straight. The sweep of flattened cheeks, the bright eyes in all shades of brown, and an air of wildness, barely contained. One smiled and nodded, as if to encourage her. Another studied her, frowning, her full lips set into a straight line. The third swept her gaze over Ilse, then immediately glanced back over one shoulder. Only then did Ilse notice the fourth woman concealed in the shadows—someone sleek and lithe and brown. Someone she had believed indifferent to politics, or the machinations of Duenne's politics.

Nadine?

Later she might ask how the courtesan had arrived in the duke's household. For now she had other concerns. She closed the last few steps and knelt before Raul's father. The old man leaned forward and held out his hands. On impulse, Ilse gathered his within hers. Unlike her grandmother's, these were strong hands, roughened with calluses from sword work. She lifted her gaze to his and saw he was smiling.

"I have long wished to meet you," he said.

"So have we all," said one of the daughters. "At last, our foolish brother chose someone with sense. And," she added, "a very nice sword. My name is Heloïse."

The rest gave their names rapidly. Marte, tall and slim and with eyebrows arcing over a strong face drawn in uncompromising angles; Olivia, a smaller, rounder version of the same. According to her older sisters, Olivia resembled their brother Johan, who had remained in Valentain to oversee the estate, along with their mother.

Terrible creatures, all of them, Ilse thought, with their laughter and smiles edged with sharp wit. She no longer wondered why Raul had absented himself from his home in Valentain. He and they were much alike, shielding their hearts beneath masks. It would be too painful, living with reflections of himself.

The essence of her thoughts must have appeared on her face, because Marte's lips twisted into a rueful smile. "We are not always so horrible."

"Oh, no," Olivia added with an innocent air. "Most times we are much worse."

Only Heloïse said nothing more, but her silent laughter was eloquent enough. Behind her, Nadine rolled her eyes.

Ilse shook her head, unable to join in their amusement. She withdrew her hands from the duke's and stood. "Your Grace, I have a letter for the king. Its contents might prove your son's innocence."

"But you are not certain," the duke said.

"No." Her gaze flicked toward the daughters, then back to Raul's father. "Your Grace, the matter concerns peace between the kingdoms. If winning that peace means your son dies . . ." She closed her eyes a moment, recovered the tattered remnants of her determination, and forged ahead. "If he dies for peace, if I do, it is a price well paid. We might fail, but we must make the attempt—for Veraene's sake."

A long silence followed. It was as though her pulse had stilled and the air were banished to another plane.

"I begin to see why he loves you," the duke breathed. "May I see the letter?"

Wordlessly, she took the letter from her shirt and handed it to Duke Kosenmark. For months, she had kept the letter itself hidden, but now, in Duenne, she knew she needed witnesses as well as allies.

The duke unfolded the paper and read through its contents. She measured his progress by the flicker of his eyes. He read it through a second time before he handed the letter back to Ilse. "A true victory for all our kingdoms. I can see that. Well, then. You must speak with the king. I can arrange a private interview . . ."

"Excuse me," Ilse said. "You misunderstand me. There can be no more secrets. I must speak at your son's trial. Can you arrange that?"

Silence followed that pronouncement. All four Kosenmarks stared at her. Then it was Marte who laughed out loud, Olivia who covered her face, as though to contain her own hilarity, and Heloïse who held out both hands to Ilse. "I am glad my brother loves you. I am glad you love Veraene. Father," she said sharply, "stop with the examination. She knows better than all of us, including Raul."

"Thank you for the recommendation," Ilse said drily.

Her words brought a flush to Heloïse's face. Olivia's dark eyes narrowed, all amusement gone. Marte, however, continued to smile warmly. "We are impossible. We know it. Which is no excuse, only an explanation. Please. Do not give up on us so quickly."

"No, do not," Nadine said softly.

It was the first time she had spoken.

Ilse glanced toward her. "Shall I trust them?"

"As much as you can trust anyone in Duenne."

Ilse nodded slowly. "Very well. Duke Kosenmark, if you cannot assist me, tell me so and I will not trouble you again. However . . ."

"I can," the duke said. "And I will."

"How soon?"

"Tomorrow. I promise you."

He lifted a hand. At once, a trio of servants appeared from the shadows. "You and your friends will have shelter here. And you, if you will permit it, will have proper clothing for your interview with the king. Do not argue. I might know nothing but these court games, but I know them well."

Humor leavened his voice.

Ilse sank into a curtsy. "Until tomorrow, your Grace."

SERVANTS LED HER away from Mann and Iani, into a grand suite of rooms, including a bedchamber with a high ceiling and vast fireplace, already lit with its own fire. She had made a swift circuit and returned to the outer rooms, still attempting to take in her surroundings, when the door opened behind her.

It was Marte, the one who had laughed.

Marte, her face now grave.

"He is afraid," she said. "My father."

"So we all are," Ilse replied.

Marte nodded. "We tend to forget that. A failing and not an excuse," she added. "Though I wonder, and please excuse the impertinence, but I do wonder if you have ever feared anything in this world."

I have, Ilse thought. *I was afraid of my father and Theodr Galt. The nights spent alone in the wilderness. I am still afraid of failing. Of bringing death instead of peace. Of spending another life or three searching for my true love.*

But when she attempted to speak, to describe the weeks and months of desperation, her throat went drier than the ashes from Anderswar's last illusion. She could only shake her head.

Marte laid a gentle hand on Ilse's cheek. "I'm sorry. I was clumsy to say what I did. But you offered us such a brave front, that I began to think you impervious to ordinary human frailty. So, come. Let us measure you for raiment suitable to your mission, and you shall present whatever evidence you must before the king."

She gestured, and a half-dozen young women streamed into the room. Some of them carried ready-made garments. Others had tape measures and pins and sewing baskets. Ilse submitted to their ministrations though it made her twitch, having so many hands upon her body. It called up sudden vivid memories of her days with the caravan, when she had not belonged to herself. But she bit her tongue, and quelled the trembling. By the end, they promised her a costume fit for an audience with the king.

"Can he manage it?" Ilse murmured, half to herself. "A public audience?"

"He will," Marte said. "He is Duke Kosenmark."

CHAPTER TWENTY-ONE

ILSE SLEPT SO deeply, she suspected Marte had drugged the water pitcher. No dreams of past lives interrupted the night, nor even an ordinary dream. It was as if she had exhausted her ability to see beyond the moment. Only once, toward dawn, did her thoughts rise toward waking, and she caught a glimpse of torchlight that reminded her of that clearing, centuries ago, where, in a previous life, Miro Karasek had captured a princess of Károví on her mission of peace.

She woke to pale sunlight streaming through half-open shutters. It was early morning, just after sunrise. The servants had opened the windows during the night, and a warm breeze grazed her face. From the streets below, she heard the clamor of many voices in many languages and dialects. Ilse stared up at the high ceiling with its paintings of women engaged in all manner of work. Stitchery. Weaving. Playing instruments. Dancing and reading. Swordplay and practicing medicine. The central panel, directly overhead, depicted a woman speaking before a grand audience that might be Duenne's Council.

Duenne. Three years ago, she had sold her body and half annihilated her sense of self, attempting to reach this city. It seemed impossible that she had truly arrived here. That she would speak before the king.

So. Let us begin.

She rose and drew on the robe hung beside her bed. The servants must have set a watch, because she had no sooner done so when a maid scratched at the bedroom door. The girl provided Ilse with directions to the baths, and promised to have a hot breakfast ready on her return.

By the time she had finished her meal, a team of maidservants brought her new clothes. Seamstresses must have spent the night and dozens of candles to finish these costumes, Ilse thought. There were three new gowns, consisting of layers upon layers of false robes sewn over a plain shift, everything embroidered along the edges and weighted with jewels in the hem. The cloth was all dark blue linen, the embroidery of an even darker hue, stitched in tiny loops and whorls. Nothing ostentatious, not as these nobles would judge it, but everything fine and costly.

Working in swift concert, the maids dressed Ilse in the first of these new costumes. Ilse barely paid attention, only enough to obey their directions to step into the shift, my lady, lift your left arm, yes, just so, now please hold still just a moment. She felt removed from the present, as though her spirit had taken a few steps outside her body and was poised to spring into the magical plane.

The door opened as the maid completed Ilse's toilette and Nadine entered, followed by a serving girl carrying a tray with carafes for tea and coffee. Nadine dismissed the maids and the serving girl with a glance.

"They have spent half the night in negotiations," she told Ilse. "Apparently Armand was ready to execute Lord Kosenmark two days ago, saying there was no evidence for the man's innocence, and he therefore saw no reason to keep him alive, in spite of the many petitions. Ah, do not weep, Ilse. Please, please . . ."

She knelt by Ilse and folded her into her arms.

"Hush. No, do not hush. Cry as you must. We are, all of us, demanding too much of you. Of that idiot you love. Of everyone I know. I told Heloïse as much, and though I had to bite her in the end, she agreed."

The picture of Nadine biting one of Raul's dangerous sisters sent Ilse into a bout of hysterical laughter. Nadine observed her, cheeks flushed, but otherwise seemingly unmoved. "I am delighted to amuse you," she said. "Now that we've sampled grief and merriment in equal measure, let us complete your toilette. Though we've no official word yet, the unoffical report is that you are to see the king and the court at noon. Therefore, this early preparation."

Ilse drew a sharp breath. "So soon."

Nadine nodded. "Just so. They wish to eliminate this last and most troublesome obstacle to their war, you see."

Ilse pressed both hands over her face. Felt warm lips on her forehead, a palm brush over her hair.

"Someday, you must tell me the story," Nadine said. "Everything that has taken place after you left Tiralien. Until then, remember that you are my first true love, if not my last."

THE FORMAL SUMMONS came within that same hour, ordering Ilse Zhalina to appear before the king and council at noon.

Ilse spent the remainder of the morning pacing from room to room.
Now she caught up the letter from Duke Karasek and read its contents one
last time. Now she paused at a window to gaze southward over an undulat-
ing sea of gray and crimson roofs, past myriad towers to the golden com-
plex of the royal palace. It was autumn already, but here in the central
plains, heat shimmered the air. Ilse drew a deep breath. She missed the
scent of salt water, the almost imperceptible susurration of the sea lapping
at the shore that had followed her through almost all her life.

Duke Kosenmark had gone to the king the night before to negotiate the
particulars for this audience, Olivia explained. She and her sisters would accompany Ilse to the palace, along with a complement of guards. There was
no sign of Nadine, or of Iani and Mann. She would have to trust the duke
to keep them safe.

At last Heloïse came to announce their departure. She and her sisters
were dressed in loose black trousers and jackets, embroidered with silver
and decorated with silver buttons and sashes of white lace, and cinched
with jeweled weapon belts hung with swords and knives.

Dangerous, yes.

They descended to the front courtyard and mounted their horses. They
would not ride alone—twelve guards took their places in a loose perimeter.
Ilse gathered the reins in her hands and attempted to collect her emotions
into one manageable bundle.

She had the letter. She was dressed as befitted an envoy from another
land.

Heloïse glanced at her. Ilse nodded and gave the signal to ride.

The party proceeded through the gates, into a small square fronting
the compound. Smaller streets branched off to either side, into the maze she
had traversed the previous night. Ahead, on the opposite side of the square,
lay a broad avenue leading south to the palace.

"No more obstacles," Heloïse said.

"Only a few digressions," Marte added with a cryptic smile.

"My sister means our progress through the streets will not be so swift
and direct as you might wish," Olivia said to Ilse.

"Politics," Heloïse said. "And security."

Clearly the matter was not as straightforward as Nadine said. With
certain misgivings, Ilse gave herself over to the machinations devised by
Kosenmark and his daughters. She quashed her impatience at their slow
pace. Nor did she object when they turned into a side street, and traveled

through a less prosperous quarter, to what appeared to be an enormous square crowded with market stalls.

Heloïse slowed her horse. The rest of the company did the same.

"Where are Baron Mann and Lord Iani?" Ilse asked her.

"At the palace. Armand wished to have their company."

"They are hostages."

"That is another word for it, yes. They agreed, because in exchange, the king allowed me to remain with my family. Negotiations have been some-what fraught, as you can imagine."

Oh, yes, she could.

"Ah," Marte exclaimed. "There is Lady Margarete and her family." She waved with enthusiasm. The parties drew rein to speak with one another—nothing but inconsequentials, but Ilse felt the weight of Lady Margarete's gaze on her. At least the Kosenmark sisters did not expect her to join in the conversation. After a few exchanges, Heloïse gave the excuse that they had an appointment, and on they went.

A second and third encounter and a fourth. Again, no one addressed Ilse, but everyone inspected her. Ilse understood. Duke Kosenmark wished to spread word of her audience with the king. This very public procession ensured she would at least attain that audience without any mysterious dis-appearance.

They arrived at their destination half an hour before the midday bells. The vast square before the palace was empty, however, as was the equally enormous courtyard within the outer walls. Ilse glanced from side to side. High stone walls lined the courtyard. The front of the palace was a blank facade, broken only by a vast set of doors, four times the height of any ordi-nary man, constructed from beaten copper and decorated with the arms of Veraene and Angersee. Beyond, towers and walls mounted upward to glit-tering domes. She tilted her head back to take in the rows of windows, the sense of concentrated power, the aura of magic that pervaded the air.

A squad of soldiers emerged from the doors to meet their company. As Ilse dismounted, the most senior officer stepped forward. The king required her immediate presence, he said, and she was to follow him at once. Her guards and escort were not necessary in the palace itself. He spoke politely, but she disliked how the other soldiers pressed forward between her and Kosenmark's guards.

"I thank the king, but I find the presence of my escort necessary," she said.

"Indeed," Heloïse said, interposing herself between Ilse and the soldiers. "We dare not abandon our charge. It is a matter of the highest protocol."

"But Lord Khandarr—"

"His Majesty will have Mistress Ilse in good time," Marte said. "Tell them that our father gives his word in exchange for our behavior. Unless Lord Khandarr holds a greater authority than Armand himself. No? I thought not. Please convey our words exactly to the king. We understand the protocol. You will have the Lady Ilse, as promised, to deliver her testimony before the court and no sooner."

The senior officer glared at her. Heloïse and her sisters smiled back, the tips of their teeth showing. With a grimace, the senior officer shrugged. "As you insist. I will relay your words to the king."

"Thank you. I would be grateful."

The soldiers withdrew. Heloïse closed her eyes momentarily, then glanced to Ilse. "Do let me know if I exceed my responsibilities."

"Not yet," Ilse said. "Though I will not be shy."

"Oh. As for that, I have no fear."

A runner in the king's own livery appeared shortly after. Ilse and the Kosenmark sisters handed their horses off to their own guards and followed the man through the grand entrance and its equally grand reception chamber, lined with ivory marble. An airy entry hall stretched before them, but with an apologetic gesture, the runner directed them off to one side and down a parallel corridor, into a small chamber.

Marte motioned for the others to wait and entered first. She glanced around, then nodded to her sisters, who then escorted Ilse inside.

The room was small, the size of a generous storeroom in Raul Kosenmark's pleasure house. Dark blue tiles covered the floor. A single tapestry, depicting a king accepting a vow of allegiance from his mage-priest, hung next to a narrow window, which overlooked a courtyard planted with flowering trees, already losing their blossoms to the autumn season. Such a plain, insignificant room, told Ilse the status of herself and her message. She didn't care. The king would hear her. It was more than she had hoped for these past four months.

Next a squad of servants appeared. They requested, in soft but firm tones, that Ilse give up all her weapons. Heloïse nodded and Ilse complied, but she noted the servants made no such demands of the Kosenmark sisters, who took up stances around the room, knives drawn, hands resting on swords.

"Where are we?" Ilse asked.

"Next to the great council room itself," Marte said. "The king will not allow you to enter armed, but the old laws permit your guardians to carry weapons."

"Such a relief," Ilse murmured.

She was rewarded by brilliant smiles from all three sisters. Olivia darted forward and kissed Ilse on the cheek. The gesture was so unexpected that Ilse flinched. Olivia paused, tilted her head as if asking permission this time, then repeated the kiss. So. Perhaps they had hearts after all. She would have to learn not to judge so easily.

The servants reappeared, clearly anxious. Ilse nodded to them, and proceeded through the door. They escorted her down the same corridor, to an entryway with double doors of polished darkwood, carved with emblems from the old empire.

The doors swung open onto a vast hall.

Ilse took in the rows of seats that circled around the floor, rising up tier by tier to the ceiling far overhead. She sensed the sisters behind her, a touch of badly needed warmth, strengthened all the more because she knew they came well armed. Ahead lay a smooth stone aisle, lined on either side by benches and chairs and richly appointed boxes; more seats rose up on either side, all of them occupied by men and women dressed in jewels that caught the lamplight and sunlight.

At the end of the aisle stood the royal dais, occupied by Armand of Angersee. One tall skeleton of a man stood behind the king, bending over his shoulder. That, she realized with an indrawn breath, would be Lord Markus Khandarr. Even from this distance he appeared markedly changed. His hair snow white. His body hunched over a stick.

If she had found the long march to Duke Kosenmark unsettling, this was ten times more so. She marched forward, down the long, long aisle, past the nobles and their minions, either seated or standing in small gatherings. She paused once to draw a calming breath and to remember Bela Sovic, Maryshka Rudny, Kathe and her beloved, so many others.

I am nothing. They are everything.

She continued on, advancing past a row of guards, past an empty moat between the audience and the king. Now she came to a second line of guards, these armed with swords drawn. One of them stepped forward to examine her. Through the gap in the line, she glimpsed a man in a drab brown tunic and trousers bent over a wooden table.

Raul Kosenmark.

Ilse stopped, her heartbeat stilled by the unexpected sight.

He sat alone, behind a plain small table, his hands clasped together before him, weighed down with chains. His face was drawn, his eyes dark from sleepless night, his mouth pinched in despair. There was no trace of beard upon his face, but there would not be. Not after Baerne extracted that most final promise of loyalty from his councillors.

One year since she had left Tiralien. Four months and more since Hallau Island.

Oh, my love, my love . . .

She had lied when she told Duke Kosenmark that his son didn't matter. He did. But if his death and hers meant peace, she would not fail, not at this last moment.

The guard searched her person for weapons. Ilse bore the indigity with trembling anger. A few yards, a few moments of speech, separated her from her goal. Once the woman finished her inspection and motioned her forward, Ilse advanced toward the dais. As if he had finally become aware of her presence, Raul lifted his head and swiveled around.

His eyes were dulled, no longer the brilliant gold of her memory. His once-black hair was streaked with gray. There was an air of defeat about him, as though he had spent these past four months in despair.

My love, she thought, with all her will.

My love, came his clear reply.

It was as though she witnessed Toc's resurrection. His eyes brightened. His lips parted in a smile beyond hopeful. Her own pulse beat quick and light with anticipation.

There was no time for more. The guard who had examined her resumed her position in line, blocking Raul from her sight. Ilse crossed to the last distance to face the king and his mage councillor.

"Your Majesty." Ilse sank to her knees and bowed her head.

"They tell me you have evidence for this man's trial," Armand said.

His voice was high and light, like a string drawn taut, but clearly a man's voice. This was the king who had determined to reinvent himself into a greater legend than his famous grandfather. She would have to tread carefully, for her sake and Raul's. And Veraene's.

"I have evidence and more," Ilse said.

She rose and advanced up the half dozen steps to lay Miro Karasek's letter at her king's feet. Armand motioned to an attendant, who retrieved the envelope from the floor and offered it to the king.

"It is a letter from Duke Miro Karasek," Ilse said. "He is— He *was* a general of Károví. While he addressed this letter to Lord Kosenmark, in truth he wrote to Veraene and you, your Majesty. On the matter of peace between our kingdoms," she added, when the king still made no move to unfold the envelope or read its contents.

Armand regarded the square of paper in his hands. "You are not one of my diplomats," he said. "Nor an envoy."

His expression was bland, unnervingly so.

"No," she replied. "I cannot claim any authority in this life. But once I was a princess of Károví, charged with the same mission. The circumstances of my life—the one before, the one today—brought me back to Károví." When he continued to study the envelope, she said, "You have heard that Leos Dzavek is dead. There is more you ought to know. Lir's jewels have departed this world. And Morennioù's queen has returned to her home-land. Once she has dealt with those Károvín who remain in the islands, she will turn her attention to the continent. She has promised us peace, but in return, we must promise her the same."

Now she had his attention.

"What queen?" Armand said. "And who made such promises to her?"

He had recovered himself quickly enough, but Ilse had not missed how his eyes had widened, nor how his gaze veered briefly to one side, to Markus Khandarr.

"The queen of Morennioù," she replied. "The Károvín took her hostage, when Leos Dzavek sent those ships east. On their return, three of the ships foundered in the shoals off Osterling Keep. The queen was taken along with the Károvín survivors. Lord Khandarr questioned her himself."

Another abortive glance toward Khandarr. Ilse felt the temptation to follow that glance, to observe Khandarr's expression for herself, but she kept her gaze locked on Armand's face. She read a flicker of doubt in his frown, whether directed at Khandarr or herself she could not tell.

"You say Duke Karasek is no longer a general," Armand said. "Which means he no longer has any influence. His letter means nothing."

"He no longer has influence, your Majesty. But the men and women he names, dukes and barons and lords, do."

And never mind the common people who held equally strong opinions. But she knew Armand could not comprehend such a thing.

Meanwhile, Armand regarded her with that same maddeningly blank expression. He still had not read the letter—he might simply make his decision on a whim. Belatedly, she wondered if she had made a mistake, coming to him so openly. Perhaps if she had listened to the duke's first suggestion, for a private interview . . .

No. All their misery, hers and Raul's and Veraene's itself, came from secrecy.

She pressed forward, trying to keep the desperation from her voice. "Your Majesty. Read the letter or not. But listen to me, please. You believe Lord Kosenmark a traitor—"

"I know it."

She bowed her head. "As you wish. I came with evidence for his innocence."

"This letter?" Armand said.

"No. My own memories."

The hall, until then abuzz with whispered conversation, dropped into a hush.

"What do you mean?" Armand said.

"Exactly what I said, your Majesty. Consult Lord Khandarr about his ability to draw the truth and nothing else from those he questions. He did so with Lord Dedrick Maszuryn. He attempted to do so with Morenniou's queen. Let me offer myself as another candidate."

The hush dropped into a deeper silence. Ilse felt the air draw tight—not with magic but with the apprehension of an entire court as it watched its king poised to make a decision. Only now did Ilse dare to shift her gaze from Armand to the man beside him.

Markus Khandarr stood hunched over a thick black staff, his hands gripping the curved handle so tightly his knuckles were pale from the effort. But what astonished Ilse the most was his face. One half slack, the flesh hanging down, as if half of him had died. The other etched with deep lines, and the flesh drawn back tight against the skull, now visible through the thinning white hair.

An old man, made unaccountably older still and weakened by a confrontation with a stronger adversary. A man permanently furious at that defeat.

His expression frightened her. If Armand granted her the right to testify under magic's influence, Khandarr would surely see that she died. It did not matter that this interrogation took place before a host of witnesses. He was a clever man. He could ensure that she died quietly in the night from a spell laid upon her now, under the guise of administering the truth spell, and no one could prove it was murder.

I must take that risk. I must deliver my evidence, persuade the king. If I die, so be it.

She rose to her feet and met Khandarr's gaze steadily. "Do what you must, my lord. I am prepared to do the same."

A strange emotion rippled over that distorted face. Contempt at her bravado? A reluctant admiration? Even the possibility of the latter unnerved her. The moment passed. Khandarr shook his head and in painfully slow, measured steps rounded the throne to approach Ilse.

"Kneel," he rasped.

"I kneel to the king, not you," she said.

The knotted half of his mouth twitched. He made no reply, but laid a hand against her throat, and despite her declaration, she could not suppress a flinch. But as he began the invocation to the magic, a voice rang out from the audience.

"Your Majesty. I claim the right to offer a gift to the kingdom's welfare."

Voices swelled in an access of surprise. Ilse attempted to turn away to face the speaker, but Khandarr tightened his grip on her throat. Magic stung her skin, and she had the impression that a single word might send the current across the divide between flesh and flesh.

Khandarr lifted his gaze to stare past Ilse and to the invisible speaker. "What gift, Lady Hanau? Amends for your daughter's treachery?"

A shock of recognition washed over Ilse at the sound of the speaker's name. Raul had told her the story of his first days at court. How the Countess Fara Hanau had rescued him from self-destruction, offering herself as a mentor at first, a friend, and though he had not said as much, a lover in later years.

Markus Khandarr saw Fara as a rival for the king's favor. He dared nothing outright, but one day, Fara took ill, complaining of a headache and dizziness. Twelve hours later, she lay unconscious in a wasting fever. But she didn't die. Not right away. Not for three months . . .

"My daughter never committed treachery," Lady Hanau said, then to the king, "Your Majesty, treason is a delicate matter to judge. Lord Khandarr's animosity toward Lord Kosenmark is well known. He is therefore unfit to conduct this interrogation. You might say my animosity toward this court is also well known. But I have a proposition. Accept the services of my personal mage. Let him question the young woman and I will no longer oppose you through my friends and allies."

Ilse glanced up at the king, but Armand's expression had turned even more remote and unreadable than before. "You will give up all claims against me and my court?" he asked.

"Against you, your Majesty, and everyone else concerned. Except," she added, "Lord Khandarr himself."

A breath of silence followed, just long enough for Ilse to sense a quickening of Khandarr's pulse through his fingertips, to consider how swiftly a desperate mage could wreak destruction. Then . . .

"I accept," Armand said. "Bring us your mage."

He gestured sharply to Khandarr, who retreated once more to his position behind the king's throne. Ilse bowed her head and breathed deep breaths. She heard, as from a distance, footsteps approach the dais, then a man's voice offering fealty to his lord and king. His name was Emil Fass. On further questioning, he said he had studied magic as an apprentice in Melnek. With a gift of money, and a recommendation from his tutor, he had come to Duenne three years ago.

"I traveled by caravan," Fass said. "I studied at the university a year before my Lady Hanau gave me a place in her household. With her permission, I have continued to study at the university, while I fulfill my obligations to her and her household."

Ilse heard little beyond the words *Melnek* and *caravan*.

I know you. And now I know your name.

This was the nameless scholar who had watched her sell her body to Alarik Brandt and his men. The same one who had dared their punishment when he gave her a stone knife to free herself. She remembered the rush of his voice as he gave her advice on how to survive in the wilderness. His last words, when he said she reminded him of his sister. "I know you," she said softly.

"And I know you," he said, his voice pitched as low as hers. "Well enough to know that you are no traitor. Nor would you lend yourself to such a cause." Then louder, "Will you allow me the privilege?"

He spoke to her, to Ilse Zhalina and not the king or Markus Khandarr. She understood. He wanted consent—true consent—before he worked any magic upon her.

"I do," she said clearly. "I will speak only the truth. All of it. I want to."

"Then proceed," Armand said.

Emil Fass laid one hand on her head, one on her shoulder. His touch was gentle, but sure. Ilse trembled, then held herself still. She had not lied.

She wanted to speak the truth. Whether Armand listened or believed, she could not do more.

"Ei rûf ane gôtter. Ei rûf ane strôm . . ."

Magic streamed around them, bringing with it the scents of crushed green grass and the electric scent of lightning.

"Ei rûf ane Lir unde Toc, ane wahrheit unde weisheit . . ."

The magic wrapped her in warmth, it soothed her nerves, and yet, she felt awake and alive as never before.

Speak the truth.

I will.

Then tell us. Did Lord Raul Kosenmark betray Veraene?

No.

Did he betray the king?

No. And because she had the compulsion to speak the truth, she added, *Not as I see it.*

Explain.

She needed no time to consider her answer. She knew what to say, as she had since Raul first spoke to her about the shadow court and its concerns.

He loves Veraene. He loves the kingdom. He would do nothing against the king, unless the king himself acted against the kingdom. Dedrick knew that. He tried to tell Lord Khandarr, but he died because—

Markus Khandarr interrupted in a harsh, almost unintelligible voice. Ilse found her voice stopped entirely, as though he had covered her mouth with a hand of magic. Fass spoke earnestly, urgently, to the king. His voice was muffled and she could not make out what he said. Armand made an impatient gesture. At once, the quality of the air altered subtly and the sense of being smothered vanished. The king nodded to Fass, who continued the questioning.

Never mind Lord Dedrick. What about Lord Kosenmark?

He wants peace.

Just peace? Nothing more?

Peace, she repeated.

What about the crown?

Ilse scowled. She didn't want to, but the magic controlled her features as well as her words. Very well. She wanted the truth. If that meant a frown, she would not resist. Meanwhile, the king and Emil Fass waited for an explanation.

He does not want it, she said. *He wants a king to rule Veraene in truth. But kingship is not the same as war. Yes, Baerne defended us. He was a great man. But there is more than a single path to greatness. Give us peace, your Majesty. Peace throughout the continent. Surely that is a legacy worth having. Read the letter, your Majesty. Look to the future and not the dead past.*

She was weeping, for Armand and the kingdom, for yet another life spent in the quest for a greater cause. No one would listen to her. Leos had not. Nor would this young king. After a few more questions, Armand flicked his hand toward Fass, who bent over Ilse and whispered the words to free her from his spell.

Magic trickled from her blood and bones. She sank to her knees before the dais. Whatever dignity she had once possessed had deserted her entirely. She didn't care. Fass spoke again. Warmth rippled through her blood, enough to take away the lassitude.

"I am sorry," he said. "I did not do better than those others."

"You are better," she whispered back. "You did what I asked. Thank you."

A CONFUSING PASSAGE followed. Numerous retainers in the duke's colors escorted Ilse from the grand audience chamber. She tried to catch another glimpse of Raul Kosenmark, but they hurried her away so quickly, she saw no more than a dark dull blur that might have been his prison uniform. Only when Heloïse whispered to her that she could visit Lord Kosenmark the next morning, did she stop struggling and allow the retainers to lift her into a chair and carry her rapidly through the palace to Duke Kosenmark's apartments.

Heloïse said much more that she had difficulty taking in, but which comforted her later. She assured Ilse that Benno Iani and Josef Mann were safe. She herself would be safe as well, housed in rooms close to their own suite and guarded by their own people—at least until the king decided otherwise, she admitted. Until then, their father would argue for her and his son.

In the midst of these explanations, Marte arrived with a tray with refreshments, and together, the sisters fed Ilse plain toasted bread and tea. They were kind, kind and gentle as Ilse had not expected from such dangerous women. "I told him the truth," she said over and over. "I do not know if it's enough."

They glanced at each other. One of them, Ilse could not remember which, nodded. "No more secrets. No more lies."

* * *

FAR AWAY, IN another quarter of the palace, Markus Khandarr attended a private meeting with the king. Hours had passed since Ilse Zhalina's audience, and the bells were ringing midnight. Both had had previous and more public obligations, Armand with his other chief advisers as they discussed the contents of Miro Karasek's letter, and Markus Khandarr, who attended that first meeting and then one of his own with various associates and allies in Duenne's Court.

Now, he and the king met alone.

A low fire burned in a brazier, sending up little warmth but clouds of fresh incense. Armand sat in a cushioned chair, his head cradled in both hands. He had a headache. Anyone would, Khandarr thought, listening to the idiotic testimony by Kosenmark's lover. Of course Dzavek's minions wished to negotiate for peace. They had no jewels, nor king, nothing to prevent Veraene from taking back the province.

Nothing, except the promise of a bloody war.

So they claimed. So Kosenmark believed.

So, if he read the signs correctly, did Veraene's king.

"She was not what I expected," Armand said softly as he massaged his temples. "Nor her message. He was innocent of treason."

"Not innocent. Remember what your people said."

"They followed a ship. On your orders," Armand said. "It led them north to Károví, yes, but we have no proof Kosenmark was on that ship, nor that he met with anyone, whether this Duke Karasek or another. Perhaps . . ." He released a long breath. "Perhaps we were wrong to promote this war. I know what I said before, but think of it. Peace between the kingdoms, and not just between Veraene and Károví, but all the nations of Erythandra . . ."

He continued in that same vein, maundering on about legacies and such, until Khandarr could not bear it any longer. He stood and lurched around the room, finally coming to rest by the half-open window. A skein of clouds obscured the quarter moon, now hanging low in the sky. From the north came a thread of breeze, colored by pine tang. It was a scent Khandarr had always associated with the palace and the doings of kings. Of influence and the exercise of absolute power. Tonight, it brought him no relief.

"Your Majesty," he said softly.

A warning. As clear as he could make it. Would Armand recognize it? He did not. Or he did not wish to hear it. On and on the boy went, his thoughts fixed on Ilse Zhalina's lies, about that damned new legacy, whatever that meant. Khandarr wished he had executed the bitch in Osterling. Instead she had escaped, and stolen away that other vicious creature, the one who now claimed she was queen of Morennioù.

His legs ached. His body was ready to collapse from weariness and frustration, and an anger he had not been able to suppress since Osterling. No, longer still. Since a day twelve or thirteen years ago, when a golden-eyed boy named Raul Kosenmark had first arrived in Duenne's Court.

"Your Majesty," Khandarr repeated, louder than before, trying to overcome the roaring in his ears. Dimly, he understood he had lost some precious ability for caution, no doubt the fault of that encounter with the Morennioùen bitch, but all too easily the rage inside overwhelmed him. And when Armand made that same dismissive gesture, he raised his staff and brought it down upon the king's head in a single hard blow.

CHAPTER TWENTY-TWO

KHANDARR STARED DOWN at the king.

Armand of Angersee lay sprawled at full length upon the dark blue tiles, as though someone had flung him there. His chair, a heavy object, had toppled to one side, dragging one silk-knotted rug with it. The small table with its sunburst pattern of inlay, which had stood next to the chair at Armand's right hand, lay in broken pieces. A trickle of blood flowed outward from the king's forehead, the only movement in this utterly still, utterly silent scene.

The destruction was greater than one blow could explain, he was certain of that. *And yet I do not remember . . .*

Time, time lost, without the excuse of magic. He could not think what that might portend. His legs trembled and the roaring in his ears grew louder. Khandarr closed his eyes and breathed steadily, stubbornly, insistently, until he had regained control of his traitorous body. He wiped the blood from his staff clean with his sleeve and stumped around the chair to where Armand lay. He adjusted his grip on the stick's round head and painfully lowered himself to his knees. His heart shuddered with the effort. He needed another moment to recover before he could make a proper examination.

Oh. No, no, no . . .

Now he could see the destruction clearly. The skull cracked and crumpled into itself. Blood seeping from eyes and ears. More blood, dark and viscous, pooled beneath Armand's cheek. Markus Khandarr reached out to touch his fingers to the king's throat. It was not easy. He had to undo layers of robes and undershirts to uncover the bare flesh. Even then, he almost fainted from exhaustion before he found the pulse point at Armand's throat.

To his amazement, he felt a faint throb against his fingertips.

He's alive. Alive. I ought to heal him. I ought to—

Before he could complete the thought, the pulse faded.

No. No, my king.

Khandarr fumbled to recapture that proof that Armand lived, that he had not committed the ultimate blunder in his long quest for supremacy over the court and kingdom. His protests died even as he felt the flesh beneath his fingers stiffen and cool. It was like the moment when spirit leapt into the magical plane—except that this soul, this king, would never return as himself. Armand of Angersee had already joined the river of souls streaming from one life to the next.

My friend, my king. I would have done everything for you. To build a kingdom, an empire. To establish your name in history. If you only had listened to me one last time . . .

He gazed uncomprehendingly at the king's body. Blood spattered Armand's face, now slack and stupid in death. More blood clotted his hair. The eyes stared back at him, blank and unseeing. Khandarr almost laughed, thinking it was a fitting description of this man, who had thrust away all attempts to see clearly. It was only in those last moments that Armand turned away to see for himself.

And for that, I killed him.

Khandarr brushed his fingers over the king's eyes. He wiped away the worst of the blood from Armand's forehead. It had the consistency of spilled ink. It smelled much worse. An animal stink and ripe with rot.

A thrum reverberated through the chamber. A chime from the sand hour globes, followed by an echo of bells outside. One hour past midnight. He flinched, suffered a moment of panic. How long had he sat there, blind and useless, with the king dead at his feet? It took him several moments before he could remember that he and the king were alone in the king's most private chamber, which was locked by metal and magic, not to mention the guards. Even the queen and her ladies could not enter without permission.

He rubbed a hand over his eyes. He was safe for the moment, but not much longer. Runners with important messages might arrive. That bastard Duke Kosenmark could demand an interview with the king, even at this late hour. And tomorrow there would be an investigation, with all the consequences that implied. Oh yes, the consequences. Khandarr could imagine a mass of courtiers clamoring for a return of their many favors. Galt would be the worst. They had given him nothing of worth, the fools. Once they heard the news, they would join the throngs in accusing him.

Only if they heard the wrong news.

Yes. That was it. The king was dead. No way to disguise that. However, no one knew of the king's death except Markus Khandarr and the gods themselves, and the gods were slow to act, as he had observed, blind Toc the slowest of all. Besides, he only needed to evade their justice for a day at the most. By then, they would be bored again and Erythandra could continue on its course to a new empire.

And a new emperor.

His breath hissed from his throat. Yes. That was one outcome. He would address that later. For now, he had to contain the panic and accusations that would surely follow the king's death in private chambers. He must make certain the queen and her children were safe from retribution. Armand's oldest child was a boy, five years old. Khandarr would ensure his safety. He would advise the boy, as he had advised the father. Soon he could regain his ascendancy over the throne.

Khandarr muttered a stream of Erythandran. The magic current drew close around him, lending him strength enough to haul himself upright. Standing, he braced himself with his feet and staff, drawing one rattling breath after another. His bones ached, his muscles cried out for relief. The sac of flesh between his legs hung heavy and cold. He wanted nothing more than to lie on his bed and let a girl massage him into sleep.

No. Time for that tomorrow, if then.

He drew the current around his shoulders, like a shroud. Half a dozen steps brought him to the first door. He leaned against its frame and laid his palm against the lock. The tumblers clicked, the spells unfolded at his bidding, and the door swung open. By force of will, and the ever-diminishing vigor leant to him over the years by magic, he proceeded through two more rooms until he gained the outer doors.

The guards saluted at once. Khandarr ignored them. He summoned a runner, one of the newly appointed men who served in the night watch, to fetch Maester Galt from his rooms in the visitor's wing. No questioning there. The man wanted to earn his place in the king's service. He ran.

To the guards, Khandarr said, "Admit no one but Galt. That is the king's command."

He retired to the inner room to wait. The fire in the brazier had died to ashes. Khandarr relit it, and scattered more incense into the flames. A cloud of sweet fresh perfume filled the room, but underneath Khandarr thought he detected the first ripe scent of decay. His instinct said to lay the body on its bed, to cover the staring face with a cloth. That was old teaching, from his almost-forgotten childhood, when his father died in the mines of northern Ournes, in the mountains between Veraene and Károví. Since those hungry days, Khandarr had learned patience and expediency. He had lost some of that necessary patience in the past six months, but never a hold on the latter.

Better to leave the king's body where it lay, he decided. It would be more convincing when he told his story of intruders and assassins.

Khandarr shut the window. Taking the king's own seat behind the desk, he busied himself writing various orders to achieve his ends. He could command the loyalty of certain officers in the guards. With the right bribes, he could remove or contain troublesome members of court and council. He needed more, however. He needed absolute control. For that he needed a first, decisive victory against his enemies.

For that, I need the blood of a king.

Just as he finished the last order, the bell rang announcing a visitor. Khandarr traversed the rooms with greater speed and energy to admit Theodr Galt. Galt had paused long enough to comb and rebraid his queue, but his air was one of fevered curiosity. At least the man showed some sense and said nothing until the doors closed and they had passed into the first of the inner chambers.

"I came as quickly as possible, my lord. You and the king wish to speak with me?"

"A matter of state. You will see."

They had reached the doors to the innermost chamber. Khandarr ushered Galt inside. He followed and quickly locked the door once again with magic.

He knew the moment when Galt saw the king's body. Galt hissed and whirled around. "The king . . ."

"Murdered. Assassinated," Khandarr said. He spoke slowly, enunciating each word with painful clarity. "Three men. They used magic and bribes. Came after I left the king. I examined the windows. Found the traces of their signatures. Duke Kosenmark hired them. He knew the king intended to execute his son."

"Then we must call the guards," Galt said. "We must—"

He stopped and stared wide-eyed at Khandarr.

"I believe I understand the situation," he said slowly.

Khandarr nodded. "I told you. I want your allegiance. You agreed. Now to prove your vow. Take this message to Baron Quint. He will arrest the duke and his family. You. Lead another squad to Lord Raul Kosenmark's cell. Execute the man. Bring his head to me. There is one thing . . ." He paused to recover his breath and to hold Galt's gaze with his own. "When the council convenes, you must confess. You worked for Duke Kosenmark.

You took a bribe. You found those men. Give . . . whatever reason you like. I will protect you. Is that enough?"

Galt's eyes narrowed. He looked a true merchant, Khandarr thought, ready to bargain. Then came a strange light smile, almost joyous, except the mage could not picture any joy in this man, except that which caused misery for others.

"I will do it," Galt said. "On one condition. Give me the girl."

"Done."

Khandarr handed over three folded papers to Galt. One was for Quint, he said. One was the formal order of execution, which Galt must present to the guards and to the prison officer on watch. The last was for Khandarr's own steward. "He will take care of the rest."

MUCH EARLIER, NADINE had begged off regular duty for the evening. Between Lady Heloïse and her two wicked sisters, she could not sit, never mind think of entertaining one of the guards, or those minor nobles who infested the palace. The steward in charge of the courtesans accepted her excuses more easily than expected, though to be sure, none of the nobles had sent for a woman or man the entire day. After the day's trial session, and the evidence produced by Duke Kosenmark for his son's innocence, they were all closeted with each other discussing politics.

Freed from her duties, Nadine collected a carafe of cold water and a bag of sausages, and settled herself in a useful niche, in a gallery overlooking Lord Markus Khandarr's suite of rooms. She waited patiently through the hours, taking note of the mage councillor's visitors. One captain of the evening guard. A woman in a silken jacket and trousers, with the look of the western provinces about her. A string of very anonymous men and women that Nadine immediately classified as informers.

But no sign of that vermin, Khandarr.

She was tempted to track him down, even if that meant a visit to the royal chambers. No. Khandarr might be closeted with the king, but she had the sense that she would lose all if she tried to chase the man through this maze of a palace.

Even so, if he does not return soon, I shall have to urinate on his doorstep.

"Nadine, my love."

It was the senior guard captain. She thought the woman had departed hours ago.

Nadine smiled and glanced upward through her eyelashes. "Katja. Captain."

"Watching our friend?" the captain said. She came originally from one of the southern provinces, dark and with thick springy hair pulled back into tight braids. On an ordinary day, Nadine would have found her irresistible. But since Heloïse . . .

Katja watched her closely, and so she smiled again, more lazily than before. "He fascinates me, my dear captain. So much influence. So much poison concentrated in a single broken body. When does your watch end?"

"In three hours. I think I shall want attention. Your attention."

Nadine laughed. She drew the captain into a kiss, which she made slow and deep and languorous. "Would you like some sausage?" she whispered into Katja's ear. "Or do you prefer ripe red cherries? I could peel each one for you, slowly and carefully, until nothing hides the fruit from view. Then I would *pop* it into your mouth. Oh, yes. That is very nice. Dear, sweet, delectable captain."

The captain drew back, breathless from Nadine's attention. "He is not there. He is with the king," she said. "Three hours. Yes?"

"Three hours," Nadine said. "Call for me in the courtesan wing."

Alone she returned to her watch. She considered her promise to Katja Keller, given so easily and meaning nothing. She cast her memory farther back, through her years as a courtesan in Raul Kosenmark's pleasure house, soft and delightful, despite the knife edge of danger that even the dimmest member of that household could not ignore.

I could have left them all, Kathe and Ilse and the others. I could have gone back to my family in the hills and led a peaceful life.

She laughed, silently, at such a picture.

Then came alert as a runner—one of Khandarr's senior runners—galloped into view. The man pounded on the grand wooden doors, decorated with gold leaf and precious gems. Nadine was certain he had flattened a god's face with his fist. Then guards admitted the runner, who tumbled inside.

A quarter hour later, six runners spilled out the doorway and hurried off in six different directions.

No Khandarr, but a message from the man. Of that she was certain.

So. Play the spy and see what scheme Khandarr has laid.

She slid through shadows and behind tapestries after the most senior of the runners. At the next guard post, the runner approached the squad captain. Nadine could not hear their exchange, but the night lamps cast enough illumination that she easily saw the man's shock, the sudden blankness she associated with a disagreeable order.

Moments later, a dozen guards streamed toward the royal visitors' wing. That was unexpected. Unless . . .

Nadine sped to the nearest servants' corridor. She crossed over to the next wing along an open-air bridge, then circled upward to the floor where Duke Kosenmark and his family had lodged at the king's special invitation. She had but a few moments before Khandarr's minions arrived.

Two liveried guards stood outside the doors. Nadine stopped and held out her hands to show she carried no weapons. "Wake the duke," she said in low quick voice. "Tell him the guards are coming to arrest . . . I am not exactly sure which of them, maybe the entire family, but most certainly the duke."

The guard's eyes narrowed as he scanned her face. "I recognize you. The Lady Heloïse's companion. Is it only the duke we should warn?"

"Everyone," Nadine said. "Now."

He nodded. "My ladies are awake. You will find them in the library at the far end of this passage. I will tell his grace." To his partner, he said, "Stay here. Do not admit anyone else, not even the king himself."

Nadine did not wait to hear the rest. She was already pelting down the corridor for the library. All three Kosenmark daughters sprang to their feet as she burst into the room. "Danger," she gasped. Panic had overtaken her unawares.

"Who?" Olivia said.

"The king," Marte said softly.

"No." Heloïse was smiling, a feral tooth-tipped smile that sent a river of cold down Nadine's spine. "Markus Khandarr. He might act in the king's name, but the plans are his. Am I right?"

"I do not know. I only know he has sent off a half dozen runners. One of them handed orders to a squad of guards, who are marching here. You and your sisters and your father must leave the palace at once."

She was up and almost away when Heloïse called out, "Where are you going?"

"To Ilse Zhalina. Go. I will find you later."

ILSE WOKE AT once to the pounding at her door. She bolted upright, heart thundering against her ribs. *The king, the duke, a messenger come with terrible news . . .* She stumbled from the bed, her feet tangled in the bed linens. The tiny room assigned to her, a servant's bedchamber, was little more than a closet, and she had just escaped from the bed when the door crashed open, and a hand seized her shoulder. Ilse grabbed her attacker's arm with both hands—it was a woman, the arm slim but strong. Ilse twisted the arm as she rolled to her feet. She shoved the woman away and swept up the knife from under her pillow, calling up the magic current.

Light flared from a candle. Nadine stood opposite her, breathing hard. Her eyes were bright and angry. She, too, carried a knife.

"Beloved," she said. "How delightful to see tokens of your adoration. Alas, we do not have the luxury for dalliance tonight. Tell me, how much do you love your idiot Lord Kosenmark?"

Ilse stared. "What?"

"I said, how much do you love that man? Because you must act now. Markus Khandarr has sent a fleet of runners off in all different directions. He nearly had the duke arrested—I say nearly because I fervently wish the entire clan succeeded in shutting up long enough to escape. At least I hope they did," she said in an edged whisper. "What you must know is this . . ."

She gave a succinct report of her spying. Ilse listened as she hurried into her plainest clothing—trousers and shirt and boots—and armed herself with the weapons she had yielded before. It was impossible that Markus Khandarr would act against the king's explicit orders. She could only think that Khandarr had persuaded Armand to break off the trial. "I will go to Raul's cell," she told Nadine. "Tell Benno and Josef. They have quarters down the next corridor. If the king had decided against us, he and Khandarr will have them arrested as well."

On impulse, she pulled Nadine close and kissed her passionately. Then she was off.

OLIVIA COLLECTED THEIR best swords and knives. Marte handed out leather helmets and the chain-mail shirts she had packed along with their other gear and clothing. It was Heloïse, however, who knew the swiftest passage to the outer gates. Within moments of Nadine's warning, they and their father were racing down and around the nearest stairwell.

All along their father protested. "We must get word to the council."

"We will," Marte snapped. "As soon as we have you safely out of the palace."

Two landings down, they emerged into a broad hallway lined by statuary. Starlight and moonlight illuminated the enormous glass windows at either end, enough to determine the hall was empty. On the opposite side, a small doorway gave into a servants' corridor that paralleled the public one. Their goal, Heloïse said breathlessly, was a courtyard near the kitchens, where the scullions loaded up wagons with trash from the palace. There would be guards, but not as many as by the public entry gates.

Down another flight of stairs to the ground floor. Then through a maze of passageways that ended in an airy public chamber, its high ceiling hung with chandeliers, and galleries overlooking the patterned floor. Silently Heloïse pointed out the small archway across the chamber. Leaning close to her father and sisters, she whispered that it would lead to the region occupied by the main palace kitchens.

They each checked their weapons. Touched hand to hand in a final reassurance.

Olivia took the lead. Marte and Heloïse flanked their father, who had drawn his sword. Halfway across, they heard an echo of footsteps to their left. "Hurry," Marte whispered.

Too late. A squad of ten guards appeared from the farther doorway. "Duke Kosenmark . . ."

"You are mistaken," Heloïse said. "We are four envoys from Ysterien."

She drew her sword. Olivia gave a warbling cry and charged forward, a blade in one hand, a metal-studded baton in the other. "Go!" she called out to her sisters.

"Not yet!" Marte, too, had her sword ready.

The fight had begun.

ILSE PAUSED ON the ground floor to catch her breath. She had stopped a passing runner for directions to the prison quarter. The boy—no older than Damek Rudny—had delivered the information in a monotone, all the while staring at her weapons. She had wanted to shake him, tell him that she was terrified as well, but when a distant shout distracted her, and he broke free, she did not try to pursue him.

It was possible, just possible that Nadine's fears meant nothing. That the king would not act against Raul. Except her own instincts yammered at her—it was not the king, but Markus Khandarr she feared. *He* might do anything.

The crash of sword against sword broke into her thoughts. Her head jerked up. Yes, it came from the same hallway as that shout.

She launched into a run for the next stairwell.

NADINE WOKE MANN with almost no effort at all. Iani she had dispatched with numerous arguments. The man was worse than any scholar she had seduced, insisting on an exact assessment of the situation. He refused her assistance in escaping the palace. He had more important tasks to accomplish. Wonderful. She left him to his own devices. To her joy, Mann asked no questions, merely requested that she permit him to follow her to whichever catastrophe required their attention.

At last, she thought. *Someone who does not argue.*

She had cause to regret that opinion within the hour.

They had descended five flights of stairs to the palace's ground floor. From there, Nadine dragged Mann through a convoluted maze of passageways that wound between the acknowledged public audience rooms, the more private interview rooms, and those others used by the courtesans when under orders from the king. She could almost tell which courtesan favored which room by the lingering scent of perfume. There was Georg, there Evanna, there the delicious Ava, who had arrived the month before Nadine and defied sexual identity.

They were approaching the outermost ring of corridors, where Nadine hoped to find a gate or doorway unguarded, when a mob of soldiers rounded the corner.

Mann never hesitated. "Follow me," he shouted, and dived through the nearest door.

Nadine dived after him. "What are you thinking?"

"I'm not," he replied with unholy glee. "I am dancing over my fate. You see, my brother said I would die. Perhaps I shall."

She grabbed his arm and hauled him into a closet, one she knew held a secret door for the convenience of servants and courtesans. Mann was laughing, she was cursing. He did not resist, however, when she kicked the next door open and propelled him through it. The passageway was cramped and dark, and the dust stirred up by their trampling had them both sneezing. Mann was babbling about his brother and the void between worlds. Once more, she wondered if she ought to have fled home to her family and spent the remainder of her years in quiet boredom.

She shook Mann by the arm. "Shut up."

He gulped down the laughter and obeyed. Soon they had reached her next goal, a ladder leading into the sewers below the palace. Just in time. From above came the shouts and curses of their pursuers.

Nadine poked Mann with her knife. He clambered down the ladder. She heard a splash and winced. Idiot. Cursing her choice of companions, she descended to find Mann hauling himself onto the ledge that ran along the main channel. She helped him to his feet and then surveyed their surroundings.

They stood on a narrow brick ledge. In the dim light from the opening Nadine could make out the low, arched ceiling, overgrown by moss and slime, the wide expanse filled by dark sludge. Her eyes burned from the stink of the channel and Mann himself.

"Which way?" Mann said.

"I don't know. Wait. To the right. That leads to the outer walls."

"And the left?"

"Does it matter?"

"Oh, yes. It all matters."

From above came the clamor of voices. More voices echoed down the passage to their right. Another moment and the guards would trap them. Mann, covered in mud and slime, laughed wildly. He drew a sword she had not realized he possessed. "Go," he shouted. "Go find the council. Find Lord Alberich de Ytel. Tell them what you know. And do not argue." Still laughing, he turned back to fight off their attackers.

"HE IS BLEEDING," Marte said to Olivia. "He cannot walk."

"Will he live?"

Duke Kosenmark lay panting on the ground as his daughters examined him, with an impersonal efficiency he found particularly maddening. Agony twisted his guts. One leg burned with white fire. A guard had smashed a truncheon against his knee. Olivia had dispatched the man before he could do more. Kosenmark had plunged his own sword into the next guard before he collapsed.

He dimly recalled the rest of the guards falling around him, like so many trees driven down by unrelenting winds. He whispered a prayer to Lir and Toc to send these men and women, who had vowed their allegiance to the king, to a more merciful life.

Olivia poked his leg. He grunted. "Find me a physician and I will live. And stop pretending I cannot hear you."

One of his daughters laughed. Marte, he thought.

Together, they raised him to standing. Heloïse slung his left arm over her shoulder. His other arm hung limp. Only now was he aware of the throbbing in his shoulder, the pain lancing through his chest. More injuries, taken while he had charged like a young bull at those guards.

"I am not dying," he breathed. "Not yet."

"Oh, certainly not," Marte said. "Else you would not complain so much. Olivia?"

"The passage ahead is clear," Olivia answered.

"Less than a mile and we are free," Heloïse added.

She did not mention their brother, but all three sisters thought of him.

ILSE VAULTED DOWN the last six steps to the prison quadrant. Guards attempted to block her passage. She glared at them. "I come in the duke's name."

"These are the king's domain. You need his authority—"

Ilse did not wait for him to finish. She gathered up the magical current and flung a fistful of fire at the guards. They all fell to the ground, writhing.

Her stomach twisted, but she could not pause for sympathy. She leapt over them and sped down the corridor, to the next intersection, down a second flight of stairs, where she veered to the right and Raul Kosenmark's cell.

Too late.

That was her first thought when she saw a knot of guards in the corridor. Four men, with swords drawn.

She slowed to a walk. If the king had decreed Raul should die, they would kill him before she could stop them with blade or magic. She had to delay them long enough for her to convince Armand himself.

One guard swung his head around. He spoke to his companions, and they all turned to face her, their weapons held ready. She drew closer, her skin alight with a fire of nerves.

"My lady," said one at last.

Ilse stopped. "My name is Ilse Zhalina. I spoke before the king today."

All of them stirred. So they recognized her name.

One glanced into the open cell. Ilse's throat squeezed shut as two more guards emerged with a prisoner between them. It was Raul, his hands manacled behind his back, his cheeks bruised and his mouth swollen and bleeding.

All her frantic thoughts of the king and his intentions vanished at the sight. Ilse glided forward to Raul, hardly noticing how the guards parted to either side. Raul's head swung up just as she reached him. "Ah," he breathed. "My love."

"My love."

She embraced him gently. His heart was beating swift and light. His skin radiated a heat far beyond what she expected. Had magic been involved? She could not tell. She only cared that she had reached him in time. Whatever Armand had decided, she would convince him otherwise. She would . . .

"Mistress Therez."

Ilse recoiled. Raul stiffened.

Theodr Galt stepped from the cell. He was dressed in dark civilian garb. He also carried a heavy sword in one hand. A strange smile lit his face.

"Your lover is dead," he said. "Or he will be, soon enough."

"By whose order?"

"The king's."

Ilse laid a hand on Raul's arm. He was trembling. So was she.

"Let me see the king's order," she demanded.

"You have no right," Galt said.

"Wrong," Raul said, and tilted his head toward the guards. "They know. A king's order is a public matter. I am no traitor, but if the king believes me one, then let the world know. Show her the papers, you miserable impostor."

Arguments followed. The king's order needed no witnesses, Galt insisted. Nor were they a secret, the senior officer replied. Besides, they had all listened to the Lady Ilse's testimony. She had a right. It was not just their own doubts about the matter, she realized. They disliked Galt for assuming authority where he had none.

"Show me the order," she said quietly. "Please. If the king has ordered Lord Kosenmark to die, then . . ." Her voice caught. "If he must die, let me say farewell."

She sank against Raul's chest and held him tight. His clothes were filthy, and he had not bathed in weeks. She did not care. She could only memorize the weight of his body against hers, the texture of his skin, all the myriad details that made up the man Raul Kosenmark. She would need all those to find him in the next life, if the gods were not kind.

"You are a master at theatrics," he whispered into her hair. His voice was higher, lighter than she recalled. He, too, was terrified.

"I am only telling the truth," she whispered back.

"That is what makes you so compelling."

The argument had died to silence. With an effort, Ilse released her hold on Raul. The senior guard waited, his expression deferential. In his hands, he held a sheaf of papers.

"The king's orders," he said. "For you to examine."

Ilse accepted them, hardly daring to believe she had been given this chance. *And what if it means nothing?*

She refused to think of that. She read through the six pages of densely written script. It was all nonsense, accusations that Raul Kosenmark had conspired to betray Veraene's concerns to interested parties in Károví. (Not the king. That much had changed since her audience.) It was as though Armand had rejected her testimony. He would do what he wished and launch a war.

The last few paragraphs caused her head to swim. Lord Kosenmark to be executed by sword. His head removed and brought as proof to the king's chambers. It was an act of cruelty, one she would not have ascribed to Armand. Except . . .

"I see no signature," she said.

"What do you mean?" Galt said.

"No signature. There is the king's seal but—"

"Nothing more is required," Galt supplied smoothly. "Nothing except his own thumbprint, which is not missing."

He was right, damn him. She had dismissed that smear of reddish brown as a wine stain. Now that she examined it, she could see the whorls of a broad fingerprint. Was it Armand's? It had to be. Even Khandarr would not attempt to forge the king's own imprint.

Or would he?

Galt attempted to snatch the paper from her hands.

Ilse struck his hand away. "One moment." To the guards, she said, "I must be certain. Please. I can prove the king's intent with magic."

The guards held Theodr Galt back from further interference. Ilse allowed herself one hungry glance toward Raul. He seemed amused, or amazed. She could not tell which. *Do you have a plan?* he mouthed.

No, she replied. *But I have an idea.*

She laid her hands over both sides of the paper. Breathed in to capture that elusive sense of balance magic required. Her whole attention spiraled down to the paper, to the spot of blood that marked the king's personal imprint . . .

Blood. That much she could tell at once. A magical signature overlaid the bloodstain, which surprised her. She had thought Armand knew no magic, which was why he required a strong mage councillor such as Markus Khandarr. The signature itself prickled at her memory. The scent of cold snow, overlaid by a sickly sweetness she did not want to examine closer. With a shock, she recognized it—Markus Khandarr's. She probed deeper. Sensed a deadness connected to the magic. Her skin itched. Signatures were not dead things. Blood was not dead . . .

Not unless it comes from a dead person.

She broke her connection with the magic and staggered backward, rubbing fiercely at her fingers where the skin had touched the blood print.

"He's dead," she whispered. "The king is dead."

"Liar." Galt lunged forward, but the guards caught him.

The senior officer's eyes narrowed. He looked unhappy and anxious. "I don't like this," he said. "You came from the king himself?" he said to Galt.

"From the king," Galt said hoarsely. "I swear it."

"No need to swear. We will ask him ourselves."

NADINE ARRIVED IN the vast wing where the senior councillors had their apartments. Mann had given her one name before he departed on his mad errand to lead the guards away. Lord Alberich de Ytel, he'd told her. Governor of Duenne City. Not the senior councillor, but a man of influence and power. He was the man to warn.

Muttering directions to herself, she turned down a side corridor, which supposedly connected this hall with another running at angles. Left and right, down three intersections . . .

. . . and skidded to a halt at the sight of palace guards with swords drawn.

She slithered back into the nearest doorway, her pulse thundering in her ears. Only when she was certain they had not sighted her did she peer around the doorframe.

Eight, no, ten guards were battling each other. In the bright lamplight, she could tell they all wore palace uniforms. Intruders? No, more mischief from Markus Khandarr, she was certain of that. Even as she came to that conclusion, one guard ran another through with his sword. The second guard jerked, then folded over with his hands clutched over his chest, blood spilling through his fingers.

Nadine did not wait. She darted back the same route she had come. She heard shouts behind her and swerved into the nearest servants' passageway. Lamps spelled with magic flickered on and died away as she passed. She knew nothing of this region in the palace, but she had her instincts, borne of many years in unfamiliar and sometimes dangerous quarters.

She exited the servants' corridor to find herself in an airy bell-shaped room, painted in vivid colors and gold leaf, with windows open to the night. And at last, a runner obviously standing duty, more proof of royalty's spendthrift notions, to place someone here in this empty spot.

The runner started to attention. "My lady."

"I must find Lord Alberich de Ytel," Nadine said breathlessly. "The palace is under attack."

Even as she spoke, the uproar from the skirmish reached them. The runner whispered, "I must get word to the palace guard."

"Those *are* the palace guards," Nadine cried. "Send word to the king himself. And tell me how I can reach Lord Alberich de Ytel. Quickly. We must find all the loyal people before it's too late."

That provoked the reaction she wanted. Without hesitation, the runner poured out directions to Ytel's suite of rooms. Then she sped off to warn the king, and Nadine went in search of the royal governor.

THE SENIOR GUARD sent a runner ahead to the king's chambers. Galt protested loudly until the guards threatened to arrest him as well. He subsided with a sour grin, but Ilse's skin rippled with cold when his gaze flicked over to her. *You kept your character a secret in Melnek,* she thought. *You were the respectable merchant, wealthy and influential. I had no reason to fear you except for rumors. If I had ignored my instincts, if I had obeyed my father and acted the part of the good daughter to marry you, I would have lived in torment the rest of my life.*

She wondered how many other young women, told that their fears were foolish, entered into marriages such as the one she had escaped.

She kept as close as possible to Raul's side during the long trek from the prison quarter and along a plain corridor that she guessed was used solely by the palace guards. No one objected to her presence, not even Galt, who continued to favor her with that eerie grin. But the guards did not remove the manacles from Raul's wrists, and they insisted she keep an arm's length away from him. *They do not trust either of us,* she thought.

Once on the ground floor, they exited the guards' corridor for a short broad passageway of plain brick and stone. At either end of the passageway, the ceilings rose higher, the walls were faced with mosaics, and she saw what appeared to be more of the palace's grand public spaces. Raul's eyes widened slightly as he took in their surroundings. "So our king has come to see as his grandfather once did," he murmured. "That is . . . interesting."

Two armed sentries stood outside a plain wooden door. When the guard made known their errand, and gave the passwords, the older sentry shook his head. "Lord Khandarr made it clear. He wants no one to pass except Maester Galt."

"It's a matter of treason," the senior guard said. He continued in a low voice, obviously explaining the difficulty. The sentries conferred with each other. Judging by their expressions, they were uneasy about disobeying the king's order, but Ilse's accusations obviously made them uncertain.

She glanced toward Raul. *What can we do?*

He shrugged, but she could sense the tension in his stance. He was about to try something desperate. So was she.

A clatter of running footsteps snagged her attention. A runner pelted around the corner, missed her footing, and crashed into the wall before she could right herself. "Treason!" she cried, scrambling to her feet. "There's fighting on the main floor. They say the king's in danger."

The younger sentry immediately vanished through the plain door. The senior guard pressed forward. "If it's a matter of treason, we must speak with the king as well."

He tried to push past the sentry, but the man set his back against the door and drew his sword. "Not until Lord Khandarr or the king tells us so—"

A muffled shout sounded from within the king's offices. Ilse felt the air draw tight over her skin. She had just registered that someone had used strong magic, when she heard a thumping noise, then a thin screech, which broke off suddenly. "Stand back," the second sentry said. He opened the door a crack and glanced inside. "Oh, sweet gods."

He flung the door wide open. "To the king!"

All the guards poured into the room. Ilse linked her arm around Raul's and they followed.

Once, the room might have been as exquisite as all the others in the palace. Once. Ilse could see nothing but the man who lay sprawled on his back, his throat torn open and the blood soaking into the carpet. It was the first sentry, the younger one. Lord Khandarr leaned against the wall opposite, next to a door that swung on its hinges. The air was heavy and rank with the scent of magic, and Ilse had the sense of falling through the ocean and the weight of water pressing against her chest.

"Lord Khandarr," the second sentry said. He stopped. Stared down at the dead man on the floor. "Lord Khandarr . . . I . . . I must speak with the king."

"The king is dead," Khandarr said heavily. "Killed by assassins."

"Who laid his thumbprint on these orders?" Ilse demanded. "The king? The dead king? And why haven't you raised the alarm?"

"Yes," Raul said. "Why haven't you, Markus?"

Khandarr gave a shout, a stuttering cry in Old Erythandran. Only a syllable behind him, Ilse cried out an answering summons. Magic burst against cold bright magic. The air rang with its explosion. Ilse fell to her knees, blinded and gasping for breath. She scrabbled against the hard tiles until she gained a purchase and crawled forward to where Raul lay. It took another precious moment before she could lift her hand to lay it over his chest. She felt the pulse of his heartbeat, the rise and fall of his chest, and she almost wept with relief. Yes, yes, he lived.

She dragged a hand over her eyes and muttered another invocation to magic. Her vision cleared, the sight horrified her. It was too much like the scene after Leos Dzavek's death. The room in shambles, its walls scorched and burnt. And worse. Five guards lying in a bloody heap, among them the other sentry and the senior guard. Markus Khandarr had vanished. There was no sign of Theodr Galt.

A shadow wavered to her right. It was the single surviving guard, obviously terrified, but determined to do his duty to the king. "Go for help," she told him. "The captain of the watch, anyone you know is loyal to our king."

She did not wait to see if he obeyed. She was already searching the dead senior guard for his keys. She unlocked the manacles from Raul's wrists and those fastening the chains to his ankles. He stirred under her touch. "Ilse. My love." Then his eyes blinked open. "Markus."

Ilse helped him to stand. He staggered on his feet, stared around at the destruction, and muttered a curse under his breath. "Where is Markus?"

"Through that door," Ilse said. "We must be quick, my love."

Raul caught up a sword from one of the dead guards and plunged through the doorway. Ilse started after him, but a hand seized her arm.

"Do not argue," Galt said. "And you will have an easier time."

He expected her to be the same as she was three years ago, terrified and unable to defend herself. That was his first mistake, Ilse thought. She darted toward him, and dug her thumbnail between his fingerbones. Galt let go, cursing. Before he could attempt to recapture her, Ilse loosed her sword from its sheath and had the satisfaction of seeing him flinch as it glittered in the lamplight.

"Never," she said in a low voice. "Never again will you torment me or any other woman."

She advanced and struck. Galt managed to fend off the first strike. He was not so lucky with the second. Ilse feinted to one side, ducked under his blade, and struck him on the temple with the flat of her blade. He dropped to the floor.

Idiot, she thought. The temptation to run him through lasted only a moment. Then she sprinted after Raul.

She crossed a second parlor and through the next door, only to skid to a halt before a curtain of fire. The tapestries and curtains were ablaze, and smoke boiled up from the carpet. She could see nothing except a few vague shadows. Ilse dropped to her knees and crawled to the nearest one. It was Armand. His skull was crushed and he lay in a pool of drying blood. Farther on, Raul knelt on one knee, covered in blood from his face to his shirt. He still gripped a sword in one hand. Markus Khandarr was splayed against the farther wall, his staff abandoned.

Raul launched himself at Khandarr. There was an explosion of magic. Ilse staggered back and caught hold of the doorframe. Her vision was smeared. Where had Raul gone? Where had Khandarr gone? She blinked, blinked again. Two shadows suspended in the air, as if painted with smoke, and she knew she saw the echo of their bodies as they leapt into the plane of magic.

She leapt after them.

RAUL CROUCHED ON a thin ribbon of brightness, emptiness all around. He would have been terrified, except his whole attention was on the man before him. Markus Khandarr's lips curled back. His face turned gray, blood smeared his cheek, and more blood trickled from the slash across his forehead. He looked as though he were close to fainting, but he glared in defiance. "If you kill me. You cannot return."

"I knew that before I followed you," Raul breathed.

He leapt forward and slashed Khandarr across the chest with his sword. A deep gash opened, down to the bone. Blood spurted out. Khandarr's face locked in surprise.

Raul grinned. "You thought I was not willing to pay that price."

"I did. Only . . . so quickly. No."

Khandarr flung his head up and called aloud in Erythandran, a long stuttering string of syllables. Magic, though they had a surfeit already in the void, swirled around them. Raul stumbled forward. Only now could he feel all his injuries. His face burned from the magic; his ribs sent spasms through his chest. He shifted his hold on his sword so that the blade pointed down. Khandarr sank to his knees, grinning at him and the blade above. "My gift to you," he said. "Remember me always."

He cried out again in Erythandran, just as Raul drove the point down into his throat. One last syllable bubbled out. Then the magic wrapped itself tight around Raul Kosenmark.

His skin was on fire with magic. His guts twisted with the agony. He fell to his knees next to Khandarr's body, jarring his cracked ribs. He pressed his hand against his side, gasping for breath as the magic coursed through his veins.

Magic. Was it possible he could bend Khandarr's magic to his own purpose? He tried to remember what little he knew about magical healing, but the current was like a live thing, squirming against his will. "Heal me," he whispered. "Heal me, dammit."

I will, said a voice like Markus Khandarr's.

Raul's throat closed. His skin shuddered and crawled. A weight pressed against his chest, squeezed the flesh between his legs. He cried out, felt a rasping in his throat, as though the magic had scoured his flesh. He cried out again, a strange deep cracking shout that wavered up and down and finally boomed out in unfamiliar tones.

He bent over double. Pressed both hands against his eyes.

I know. I know what he's done.

ILSE ARRIVED IN the void, her sword still gripped as if to parry another attack. All was dark. Empty. She saw nothing, not even the stream of souls on their journey from life to life. A true void, without scent or sound or any movement. Once more Anderswar defied her expectations.

I have lost him. Oh Lir, please show me where he has gone. If you love your children, have pity on us. Oh Toc . . .

She pressed a hand over her mouth and closed her eyes, shuddering in terror and grief. Two points of light flickered against her eyelids, then faded into a darkness more profound than before. Was this how blind Toc saw the world? He had sacrificed his eyes to create the sun and moon. In her grief over his death, Lir had wept, and her tears became the stars.

A silvery mist curled around the edges of her vision. She took a faltering step forward. The mist brightened and surged upward to bury her feet. The blackness overhead grew dimmer and she saw a pale stream of what might be the river of souls as they crossed the void. Her eyes still closed, she turned around to see the fog rising up in streamers. And there, just ahead, movement stirred.

She hurried forward a few steps. Stopped and sank to her knees in shock. Markus Khandarr lay sprawled at length, blood leaking from throat and chest, coloring the mist dark crimson, his eyes blank with death. Raul Kosenmark crouched next to the body, his sword forgotten by his side. Even as her pulse beat faster in joy that he lived, Raul gave a jerk and collapsed.

Ilse flung herself to standing and ran to his side. No, no, no. The gods could not be so cruel to let him die. She touched her fingers to Raul's throat. His pulse beat steadily, but his shirt was sticky with blood, and his skin burned with fever.

He stared at her with golden eyes dimmed and cloudy. "Ilse?"

"My love. What happened?"

"It's . . . it's what he said before. He . . ."

He mumbled but she could not understand him. He had lost too much blood. She had to get him back to Duenne as quickly as possible. She nearly laughed to think of time, here in Anderswar. She had to bite down on her lip to break the panic. *Come, my love. I will not fail you now.*

Her heartbeat slowed. Her vision spiraled down to the point between breaths, the point between magic and the mundane, between terror and courage. She had forgotten Anderswar and its void. She could think only of Duenne and its towers. Of the streets filled with bellsong and a wind that carried the scent of Veraene's endless plains. Of a golden palace where Tanja Duhr and her beloved once lived.

The mist ebbed from them like the tide rolling out. Once more she saw the worlds wheeling beneath them. Above, bright points marked where souls journeyed to their next lives. Ilse gathered Raul into her arms.

"Ei rûf ane gôtter," she whispered. *"Komen mir de zoubernisse. Komen mir der wërlt."*

CHAPTER TWENTY-THREE

HER BODY HAD turned numb. Her breath had frozen inside her. Her thoughts came to her in single words, collecting like raindrops from the mist, until they gathered the weight to plummet from nothing into substance, into the pool of consciousness.

Black. Void. Death and blood. A senseless babbling in her ears.

It was like a game of word links drawn from the nightmare that was Anderswar.

Gradually, as though from a distance, she became aware of her surroundings. She drew a deep breath and felt an ache deep within. Voices thrummed in her ears, like that of Lir's jewels before they returned to magic's plane. Raul lay motionless in her arms, his skin burning with fever. She pressed her face against his chest. If he was so warm, she told herself, he could not be dead.

A hand gripped her shoulder. "Ilse."

She jerked her head up. Benno Iani bent over her. His eyes were buried in darkness, lines etched into his face. And that look on his face, as though he had witnessed something impossible.

"You are home," he whispered. "Home. Do you understand?"

She could barely comprehend what he said. *Home? What did that mean?* She blinked and tried to take in her surroundings. She was dimly aware of many, many people gathered around. There was the gleam of swords, and the brighter, sharper glitter of jewels. She lifted her head to see a vast open space. The palace, she remembered. They were in the middle of the grand audience hall where she had argued for Raul's innocence.

"Benno," she whispered. "How . . ."

"You and he vanished five days ago. Your shadows appeared in this chamber yesterday. I've been waiting." In milder tones, he said, "You must let him go."

Ilse released her grip on Raul. She fell backward, into a cloud of scented silk. Her head lay pillowed on a woman's breast, and a gentle hand brushed the sweat-soaked hair from her face. "You must never, ever frighten us so,"

Nadine murmured into her ear. "I am a selfish creature, remember? I cannot bear to spend a lifetime thinking I might have saved you, but did not." She kissed Ilse lightly and her breath fluttered against Ilse's cheek. "My love, my brave and true love. Do you know what you have done? You have saved the kingdom. Come. Do not weep. Lord Iani will cure your beloved of whatever ails him."

"I will hold you to that promise," Ilse whispered.

Nadine laughed and helped her to stumble over to Iani's side. Iani barely acknowledged them. His attention was locked on Raul, who lay shuddering and sweating on the marble floor. Raul's shirt was soaked with sweat and blood, his golden eyes staring upward as though he could see to the river of souls and beyond. All around the magic shimmered in a thick cloud.

"A curious knot," Benno murmured. "I wonder . . . Ah."

He rocked back onto his heels, his face gone blank with amazement.

"What is it?" Ilse said. She clutched at his arm. "What is wrong, Benno?"

Iani did not respond at first. He rubbed his free hand over his eyes, stared again at Raul. "I did not think it possible . . ." Then he glanced around, as though suddenly aware of the audience that surrounded them. "He is ill," he said in a louder voice. "He needs quiet and rest. With that, he will recover soon enough."

He stood and, with an air Ilse had not thought possible from the man, barked out orders. A litter for Lord Kosenmark, another for Mistress Ilse. They were to take both of his patients at once to the duke's new suite of rooms. Tell the kitchens to send up trays with food fit for invalids. He flung out his hands and runners scattered to obey. Then Iani reached down to Ilse. "Come. I will tend you both together."

The litters arrived. Benno oversaw the carriers settling Raul and Ilse on the cushions. Nadine covered Ilse with a blanket and smoothed her hair from her face. "Do not kill her from neglect," she said to Benno Iani in a soft silken voice. "Or I shall hunt you down."

"That I believe," Benno said just as quietly. "You forget, however, that she is just as much my friend as Raul Kosenmark is."

THE CARRIERS RAN without pause through the corridors, up a winding staircase, and into a different wing, one far grander than the one Ilse remembered. A dozen men and women in the royal livery stood guard along its length. More guards in the Valentain uniform flanked the double doors that marked the Kosenmark suite. One lifted her into his arms and carried her through the doors, into an apartment that might serve a prince, if not a king.

Once inside, attendants took over and laid Raul on a bed of soft linens and feather quilts. The guard carrying Ilse set her on a second bed. She struggled to stand up, but her body refused to obey, and she collapsed into a heap. Iani came to her side at once. "You and he spent days between Anderswar and the ordinary world," he said. "You must have nourishment. And speaking of which . . ."

Servants arrived with bread, hot broth, and watered wine. Nadine had insinuated herself between them and knelt beside Ilse. "Allow me," she said. She raised Ilse and arranged the pillows so that Ilse could sit upright, then fed her spoonfuls of broth. Her manner was brisk and gentle as she coaxed Ilse to take yet another sip of the broth.

"When did you become a nurse?" Ilse whispered.

"Since my brother took ill and our mother could not spare any attention from the harvest. You did not know I had a brother. I did. A horrible mischievous brother. Also, two sisters and a dozen or more useless cousins. My father remains a mystery, alas, though we considered him a valuable source for the stories we told on winter nights."

Nadine prattled on about her brother and sisters, and her life in the hill country of Veraene's northern province of Ournes. She kept her voice pitched low and soft and soothing, while she broke up pieces of bread and soaked them in the broth. "You must eat," she said, when Ilse objected. "Eat so that you can be strong."

"But Raul."

"Hush. Let me poke our Lord Grand Physician."

A short whispered conference took place between Nadine and Benno Iani. Ilse could overhear enough to know the extent of Raul's injuries. Two broken ribs, several others cracked or bruised. Markus Khandarr's cold magic had seared Raul's face, leaving it raw and bleeding. The deepest wounds were gashes, delivered with the precision of a surgeon's knife, one over Raul's left eye, another on his thigh. He suspected internal injuries as well, which accounted for the gray pallor and weakness. And then there was a fever . . .

"Is he dying?" Ilse said.

Benno's gaze jerked up to meet hers. "No."

"Then what is wrong? What is *not possible*, as you called it?"

Benno glanced to one side, clearly uneasy. "He's lost a great deal of blood. Khandarr might have killed him outright, but he did not."

His lips pressed together, he gestured toward Raul. Ilse waved away Nadine's hand and crawled to Raul's side. It took her a moment before she could focus properly and another moment before she could take in the significance of what she saw.

Raul's cheeks were rough with an unshaved beard. A soft down of fur covered his chest, what little she saw of it. When she at last understood the import, her breath came short with shock.

Oh. Yes.

There was one injury, chosen by Raul when he was too young or headstrong to understand the consequences. The reason he never returned home, after Baerne of Angersee died and his grandson Armand dismissed his inner council. Raul had spent thirteen years reinventing himself as the man who spoke as a woman, and pretending it did not matter.

"Khandarr has changed him," she repeated in a whisper. "Yes. Now I understand. Oh, my love," she whispered, and pressed a kiss upon his feverish lips.

Raul's eyelids fluttered open. "My love."

His voice was harsh and deep, at once strange and familiar.

"My love," she said. "You are—"

"An ugly man, from what Benno said."

She tried to laugh, but could not. "Oh, no. You were much uglier that other time, when we nearly died in Tiralien. Do you remember?"

His mouth, swollen and discolored, quirked into a smile. "Which one was that? There were so many, as I recall."

She heard a muttered exclamation from Nadine, but she paid no attention to anyone but Raul, who lay before her transformed and yet the same man she loved from life to life. "You must remember," she said. "It was the time Markus Khandarr lured you into the streets with a false message. Dedrick and I ran to warn you. We were nearly too late."

"Ah, that time." His tone was pensive. "I remember. I led my people to death. And Dedrick. I failed them all."

His gaze went diffuse, as though he had lost sight of this world, and now gazed upon the souls of those dead men and women. Ilse gripped his hands within hers, willing him to remain in this life, in this moment.

"If you remember that, do you remember what you told me?" she asked fiercely. "You told me not to grieve. We make mistakes, you said. But we shall not make the same ones ever again. You live, my love. You and I live. Let us rejoice."

She leaned forward to kiss him, but Raul turned his face away. "Do you know what Markus did to me?" he said.

"I do. Does it matter?"

"I don't know. I feel . . . as though he stole my body and set a stranger in its place."

Now they had come to the crux of the matter.

"We are changed, you and I," Ilse said. "Changed by death. We fall into each new life weak and helpless, and yet we overcome. This is no different, my love."

She leaned over Raul once more. This time, he did not turn his head away. Their lips brushed, his were fever warm and dry. She started to pull back, but Raul lifted a hand to her cheek. "Not yet," he whispered. "Not quite yet." And kissed her once more.

ILSE SPENT THE next three days recovering, while Nadine and the Kosenmark sisters tended to her needs. The Kosenmark family had taken her under their protection within their extensive suite of rooms, with the assurance that once she had recovered, she might petition the Regent Councillors for her own quarters. Until then, they would provide her with whatever she needed.

What Ilse needed was sleep and information. The sleep she could manage for herself, but for the information, she depended on Raul's sisters. From them she learned what had transpired during that mad and chaotic night and the five days after. Duke Kosenmark had survived, battered, bloody, and more than a bit bruised, but alive. Baron Mann had vanished, only to reappear two days later from the depths of the sewers, his strange manic energy having leaked away and leaving him subdued.

"He is very glad to know you have returned," Marte said. "If I did not know him better, I would say he was smitten with you. As it is, I can only say that you have earned his allegiance."

Ilse ignored her comment. "What about Galt? I struck him down, but—"

Olivia smiled grimly. "He lives. The guards took him prisoner, and the council holds him as a vital witness to the events that night. For that reason alone, I am so glad you did not kill him, though I would have understood."

Ilse wanted to laugh, but her throat hurt too much. She had spent all her courage and strength. Even weeping was beyond her.

Raul himself mended more slowly. Benno Iani healed the worst and most obvious of his injuries—the burns and broken bones. The fever took longer to expel and even once he could eat without vomiting it back, he was unable to stay awake longer than a few hours at a time. They had had to shave off his hair to dress his wounds. After that, he had insisted on keeping his hair shorn close to his skull.

Three weeks after Armand's death, the trials commenced.

Ilse received her summons at night, after her daily visit with Raul.

"Do they think me guilty?" she said to Olivia.

Olivia shook her head. "I doubt that. But the city is in a panic. Our king is dead. We . . . I had not told you yet, but we have no heir. The queen and her children have vanished. My father believes they have escaped, but we've had no reliable news about them, only wild gossip. Lord Alberich de Ytel has organized a search for the heir and has vowed to uncover all plots against the king. That is in your favor, and my brother's. Once we prove your innocence, no one can accuse you in the future."

Ilse was not so certain, but the following day, she dressed in her new clothes, provided weeks ago by Duke Kosenmark, when she first appeared in his household. She would not give her own testimony until the third day, but she wanted to learn more about the events of the night Armand died and the days after.

The palace guards were summoned first. From them, the council learned of orders, ostensibly given by the king, commanding them to arrest Duke Kosenmark, his family, and other nobles connected to a supposed plot to murder the king. Did they have the orders directly from the king? Lord Ytel asked. No, but that was not unusual. The orders carried the imprint of Armand's thumb, and came from Lord Markus Khandarr or his secretary.

A straightforward explanation, except that other squads had been ordered to arrest various different squads. The soldiers, those who had survived the night, remembered nothing more than a vague accusation of treason. Except the commanders for those squads testified to their loyalty, and insisted they had never received notice for such an arrest.

He wanted to create confusion, Ilse thought. *He wanted to disguise his own actions while he eliminated all his enemies.*

On the third day, Ilse was called to give her own story.

"Why did you come to Duenne?"

"To deliver a letter from Duke Karasek of Károví and to give evidence of Lord Kosenmark's innocence."

"When did you last speak with Duke Kosenmark?"

"The night before I stood before the king and council."

"And with his son?"

"Before I brought the letter? On Hallau Island, where we hoped to send the queen of Morennioù home. If you mean in Duenne, I last spoke with Lord Kosenmark when he stood in chains, with a false order for his execution."

A loud chatter rose from the audience. The council had to wait until that subsided before they could proceed with their questions. When they did, they were far gentler than Ilse expected. They requested, and she gave them, a precise account of that night, from the moment Nadine came to warn the family, to Ilse's inspection of the orders for Raul's execution, and then the events outside and within the king's offices.

"Do you wish to know what happened in Anderswar?" she asked.

The chief questioner shook his head. "That is not necessary."

Ilse held her breath a moment. Did that mean they knew how Markus Khandarr had died, and did not care? Or did they have other witnesses, to argue against her testimony? All the guards had died . . .

Dismissed, she took a seat in the gallery beside Nadine and Heloïse Kosenmark. "I should go."

"No," Nadine said. "We must hear this next man. That includes you, my love. Especially you."

The next witness was a prisoner, bound in chains and surrounded by a half dozen guards. Ilse could not fathom who that might be. Another mage? An influential noble, once aligned with Markus Khandarr? It was an older man, with hair streaked in gray and white, and dressed in the same dun-colored prison garb Raul Kosenmark had worn.

The guards took hold of their charge and thrust him into a wooden chair, where they bound him securely.

Ilse drew a sharp breath as she recognized the man.

Theodr Galt.

He had changed since that evening, long ago, when he entered her father's house. No longer the finely dressed gentleman, he sat bent and broken in the witness chair. His face was gaunt and discolored by bruises. His hair lay in gray and white clumps. He scanned the council chamber with furious eyes. When his gaze caught on Ilse's, he stopped. His mouth moved and he attempted to rise. The guards thrust him back into his seat.

"Do not be afraid," Olivia said.

"I am not afraid," Ilse said. "I am angry."

Galt did not wish to testify, that was obvious. He clamped his mouth shut. When the guards slapped him, he laughed, a high-pitched laugh that made Ilse grow cold.

"Why should I give you the satisfaction of obeying?" he said. "You will execute me no matter what."

After a brief consultation, the council summoned a mage. Ilse could not tell who she was. She had silver-white hair, and her robes were dyed in the deepest blue. She laid a hand on Galt's forehead. He struggled to escape her, but she merely smiled. *"Ei rûf ane gôtter. Ei rûf ane strôm . . ."*

She bound him with magic and ordered him to tell the truth.

"The truth?" he whispered. "All of it?"

"Everything," she said.

He did. He talked of his desire for Therez Zhalina. His fury at her escape. How he joined the trade delegation from Melnek and how his path had crossed that of Lord Markus Khandarr. Many of the details sickened Ilse. She forced herself to listen, however, as he recounted his dealings with the Mage Councillor, Markus Khandarr. Treason, she thought. Treason to the king and kingdom, all for the sake of a few coins in taxes, and the satisfaction of revenge.

"Ilse, Ilse are you well?"

Marte, sounding anxious.

Ilse nodded. "I am. But I wish to go."

"So do we all," Heloïse murmured.

They hurried out a side door, and up the stairs to their private chambers.

THE INTERIM COUNCIL sentenced Theodr Galt to death. His execution would not take place immediately, however. He would spend a year in prison, in a cell deep below the palace, where he would be permitted no light, nor any visitors other than the guard who brought him a daily meal of bread and water.

Ilse heard the news without any joy. Death only meant death, not redemption. Would he comprehend, in his next life, the mistakes he had made in this one? She doubted it.

A week after that, the queen's body was discovered in the river. The children's bodies, all three, were recovered from a grave outside the city. Ilse tried not to consider which political factions would benefit from these deaths.

To her relief, the next few days distracted her from the matter of

Theodr Galt and the queen. At Duke Kosenmark's request, the council had assigned her new quarters, and the duke himself had settled a temporary allowance on her. When she protested, the duke waved away her objections. "You cannot be beholden to us. You do not need to be. The council knows you have served Veraene, and they are happy enough to provide. Besides," he smiled at her with a dry amused smile that said he was nearly recovered, "you will have money from your family soon enough."

Money. From Ehren.

A letter confirmed the duke's words. The money she had inherited, which Ehren had in turn inherited from her when everyone thought her dead, returned to her once more. She accepted the new rooms gladly and hired a maid to oversee her clothes and the rest. Theda had served other nobles in the palace. She took on the task of hiring the several underservants Mistress Ilse would require.

Those were the easiest decisions Ilse faced. Soon after she gave testimony, a runner came to her with a letter requesting her opinion on matters between Károví and Veraene. It was signed Duke Feltzen.

I know you, she thought. *You came to Raul asking for his advice. When he did not prove an easy target, you attached yourself to Armand of Angersee.*

She wrote back, "If you wish a capable emissary, and that is what I advise, then speak with Baron Mann."

"I thought you loved politics," Nadine said, when Ilse told her about the exchange.

"I do," Ilse said. "I dislike political games, however. Baron Mann is adept at both. Besides," she added, "he will see the situation with fresh eyes."

She was not free of further importunities so easily, however. Others invited her to informal discussions about the kingdom—Duke Kosenmark, other members of the council, and others on the outskirts of power. They had recovered Duke Karasek's letter from the king's office, burned but still legible. Károví was in turmoil. Several key members of the nobility were gaining control, among them being Duke Markov, which Ilse expected, but also Ryba Karasek, now the duke of Taboresk. Ilse attended these sessions and found herself consulted in matters of state. She discovered a new joy in using her knowledge of Veraene and Károví and even Morennioù.

Meanwhile, Baron Eckard and Emma Iani arrived in court. Letters had gone out from Duenne's Council, notifying the provinces of the king's death. Baron Eckard, held in prison, was freed. Emma Iani and the rest of Raul's shadow court had come out of hiding. Kathe and Gerek had taken possession of the old pleasure house in Tiralien. Their plans, at this point, were uncertain.

Through all these weeks, Ilse had visited Raul Kosenmark daily.

He had gained in strength. There had been a setback after his own testimony to the court, but since then Benno Iani reported constant progress, at least in the physical. However, Ilse could not convince Raul to speak of anything except inconsequentials. It was as though he had abandoned the kingdom for . . .

For nothing, she thought.

"He is afraid," Emma Iani said as she sat by Ilse Zhalina's fireplace.

"Does that surprise you?" Ilse asked.

Emma shook her head. "I would be surprised at the opposite. He wants the crown. But he cannot take it without believing himself a traitor."

Heloïse lifted her head, but when Nadine laid a hand on her arm, the other woman pressed her lips together. Secrets, Nadine once said in an unguarded moment. It was enough of a clue for Ilse Zhalina that she directed the conversation in a different direction. Later, when she attempted to speak with Heloïse alone, she found the woman had disappeared, leaving behind Nadine in her most brittle mood.

In the weeks that followed, she wrote letters. She sent long overdue reports to her brother Ehren, to Kathe and Gerek in Tiralien, and eventually an indirect account to Alesso Valturri in Fortezzien.

We are all waiting, waiting, waiting . . .

AUTUMN SPUN INTO winter, leaf by wind-blown leaf. The bright gold grasses of the plains had darkened to brown, crimson speckled the northern hills, where oaks grew among the pines, and the color bled from the skies, the brilliant blue of autumn turning into winter gray.

Early one morning, a runner came to Ilse Zhalina's quarters. Her newly hired maid, Theda, passed the man into the formal parlor where Ilse sat with Marte and Olivia at breakfast. "My lady." He knelt before her and held out a thick envelope of ivory parchment, wrapped in silk ribbons and carrying the seal of Duenne's Court. The scent of magic hung in the air.

Ilse stared at the letter. "What is it? Do you know?"

The runner was silent. She reached out and took the envelope cautiously. Magic bit at her fingertips, sharp and strong, as though her touch had unleashed a spell much more powerful than the ordinary one used to seal a letter against all but the intended recipient. Ilse dropped the letter back into the runner's hands.

Olivia smothered a laugh, but Marte's eyes were wide with curiosity. "I know the seal. It's not for ordinary council business, only matter of state. Open it, Ilse."

Reluctantly, Ilse took up the envelope a second time and touched her fingers to the seal. The magic surged through her veins, more bearable now. It immediately subsided, and the pages unfolded into her hands.

My Lady Ilse Zhalina, I write first to offer my apologies that our council has acted so slowly in recognizing your extraordinary efforts for the kingdom. You have gifted us with the opportunity for peace and prosperity. You have offered testimony without regard to yourself, and only for the truth, demonstrating a greater honor than any noble. It is with the full consent, therefore, and unanimous agreement of the Council of Duenne, that I offer you a title of the realm . . .

"No," she said. "No and no and no. I do not need it."

"What is it?" Marte asked.

Ilse laid the pages on the table and stared at them. "A bribe. Or so it appears. Duenne's Court confers the title of Lady upon me and my heirs, not to mention . . ." She scanned further down through the letter. "Certain holdings, located in the northern district of Duenne itself, and the income that derives from such. Such title and holdings grants me a place in council, if I desire it. Oh, and full and free pardon for my part in assisting Morenniou's queen to freedom."

She glared at the runner. "Do they expect an answer?"

"No, my lady. But if you wish to send one—"

"Don't," Olivia said before Ilse could speak. "Not yet." She gestured for the runner to go. He glanced at Ilse who reluctantly nodded. Once the door had closed behind the man, Olivia said, "Accept the title and lands. Everything. You will find them useful."

Ilse eyed her doubtfully. "Useful how?"

"For following your heart's desire," Marte said. "Whatever that might be."

Ilse released a long slow breath and glanced from them back to the letter. She reread its contents more closely, taking in all the details of the proposed title, seeing them now against Marte's and Olivia's words. The signature was from Lord Alberich de Ytel himself, Regent to the Council. She tried the title out on her tongue. Lady Ilse. It felt awkward, wrong. She tried again. Lady Ilse, member of the court. That went better. She had earned a place among the advisers in court, but nothing official. Perhaps this was the means for her to step from the shadows at last.

"You are right," she said.

"Of course I am," Olivia said.

Ilse hardly paid her any attention. She attempted a third pass through the letter, but though she had nearly memorized its contents by now, she found herself unable to truly assimilate its meaning for her and her future. She started up. "Excuse me. I must go."

She made directly for Raul Kosenmark's apartments.

Once Iani had declared his friend recovered, Raul had requested, and received, separate quarters from his father and sisters. They lay on an entirely different floor, in a different wing, which Ilse could see from the balcony of her own rooms. The appointments for these new quarters seemed relatively plain and small compared to the Kosenmark family suite. A modest entry hall, leading into a sunny parlor, with a second more spacious sitting room that served as his library.

Ilse found him in the sitting room, dressed in a plain shirt and loose trousers. His sword lay on the cushions next to him, along with various tools for sharpening and cleaning. Almost three months after his ordeal in Anderswar, his flesh and bones had healed, though he still tired easily. It was the new hesitation in his manner, the gravity that had overtaken his passion and joy, which troubled her.

He smiled as she came into the room. "My love."

"My love," she replied.

She was tense and breathless, uncertain how to proceed.

"You seem anxious," he said at last.

Ilse laughed softly. "That is because I received a most interesting letter this morning."

"About your pardon?" He smiled faintly. "I have mine as well."

"That and more." She hesitated a moment, not certain how to relay the news, nor how to frame the questions that came with it. "The council . . . It appears the council wishes to confer a title on me."

His golden eyes widened and there was a quirk at his lips that reminded her of the old Raul Kosenmark. She wished she could leave the matter at that, but she could not. *The truth,* she told herself. *No more secrets, especially not between us.*

"Was that your doing?" she asked lightly.

The quirk vanished and he shook his head. "Not mine, nor my father's. You have won this on your own, my love."

So. He understood. She glanced at his sword. There were rust stains on the blade, as if it had been stored away without proper attention. Raul had the cloth and oil and tools ready to clean the weapon, but he had made no progress, and she wondered how long he had sat there, dreaming and doing nothing.

"Will you take up drill again?" she asked.

He shrugged. For that one moment, he had seemed alive and amused—ready to engage with the outer world—but the animation had leaked away, and he was staring at the sword as though it were an alien thing.

A rack of weapons stood by the wall, including two wooden swords for practice. Ilse took the shortest one from its hook. Its grip felt familiar, and she thought that it came from the old pleasure house in Tiralien—a coincidence, but one that confirmed her impulse. "Perhaps I should challenge you," she said. "Lady to Lord."

Raul glanced up, startled. "Ilse . . ."

She smacked him on the shoulder with the flat of the blade. "Get up. Show me you haven't forgotten."

Another hard smack sent him scrambling from the chair. He caught up the second wooden blade, but not before she landed another blow.

Raul grabbed her wooden blade. "Stop. I know what you're doing."

"Do you?"

She yanked her sword free and circled the chair to launch a flurry of strikes. Once and twice she penetrated his guard, but he managed to block the rest. Now he pressed forward to force her retreat. She circled around the table and chairs. Perhaps she ought to suggest a new drill to Benedikt Ault—swordplay with obstacles. It would prepare a student for a genuine skirmish, she thought, remembering her first true battle, the terror and confusion, the sick feeling when she killed a man, and how she nearly died.

She lunged forward, only to have Raul catch her blade on his. Before he could return the attack, she danced backward and out of his reach. Raul was grinning now. She laughed. When he flung down a chair between them, she leaped over it to engage with his blade. This time she was not quick enough. He caught her blade near the hilt and twisted his around, sending her sword spinning through the air.

Raul closed the distance between them and caught her in his arms. He bent to kiss her.

And stopped, his mouth inches from hers. With a muttered exclamation, he spun around and dropped the sword to the floor. "I'm sorry. So sorry."

"What's wrong?" she asked breathlessly.

He threw his head back and stared at the ceiling. He was breathing hard, trembling, too. "Nothing. No, I am wrong. Different. I can't—" His voice broke. "I cannot tell who or what I am. He won, Ilse. Yes, he died, but he won."

"No," she said. Then in a louder voice, "You are wrong, my love. Markus Khandarr is dead. You killed him in Anderswar. We lost the king but not the kingdom. As for you . . . You will survive."

"You cannot know."

"I do know," she said. "You, of all my friends, you ought to understand how much I appreciate your situation."

She had caught his attention at last. "How?"

"How?" Her voice ticked upward. "How could I not? I gave myself to Alarik Brandt, just as you gave yourself to Baerne of Angersee. I thought I understood the trade. I did not. Nor did you, you poor child, scarcely fourteen years old. You thought you comprehended the world, or if not that, the world of Veraene's Court. I thought I comprehended my own body. Whatever our beliefs, whatever our expectations, you must admit we both made a bad trade. And we both . . ." Her voice edged into tears, which she brutally suppressed. "We both struggled through, my love. We both survived."

She said that last word in a breath, nothing more.

"We survived," she repeated. "You transformed yourself. You fitted your body, your manners, everything to act as though you did not care that you had sacrificed your manhood, only to find that sacrifice discarded. I sacrificed myself to gain freedom only to find that Alarik Brandt had lied to me. Eventually, I discovered that his lies didn't matter. I had myself. I had my life, my desires, my soul restored.

"The same is true for you. Baerne of Angersee and Markus Khandarr no longer matter. Your future is yours. Choose well, my love."

She had no more words to speak. She could only stare at him, terrified and shaking with all the admissions she had never dared to speak before. Not even to him.

Raul remained with his back to her. "And you? What will you do now, Lady Ilse?"

"I will serve my kingdom," she said. "However my kingdom wishes me to serve."

Raul bowed his head but did not turn around. When he continued to be silent, she laid the wooden sword on the floor and silently left the room.

*   *   *

LATER THAT AFTERNOON, as she sat alone in her quarters, gazing over the sun-drenched rooftops of Duenne, a runner brought her a message.

No wax. Magic alone sealed the edges of paper.

Ilse touched her fingertips to the envelope. A fleeting glimpse of dark blue silk, rippling through the night, Raul's magical signature, then the sheet of paper unfolded, and she was reading the message within:

I failed to give you a proper answer before you left me this morning. I did not have the words then, I am not certain I have them now. I can only say that once more you are the one friend I can trust to tell me the truth. For that I am grateful. I will take my place in council tomorrow.

CHAPTER TWENTY-FOUR

THROUGHOUT HER YEARS in Lord Kosenmark's pleasure house, Nadine had never once considered what Duenne's Court and Council might be like. Oh, she knew about the dangerous game Kosenmark conducted, and she spied on others herself whenever possible. All that was a personal matter, for her own preservation. In her mind, the thing called politics was merely an excuse for ambition or outright murder, and she wanted no part of it. Even those who claimed to serve a noble cause, Kosenmark among them, had committed several unspeakable acts in the name of government.

Today, however, she was in the heart of it all.

It was Heloïse Kosenmark's fault. They had retired late, after an extended and useless conference with certain members of Duenne's Court. Nadine had not paid much attention to the conversation itself. She only knew that Heloïse had wanted a great deal of soothing afterward before they could both sleep.

She was in the midst of a sensuous dream from past lives and lovers when her instincts woke her. She blinked and rolled over to see the lamp-light dancing over the ceiling above. Sunlight glittered through the half-open shutters, a cascade of white and pale yellow. Heloïse bent over a cushioned bench, sorting through a pile of clothing.

Nadine watched from under the blankets, unwilling to emerge from her nest. Winter in Duenne was nothing like the hill country where her family lived, but she had come to love warmth and comfort during her time in Tiralien. She watched Heloïse pick up one gown, then set it aside in favor of another, and another—wisps of cloth and robes and trousers—as though mere clothing made a difference to one's life.

"What is it?" Nadine asked. "What are you doing?"

Heloïse paused. With the sunlight at her back, her face was invisible in the shadows, but it was easy to read the tension in her sudden stillness. "Nothing. Go back to sleep."

"Not until you tell me. What is wrong?"

"Nothing, I said. I just— I am going to observe the future, my love. A matter of the kingdom, if you must know."

Lies. The entire family was built upon the tradition of lies and secrets. And yet Heloïse was not entirely like her father and elder brother. It was for this reason that Nadine slid from the bed and wrapped her arms around Heloïse in a loose embrace. "I shall keep you company."

Heloïse did not object, which was answer enough, and so Nadine dressed with the speed and ease she had learned as a courtesan, in her best gown of silk, the embroidered outer robe styled in the finest of Duenne's fashions, and a heavy sash. She needed only her slippers, and they were on their way.

Their destination was a tiny row of benches, tucked underneath the ceiling itself, that overlooked the grand council chamber of Veraene's Congress. This was where Armand of Angersee had tried Lord Kosenmark for treason, where Ilse Zhalina had given her testimony, where the Regency tried Theodr Galt. Since then, the chamber had remained unused, but as Nadine settled herself next to Heloïse, she saw an enormous crowd gathered below. Courtiers. Attendants. The councillors themselves stood in smaller knots or took their places around a series of benches, ranged according to rank, that circled the dais and its empty throne.

A matter of state, Heloïse had called it.

A matter of kings, Nadine thought.

She half rose, thinking she did not wish to observe today's spectacle, when Heloïse twisted about. "We must have coffee," she murmured, "if we are to endure the session. Oh, thank the gods." She gestured energetically to a young man in servant's livery, who carried a tray with small squat mugs. Money exchanged hands, and soon Nadine sipped from a cup of hot chocolate, while Heloïse savored her spiced coffee, making small satisfied noises, like a cat.

She was an extraordinary woman, Nadine thought. She had the grace of Lord Kosenmark, and his height, but on a far leaner scale. Golden eyes, black hair, the cheeks drawn in swift, uncompromising angles, and her wide mouth alight with humor, or the promise of it.

"You are staring," Heloïse said.

"And so I should," Nadine returned lightly. "You are a spectacle."

Heloïse's laugh was low and rough, like water rushing over stones. "I am not, but I could arrange for one."

Nadine dropped her gaze. "Naughty child."

"Hardly a child," Heloïse replied. "But look. Lord Ytel has made his appearance. Now we ought to see something interesting."

Nadine drained off her cup of chocolate and leaned against the railing. The swarm of dots parted. A tall bent figure proceeded slowly along the path cleared before him. Lord Alberich de Ytel. She had spoken with him only a few moments that mad night. Her impression of the man was that little could overset him, even when dressed in his nightclothes. Today, he wore layers of stiff robes, with the chains of his office around his neck, and his gray hair drawn into a tight, old-fashioned queue. He took his place among the councillors and lifted a hand.

All conversation ebbed to near silence. Ytel began a long speech, delivered in a low, sonorous voice, about the kingdom and its future and how the council would endeavor to sift through the many names proposed . . .

Names for the next king, she realized.

"I hate this," she said suddenly.

"So do I," Heloïse said. "That is why I never came to Duenne before. Never once wrote to my beloved older brother during his exile. I am ashamed of my cowardice. No matter how stupid Baron Quint and his like might be, it doesn't excuse me."

"Do you blame—"

"I blame no one. I only speak for myself."

Heloïse turned her bright gaze to the council floor. Lord Ytel had retired. Lord Thonis took his place and bellowed out a speech. Others bellowed back. Yatter, yatter, yatter. From Heloïse's recent comments, Nadine understood that the council wished to settle the question of kingship properly, but to Nadine, these debates all seemed pointless. The rich nobles would do as they pleased. Armand, that poor toad, might be dead, and Khandarr, too, but politics would proceed as usual. She leaned back and closed her eyes, abruptly unable to bear the spectacle. Perhaps she could persuade Heloïse to return to their rooms. From what little she had glimpsed through the windows during their swift progress to the audience chamber, it promised to be a splendid winter's day. They might obtain horses and ride through the hills above Duenne, or simply wander through the various districts of the city . . .

A sudden silence washed over the hall.

Nadine's skin rippled in sudden apprehension. It was nothing, she told herself. A pause in the idiocy, nothing more. But then she heard the tread of slow and heavy footsteps. Her eyes still closed, she tried to guess the newcomer's identity. An old man, she thought, given to self-indulgence. No doubt someone with more rank than sense.

Next to her Heloïse hissed. "He has come. I knew he would."

Nadine opened her eyes reluctantly. Heloïse was pressed against the railing, tense and alert, her gaze fixed on the floor below. Silently, Nadine came to her side.

Raul Kosenmark emerged from the silent crowd. For a moment, he scanned the audience, but the act was clearly perfunctory, because he merely shrugged before he took his place among the other councillors.

This was not the Lord Kosenmark that Nadine knew from her years in Tiralien. He was dressed in an almost plain costume of dark blue trousers and shirt, over which he wore a sleeveless robe that swept the floor. His only concession to fashion were the dark blue gems he wore around his throat and hanging from one ear. But it was his manner that struck hardest— slow and ponderous, as if each gesture came at a cost.

And so it does.

"I thought he had forsworn the general council," she murmured.

She knew Raul had begun to attend council the previous few weeks. He had entered into sharp debates about certain matters—trade negotiations with neighboring kingdoms, aid to the poor, improvements to the kingdom's universities. On all the larger matters of state, however, especially those concerning Károví, he was silent.

"So had I. But I hoped—" Heloïse broke off and shook her head. "Let us listen to what he says."

Raul took his seat, but he had no sooner done so when three men and two women approached the central circle. They paused at a signal from the guards. The chief minion, as Nadine thought of him, signaled to a lesser minion, who struck an enormous metal disk with a hammer. Nadine pressed her hands over her ears, breathless from the noise.

One man stepped forward. He was old, Nadine could see that plainly, even from this distance. Old and white haired and built like a square of marble quarried fresh from the mines. Unlike the self-important idiot of Nadine's earlier imaginings, this old man strode forward with intent. It was Baron Eckard. She had met him just once before, at the pleasure house in Tiralien, but she knew his name from countless secret conversations she had overheard. Eckard turned and called out, in a voice that carried easily to the highest benches, "My lords and ladies, I have a petition to make."

"To whom do you make it?" the chief steward replied in an equally loud voice.

"To the king."

Suddenly Nadine found it difficult to breathe.

"The king is dead," came the reply.

"Then who should follow him?"

The steward swung around to the councillors. "What say you, my lords and ladies? Do we have a king?"

A queen, Nadine thought. *What about a queen?*

But even while she protested this seeming blindness, she found herself gripping Heloïse's arm.

One of the oldest councillors rose to his feet. "The king is dead, and the king's heir as well. We must choose another."

"Shall we ask the delegation their choice?" the steward asked.

To this point, they had all spoken as if by formula, but with this question, the councillors fell to muttering among themselves. Now Nadine could pinpoint Raul by his silence and stillness. It was all a great pretense, choreographed to make it seem as though he accepted only reluctantly. She hated him at that moment. In spite of all her bitter raillery, she had thought him above such petty machinations. She started to rise.

"Wait," Heloïse whispered. "Please."

Nadine sank back into her chair and laid a hand on her beloved's arm. Heloïse was trembling. "Are you afraid he will refuse?"

"No. Not that. Just the opposite. And yet, if he does not . . ."

The other two men and women of the delegation joined Eckard. Baron Mann. She had last seen him covered in blood and slime, laughing with the edge of madness. After him came Benno and Emma Iani. Luise Ehrenalt, as well. His oldest friends, the heart of the shadow court.

"This is too much," Heloïse murmured.

"Then he should refuse," Nadine said.

"He . . . I have no idea what he might do, but I cannot watch."

Heloïse seized her by the hand. Nadine resisted a moment longer. Raul had stood and faced off the delegation. There followed an intense debate, conducted in low tones that Nadine could not follow, and she wished in vain for the listening pipes of Kosenmark's pleasure house.

"Wait," she said. "Isn't this why you came here today?"

"I was wrong," Heloïse cried. "I cannot bear to watch. It will do no good for him, whatever he says. Please. Come with me, Nadine. Please."

They fled down the back stairs, back through the maze of corridors. It was not until they had closed the doors of their apartment that Heloïse released a sobbing gasp. She was weeping, had been for many moments.

Nadine touched her fingers to Heloïse's wet cheeks. "I love you."

Heloïse wrapped a hand around Nadine's neck and drew her into a kiss, one that lasted so long that Nadine gasped for breath when Heloïse released her. "Marry me," Heloïse whispered. "Please. I want you. I need you. I will love you for all of this life and a hundred more to come. I promise."

Nadine drew back in surprise. "I thought . . ."

"You thought wrong, my love."

Heloïse was laughing, a low gurgling laugh. If Nadine had not known her better she would have missed the edge of desperation in her voice.

"Marry me," Heloïse repeated.

I should not. She doesn't know what she is saying.

Oh, but I love her.

She hooked a hand around Heloïse's neck and drew her into an even deeper kiss.

"I will," she said hoarsely. "For now and forever. For all our lives to come."

IN THE SILENCE of the audience chamber, Emma Iani approached those final few steps to stand beside Baron Eckard. She and Eckard had rehearsed the exchange throughout the past two weeks, refining and revising the challenge to Kosenmark and the council. Even so, it took all her courage to face Lord Raul Kosenmark today.

His gaze settled upon her. Easily, one might have said, except for the quick pulse at his throat, and the paleness of his face. When his lips drew back in a lupine smile, she scowled and had the gratification of seeing the blood flush along his cheeks.

"I told you, I will not," he said.

"A child's answer," she said. "A stupid, selfish answer, from a man who wishes to avoid any responsibility."

"You think—"

"I think nothing," Emma Iani said. "I merely observe."

For a very long moment, they stared at each other. *I should be afraid,* Emma thought. *If I succeed . . .*

Raul blew out a breath and lowered his head. "You think me a coward."

"Of course. What else would stop you from taking the throne, when no one else could? Self-doubt?" She laughed softly. "You doubted yourself once and a dozen times, but surely the support of many dozens of nobles, and many more thousands of citizens, should overcome that doubt."

He shook his head. "You do not understand. I do not wish the crown."

"There are many things I do not wish," she replied sharply. "My husband's grief and illness. Lord Dedrick's death. If I had what I wished, you would not have sent Benno into Markus Khandarr's traps."

"So you claim I owe you a debt."

"No. I say you owe the kingdom a debt."

For a terrible moment, she feared she had overreached and he might walk away from this council chamber and Duenne itself. If she could have summoned magic to bind him to her, she would have in this moment. But it was Benno who had mastered such spells, not she. All she could do was silently urge Raul to accept the crown.

His mouth curved in a mocking smile, as if he could read her thoughts. "Then you claim it is what the gods require. How interesting."

"No," she said quietly. "It is what the citizens of Veraene wish, and you know it. Raul . . ." She drew a long breath, considered once more how to convince this stubborn man to give over his useless and dangerous doubts.

He tilted his head and regarded her with narrowed eyes. It was as if they stood alone in a room, not before a thousand nobles, all watching and straining to hear their words.

"I would beg," she said. "I would grovel. Do anything. Not for myself. Certainly not for you, my friend. We are nothing, except as we serve the kingdom. That is why I joined your shadow court. That is why I am here today. I and Benno and all your other friends—"

"But not Ilse Zhalina."

That checked her. "No," she admitted. "Ilse would not, though I asked her. She told me she would never build a cage for you of her expectations. You must choose freely. I am not like her. I will stand here until you truly and honestly consider the matter, even if, in the end, you still choose to abandon the kingdom to another's rule. But Raul . . . *You* are what Veraene needs. It is not wrong for you to take power, as long as you use it for what is right."

"Ah," he breathed. "That is the true question."

He bowed his head and said nothing more. All around them, voices swelled up in a hundred different conversations, the steward was calling for order, while the councillors demanded a formal vote on the matter. Raul seemed oblivious to it all. Only when Baron Eckard came forward and laid a hand on Raul's shoulder did he finally lift his head. The two exchanged a look—old friends, even older than she and Benno. Eckard bent close and murmured something inaudible. Raul finally smiled, albeit a painful one. Then he nodded.

Emma released a shaking breath. She felt Benno's warm hand clasp hers, steadying her.

I have done it. All of us have.

CHAPTER TWENTY-FIVE

THAT SAME DAY, Ilse woke at dawn. Bells whispered in the distance, a soft silvery chorus that reminded her of courtiers massed together. Five bright clear tones rang out—five hours past midnight, two hours at least until the sun rose.

The air in her bedchamber was cold and damp, a true midwinter day in the central plains. Her maid had banked the fire and closed the shutters for the night, but enough of the early dawn light leaked through for Ilse to make her way from the bed to her wardrobe. She huddled into a woolen robe and slippers, then lit a candle and rekindled the fire. The water in her basin stung with cold when she splashed a handful over her face.

Midwinter. One week until Long Night. Three months and more since Armand died.

And today Duenne's Council would begin its search for a new king. A long and arduous task, she suspected.

Will you attend? she had asked Raul.

I must, if only to represent Valentain.

A hundred different factions would observe the council's debate, of course. A hundred different members of those same factions had fluttered around Ilse, attempting to gain her support for one candidate or another. Even her friends were not immune. The night before, Emma Iani had come to Ilse privately, to request her presence while they badgered Raul into accepting the crown. Of course Emma had phrased the question far more delicately. "We would like you to stand with us," she said. "Nothing more."

"I cannot," Ilse had replied. "You know that, Emma. The choice must be his, freely decided."

She stared blankly at the wall, her arms wrapped tightly around her body, while the fire hissed and crackled. She would not attend the council session, no. Nor could she take refuge in yet another committee meeting. There would be none today, not until a new king was chosen.

Which might not take place until Long Night or beyond, given the many fierce and uncompromising divisions within court and council.

Abruptly impatient with herself, with Emma Iani and all the rest of Veraene's politics, she unwound her nighttime braid and brushed out her hair vigorously until her eyes watered. She twisted her hair into a knot, which she pinned securely, and dressed in layers of silk and wool, practical clothing for riding in rough country, and all newly supplied by the seamstresses recommended by Heloïse Kosenmark, and paid for from her own funds, recently transferred by her brother to her newly hired agent in Duenne.

She pulled on a quilted jacket and a wool cap lined with fur. The act of dressing had confirmed her impulse. She would ride. She would escape the palace for the open plains beyond the city walls. Once Long Night came, winter storms would make the roads impassable. She had to take the chance that today offered.

Her maid Theda was awake and relighting the fire in the second of Ilse's outer rooms. "Send a runner to the stables," Ilse said. "Have them saddle my horse."

"Of course, my lady. Will you have breakfast here, or would you like the kitchens to prepare a basket?"

Ilse had intended a brief ride, no more than an hour or two, but at Theda's question, she had the sudden glorious vision of an entire day free from all constraint. "The second, please. Tell them I shall want provisions for a full day's outing. Let the stable master know that as well."

She drank a cup of tea and ate a few biscuits at Theda's urging, then followed one of the less public routes to the palace stables. Few were about at this hour; the corridors and stairwells were still dark, lit only by a few torches. A monster slumbering, she thought. Once she came to the main floor, however, more servants were about, and the stables themselves teamed with activity. A senior hostler waited with Ilse's horse already saddled. Next to him stood a young woman, also dressed for a winter ride, with several bulky saddlebags on her own mount.

"My lady." The woman bowed. She was short and stocky, her thick black hair tucked under a knitted cap, and she wore several visible weapons, including a short sword on her belt. Ilse guessed a search would uncover more.

"I had not requested an escort," she said.

The woman shrugged. "If you wish me gone, my lady, you have only to say so. I hope you do not. The weather can be treacherous this late in the season. And we thought you might like a guide who knows the best sights."

A guide who carried herself like a soldier, with weapons at her belt and boot. Ilse thought she detected Duke Kosenmark's hand in this. He had reminded her, more than once, that the old factions continued to operate in secret. Ilse knew his concerns were borne out by incidents over the past three months, so she did not argue.

"Have you guessed my destination then?" she asked.

The woman's mouth tucked into a cheerful smile. "Oh, dear no, my lady. I would never presume to guess. However, I trust I have come to you well prepared. My name is Guda Decker, if you should like to address your curses and commands more directly."

It was impossible to resist her good humor, and Ilse smiled in return. "Then let us put your preparations to good use, Guda Decker."

They mounted and rode through a series of courtyards, each a pocket of cold air surrounded by walls and towers, and the covered passageway that dipped under the outer wings of the palace, and through one of the many smaller side gates into the busy avenue beyond. The bells were ringing seven, and the skies had brightened, but the streets themselves were thick with fog and shadows, and most of the wagons carried lanterns to light the way.

"Do you wish to visit the winter markets?" Guda asked. "I know a stall with the best grilled sausages."

Ilse surveyed the streets. The number of guards inside the palace itself had increased over the past month, and more patrolled the streets. The city was restive. Its mood would turn even more uneasy while the council debated the matter of kingship.

"Another day," she said. "I would like to see something of the countryside. Will your preparations go far enough for that?"

Guda bowed in her saddle. "They will indeed, my lady. Give me a direction and I shall find you the closest city gate."

Ilse tilted her head back and scanned the cloudless skies.

When she had first come to Duenne, she and her companions had leapt through the magic planes. It was as though a seamstress had snipped a length of cloth, and stitched together its ends, removing in a few deft movements a hundred or more miles of land. Which part of that missing journey to visit first? East lay Tiralien. She had traversed those hills twice, both times in hunger and panic. North lay a region she wanted to explore some day, but for now, she had enough of hills and mountains both. "South," she declared. "Over the open plains."

"As you wish, my lady."

Half an hour later saw them exiting the city gates for a highway leading south. They passed through the outer city, as Guda called it, crammed with small shops and yards for sheep and goats. Beyond that lay a ring of smaller farms, so it was not until the sun rose above the horizon that Ilse could count herself free of Duenne.

The plains spread outward before her, like a pale ocean that undulated toward an impossibly distant horizon. There were no forests, no mountains, nothing but an endless expanse that glittered with frost under the winter sun. Above, the skies were a burnished gray, clear and seemingly as limitless as the earth below.

Ilse urged her horse forward at a trot, and Guda followed. Their highway swung to the southeast, between a few outlying farms, then into the frozen sea of grassland. If they were to continue in this direction, they would reach the provinces of Pommersien within three weeks. Other highways branched off from this one, to Fortezzien, Tiralien, and other coastal cities. But she wanted no grand destination today, only a momentary refuge where she might think through her future.

Sooner than she expected, they came to a narrow track that angled to the right. Perhaps a smaller city or town lay at the end. Perhaps a farm settlement had paid the kingdom for this road. Ilse drew rein and considered the possibilities. From here, she could see a line of trees, and a faint blue mass that could be a village or farm. Dark shadows marked a drifting herd of cattle, and on the horizon, a swiftly moving speck of shadow that might be a horse galloping free.

"Let us ride, ride onward into infinity," she murmured.

"My lady?" Guda said.

"A test for your preparations, Guda Decker. How fast can you ride?"

Without waiting for an answer, she gave a shout and urged her horse into a gallop. The horse surged forward happily, willingly, hooves pounding over the frozen ground. Ilse yipped in delight and bent over her mount's neck, the cold wind burning against her face. She hardly cared. She was riding into infinity, into an unknown future. From far behind, she heard Guda shouting after her.

She had surpassed the herd of cattle before she leaned back. Her horse slowed to her touch of the reins, and they circled around into the fields to meet up with her companion, who appeared torn between laughter and dismay.

Ilse grinned at her. "Are you hungry?"

"But my lady . . ."

"*I* am hungry," Ilse said. "Let us investigate your preparations, Guda Decker, and what the kitchens have provided us."

Her guide and guardian laughed, then shook her head. "Yes, my lady. Just as you ask. But not exactly here, if you please."

There was a traveler's camp another mile down this road, Guda told her, where they and the horses would be far more comfortable. Ilse could hardly disagree. A short interval later, they dismounted in the camp, which was a circle of bare dirt, with a well-used fire pit and a shelter of stone covered by a thatched roof that needed repair. A stream meandered past and disappeared into the frozen grass.

Guda built a fire using dry wood from the shelter, while Ilse walked their horses, then rubbed them down. By the time she finished, Guda had coffee brewing and was grilling bread and cheese. Ilse sorted through their saddlebags and discovered several sealed pots. One held a mixture of rice and spiced lamb, another porridge, another yet a thick soup of lentils and greens. There was also bread, dried figs, more cheese, and a plentiful supply of black tea leaves and dried meat—enough for an entire day, just as she had asked for.

She and Guda ate the bread and cheese first, then the porridge, and drank down a pot of hot coffee. Once they had finished, they washed their dishes and tidied up the camp.

"What next, my lady?" Guda asked.

The day had turned clear and bright. The air was crisply cold, with the scent of snow in the air. Ilse blew out a silver-bright breath. They had six hours until sunset.

"West," she said. "I have an urge to see the compass."

They left the roads and trails and rode west until the sun hovered directly overhead. This time there was no traveler's camp nearby, but Guda knew of a ravine with a reliable stream and trees for shelter. Once more they built a fire and set water to boil. Ilse fed hot mash to the horses, while Guda constructed a shelter from canvas and sticks. Just as she finished, a wind kicked up from the north.

Crouched under the shelter, they consumed the lentil soup cold. Ilse accepted a mug of hot tea, grateful for the rush of warmth. She picked over the lamb and rice, however, finally setting the dish aside.

I cannot gallop forever.

Soon, she would have to return to Duenne, where her obligations to the crown awaited. There she would learn Raul's decision, and from that she could make her own choices about the future.

He might say no.

He might agree, and the council, too. If that is so, they will want a noble queen. Or they will want someone with connections here and abroad.

Her heart constricted at the thought of Raul with another, and yet . . .

If that meant Veraene's salvation, how could she argue? She had spent a lifetime and more seeking peace between the kingdoms. Raul Kosenmark would make a fine and wonderful king to Veraene.

She had choices, too, she told herself. She had earned a place in Duenne's Court on her own. She had an income that offered independence. If she decided she could not bear . . . that is, if she hated politics, she could retire to Melnek or Fortezzien, or even to Tiralien. She could leap by magic to some unknown destination. And, and, and, they were not at the end of all their lives. If victory meant a delay, then so be it.

Ilse brushed the tears away with her gloved hand. She stood and paced along the edge of the ravine. Off in the distance, a thin blue ribbon marked Duenne's presence. She stood, hands clasped behind her back, and stared northward. The horizon swept along until it reached a bump, another, then stuttered upward into the hills. Through that open gap the first outriders of Erythandra's hordes had appeared. In the hills themselves, Tanja Duhr had chosen to spend her final years.

"My lady."

"Another hour, Guda Decker, no longer."

Ilse tilted her head upward, still restless, still uncertain.

It was a day for impulse. She would never have another in this lifetime.

"Ei rûf ane gôtter!" she called out. *"Ei rûf ane Anderswar!"*

Challenge given, challenge answered.

The air drew tight. A strong green scent flooded her senses. Ilse blinked and Veraene disappeared. She stood on the edge of nothing, while the universe spun below. A stream of bright stars rippled overhead, souls in transit to their new lives.

Her beast crouched opposite, the same mad patchwork of feathers and fur and claws, as though a furious god had created it in retribution for some grave wrong. Its claws clicked against nothing, loud and sharp. Its sex hung heavy and low and full.

I am the creature of your expectations, it said.

She acknowledged the truth of that with a nod. *I know that now.*

So you are stupid, but not without redemption. Why have you come to me today?
No reason.
You think you can bid me farewell? Order me to begone?
Ilse laughed. *Hardly. You and I will have more dealings over the years. No, I am not running away from you, or Duenne, or myself. Not any longer.*
Then why did you call me?

Ilse held out a hand. The beast rose on its bent legs and skittered closer. It took all her self-control not to tremble in terror. Expectation or not, this was no tame creature. When it reared to embrace her, she felt a rush of bitter cold, as though Veraene's winter had invaded the magical plane. She lifted her chin and met the beast's lips with her own. Its beak was hard and sharp. The next moment, its flesh transformed into an almost human mouth.

My love, it whispered in a low, rasping voice.

No, she replied. *My love is a man and not a beast. But I know that you are a necessary part of me.*

Its lips peeled back into a grimace, at once terrifying and alluring. Another point to consider, she thought. *I begin to think I have underestimated you,* the beast said. *Farewell, Ilse Zhalina. Farewell until you have need of me again.*

It lifted its muzzle and howled. The magic current surged around them. With a sudden jolt, the void disappeared and she crouched on a cold hard surface. Ilse inhaled sharply, smelled mud and wood smoke and the scent of horse. Ordinary scents from an ordinary world. Even now the indication of magic was fading. All was dark, except for the bright blaze of a fire. Overhead, clouds obscured the moon and stars. A thick snow was falling.

She lurched to her feet, but her legs buckled and she collapsed. A woman caught her in her arms.

"My lady! You're alive."

Guda dragged Ilse closer to the fire. Snow blew past their campsite in streamers, but the canvas shielded them from the worst. Dimly Ilse became aware of the biting cold, the horses stamping and blowing gouts of steam, and the beckoning warmth of hot tea that Guda held to her lips.

"Drink, my lady."

Ilse drank, grateful for the warmth. "Thank you. I'm sorry, Guda. Sorry I didn't warn you."

Guda was trembling, but she managed a smile. "My lady, you did ask if I were prepared, so did the duke, only I never thought—"

"None of us thought. I'm sorry. Here, drink the rest of the tea and let us consider what to do. How late is it, do you know? Shall we ride for Duenne, or do we remain here?"

"No later than six bells, my lady. Let us ride for Duenne. We can make it before the roads are impassable."

It was a near thing, in spite of Guda Decker's assurance.

They extinguished the fire and set off to the east, using a lamp Guda had brought to light their path. When the snow turned thick and impenetrable, Ilse called up magic to burn a path before them, but it was close to midnight before they regained the city walls, and another half hour to the palace itself. Stable hands on watch took the horses and bundled both women into warm dry clothing. They had strong spirits and tea at hand, and administered both in small doses until both women had ceased shivering.

Ilse clasped Guda Decker's hands in hers. "Thank you, Captain Decker. Oh, yes, I could guess your rank. If I could have petitioned the gods for a companion for today, you would be her."

Guda returned the grip. "And you for me, my lady. Though . . ." And she was laughing, though it was a high, tremulous laugh. "I would have asked for more warning about the magic."

Ilse hugged her close and kissed Guda's cheek. Then she was hurrying to her rooms, to where Theda no doubt waited anxiously. The day had changed nothing, while she did not know her future, a strange exhilaration had taken hold of her. She hardly noticed the emptiness of the hallways, or the stares from guards as she passed.

Theda waited in the corridor outside her rooms, her hands knotted together. At Ilse's approach, she gave a smothered cry. "My lady. They sent word you had returned. I am so glad. You have a visitor."

"A visitor?" Ilse paused and took in Theda's agitation. "Who is it? What has happened?"

Theda gestured wordlessly at the doors. *A death,* Ilse thought. *Assassins. The duke himself or Raul . . .* Her pulse leaping, she ran through the entryway, which was dark and quiet, and into her public sitting room.

Raul stood with his back to her, facing the series of high narrow windows that overlooked the eastern quadrant of the palace grounds. The shutters stood open, and a storm of snow blew in an unending cascade against the glass. A fire blazed in the hearth; on a sideboard stood a branch of candles. As she crossed the threshold, he turned and stepped toward her. Gems flashed in his ears. Firelight streamed up and around his collar, picking out the layers upon layers of formal robes.

"Ilse."

He was like a ghost of shadows, edged by silver and firelight. She . . . she had no idea how she appeared. She only knew that her breath came short and sharp with sudden apprehension.

"What is wrong?" she whispered.

They both stared at one another. She wished she could read his expression, but the fire at his back made that impossible. He was like Toc in the everlasting dark, like a soul wandering through an endless void.

"They have made me king," Raul said at last. His voice was harsh and soft and deep. Nothing like the contralto voice she remembered from years past. He gestured sharply, the firelight rippling over the gems he wore. "No, that is wrong. They offered. I accepted." In a softer voice, he said, "I never thought they would. I never thought I would agree."

He was shaking. His face was drawn into a mask.

"Sit," Ilse told him. "I will fetch wine."

He dropped into the nearest chair, quickly, as if a god had snipped the strings that held him upright. Ilse touched his hand, which felt cold, then glided out to where Theda waited. "Wine," she said. "Wine, water, cups . . ."

"I sent for them already, my lady."

Ilse hurried back to the sitting room where Raul had not stirred. She watched him, thinking she had not seen him so unstrung since Benno Iani came with news of Dedrick Maszuryn's death.

Has he come for comfort? Or wisdom?

She did not think she had either to offer. She paced back to the front door. Runners had arrived with carafes of water and wine. Ilse took the tray and dismissed her maid for the night. She carried the tray into the sitting room where Raul sat, head resting on his hands.

"Your wine," she said softly.

His head swung up. He watched as she poured two cups, then accepted one from her hands.

"I worried," he said. "They told me you left the palace before sunrise."

"And never returned. Did you think I had run away?"

"Yes."

Ah. Oh. She ought to have left word. Except she had not known herself how long she had intended to be absent, nor had she predicted that impulsive visit to Anderswar. She certainly had not expected Duenne's Court to choose a king today.

"I'm sorry," she said.

He made an airy gesture with one hand, as if to say it didn't matter. On impulse, she caught his hand and kissed it.

Raul flung his wine cup to one side and gathered her into his arms.

"I love you, I love you, I love you," he murmured. "Please. If you must go, please tell me first. I will never make a cage for you. I promised you that. I keep my promises. I swear it. Only . . . I have lost you so many times."

He was about to withdraw from their embrace, but Ilse held him tight. "I love you," she said. "I would leave if you needed me to. Not before."

"That explains a great deal," he said softly.

His own cup lay in fragments over the floor. Taking up Ilse's, Raul handed it to her and drew her through the doors onto the balcony where snow blew and drifted over the stones. More snow streamed down from the skies. With a word in Erythandran, he created a bubble of warmth. It was exactly like the one Bela Sovic used when she first encountered Ilse. Ilse found herself wishing she knew Bela's fate.

Raul led her to the edge of the balcony. A few dim circles of lamplight interrupted the darkness, but otherwise, all of Duenne was a blanket of blackness. The air would be frigid, but Ilse felt no cold. She settled onto a bench near the wall, with the wine cup cradled in her hands. Raul stood with his back to her, facing the expanse of darkness that was Duenne City.

"I love you," he said.

She was glad she sat, because the statement, delivered so plainly, robbed her of all strength. This was no sophisticated declaration. It was a cry of desperation.

"They told me I must marry," he went on. "That as the king, I must have heirs. And now . . ." His voice edged higher, softer. Almost like the woman's voice he once possessed. "Now I can."

"What are you saying?" she asked.

"That I love you," he said. "That I cannot marry anyone but you. If that means I give up the crown I will. And yet, I hope you will say yes. I know what I ask. Ilse—" He spun around, hands held out to either side. "Ilse. My love. Once, long ago, we talked about Anike and Stefan. We would be ordinary people, with no ties or obligations to Veraene's Court. That is no longer possible . . . if you marry me, if you will be my queen and my partner. You must forget Anike and all our dreams of anonymity."

Oh. Oh, my love.

Ilse stood and faced her beloved. She dipped a finger into her wine and ran it along the cup's edge. In old Duszranjo, this would symbolize an oath of allegiance. *Water from my body, wine from my cup, thus we are bound together.*

"So I vowed to you two years ago," she said softly. "When Maester Hax died, and you asked me to take his place."

"I remember," he said. "Do you remember my reply?"

She did. He had completed the ritual, though she had only meant to vow her allegiance to him.

"I love you," he said. "I cannot be king without you. If you refuse the crown, then I will as well. Let another have it."

He dipped his finger into the cup she held. His gaze fixed on Ilse's, he ran his fingertip along the cup's rim. "Magic from my body to yours, wine from a single cup, this binds us together. Ilse, I love you. Will you marry me? Will you be my queen?"

"I love you," she said. "I will gladly serve Veraene with you. We are joined as partners, we always have been."

Her hand lifted to his cheek as he bent down to kiss her lightly. His lips were warm. His scent pervaded her senses. Cinnamon and sandalwood. The fresh clean scent of male. Of Raul Kosenmark and no other.

Yes, and yes, and yes forever.

CHAPTER TWENTY-SIX

THE KINGDOM OF Veraene had existed for almost four hundred years, the empire of Erythandra another five or six hundred years longer, depending on which historians you believed. A thousand years of history, then, each one adding to tradition, pebble upon pebble, building up to an inexorable mountain.

But theirs was no private marriage, Ilse thought as she and Raul worked through the endless preparations. Ordinary people might join their lives with a simple promise, but she and Raul would be more than husband and wife, they would be king and queen. The ceremonies of wedding and coronation were signposts to history.

Seven months passed, then the day itself arrived.

She rose before dawn. Her attendants—she had dozens now—slept in the room outside her own bedchamber. Ilse moved silently to the window. She wanted just a few moments alone before the madness began.

Her rooms overlooked the eastern quadrant of the city, which was almost invisible at this hour lost in indigo shadows. Above, stars spangled the sky, but a scarlet line marked the far horizon. Even as she watched, light rolled over the plains, like the tide rushing toward shore, revealing farms and pastures, open fields, the Gallenz River as it looped around and through Duenne, and the city itself.

A breeze filtered through the open window, carrying with it a mélange of scents, like voices of the city whispering to her. Wood smoke. A thread of incense. Traces of perfume from her bed linens. The breeze curled around her, and she caught a whiff of another, well-remembered perfume.

"Are you thinking of running away?"

Nadine's voice held a hint of laughter, barely suppressed.

"Hardly," Ilse said. "Unless I could persuade Raul to flee with me. How did you evade my guards?"

"I seduced them one after another. They were too grateful to demand mere money. As for your royal beloved, he might agree to an elopement. I saw his expression last week, during that dreadful meeting with the chief steward."

Nadine had not officially attended that meeting, but Ilse had long ago suspected Nadine had infiltrated all the secret passageways within this palace. Or not all of them—that might require a lifetime—but certainly the ones that let her observe such meetings. No doubt she and Heloïse used those dark corridors for other nefarious activities as well.

Ilse turned, expecting to see Nadine's usual mocking smile.

But no. Nadine's mouth tucked in at both corners, and her eyes were bright with unshed tears. "I remember," she whispered. "I remember when you first came to us in Tiralien. I—please do not hate me for this—I saw you bruised and bloody as our beloved lord carried you from the doorstep. You should have seen how he snapped at Lord Dedrick and the others." Here she tried for a genuine smile and failed. "No. Perhaps not. However often I wished to smack Lord Dedrick, he was a true and honest lover, and I grieve for his end."

She blinked. The tears vanished, as if by magic, and once more Nadine was the elegant courtesan. Ilse knew how to see beyond that mask, how-ever. "I love you," she said, and touched Nadine's cheek. "I am glad to have you as my friend. Will you and Heloïse marry here, or wait until you return to Valentain?"

Two dancers, in the complicated dance of love and friendship. Nadine tilted her head, accepting this new direction for the conversation. "I told her I was unfit for marriage."

A pause. But Ilse had learned how to wait.

"This winter," Nadine said quickly. "We stay in court another month, then return to Valentain with the duke." Her gaze dropped to the tiled floor. "I am afraid. Laugh if you like. You should. But I am terrified. My only courage comes from you and the example you give me. Yes, you. I have watched you confront kitchen girls and kings without flinching. I hope merely to face my beloved's family when they no longer have matters of state to distract them."

Ilse clasped Nadine's hands. "I am happy for you."

Nadine stifled a laugh. "And I am for you. Now"—she expelled a breath—"let us wake your indolent attendants."

And so it began, the hours of formal ritual. Trailed by her senior atten-dants, Ilse marched in a formal procession to the grand formal baths in the lower levels of Duenne Palace. There she immersed herself in warm water mixed with oil and scented with herbs, the same as Armand's bride had, and all the other queens of Veraene and Erythandra, a tradition recorded as far back as the times when the Veraenen tribes still lived in the northern plains.

Cleansed as ritual required, she submitted to her attendants, who wrapped her in bleached towels of new linen, woven especially for this day. She and they mounted the stairs to her new chambers, the ones formally assigned to the queen, where her bridal clothing awaited her.

But first, more rituals, more tradition. Her hair brushed dry and tied with white ribbons, so that it fell in a dark cascade down her back. A long loose tunic of new linen donned. It barely hid her body in the full sunlight, but she would not leave this room. Only her attendants and Raul himself would see her.

A barbaric custom and costume both, he had murmured, when they were first confronted with this oldest of all traditions.

Yours or mine, she had whispered back.

He had smirked at her response, but as he entered the chamber this morning, she could see that all pretense of amusement had leaked away from his face, leaving him pale and grave. He, too, had endured a cleansing bath, and he, too, was dressed in unbleached linen, his costume a robe caught around his waist by a hemp rope, and nothing else. As he strode forward, the cloth rippled back. He might as well have entered the room naked.

The attendants all glanced away. Ilse met his gaze, saw his face suffused with embarrassment. "That is not like you," she whispered.

"I am growing old," he whispered back.

She laughed.

He grinned back and took her hands.

"That, my lord and almost king, is not part of the ritual."

Raul leaned toward her. "You have no idea what damage I wish to inflict upon ritual at this moment," he whispered.

Her cheeks flooded with warmth. "I can guess."

Servants brought unadorned stone mugs, an equally plain jug, and baskets woven from reeds that contained their breakfast, then they withdrew, along with all the attendants. Ilse and Raul partook of a plain meal, unleavened bread dipped in oil and sweet herbs, plain white cheese, and coffee brewed thick and bitter. Later, after the marriage and coronation, would come the grand feast with royal guests, nobles from court, and emissaries from other kingdoms and republics, but for this hour, the future king and queen were ordinary citizens, or as much like them as possible.

Raul poured coffee into their mugs. "Anike," he said.

She lifted hers in salute, her hands curled around the rough surface. "Stefan."

The names they had used, so many years before, when running from Markus Khandarr's assassins. It would be their private signal, a sign that despite the demands of kingship and queenship, they could maintain a secret bubble for themselves alone.

THE BREAKFAST DONE, Raul vanished to his own quarters to dress for the public ceremonies. Another bout of panic overtook Ilse, and she wished she had Nadine to mock her, Kathe to talk quietly and sensibly, but she knew both her friends were busy with their own preparations. And so she submitted to her attendants, who anointed her with rosewater perfume, who lined her eyes and lips with golden paint, and who guided her into the many layers of her bridal costume: the linen shift, undergown of patterned ivory silk, the long tunic that fell to her knees, the grand robes of gold cloth that overlaid the rest. They unplaited her hair, brushed it smooth, and worked it into tighter braids, which they wound around into a low crown to echo the golden crown she would receive later that day. The rest they let fall in a loose waterfall down her back, which they adorned with miniature diamonds. That, too, was a custom, a reminder of Lir's tears spent on her brother's, her lover's, death and set as stars in the sky.

A second breakfast followed, one attended by the senior members of Veraene's Court, both from Armand's reign, as well as those who would serve Ilse and Raul. Next came a ceremony dedicated to Lir and Toc, held in a small chamber with those same councillors as witnesses, then another in memory of all the past kings and queens of Veraene.

How many died by treachery? Ilse wondered. *How many by undiscovered rebellion?*

An unprofitable line of thought. Raul must have guessed, because he pressed a hand against hers, and when she glanced up, he smiled wryly.

Back to their separate rooms, where attendants washed and dressed and adorned them a third time. More jewels. More paint, with silver to accent the gold. Ilse thought she might weep from exhaustion, but then she remembered she loved Raul and wished to marry him, and that sustained her.

And then it was time.

The bells of Duenne chimed the hour, a bright cascade of melody pouring over the city, like sunlight over the horizon. Ilse's senior attendant scanned her one last time. She touched her fingertips to Ilse's cheek—and now her expression changed from remote to amazed, as if she suddenly realized herself what the day portended. Ilse drew a deep breath and smiled. No longer a fixed one, or one she summoned for the moment, but one in truth.

It was time and past.

Ilse proceeded forward. An attendant accompanied her on either side, unobtrusive guides along the web of corridors and passageways. They passed from the royal wing into a more private region in the center of the palace, through another series of corridors, and then at last to the grand public chamber where kings and queens had bowed for their coronations.

Raul had arrived first. He stood to one side, clad in darkest indigo, with no other decoration except diamonds set in both earlobes. His glance swung up, pinned Ilse with an expression of joy and desire combined.

She stepped to his side. "My beloved."

"My beloved and my queen."

The ceremony they had arranged months before, in spite of arguments with all their advisers. Even now, Ilse was not certain the guardians of tradition would relinquish their hold upon the old and honored ways. Only when her attendants, and Raul's, stepped aside, leaving them to march toward the thrones by themselves, could she believe they had done it.

Down the aisle, with all the guests watching, from either side and from the balconies above.

Up the seven steps to the dais. There, the thrones awaited, and on their cushions, the two plain crowns that she and Raul had insisted upon.

"My beloved," Raul said. His voice was clear and loud. "Will you be my wife?"

Her throat caught in sudden happiness. She swallowed and managed a smile. "I will. And you, my beloved, will you be my husband?"

His voice wavered, steadied. "I will."

They lifted the crowns from the thrones. Facing each other, they knelt. It was a maneuver they had practiced a dozen or more times, but Ilse's hand shook as she set the crown upon Raul's head, while he did the same for her. The haze of terror and amazement lifted a moment, and she saw that he was trembling, too.

"You are weeping," Raul whispered.

"For joy," she replied in a voice as soft as his. Then she reached up to cup his cheek, which was damp with tears as well. Without a thought, she drew him close and kissed him on the lips. He wrapped both arms around her in a tight embrace and returned her kiss.

That last was not tradition, but she hardly cared.

THE CEREMONY CONTINUED with each ranking noble and all the servants of the court kneeling before the new king and queen, and vowing their allegiance. First came the regional governors in order of seniority. Lord Alberich de Ytel of Laufvenberc, governor of the city of Duenne, led them all, having served Baerne of Angersee as commander, then in court and council, until Baerne had appointed him to his post as governor. Lord Alberich's skin lay in deep folds, his complexion mottled with brown and black spots, but his eyes were keen as the servant assisted him up the steps and onto his knees.

I am too young, too ignorant to accept this man's allegiance, Ilse thought.

Nevertheless, she clasped her hands around his, and listened with at least the outward seeming of calm as he recited his vows.

"My queen, my liege, my sovereign, and mother to our people, I offer my heart, my honor, my strength. All that is mine to give, in this life and all those to come, I lay before you . . ."

It was an ornately worded formula, thick with imagery. The words had not changed since that first vow, spoken by the clan chiefs to the first king of Erythandra. Lord Ytel spoke in halting phrases, his voice breathy and almost inaudible, but Ilse had the impression of a great will behind that frail mask of flesh. What he swore was the truth, in Lir's name and Toc's blood. She could do no less for him.

"My servant, my brother and child of blood, I swear my allegiance in turn, heart and body and soul, to you and to the children of your flesh and of your soul, in service to our kingdom and its welfare . . ."

She almost faltered when she declared herself his mother. Merely symbolism, she told herself. The heart of that vow was not beyond her. Her heart and life *were* the kingdom's. The words themselves were merely confirmation.

She was glad, however, when she could withdraw so that Raul could receive the man's vows and give his in turn. Only when the servant approached once more to help Lord Ytel stand, did the old governor send her one searching glance, a slight nod, before he turned to descend the many steps and allow the next governor to approach.

More governors—Stephane Tomassi of Pommersien, Vieth of Gallenz and Tiralien, the rulers of various provinces—Ournes, Morauvín, Juraz-mec, and more. Ilse thought she would become numb to the ritual, but no, each time her hands reached out, she felt a shiver run through her, scalp to toes, as if Lir and Toc had laid their hands upon hers as well.

Only twice did the smooth procession pause. Once, as Nicol Joannis from Fortezzien mounted the steps. He kept his eyes lowered as he knelt before Ilse and gave his vows, but just once, as he shifted to face Raul, his gaze flicked up. Raul's expression, already painted smooth and impassive, took on an even more remote cast. Ilse could almost hear their unspoken conversation.

You abandoned me. You abandoned us all.

I was afraid. I have no other excuse.

Then, almost imperceptibly, Raul's stiff expression relented. He pressed his hands around Nicol Joannis's, who in turn bowed deeper before his new king. Ilse breathed a sigh of relief. *We are no longer enemies or conspirators. We are king and queen and liege. So we must act for the good of the kingdom.*

The second pause came once the queue of governors wound to its end, and the first of the ranking nobles came forward, in an order determined by yet another arcane formula dictated by eight centuries of custom and pride.

First among them was Duke Alvaro Andreas Bertold Kosenmark, who marched haltingly up the steps. In spite of the mage surgeon's efforts, Raul's father still limped, and his knuckles were pale as he gripped his cane. He waved away the hovering servants, and dragged his left foot up the last step. His gaze met his son's in a brief and searching exchange. Then the old duke eased himself onto his knees before Ilse to give his vows of allegiance.

And so it continued throughout the morning, the line winding to its end as the sun crossed overhead. When the last minor lord gave and received his oath, and withdrew, Ilse closed her eyes for a moment. Only now was she aware that her feet throbbed from standing.

Raul pressed his hand against hers. "Tonight," he murmured.

"If we survive the remainder of this day," she answered softly.

"Oh, we shall. I swear it. I have," he added, "a great deal of practice in making vows."

She would have laughed, except she knew she must not laugh in front of the vast audience witnessing this event. She only smiled, and pressed her palm briefly against his, turning the gesture into one more formal as they clasped hands and lifted them as though to start a dance.

A dance it was, she thought, as they descended the steps. The masses of nobles and courtiers parted before them—she was dimly aware of many,

many faces to either side, all of them in constant movement as the audience flowed away and to either side, to take their places in a grand procession from the vast throne room to an even more enormous hall where the first feast would commence.

The feast. The speeches given by various lords to Raul and Ilse, and theirs in return. The formal exchange of wine cups between king and queen, between the new rulers and their honored guests at the first table. The whispering of magic, like a cool stream, to relieve the sweltering summer air. The servants bearing dish after opulent dish, while musicians, placed in small groups throughout the hall, played a complicated tune upon oblique and transverse flutes, connected through part and counterpart, while a single water flute threaded its voice among them. Theirs was but one feast among others, too. A dozen more took place within the palace itself, and more yet throughout the city. Each one linked to another, Ilse thought, like a chain of words linked together, like a river of souls throughout history.

As twilight dropped over the city, Ilse and Raul stood for a last exchange of wine cups. Servants removed the tables from the hall, and the musicians took up new stations in corners and alcoves. Dancing commenced with the king and queen, a simple pattern of steps, palm against palm, circling around the center of the floor. One by one, other partners joined them, and the pattern grew to include them. Nadine and Heloïse, both shining with giddy joy. Raul's other two sisters, Olivia and Marte. Emma and Benno Iani. Baron Mann. Klara. Baron Eckard. And off in a far corner, Kathe coaxing her husband, Gerek, to dance.

It was not until the bells rang midnight that Ilse and Raul departed from their guests, and returned with slow weary steps to the king's chambers. As they passed through the outer rooms, a dozen attendants rose to their feet. Raul dismissed them with a silent gesture. Then he and Ilse passed through the doors into the bedchamber.

He closed the door. Ilse turned toward him and felt her heart leap high against her chest. "My king."

"My queen." His voice was breathless with laughter. More. Anticipation.

She thought she knew the reason.

They were not new lovers. They knew each other's bodies, in this life and in countless others. But all had changed in that promise given each to each. Now they were husband and wife, king and queen.

Raul laid his crown upon a table, raked his fingers through his cropped hair. He glanced up, a laughing smile breaking through the gravity that had clothed him these past seven months. It was like the sun flooding a cloud-streaked sky. Her breath came easier. "My love," she said.

"My love," he said. "I come to you unadorned. Incomplete. Will you have me?"

"I will. And you?"

"With all my heart." As she lifted a hand to remove her crown, he shook his head. "Not yet."

She waited, suddenly breathless again.

He removed the diamonds from his earlobes. Laid them beside the crown. Next came the long coat of stiffened silk and its belt. Ilse watched with quick-beating pulse as he undid the buttons of his shirt, his trousers. Piece by piece, he removed all decoration, all clothing, until he stood before her bare-skinned, the candlelight painting his body with silver and gold.

"Unadorned," he said. "Whatever I am, tonight I am nothing more than a man. Not even Stefan, because I would take nothing as a shield, not even a false name. I am only Raul. Will you have me?"

Ilse wet her lips. "I will. Tonight and forever."

She took his hand and led him to the bed.

CHAPTER TWENTY-SEVEN

IT WAS A day, a moment, she could not have foreseen, and yet she knew every detail in advance.

The bed was a monstrous thing, easily large enough for ten lovers, as if a monarch required a greater stage than ordinary folk. There was no canopy, just a vast open expanse of white linen, overspread by layers of indigo and emerald silk. Servants had lit five branches of candles. A chandelier hung from the high, arched ceiling. Unseen, a brazier burned incense, sending up clouds of a fragrant cedar scent. It was too, too much, Ilse thought. It was fitting, however. A chamber this overwrought was like an echo of her emotions.

She pointed to the bed. "Lie down."

He obeyed, his mouth twitching in amusement. Long-limbed and graceful, he climbed the steps and eased himself onto his back. His bare skin gleamed in the candlelight, and he stared back at her with impossibly bright eyes.

"Not yet," she said. "Do not move."

"Is that your command?"

"It is."

She ran a finger along his cheek, touched the corner of his mouth, then brushed her hand over his throat and down his chest. The pulse at his throat beat faster, but otherwise he remained motionless. Only when she pressed lightly upon his stomach did his chest rise and fall in a breath caught suddenly.

His body, so familiar, so different. As if the gods had brushed him with shadows, within and without. She missed the long fall of hair, how it would tumble over his eyes when she loosed its ribbon. Now, his hair was cropped close, and where his chest once had been as smooth as a boy's, she could run her fingers through fine dark hair running over his chest and down to his groin.

Raul closed his eyes and whispered something unintelligible.

Ilse paused, her hand resting over his belly. Watched as his penis thickened and stood upright. She curled her fingers around it, then slowly let her hand drift downward to the still unfamiliar sacs of flesh underneath. Then she bent down and kissed Raul's chest, breathing in the musk of his perfume, and the stronger musk of his desire.

Tonight, she thought. *Tonight we make love, and if the gods will it, a child.*

She straightened and withdrew her hand. Raul's eyes fluttered open.

"Almost," she said, setting her crown next to his on the table.

Just as he had, she undressed, item by item. The gold-embroidered slippers. The grand robes and jewels, in which she had married, accepted a crown, and vowed her life and service to her subjects. The long tunic underneath, and all the other layers, each one removed and folded and set aside, until she stood clad in her shift alone. As she reached up to her hair, Raul sat up. "Grant me this favor, please."

One by one, he took the diamonds from her hair. When the last lay on the table beside her crown, he plucked out the pins holding her hair and let it fall in a glorious cascade over her shoulders.

"The candles?" he asked.

She shook her head. "I want them lit."

She drew off her shift and climbed the steps to the bed. When Raul made as though to draw her into an embrace, she pressed both hands against his shoulders and pinned him against the bed. "I have always wished to do this," she whispered.

His eyes widened. His mouth opened in a half-laughing smile. "So have I."

He was more than willing, more than ready, as was she. She lowered herself slowly, biting her lip to keep herself from rushing. Then came the moment when she could not hold back. A sharp sudden push down. She flung back her head and a cry burst from her throat, answered by his. Already their bodies found the rhythm, its pace rising ever faster. Ilse was babbling, laughing, and weeping. Raul, speaking in old Erythandran, then suddenly in Károvín, Veraenen, and others she could not identify, as though his memories swung from this life to the past and all the way to the present again. There was no time when they had not been lovers. Each life, they would discover each other anew. It was like a dance with patterns unfolding, each one leading to the next, each step and step a reflection of the past and yet a new thing altogether.

A final surge of hips against hips, a long moment when they went still in passion complete. Another moment before the breath trickled from Ilse's lips, and her muscles unlocked. Her blood thrummed in her temples, her body trembled, and her skin was slick with sweat.

Raul curled a hand around her neck. His gaze locked with hers as he drew her into a kiss so deep, she thought she might drown. *I love you*, she thought.

"I love you," he whispered hoarsely. "I shall love you forever."

CHAPTER TWENTY-EIGHT

DAWN WOKE HER, the swift light touch of sun upon her eyelids, followed by the unexpected trill of birdsong outside an open window. Gentle. Persistent. Inexorable.

Ilse lay with her eyes closed, taking in each detail of this new day—the linen sheets entangled around her legs, the scent of her own perfume, of rosewater mixed with sweat and the sharper scent of sex, and the fainter ones of incense and beeswax. The familiar weight of Raul's arm over her hip. The still unfamiliar roughness of his unshaven cheek against her back.

A warm breeze drifted through the window, carrying with it the muted noise of the city beyond the palace grounds. Duenne. At last.

She shook with silent laughter. She had come to Duenne ten months ago. And yet it was not until today that she had a sense of completion, as if the coronation and wedding signaled the end to some long-delayed endeavor.

Raul stirred. His hand slipped along her leg and he murmured something truly salacious. Ilse's breath caught in a sudden access of desire, even as she stifled more laughter. So much had changed. So much had not.

She slid from his embrace and sat up, the better to indulge herself and stare besottedly at his sleeping face. His dark hair, shorn by the physicians and which he continued to wear in that style, was like a velvet hood over his skull. Silver shimmered among the blue-black. Scars ran in a pale network over his neck, chest, and shoulders—a remnant of his last battle with Markus Khandarr. He was still beautiful in her eyes, but she could not ignore the signs of age, of anxiety. Nor the other signs of that last battle. A shadow of beard painted his cheeks and chin, dark limned with silver. The silken cloud over his chest and belly, between his legs. Not quite a grown man's, nor yet the sign of youth.

Whatever Khandarr intended, Raul Kosenmark would never return to his childhood, nor would he leap beyond the years to become a man like any other. He would be forever himself.

In the past few moments, the sun had lifted a few degrees. Now it poured through the openwork shutters, casting a lattice of shadows over Raul's face. He wrinkled his nose, as if the light tickled, then breathed out a sigh.

My beloved, my king.

He had wanted kingship, had thrust it away because he feared his own ambitions. At the last, he had accepted. Emma Iani believed the victory was hers. But in the end the victory was Veraene's, the decision Raul's.

They had both made their choices. More and more would come, until each minute turning of each day revealed itself in the grander pattern of a life, of lives, of history.

It was this quote from Tanja Duhr that drove her from bed. Ilse washed her face in the waiting bowl of water. (Warmed with magic, scented with herbs.) By the king's and queen's order, given the night before, no attendant waited to help her dress. Someone had left a gown and robe waiting for her. She dressed in them and headed toward the outer chamber.

The doors swung open—as if impelled by magic, she thought. Three attendants and six guards waited outside. All of them sank into deep bows.

"Your Majesty."

I am queen, she thought. *Queen of Veraene.* Her pulse beat impossibly fast. If nothing else convinced her, this one gesture did.

"I would walk," she said at last. "Let the king know where I have gone."

She did not need to give her destination—indeed, she did not know it yet—but she felt certain that Raul would receive word when he needed it. She set off in a flutter of robes. A moment later she heard the echo of booted feet.

They were her guards, charged with the queen's safety.

I could order them away.

Or not. It might be a custom beyond her power, or Raul's, to keep the guards away from Veraene's kings and queens.

Gradually her pace slowed, as did her pulse. It was not fair for her to take out her whims on those charged to protect her. She would have to accustom herself to constant vigilance and the presence of watchers, observers, gossips, and minions.

She blew out a breath. (And wondered if someone watched and noted her behavior.)

I shall go mad if I worry about who sees what.

At the same time, she could not ignore it.

Ilse ran a hand over her face. No smile, not yet. But she knew at last where in all of Duenne's palace she wished to go.

* * *

MIDMORNING. THE SUN poured down from the cloudless sky, inun-
dating the city and its palace. Already heat shimmered from the stonework,
reflected from the clouds of dust stirred by traffic in the streets, until the
city appeared to float upon a golden haze.

Ilse sat tucked beneath an overhanging ledge, on an almost-cool patch
of stone, with the shade shrinking about her. The city of Duenne spread out
from her feet. South. East. West. Through the haze of dust and sunlight,
she could make out the broad Gallenz River as it circled around the older
districts. She could mark the progress of history by the various walls, the
different colors of brick and stone, the shape of the buildings.

"Good morning, my queen."

Raul dropped onto the sun-warmed bricks beside her. He wore a dull-
brown tunic and trousers and was barefoot. He was smiling, a small smile
that radiated contentment.

"My guards were dutiful and told you how to find me."

He shrugged. "I would have guessed, no matter."

That surprised her. "How?"

"Because I know the history of this palace."

Of course.

She had asked the way, he had known from earlier years, where Tanja
Duhr met her beloved soldier. Not her first lover, but the one she remained
true to, from death to death, and if legend were correct, into life beyond.

It was a splendid place to meet one's forever love. Tanja Duhr and Adele
Visser. One the poet of the empire, the other a soldier and guardian of the
realm. Of course Raul had guessed she would come here.

"Who am I?" she asked.

He shrugged. "Who was I? A pirate. A minor diplomat. A scholar in
the service of Leos Dzavek. What matters now is that we are queen and
king."

The truth. She recognized it, even as she shuddered away. One story
winding to its end, another beginning. Dzavek dead. Armand of Angersee,
as well. So many others, who had cast their loyalty to one side or another.
Others had survived and would grow into new lives and families. So and
so. It was true. Seeds did sprout. New trees sprang upward to the sky,
branching, arching, interweaving, like the walls of a temple summoned by
the gods. Oh, yes, she remembered how the gods had visited her, and Miro
Karasek, and Valara Baussay, in the far north of Károví. It would never do to
forget the gods.

She thought next of Valara and Miro, who had fled to Morennioù, still hiding behind its veil of magic, and of Károví, which hovered on the edge of chaos without its immortal king.

"We are not done, are we?" she said.

Raul smiled, as if he guessed her thought. "No, and never shall be, not until our souls depart this world forever, to join the gods in their eternal delight."

Duhr again. No, not Duhr, but a later poet that some said was Duhr reborn.

Ilse stood and held out her hand to her husband. "Come," she said. "Let us begin the new day."